Shameless EMBRACES

New York Times and *USA Today* Bestselling Author

LORA LEIGH

Ellora's Cave
Romantica Publishing

What the critics are saying...

"Yet again, Lora Leigh shows her mastery of the craft of erotic romance." ~ *Romance Junkies*

"The story of two such strong passionate characters was sheer pleasure to dive into. Don't miss this one." ~ *A Romance Review*

"Shameless is the seventh book in Lora Leigh's Bound Hearts series, and like its predecessors, Shameless is a veritable sexual feast of love and lust." ~ *The Romance Studio*

"Shameless is the best of the series so far, with Ms. Leigh raising the bar even more with each installment. Thankfully she has always risen to the challenge." ~ *Fallen Angel Reviews*

"A story full of heart and soul and an absolute must read." ~ *Cupid's Library Reviews*

"Sax is one of the sexiest things on two legs; his intense sensuality will make you sweat and your heart pound." ~ *Romance Junkies*

"Bound Hearts: Embraced features one of the hottest heroes in the series so far, Saxon Brogan. As a hero, he is everything you can ask for: strong, sexy, forceful, passionate, caring, and a gentleman." ~ *A Romance Review*

"The Trojans, as they are called, are alpha men who conquer their women and provide them untold pleasures in a ménage setting!" ~ *Cupid's Library Reviews*

An Ellora's Cave Romantica Publication

www.ellorascave.com

Shameless Embraces

ISBN 9781419954658

Edited by Sue-Ellen Gower.
Cover art by Syneca.

This book printed in the U.S.A. by Jasmine-Jade Enterprises, LLC.

Trade paperback Publication March 2007

Also by Lora Leigh

A Wish, A Kiss, A Dream (*anthology*)
B.O.B.'s Fall (*with Veronica Chadwick*)
Bound Hearts 1: Surrender
Bound Hearts 2: Submission
Bound Hearts 3: Seduction
Bound Hearts 4: Wicked Intent
Bound Hearts 5: Sacrifice
Cowboy & the Captive
Dragon Prime
Elemental Desires (*anthology*)
Ellora's Cavemen: Tales from the Temple I (*anthology*)
Feline Breeds 1: Tempting the Beast
Feline Breeds 2: The Man Within
Feline Breeds 3: Kiss of Heat
Law and Disorder: Moving Violations (*with Veronica Chadwick*)
Legacies 1: Shattered Legacy
Legacies 2: Shadowed Legacy
Legacies 3: Savage Legacy
Manaconda (*anthology*)
Men of August 1: Marly's Choice
Men of August 2: Sarah's Seduction
Men of August 3: Heather's Gift
Men of August 4: August Heat
Sealed With a Wish
Soul Deep
Wizard Twins 1: Menage A Magick
Wizard Twins 2: When Wizards Rule
Wolf Breeds 1: Wolfe's Hope
Wolf Breeds 2: Jacob's Faith
Wolf Breeds 3: Aiden's Charity
Wolf Breeds 4: Elizabeth's Wolf

About the Author

Lora Leigh is a wife and mother living in Kentucky. She dreams in bright, vivid images of the characters intent on taking over her writing life, and fights a constant battle to put them on the hard drive of her computer before they can disappear as fast as they appeared.

Lora's family, and her writing life co-exist, if not in harmony, in relative peace with each other. An understanding husband is the key to late nights with difficult scenes, and stubborn characters. His insights into human nature, and the workings of the male psyche provide her hours of laughter, and innumerable romantic ideas that she works tirelessly to put into effect.

Lora welcomes comments from readers. You can find her website and email address on her author bio page at www.ellorascave.com.

Tell Us What You Think

We appreciate hearing reader opinions about our books. You can email us at Comments@EllorasCave.com.

SHAMELESS EMBRACES

EMBRACED

Trademarks Acknowledgement

The author acknowledges the trademarked status and trademark owners of the following wordmarks mentioned in this work of fiction:

Lexus: Toyota Jidosha Kabushiki Kaisha Corporation Japan 1

Prologue

It was crazy. The worst possible idea imaginable. She had spent three years denying the desire, denying the truth of her own feelings. If she walked up to that room, then it would change things forever.

Marey pulled her little car into the parking lot of the motel and stared at the exterior nervously. Was she brave enough to do it? Could she actually walk in there and give in to all the desires she had kept hidden all her life, and then walk away as though it had never happened?

Her hands gripped the steering wheel, her fingers curling around it in a death grip as she fought the tremors that quaked through her body. She didn't know if she could do it. She had spent too many years fighting it. Unlike her friends, the merry five who had entered into marriages with infamous Trojans, Marey knew she likely didn't have what it took to carry this off.

It was one night, her hormones screamed at her. One stupid night of wild, hot sex, stop philosophizing over it. She could do this.

Couldn't she?

Of course she could. She was thirty-five, not twenty, and she hadn't been a virgin for a long time. Damned good thing, she reminded herself—Saxon Brogan would terrify a virgin.

She laid her head against the steering wheel, groaning pitifully as she tried to force herself from the car. *Wasn't this what she wanted?* she reminded herself. One hot, wicked night with the man of her dreams before reality came with the rising sun and she went back to the staid, sterile life she lived.

Why? Something snapped within her then. Why did she have to return to anything? There was no husband. No children. No parents to catch her in some naughty act. All she had were her friends. Friends that one by one had fallen into the clutches of a lifestyle that Marey might not understand, but didn't condemn. And it wasn't as if she was doing anything illicit.

She ignored the flashing thought of the underclothes she was wearing. Or those she wasn't wearing, she reminded herself.

She could do this. She raised her head, nodding firmly. There was no law that said the man who fucked you had to love you, was there? Of course there wasn't. Besides, she loved Sax. The admission was one she rarely allowed herself to make. One she hid from herself as much as possible.

Fear had held her hostage for years. The fear that her ex-husband, Vince, would finally slip his hold on sanity and kill her. The fear that she was making another mistake, that her heart would pay the price this time. Her pride had been sacrificed to her ruined marriage and Vince's fury. But her heart. If Sax broke her heart, could she survive it?

She breathed in roughly. She would have to survive it. Now, dammit, she had waited too long. Fantasies could only sustain a woman for so long, and toys were a poor second to what she knew was waiting for her.

Sax, with his quirky little smile, his dark eyes, his voice whispering his need for her. The sight of his hands, so much darker than her pale flesh, coasting over her body, bringing her a pleasure she had never known before. Dominant, commanding, he was part of the exclusive men's club that had been nicknamed Trojans. They were dominant, forceful, but even more, they practiced sharing their women, bringing them to heights of arousal that were rumored to leave their women weak for days.

Her friends had married into the club. And though getting details was like pulling teeth without anesthesia, she had managed to pry out enough to fuel her own midnight fantasies.

Was she brave enough? If she could fantasize about it, then surely she had the courage to do it. To go to Sax and take the pleasure she knew awaited her. To see if a future was possible, if the fantasies were a pale excuse for reality, or vice versa.

She pried her fingers from the steering wheel, grabbed her small purse and opened the car door before she could change her mind. She was a grown woman. A mature adult. And if there was one man in the world who could trip her switches, it was Sax. So what if he didn't love her, if he was miles out of her league. He wanted her. For tonight at least, she could be the woman she wanted to be, with no fear of gossip or reprisals.

Squaring her shoulders, she moved across the parking lot and up the stairs to the second landing. Room two twenty-nine. She pulled the key card from the side pocket of her purse and gripped it with tense fingers. Nerves shook her body, pounded through her bloodstream. Adrenaline was a crashing crescendo in her ears as she approached the door and drew in a hard, deep breath.

She could do this. She had waited years, lusting after a man she feared she couldn't keep. Besides, it was almost Christmas—well, almost Thanksgiving anyway. She could treat herself to something a little different this year. Something hot and wild, something she could carry with her forever, no matter what the future might hold.

She slid the card into the electronic lock, waited until the light flashed green, then turned the handle slowly.

See, she could do this. She pushed the door open slowly, and stepped in before coming to a shocking, mind-numbing stop.

* * * * *

"What the hell happened?" Sax Brogan was enraged as he entered the ER, coming to a stop as James Wyman rose from one of the plastic seats and moved quickly to meet him.

He wanted to hit something. Someone. Every muscle in his body bunched, tightened with the impulse as the other man approached.

An hour at the police department hadn't improved his mood. Being suspected of physical assault and attempted rape had been more than shocking. When he learned who he was accused of assaulting, he had nearly lost his mind.

His only thought was to get to her, to make certain she was okay, to see with his own eyes the damage done.

"She's conscious now," James murmured as he reached him, then waved him toward the elevators. "They have her sedated, though. The injuries aren't that bad, the concussion is mild. The doctor thinks she'll be fine."

"That crazy ex of hers?" Brogan clenched his fists, fighting his fury. He couldn't believe this. It was inconceivable.

"Unfortunately," James sighed as they entered the elevator. "The detective called a few minutes ago. They have him in custody now, but I don't know if that's going to help Marey when she faces you."

Sax glanced back at James with a frown. The investigator had told him Marey called the station herself, giving a statement over the phone and securing his release.

"She knows you're aware of what happened. That you know she thought she was meeting you in that motel," he explained patiently. "You know how she is. She's fought this thing between you two for too long. This isn't going to help things."

Sax remained quiet. He stared at the elevator display panel, ticking off the floors until the muted bell sounded and it came to a stop.

The bastard ex-husband had found her weakness, just as they had all known he would.

"She'll get over it," he finally said, reining in his need for violence. "Starting now."

He had stayed away from her out of respect for her, because she had asked him to. Her soft voice, her gentle gray eyes had pleaded with him not to press her, and he hadn't.

Squire Port, Virginia, home base for Delacourte and Conover Electronics was a small little community. Everyone was at least acquainted with every one else, and many knew each other well. Delacourte Electronics promoted a friendly, casual atmosphere with its employees and their families, and because of that, Sax had known Marey for years. Before the messy divorce and her withdrawal from all but her closest friends. He also knew her ex well enough to know that any relationship he began with her would be marred by the man's possessive insanity.

"How did he know to use me?" He stopped at her hospital door, keeping his voice low as he glanced at James once again.

Sax knew he had been careful, very careful over the past years, to heed Marey's wishes and stay away from her. He hadn't liked it. Hell, he hated it to his back teeth, but he had respected her wishes. So how had Vince known she would drop her guard for a secret assignation with him?

"We don't know." James shook his head, shoving his hands in his pants pockets and staring back at him somberly. "We just don't know, Sax. The police found a note, signed with your name, asking her to join you in that room. Her screams alerted a couple in the next room who called the cops. When they found her, she was unconscious. I think he meant to kill her."

And blame Sax for the crime. Son of a bitch. He ran his hand over his shaved head and breathed out roughly.

"I have to make sure she's okay," he said roughly, his throat clogging with pain at the thought of what had been done to her. "I have to see her."

"I knew you would." James nodded slowly. "When she woke up, and Terrie explained what happened, she was horrified. She called the police herself. But she hasn't said much since. She knows you're coming."

Sax nodded then reached for the doorknob. He turned it slowly, pushing the door open and stepped inside quietly.

Terrie, James' sister-in-law, came to her feet, her face still damp, her eyes red-rimmed as she stared back at him.

"Come on in," she whispered, glancing at the sheet-draped bed that Sax could only glimpse the bottom of. "She's resting. For now."

Sax entered the room, moving slowly as he passed the bed.

"I'll be outside." She patted Sax on the arm gently as she passed him.

As the door closed, he turned, swallowing tightly before allowing himself to see the damage done.

God help the bastard, he thought when he saw her face, because he was going to kill him. Her face was horribly bruised, her eyes and lips swollen. Sax prayed that Vince Clayton wouldn't manage to get out of jail, because if he did, he was a dead man.

Her soft, pale blonde hair framed her face—a face he knew was softly rounded, inquisitive, stubborn.

"Looks bad, huh?" Her voice was raspy, groggy as she opened her eyes, the soft gray barely visible through the swollen lids.

It was all he could do to restrain himself, to hold back. He wanted to pull her into his arms, hold her against his chest and swear he would never let it happen again. That he would protect her, keep her safe. But he was smart enough to know she would never accept it.

"I'll kill him, Marey." He pushed his hands in his pockets, his fists clenching as rage ate through him. "I swear I'll kill the bastard."

Her breathing hitched as she grimaced painfully.

"It was my fault." Tears clogged her voice then. "I should have known better." A bitter laugh escaped her throat. "It was stupid of me not to check with you."

He moved to the side of the bed, his chest tightening with emotion. He couldn't believe this had happened, couldn't conceive that anyone would do this to her.

He sat down slowly in the chair beside her, shrugging off his suit jacket and flexing his shoulders as he sighed wearily.

"I've considered it a time or two," he finally admitted with a grimace. "Actually, kidnapping you and tying you to my bed for a week was my favorite fantasy."

A short, groggy little laugh left her throat. "Trojans and their whips and chains," she said with a little sigh.

He picked up her hand, noticing the flinch as he did so. It wasn't from pain.

"Don't." She pulled back from him, swallowing tightly. "I'm sorry about what happened. I'm just sorry. But I can't—"

"You came to that motel thinking I would be there," he said gently, staring down at the soft creamy flesh he gripped in his much darker hand. "I wouldn't have expected that, or I would have had you years ago. You can't back out now."

"I already have." Despite the drugs and the pain, her voice was firm.

"You might think you have." He picked up her hand again, his fingers holding it in place as she stared at where they met. "But Marey, I can be relentless. I won't let you go now, not knowing this."

Panic flared in her eyes.

"And he will never hurt you again." He leaned close, staring back at her intently, determination thundering through him. "Do you hear me? The bastard will never touch you again, because to do so, he will have to go through me. You're mine, and when you get out of here, I intend to claim what belongs to me, Marey. Every sweet beautiful inch of you. Mine."

Chapter One

One Month Later

"What are you doing here?" Marey leaned against the doorframe, staring up at Sax as he stood on the stoop, looking too damned sexy, too tempting for so early in the morning. "This habit of yours is getting on my nerves, Sax. This is too early in the morning to be out of the bed."

In the past four weeks, if he had missed half a dozen mornings showing up for coffee and trying to wheedle breakfast out of her, then it would surprise her. And he was getting bolder. Touching her as she moved around the kitchen, stealing kisses when she couldn't avoid him, laughing at her irate expressions and teasing her when the morning grumpiness got the best of her.

"You should be used to it by now." His teeth flashed in a smile that made her pussy weep in loneliness as he stepped into the house, pulling the door from her grip and closing it softly.

He was going to drive her to an asylum before it was over with. The man was like an unstoppable force once he got something in his head, and since her attack, he had appointed himself her personal bodyguard whenever he deemed it necessary.

She sighed wearily. She was exhausted. Sleep was a thing of the past and paranoia whipped through the night like the rattle of ghostly chains.

"Vince call?" he asked as he moved into the kitchen, heading straight for the automatic coffeepot. She had learned to time it for his visits.

She stood still as the question filtered through her morning grogginess, holding her still in shock.

"How did you know he was released?" She frowned in irritation as she followed him. "And since when did you decide to just make yourself at home here?"

He pulled one of the mugs from a hook under the cabinet and poured the coffee with the ease of a man comfortable in his surroundings.

"Stop trying to sidetrack the conversation," he retorted calmly. "Why didn't you tell me when you found out he was released? It's been a week."

She pushed her hands deep into the pockets of her baggy flannel pajama bottoms and hunched her shoulders defensively.

"Because it was none of your business?" she suggested mockingly. "I didn't make his bail for him and I'm not taking his calls. There's nothing else I can do until the court date."

"He's been calling?" The cup lowered back to the counter as his voice lowered dangerously.

Hell. It was too damned early to deal with this crap.

"A few times," she answered waspishly. "Let it go, Sax. You're not my father or my husband."

His eyes narrowed. The deep chocolate depths of his gaze sent a shiver of sensation through her. So far, he had been gentleness itself as she healed from Vince's attack. He hadn't really pushed her for anything other than breakfast, and though his sexuality was always present, he kept it reined in for the most part. She had a feeling, based on that look, it wouldn't last for long.

"I'm not going to sit idly by while he beats the hell out of you again, either," he informed her, his voice cold, his expression shuttered as he watched her. "And look at you, you aren't even sleeping anymore. Do you think I don't know what those shadows under your eyes mean, Marey? Why are you being so stubborn?"

She breathed out roughly as she stalked to the coffeepot herself. No one should have to deal with this without that first cup of coffee.

"Don't start again, Sax," she snapped. "I'm not moving in with you. It's not happening, noway, nohow."

Especially not now. She poured her coffee, reining in her own fury at the circumstances. To be honest, she had been giving in, considering the offer he had made after she came out of the hospital, tempted by the hot looks, the promise of passion and heat in his eyes. Vince's release from jail had canceled even the consideration of such a move. There was no way she would dare to push him that far now. The instability she only glimpsed during their marriage had become terrifying.

She poured the steaming liquid into her cup, ignoring him as he crossed his arms over his chest, straining the white silk shirt he wore and making him look impossibly strong. It was obvious he hadn't grown lax in the four years since he had left the Army and joined Delacourte. His body looked just as tight and hard as it had when he came home.

A woman really, *really* shouldn't have to face this so early in the morning. This amount of sex appeal, dominance, and pure male presence should be reserved for fantasies alone.

As she turned away, she stiffened as she felt the whisper of a touch over the curve of her rear. Balancing the hot coffee, she shot him an irritated glare.

"That was dirty and low," she snarled as he grinned back at her unrepentantly. "Keep your hands to yourself."

He snorted at that, a male sound of disbelief. "That's not going to happen, Marey. And we're not finished discussing this Vince thing, either. If you won't move in with me, then I'll park on your doorstep instead."

"And I'll have the sheriff drag you off." She sat down at the small breakfast table, her cup thunking on the glass top as she flicked him another irate look. "Sit down and drink your coffee, Sax. It's too early in the morning to argue with you."

"Add that to the fact that you haven't slept in weeks." He frowned back at her. "Yes, I can see where your patience would be wearing thin. Aren't you sick of it yet? Being too damned scared to reach out for what you want?"

"You being what I want, of course," she suggested sarcastically. "Don't you get tired of running after women who don't want you?" Lord forgive her for that lie. It was a whopper.

He laughed at her then. A low, deep chuckle that stroked over her senses and had her clit reminding her voraciously just how much it longed for his touch. It was swollen, sensitive, just as her nipples were, her breasts—hell, every cell in her body was aching for him.

"You're almost awake enough this morning to pull that lie off." If his frown was anything to go by, he was less than pleased. "Try getting some sleep tonight and maybe I'll pay attention tomorrow."

Maybe pushing Sax at seven-thirty in the morning wasn't a good idea, she thought a second later as he pulled her from the chair, one powerful arm hooking around her waist as he brought her flush with his very hard, very aroused body.

"Sax..." She meant to protest. Really, she assured herself. She was outraged that he would be so dominant, so sexually determined at the drop of a hat.

Of course she was, her conscience mocked her as her lips opened beneath his, a moan shuddering from her chest as his tongue licked at her lips, possessive and intent on claiming the territory beyond.

She was going to protest this. She was going to tell him just how arrogant and completely, impossibly unfair he was being and all the reasons why this was a really bad idea.

Sure she was, she mocked herself as her hands gripped his shoulders, her lips opening beneath his as she felt his hands moving slowly beneath the loose material of her nightshirt, pressing against her stomach as he played with the strings that tightened the waistband of her pajamas.

He felt so good. So good and warm, and strong. All she wanted to do was immerse herself in it, let the sensations whipping through her body carry her wherever he wanted her to go. Just this, just for a brief time. Then she would make him stop. She would be strong again and she would reset the boundaries she knew she had to have between her desire and what she knew would protect them both.

For now, she was lost and she damned well knew it. This was why she kept as far away from him as possible. This was the reason she had fought the desire between them. Because of this, the pleasure, the incredible fiery sensations that traveled not just through her body, but through her soul as he lifted her closer, grinding her against him, the hard wedge of his erection pressing firmly into the engorged nubbin of her clit.

"So sweet," he whispered as his lips nipped at hers then, his teeth tugging at the bottom curve, his tongue licking over it as she fought for his kiss again. She didn't want to think, didn't want to let go of the incredible pleasure consuming her.

It was happening too fast, a part of her screamed. If she didn't stop now, she wouldn't be able to later.

Shut up! The aching core of her pussy wasn't having it. It flared with renewed demand, weeping its thick juices as he lifted her closer.

She sought his kiss again, her head tilting, her tongue licking at his lips, a moan shuddering from her chest as he gave her what she sought. Hot, moist, his tongue ravaging, his hands possessive as he lifted her, settling her against the table as he pressed between her thighs. Her bare thighs…

Oh God, she was so lost. How had he removed the pajama bottoms without her even noticing?

"Come here, baby." He moved back despite her protest, his hands lifting the shirt, pulling it over her head before she could form a protest.

"Sax… Not fair…" she cried out as he bent her backwards, his lips covering the hard tip of her breast as the words echoed around them.

She was going up in flames. She couldn't survive pleasure like this. It was too much. Too intense.

Her hands gripped his head, feeling the slick, shaved contours beneath her fingertips as she held him to her, gasping, crying out, fighting for breath as the intensity of his touch swirled through her.

This was what she had gone to that damned motel for. Because she couldn't resist the allure, the fire, the cascade of pleasure that infused every particle of her being.

"No, it's not fair," he growled, his lips raking over the incredibly sensitive tip of her breast. "I'm at your breasts when I'm dying to eat your pussy."

Shock held her motionless as he jerked a chair from under that table and pulled it to him. Sitting down, he spread her thighs, his eyes on hers as his head lowered.

"Breakfast," he whispered. "I always did prefer sweets first thing in the morning."

His tongue swiped through the ultra-sensitive slit of her pussy. When his tongue reached her clit, he circled with a hum of approval, licking around it, causing her to arch closer, a strangled scream of pleasure tearing from her throat.

She wasn't allowing this, she assured herself. She wouldn't allow it. It was dangerous. Not just for her peace of mind and her own heart, but for him as well.

But she was, and she was glorying in it, she realized distantly. Her thighs were spread for him, her hands gripping his head, holding him to her as he devoured her with lustful greed.

His hands were just as busy as his lips, and he was proving the rumor that he was definitely an ass man where a woman was concerned. His fingers were caressing from her pussy to the small entrance of her anus. And though Marey had been certain that particular fetish wouldn't infect her as it had her friends, as his fingers massaged, caressed, pressed, she found her curiosity and arousal heightening.

His mouth kept her pussy from missing the touch of his fingers, allowing his fingers to spread the slick cream that wept from her vagina back to the small entrance to lubricate and prepare it for the gentle impalement of his finger.

"Sax..." She was panting with the pleasure, unable to focus, no longer able to think. She could only cry out his name, lifting for him, poised on an edge of sensation she was certain would destroy her.

"There, baby," he crooned against her pussy, his voice vibrating against her clit. "Just enjoy. Let me show you good it can feel."

Another finger joined the first. She wasn't certain if her strangled cry was one of protest or encouragement, but she knew the slow, even thrusts of his fingers inside her—first one, then two—were pushing her past any boundaries she could have conceived.

He moved, shifted as his tongue dipped into the opening of her vagina, tracing the entrance, flickering over the sensitive tissue as he licked at the juices easing past it. She was so wet, so hot, it should have been humiliating.

Her eyes widened in shock as she felt his finger move back, felt the tip of another joining it. Cool, slick gel eased his fingers inside her, assuring her he was more than prepared for whatever his desires were that morning. Desires that were quickly becoming her own.

He prepared her slowly, easily, keeping her poised on pleasure so intense she was certain flames were going to begin rolling over her. Perspiration dampened her skin, fingers of heat ran over her repeatedly as the band of intensity tightened in her womb and the stretching fire increased in her rear. Fire that burned with a pleasure so mind-consuming there wasn't a chance of denying it. So soul-destroying that when he rose to his feet, releasing the straining length of his cock and pushing the waistband of his slacks around his thighs, she never thought to protest, never thought to consider that she was crossing a line she might never be able to return from.

"This is what you're denying yourself, Marey. Only a part of what you're denying us both."

He pressed the head of his cock against the stretched opening of her anus, lifting her to him, his hands spreading the cheeks of her buttocks apart as she felt the thick crest begin to penetrate the little opening.

Pleasure and pain collided as his gaze caught and held hers. She felt him enter her slowly, unbearably slowly, stretching her impossibly, sending her senses screaming with the conflicting sensations.

She had never believed that line between pleasure and pain would tempt her, would draw her to the extent that nothing mattered except pushing that boundary further.

"Breathe, baby," he whispered. "Deep breaths. Close your eyes and press out for me. Let your body milk me in, don't force it."

Her head thrashed on the table.

It was decadent. Splayed out on her breakfast table, Sax's cock slowly filling her ass as she stared back at him beseechingly. Her most perverted, most depraved fantasies were being played out, stripping her of control, leaving her pliable, willing, eagerly embracing the broad erection impaling her.

"Good girl," he crooned, his face twisted into a mask of pleasure. "You're so fucking tight, Marey. It's like being consumed by flames."

She was the one being consumed. Inch by inch as he worked his cock inside her, filling her, stretching her until he sank in to the hilt.

She couldn't breathe. She could feel the muscles of her anus convulsing, flexing and rippling around the length of flesh filling her. It was more pleasure than she could have envisioned. Deeper, more intense than the vibrators or plugs she had used there.

"Think of this, Marey," he growled as he began to move, holding her to him, sending her senses careening as he began to fuck her slow and deep. "Think of this, baby, the next time you're telling me I'm chasing a woman who doesn't want me."

She screamed as his movements began to quicken, one hand moving from her buttocks, his fingers going to her aching, empty pussy. Two fingers pressed inside, moving in tandem to his thrusts up her ass as reality began dissolve. The world centered on the dual penetration. His fingers moving inside the ultra-tight depths of her pussy, his cock fucking her ass with long, smooth strokes that steadily quickened, grew harder, more intense.

She writhed beneath him, straining toward release, begging for it, pleading as her body tightened to what she was certain was a breaking point.

"Now, Marey." His voice was strained, rough as she felt his cock flex and throb inside the sensitive channel.

His fingers moved faster inside her pussy, his thumb moving to her clit, stroking it, pushing her higher, higher…

She screamed as she fell over the edge of oblivion. Ecstasy washed through her body, burned along her nerve endings, sending her flying into rapture as she felt him explode, the heat of his semen filling her as he thrust in hard and deep one last time, groaning fiercely as he came inside the hot depths of her ass.

She settled down to earth long moments later, her eyes opening as he slowly withdrew from her. She watched as he fixed his slacks then reached to the counter to tear a handful of soft paper towels from their holder.

He cleaned her gently, watching her with those chocolate eyes that seemed to see clear to her soul.

"You can't turn back," he told her as he eased her up, holding her steady as she stood naked before him, fighting to find reality once again. "I won't let you."

"No matter how much it hurts me?" she asked him then, her voice hoarse, filling with tears as realization began to wash over her. "Does that matter, Sax? Does it matter at all how much it's going to hurt me?"

Chapter Two

"She has to be the most stubborn, independent, irrational woman I've had the misfortune to meet."

Sax slammed the file drawer in place, ignoring James' mocking snort behind him as he slapped the file he had pulled out on the desk between them.

He was irritated, horny as hell, and damn if he wasn't suffering from a guilt trip of major proportions.

No matter how much it hurts me? The words wouldn't leave his mind, ricocheting in his head as he fought against the pain he had glimpsed in her eyes.

"You act like you're surprised, buddy," James laughed as he leaned back in the chair in front of Sax's desk and watched him with amusement. "You've been chasing her for three years and just figured that one out?"

Sax sat down heavily in his own chair and regarded the other man with a frown.

"I don't appreciate the amusement you're finding at my expense, James," he snarled back. "Dammit to hell, she enjoyed every minute of it. Drenched my fingers when she came and still had the nerve to try to guilt me out of her life. I should tie her to the damned bed for a week and fuck her until she's too tired to guilt or deny me."

James chuckled at that one, not that Sax could blame him. Sax had been making that same threat for three years now.

"Vince is out on bail," Sax sighed then, worry and fury clashing at the thought of all the ways he could hurt Marey. "He disappeared within hours. If she doesn't ease up on the stubbornness, he's going to kill her."

It was his worst nightmare, that Vince would attack her again, taking her from him forever. It was hard enough waiting on the sidelines all these years, certain she would give in eventually. But now...Sax knew the waiting was over. The question was would the fragile bonds of emotion between them survive the dominance rising inside him? He was sick of waiting. And he was sure as hell sick of her denying the very thing he knew both of them craved.

"Vince will self-destruct eventually," James agreed. "All we can do is watch her, Sax. Daniel will look for him, Drew Stanton owns the security agency she's using—he has priority watch on her. The sheriff will keep a closer eye on the house during his patrols, and when he comes up for trial, Caleb will make certain he spends plenty of time behind bars. The members of The Club won't desert her. We watch out for our own, you know that."

Caleb Embers was the prosecuting attorney assigned to the case, and a member of The Club. Sax was well aware of the fact that if Vince made it as far as trial, then Caleb would fry his ass.

"Keeping him the hell away from her until he gets to trial is what worries me," Sax bit out. "She's so determined to deny us both that she could end up giving him the opening he needs. I swear to God, James, I can't understand her. It's as though she thinks she has to deny herself. As though she's paying penance for something that only she's aware of."

"Or terrified of a pattern repeating itself," James suggested then. "She put her life on hold for her parents. When they died, she wasn't a teenager any longer. Loneliness can do strange things to a woman, Sax. She married the first man who offered and learned within weeks the mistake she made. I have a feeling you're something Marey couldn't bear losing. So she's going to fight you harder."

Which was no more than he expected. But damn if it wasn't grating on his nerves.

"Tell you what." James leaned forward in his chair, watching Sax with a knowing glint in his eyes. "Let's head to the house for dinner. We'll have a drink and see if Ella has any ideas how to break her friend's control. She knows Marey better than anyone. If anyone knows how to find her weakness, it's my wife."

Sax tapped his fingers against the leather arm of his chair. He was right. And Ella would help too. She was worried as hell over Marey. She would make a great conspirator.

He moved quickly to his feet, ignoring James' amused laughter as they pulled on their suit jackets and headed for the door.

"So, who's your third lately?" Sax finally thought to ask his friend as they neared the door.

James snorted. "Ian came out of hiding. I think he's running though. Damn if he's not desperate to get as far away from his own house as possible since Dane's daughter moved in with him. Have you seen her?"

Dane Mattlaw had been Ian's best friend while he lived abroad in his younger days. The older man had been a steadying influence, while also helping to develop some of Ian's sexual tastes in the high-class brothels they frequented before Dane's marriage.

The daughter was a vixen. Not that Ian had introduced any of The Club's members to her.

"Mattlaw will kill him." Sax grinned when James' comment finally registered. "If he's running from her, then he's a little too interested."

"Too interested and denying it too hard," James laughed as they left the office. "Watching him fall is going to be fun, Sax. He's a little too superior in his attitude toward the rest of us after our marriages. We're all cheering for her. She's going to put a hurting on that boy that will bring him to his knees and make him cry for mercy."

That reminded Sax much too much of what Marey was doing to him. Damned woman.

* * * * *

"He's driving me crazy." Marey stomped into Ella's house hours after the kitchen interlude, ignoring her grinning friend as she made her way to the kitchen and the wine Ella kept in steady supply.

Hell, she was married to a Trojan, a dominant, woman-sharing, sex-perverted male that likely made Ella as insane as Sax was making her at the moment.

"He's a sweetheart, Marey," she laughed as she came behind her, moving to slide two wineglasses from their position under the cabinet and set them on the work island.

A sweetheart. Yeah, he was a sweetheart all right, and he was making her fucking crazy proving it. Keeping an eye on her, checking the house all the time, calling to make certain she was okay. The sound of his voice, that deep baritone, rasping over her senses, had nearly been her undoing several nights in a row.

"You should know," Marey finally snorted mockingly. "Wasn't he James' little buddy that first time?"

Ella cleared her throat, a light flush working over her cheeks at Marey's reply.

"If I had known you—"

"Oh, shut up." Marey waved the small guilt-ridden sentence away. "I don't have a problem with it. I just need solutions here. How do I get rid of him?"

She poured a half glass of wine, considered the amount then filled the glass. She needed definite liquid courage here. She smacked the bottle to the counter, lifted the glass and took a healthy swallow. She needed the strength right now, not to mention the balm to her nerves. The balm to her nerves was a definite must-have.

"Wine is for sipping, whisky is for swilling," Ella said mildly, watching her warily. "So why don't you care if I fucked Sax?"

Marey was in the process of sitting her glass back down. She paused, glanced at her friend and lifted it for another healthy swallow. Ella's timing sucked.

"Just don't let it happen again," she muttered as she refilled the glass moments later. "I might not be so forgiving now."

That was an understatement. She would be damned pissed, but she knew that Ella would never consider it after suspecting the feelings Marey had for him. Marey could confidently pat herself on the back that she had hidden her feelings for the man from even her closest friends. Ella had no idea until several weeks after she returned from her honeymoon. During one of Marey's late-night let's-consume-a-bottle-of-wine visits, Ella had revealed that Sax had been the third in the Trojan ménage James had set up.

Marey flushed uncomfortably at the memory of what she said in reply.

Touch him again and I'll rip your tonsils out! she had informed her friend haughtily. *James wouldn't find you near as attractive then.*

She sighed wearily. She had fucked herself there. Ella had tried to throw her in Sax's company ever since.

"But you don't want him?" Ella lifted a perfectly shaped brow with mocking inquiry.

"Don't start lecturing me, Ella," she snapped, pushing her fingers restlessly through her hair and wishing she had taken the time to confine the long, blonde strands to a braid or something. Anything to keep it out of her face. It was aggravating her, and she didn't need the additional frustration.

"Who's lecturing you?" Ella shrugged as she poured a half glass of wine, refilled Marey's then picked up her glass and gestured to the living room. "Let's at least argue in comfort. Why do you always have to come here looking for a fight? I have better things to do than fight with my friends."

Yeah. Like fuck James Wyman with Saxon Brogan as a third in a ménage that made Marey crazy to think about. Not that the past exploits bothered her. Ella was her friend—more like a sister—and really, if she had to share a man in such a situation, then it would be Ella she would choose, she thought whimsically.

Damn, that wine must strong.

Sighing, she plopped down in her favorite leather chair, wiggled a bit and then cast Ella an accusing stare.

"James has been sitting in my chair," she sniped. "He's messing it up."

She watched Ella smother her chuckle. No one was taking her seriously anymore.

"Well, sometimes, we share it." Ella wiggled her eyebrows suggestively as Marey gaped back at her.

"Eww." She jumped from the chair. "You fucked in my chair?"

"Well, I cleaned it later." Ella was definitely laughing now. "Don't worry, there's no evidence left of the event."

Marey shuddered and moved to the less comfortable recliner. "Have you fucked here too?"

"Honey, every square inch of this house has seen action this year." Ella leaned back in her chair, her eyes sparkling with laughter as Marey grimaced in distaste.

"I guess even the floor is grotty," she sighed as she collapsed back in her favorite chair. Dammit, she didn't want to think about sex right now. Didn't want to hear about it or know about it.

"Yup, even the floor is grotty," Ella laughed at the description. "Now tell me, why would it bother you if I fucked Sax now, if it didn't bother you before?"

Marey shot her an evil look. She deserved it. She was so damned confident and sexually wicked now that she should be burned at the stake.

"Women like you were stoned a hundred years ago, Ella," she reminded her with aloof distain.

"That was two hundred years ago, dear," Ella pointed out, toasting her with her glass. "Aren't you glad we were born during a much more sexually aware time?"

"You do not want me to answer that right now," she sighed wearily, staring back at her friend with a mixture of irritation and fondness.

"Answer me, Marey," Ella demanded softly. "I won't leave you alone until you do."

Marey sighed in resignation. "Hell, I don't know. Maybe I'm just as perverted as the rest of you." Ella shot her a disapproving look. One Marey ignored, just as she always had.

What the hell was she supposed to say? That jealousy just didn't come into it? She was smarter than that. Friends lasted forever, men didn't. Besides, she knew that Ella would have never let Saxon touch her if she had known Marey was even the least bit interested in him. Being angry over it now was nothing short of ludicrous.

"Then what is your problem?" Ella lifted her glass, sipping at her wine as she watched her with those probing blue eyes of hers.

Ella had always seen too much. She had known when Vince was abusing her, when she had taken enough and was preparing to leave, when she began to fear for her safety because of his threats. They had known each other for years, their parents had been best friends, and despite their age difference, they had always been close. That bond of friendship had only strengthened as they became adults.

"Ella, you have to make James talk to him." Marey finished off her wine before leaning forward and extending the glass for Ella to refill. "He's making me insane. He calls. Checks the house every night. And this morning, he had the nerve to show up demanding breakfast. He's trying to take over."

"I see..." Ella nodded somberly. "This would be a problem."

"It's horrible," Marey snapped, furious at the gleam of laughter in Ella's eyes. "I don't want him there. James is going to have to talk to him."

"Vince made bail the other day, didn't he, Marey?" Ella said then, her voice gentle, but knowing.

Marey leaned back in her chair, lowering her head to stare into the pale liquid that filled her glass.

Yes, Vince had made bail.

"That has nothing to do with it," she whispered. "I'm not a coward, Ella."

But she was. She could feel that knowledge crawling through her mind, mocking her with the sterile, lonely life she led.

"I never thought you were a coward, honey," Ella sighed. "Just frightened. And I never blamed you for that. But you have to fight back sometime."

Marey avoided her gaze, shaking her head as she swallowed past the lump in her throat.

"He would go after Sax," she finally whispered. "Not me."

And she couldn't bear the thought of that.

"And Sax is man enough to rip his face off," Ella snorted. "Come on, Marey. Vince only whips on people who are smaller than he is and you know it. Sax would grind that little bastard into dust."

"Or Vince would hurt someone else, and frame him again," Marey snapped. "Or do something to cause his brakes to fail, or any number of things that could end up destroying him. Dammit, Ella." She stared back at her miserably. "I can't let that happen. Can't you see that?"

"Vince is out on bail. Once he goes to trial, he'll go to jail," Ella pointed out.

"For how long?" Marey sneered then. "A year? Two?"

She sat the glass of wine on the table that separated their chairs as she rose to her feet. Crossing her arms over her chest she paced to one of the wide windows on the other side of the room before turning back to face her friend.

"I've grown used to being alone—"

"You're full of shit," Ella snapped. "You've grown used to hiding, Marey. Risking nothing and having nothing, and letting Vince terrify you. I won't have James talk to Sax." She lifted her chin stubbornly. "I think he's doing the right thing, and I think he's the right man for you. So forget it."

"You're such a bitch!" Marey snarled.

"Takes one to know one," Ella snapped back childishly, frowning back at her mulishly. "Maybe you'll get lucky and Sax will spank it out of you. Oh, but you might enjoy that. I'll tell him to hold off on it for a while."

Marey narrowed her eyes warningly. Ella's response was a cool little smile as she moved to her feet, facing her defiantly.

"That's low," Marey growled furiously.

"No, dear, low is telling you what a magical tongue he has," she sighed mockingly. "And how much he fairly loves to eat pussy. The man is a connoisseur. He can go at it for hours, and leave you screaming for more."

Oh, she didn't need to hear that. Her pussy flooded, her juices easing from her vagina to coat the bare, waxed folds beyond as she remembered just how good his tongue was.

Ella's expression was mockingly ecstatic, her eyes gleaming in confrontation, her lips curved into a satisfied little smile.

"And he has stamina..." She drew the word out pleasurably as Marey breathed in slowly, reining in her response. "His cock stretches you, makes you burn, makes you beg..." She closed her eyes dreamily. "He's almost as good as James."

"Glad to know I rate in there somewhere."

The sound of James' amused, deep voice had both of them jumping in startled awareness as they turned to stare at the door.

He lounged against the doorframe, incredibly handsome, sinfully sexy. Marey well understood why her friend had been so besotted with him for so many years.

"This is a private conversation." Despite her furious blushes, Ella drew herself up haughtily and faced her husband. Though Marey had no problem seeing the arousal that flared in her eyes.

"So I heard." His lips curved in a smile, his eyes gleaming with laughter. "Very interesting one as well," he mused as he crossed his arms over his broad chest. "Should I let Sax know you're up for a visit?"

"No!" Marey's furious exclamation joined Ella's as they both faced him now.

He chuckled in response.

"Go play or something, James." Ella waved her hand at him dismissively. "This is girl talk."

"So I heard," he drawled. "But maybe you would both like to know that Sax is due here in about ten minutes to go over a new product that's in design at the moment and to share a beer while he bemoans a certain woman's stubbornness. Marey might want to run while she has the chance. He's just waiting to catch her out of that fortress she owns, and she looks pretty primed right now."

He glanced to her breasts and Marey's gaze dropped to the royal blue silk covering the full mounds. Her nipples were poking against it like a four alarm signal for an all-night fuck.

Her gaze flew to Ella's in horror.

"This is your fault," she snapped. "I didn't need to hear any of that."

"But you still love me." Ella grinned.

"Bitch," Marey snarled again. "And yes, I still love you. But I am gone like the wind."

And she wasted no time in running. Sax was on a very, very short leash right now, and she knew it. As much as she loved Ella, there wasn't a chance in hell she was sticking around to see him. Because her own desires were on an even shorter leash, and growing fiercer by the day.

Chapter Three

She locked her doors when she got home. Ignored the doorbell, thanking God that Ella hadn't given Sax the code into the house as she had the gates. The next morning, she did likewise. Cowardice? Hell yes, she told herself fiercely. Sax terrified her where her weakness to him was concerned.

She finally slipped out around noon, unable to cancel her meeting with Ella at Delacourte to complete the planning for the annual Christmas party. She slipped in without incident. Getting out wasn't as easy.

"When are you going to stop running from me, Marey?"

Damn.

Caught in the empty outer office where James' secretary should have been standing guard, but was absent instead.

"I'm not running from you," she denied the charge calmly, despite the fact that she knew she was running. Every chance she could get for now on. "I was heading home. I'm finished for the day, Sax."

He stood in front of her, too close, but she refused to retreat. She had run from her ex-husband for years—that was humiliating enough. She wasn't going to back down from another man. Especially one she knew as well as she knew Sax. One that could make her senses sing with pleasure. Her body rock in orgasm. Her mind dissolve with no more than a touch. God, she was hopeless.

He towered over her, tall and broad, his shaved head gleaming in the light above them. Teak dark flesh was emphasized by the charcoal gray of his suit and his dark, chocolate eyes. Eyes that warmed as he watched her, just as his smile did.

How was she supposed to fight him and herself?

"I'm getting tired of waiting on you, Marey." Sax didn't beat around the bush. "You're tempting me into that little kidnap fantasy we discussed before. You might think hiding from me is achieving whatever objective you've set, but I can assure you, baby, the day is going to come that I'm not going to let you run any longer after yesterday."

She felt the flush that suddenly washed over her face.

"You really need to forget about that," she muttered, crossing her arms over her breasts as he braced his arm against the doorway, leaning against it casually.

He was about as completely yummy as a man could get. Yummy enough that her mouth watered with the thought of tasting him, her hands itched to touch him. And she knew every muscle under that skillfully tailored jacket was as hard and tight as that bulge behind the zipper of his slacks. A bulge well capable of satisfying a woman in any and every way.

She risked a quick glance down. Oh, hell yes, definitely yummy.

"You can touch if you want." He was openly laughing at her as her gaze flew back to his. "After yesterday, there's really no sense in being shy, honey."

Marey cleared her throat, not so much embarrassed and never shy, as she was aware of the tightrope she was walking. Fighting herself was hard enough. She didn't know if she could fight him as well.

Not considering the years of dreams and the silly emotional attachment she had developed to him after her divorce. Why she was running now made no sense to her, and she doubted it would make any sense to anyone else.

"That's all right," she finally replied calmly, refusing the invitation to touch him. "I do need to leave though, if you don't mind."

"Leave with me."

The offer left her stunned. Her eyes widened, her breath stuttering in her chest as he stared back at her somberly, intently. It was tempting. So very, very tempting.

"That's not a good idea, Sax," she finally whispered. "You know it's not."

"You can't keep running," he finally sighed. "And I'll be damned if I'm going to keep chasing after you. How long are you going to let Vince run your life like this?"

She glanced away from him, turning back as he straightened from the doorway and came closer. She stepped back, then stopped. She wasn't going to run from him. But God, how could she handle…

Her swift indrawn breath was fully audible as his hand lifted, smoothing down the silk covering her arm. The caress had her nerves tingling, but when his hand gripped hers where it rested on her other arm, she shuddered in response. The back of his hand brushed her hard nipple, sending shards of awareness whipping through her.

Her clit caught fire, swelling, burning out of control from no more contact than the back of his hand brushing the hard point. Her pussy clenched in empty hunger, reminding her that even her vibrators suddenly lacked the satisfaction she had once found with them.

"Sax, this isn't smart," she whispered. "You know it's not."

His head lowered, his lips smoothing over her forehead as she stared up at him. The warmth, the velvet roughness of the kiss had her eyes closing and weakness sweeping over her.

"I want you, Marey," he whispered as his lips moved along the side of her face to her ear. There, his teeth caught the sensitive lobe, tugging at it erotically as she shivered, her arms unfolding, pressing against his hard chest, her fingers curling in the silk of his shirt. "Yesterday was just a small treat. I want all of you. Hot and wet, moaning beneath me as I show you just how good we can be together. Wouldn't you like that, baby?"

She stood, dazed, pleasure sweeping over her as he lowered one hand to the curve of her buttock, his fingers shaping the flesh as his teeth raked her neck.

"Do you remember how good it was? I do. Buried snug and deep up that sweet ass. I want to bury in your hot little pussy next. Deep and tight while I feel you milking me, hear your wild little moans in my ears."

"You're not playing fair," she whispered, feeling the pleasure streaking through her womb, striking between her thighs and making her clit swell and throb with arousal.

She was so weak. Too weak.

"I'm not playing," he whispered a second before his teeth raked her neck again and his hand clenched the flesh of her rear. "Not in the least. Remember that, Marey. This isn't a game, and the next damned time you refuse to open that door to me, it's coming down. You can say no if you don't want to be touched, but I'll be damned if I'll worry if you're lying in that house bleeding to death or already dead. Don't make that mistake again."

His voice had her shivering in trepidation. He was serious. Too serious, and she knew it.

He straightened then, staring down at her broodingly, his eyes glittering with a sensual hunger and an emotional intensity that shook her to the tips of her toes.

"Hurry and run," he said mockingly. "Or you might not have the chance to get away again. The next time I have you cornered, I'm going to fuck you until you never dare to run from me again. You won't be able to breathe, let alone deny what we both want."

She blinked in shock. Run.

She moved quickly around him and did just that. Reluctantly. Straight home, to her room, to her bed, eyes closed and vibrator running as she fought to ease the craving for Sax's touch.

Sax breathed out roughly, as she did just as he suggested—she ran. He was growing tired of this. She was more skittish now than she had ever been before. And it broke his heart. He could see the yearning, the pain in her eyes, and wanted nothing more than to ease it. To love her until the pain vanished and the happiness shone through, as it did with Ella.

Dammit, he wanted her to choose, and there lay the bitter truth. He didn't want to force her to accept him, he didn't want to overcome her objections or override her shyness and fears. He wanted her to come to him. Arrogance? He snorted at that thought. Probably. But she had been running for so damned long that it was starting to grate on his ego.

"She'll stop running, Sax." Ella stepped from the office she had been meeting Marey in, her voice concerned, compassionate. "Sometimes she gets stubborn and you just have to let her wear herself down."

A smile quirked his lips. Ella had been defending her friend for months now. That had begun about the same time James had informed him that Ella had refused to participate in another ménage with him.

"I've waited a long time, Ella," he breathed out wearily. "I'm going to get tired of waiting soon. When I do, she might have more to worry about than Vince. She's going to have to worry about me."

Ella ducked her head, though he caught the amused curve of her lips.

"It's something that perhaps you should consider," she finally said as she raised her head, her gaze direct then, somber. "Marey doesn't always reach out for what she wants, Sax. She's too used to having it jerked away, just as she's within reach of it."

He wanted her to come to him. She had asked him, pleaded with him years before to leave her alone, to stop his campaign to seduce her, to hold her. He had promised himself then that when the time came, it would be Marey's decision. Perhaps that was where he had made his mistake. He hadn't known then the things he knew now. Her determination to hold herself aloof, to ensure she never lost anyone, nor was betrayed again.

He pushed his hand into the pocket of his slacks as he stared back at Ella, seeing the confident, sensual, loving woman she had become over the past year. She had run from James for nearly a decade, just as stubborn and determined as her friend was. She was happy now, glowing with it. Could he fill Marey's eyes with the same satisfaction, that glow of a woman confident and well satisfied with what she found in her lover's arms?

He lowered his head, staring at the rose carpet of the outer office as he fought to restrain the impulses that had been rising inside him for weeks now. After Vince's attack on her, he hadn't wanted her to feel as though she was confronting another extreme situation, a man unable to let go.

Perhaps instead of giving her the space to find the answers, he was doing as Ella suggested instead. Giving her a chance to hide. Marey didn't need to hide anymore. She had been hiding for far too long.

Chapter Four

Someone was in the house.

Marey jerked up in bed later that night, terrified as she heard the sound downstairs. What the hell was it? Why hadn't her alarm gone off?

There it was again. She blinked in the darkness. Was that a whistle? She stared into the dark bedroom, her heart racing, the sound echoing in her ears as she fought to wake up, to make sense of the sudden panic ripping through her again.

The new alarm system was supposed to be foolproof. Alerting the police and sounding a wail that would raise the dead if the house was breached. Evidently, it wasn't as secure as the salesman had promised her.

There it was again. It was a whistle. And she knew that sound. The grating little tune was one Vince was fond of. He would sound it for hours at a time, working himself into a rage as he did so. It always heralded another accusation, another rage, and in those final weeks of their marriage, another physical blow against her.

Shit. She jumped from the bed, jerking her robe on as she grabbed her cell phone from the bed and punched in the sheriff's number. This was insane. How the hell had he managed to get through the alarm and into the house? And why was he being so stupid?

"Sheriff's office." The dispatcher answered on the first ring.

"Janey, it's Marey Dumont," she snapped, her voice low. "Vince has broken into the house."

She had gone to school with Janey, knew her husband and her kids. None of them liked Vince. Not that she could blame them.

"Stay with me, Marey, I'll get someone on the way out there."

Marey listened as Janey's voice became more distant, imperative, as she called in the report.

"I have a car on the way, Marey," she came back, her voice calm, cool. "I want you to stay on the phone with me, honey, till they get there. You say the alarm didn't go off?"

"Not a peep," she whispered. "I just happened to wake up when he made a sound downstairs. I don't know how he got through."

It didn't make sense. Vince wasn't the brightest light in the house, and electronically, his skills were nil. He would have needed the code to the gates as well as the door.

There was a crash downstairs.

"You fucking whore!" Vince screamed from the bottom of the stairs then, as something else could be heard shattering against a wall. Dammit, he was breaking her vases, she thought miserably. She had paid a lot of money for those damned things. Her insurance company was going to scream.

"Shit. Janey, tell them to put some lead on the gas," she breathed out harshly. "He's drunk and he's pissed. How the hell did he get past my alarm?"

She moved quickly to the bedroom door, locking it before pushing the large, wing-backed chair over to it, and tilting it until the back was forced beneath the brass knob. It was the only security she could think of. Tomorrow, she promised herself, she was buying a gun.

"They'll be there fast, Marey, just stay calm," Janey assured her quietly. "I want you to stay back from the door. Hide in the bathroom and lock the door there. Get as far away from him as you can until help arrives."

She could hear her voice fade as Janey turned to the radio and called in to report to whoever was headed to the house.

She stood indecisively in the middle of the bedroom, staring around it in regret. She couldn't stay here. Vince was evidently insane. First the attack at the motel and now this. She couldn't, she wouldn't live this way.

"I'll kill you this time, you fucking bitch." He was at the door, his fists hammering on the door as Marey began to tremble nervously. "What makes you think you can whore around on me? I'll kill you for even thinking of letting another man touch you. You fucking slut. You're a dead woman!"

Enraged, almost incoherent, his curses slammed into her, making her stomach knot in fear as she bit her lip to hold back the cry of rage that built in her throat. They had been divorced for years, and she had been careful. Very careful to make certain he had no reason to torment her as he had that first year after their split.

His fists hammered into the door again, shaking the panel. He was a brute of a man. The door was heavy but she had no doubt he would get through it.

"Janey, this is getting serious," she breathed out, her voice shaking as she moved to the bathroom and locked the door there as well. There were no chairs to place against the door, nothing to hold him back. "These doors won't keep him out."

"Two minutes, Marey," Janey promised her calmly. "You can hold on two minutes. Get a can of hairspray, anything harsh. If he makes it past the doorway, spray his eyes full. Do whatever you have to. Sheriff Richards and Deputy Carlson are almost there. You'll hear the sirens soon and so will he. Maybe it will run him off."

She was right. Seconds later the sound of sirens wailing in the distance could be heard. Relief poured through her as tears filled her eyes. Her nerves clashed as she felt the jolt of Vince throwing himself against the door.

"The gates are locked," Marey told Janey, moving along the wall as she heard him crash into the door again. "The code is six, four, eight, three, two, nine. That's going to delay them."

Janey relayed the code to the sheriff before coming back.

"You hear them now?" The sirens were growing louder.

"You fucking whore. You slut," Vince screamed then. "I'll get you, bitch. When I do, I'll kill you. That damned sheriff won't save you every time."

The sound of running feet down the stairs assured her he was leaving. Breathing a sigh of relief, she collapsed against the wall, a tired, nervous little laugh escaping her throat as tears tightened her chest.

"He's gone," she whispered then. "Janey, he's going to fucking kill me. What the hell am I going to do?"

The house was a mess.

Evidently Vince had found quite a few ways to amuse himself before she woke up. Curses had been spelled out in lurid detail in black and red permanent marker across the walls. Her living room furniture was slashed, vases and heirloom glassware shattered. Some of the items Marey knew she would never be able to replace.

She stared around at the destruction, dressed in jeans and a sweater to ward off the chill that filled her body as the sheriff and his deputy filled out their reports and called the security company. Within hours, the house was filled with people, and all Marey could do was stand and stare around in confusion at the mess her ex-husband had made.

"You need to find a hotel, or stay with a friend for a few days, Marey." Sheriff Richards stepped around the mess in the entry hall as he moved from the living room. "The security system is intact, but he obviously has the codes. You're not safe here."

Duh. No shit.

Marey kept the sarcastic comment to herself as she stared back at the sheriff.

"What are you going to do about him?" she asked him carefully. "They let him out on bail. He could terrorize me further, Sheriff. Now what the hell are you going to do about it?"

He sighed roughly, propped his hands on his hips and shook his head. As handsome as the man was, right now, she wanted to kick his teeth in. He was being of no help whatsoever.

"We'll pick him up. He's violated the terms of his release, so the bail will be revoked. But until we catch him, you're not safe."

"She will be."

Marey froze at the dark, dangerous voice behind her. She turned slowly toward the open front door and stared back at Sax Brogan with a sense of fatal resignation.

Now, why hadn't she guessed he was going to show up?

A man shouldn't be so sinfully sexy, she thought. He shouldn't steal a woman's last breath with a frown, or make her knees weak from one of those hot little looks from dark, chocolate brown eyes. And he sure as hell shouldn't make her pussy burn in the middle of a situation that was precarious to say the least.

"Hello, Sax, it's good to see you again." Sheriff Richards nodded back at him as Sax stepped into the house. "I hope you're going to convince her to get out of here until we pick up Vince. She's getting a bit testy on me." He cast her an amused look.

Marey frowned back at him.

"I am neither testy, nor a child, Sheriff," she snapped. "And I don't need a man to take care of me. I can make decisions fine on my own."

She hated it when men acted as though a woman was only safe if she had a man in front of her. In Sax's case, if things went the way he wanted, she would have one behind her as well.

"Of course you can." The sheriff nodded. "Which means you're going to take my advice and get the hell out of here until I let you know we've caught Vince Clayton. Aren't you, Marey?"

Why did men always think *they* were right and she was wrong?

"Pack some clothes, Marey," Sax said easily, though she read the tense readiness in his body. "I'll take you to Terrie or Ella's, but you are getting out of here. If I have to carry you out."

His dark face was set in lines of determination and resolve. Marey glanced away, knowing that if she left with him, he wouldn't leave her anywhere else. She would be going to his house. His bed.

She glanced back at him knowing she was losing a battle she didn't really want to fight any longer. She had set this in motion when she made that trip to the motel, when she had let her desires and her needs overcome her common sense. She had no one else to blame but herself.

"Go on, Marey," the sheriff urged her. "We have an APB out on Vince, we'll have him in custody soon. Until then, protect yourself. Get the hell away from the house."

Like she had a choice at this point? She was well aware of the fact that she couldn't stay at the house, and she wasn't endangering her friends either.

Gritting her teeth in fury, she slanted Sax a fulminating look as she turned and stalked to the curved staircase.

"You're taking me to a hotel," she snapped, though she was careful to keep her back to him. "No questions, no alternatives. A hotel."

"Whatever you want, Marey," he called back, his voice carefully neutral.

Pausing, she turned back to look at him.

His expression was pure sin, sex in its most undiluted form. His dark eyes gleamed with it, his expression was filled with it. She was so fucked. Unfortunately, she had a feeling she was going to enjoy it. Too much.

Chapter Five

She knew he wouldn't do as she asked. How had she known? She was psychic, she sneered to herself. She had known because she knew Sax Brogan. Three years before, he had claimed her with no more than a kiss. A dark, sultry earth-shattering kiss that had filled her senses with visions of hot, carnal delights and her mind with her own screams of lusty need.

She had held him off with a simple request. A plea. And for years he had abided by it. Until the day he was arrested because she was attacked during a meeting that she thought would involve him. She had known when she stepped into that motel room that she had made a grave, tactical error. Not only was she losing the battle with Vince, but she had known, if she survived, she would lose another, much more personal battle, with Sax.

He didn't say a word after loading her large suitcase into the back of his Lexus and helping her into the passenger side. He had loped around the car, got into the driver's seat, put the car in gear and driven away from her home. Straight to his. A beautiful two-story contemporary home on the outskirts of the city, surrounded by trees on two sides and the haunting melody of the ocean on the other. It was as rugged and strong as he was.

And she had kept her mouth shut. She hadn't demanded he drive to the hotel. She had sat in the car, silent, watching the night pass by as her pussy grew wetter by the second.

"Nice place." She finally found the courage to speak as he closed and locked the door behind them. The room they stepped into was huge. There was no entryway, just a large, open ceiling living room that was roomy and comfortable and at the same time as enduring as she had always thought Sax was.

"It's home. The bedroom is up here." He led her to the double doorway, stepping into a short hall with a tall, oak staircase that led to the upper landing.

Like the living room, the hallway had an open ceiling allowing her to glimpse the railed hall above. She followed him up the stairs silently, her heart thundering in her chest, knowing she wouldn't, couldn't fight him any longer.

The bedroom he led her into was obviously his. The stark masculine furniture, a huge king-sized bed, tall, wide dresser and a low, mirrored chest. One wall was open, with a sturdy railing and a view of the living room. Beside it was a computer desk, the computer sitting atop it was still running, the last instant message he had received still displayed.

From Wicked, *Janey just called Tally. Vince hit the house. Get there now!*

"Well, so much for confidentiality," she remarked as she stared at the screen. "I thought dispatchers were sworn to secrecy or something?"

He moved to the computer and flipped off the screen with a snap before turning away from her and tossing her suitcase on the low chaise lounge that sat in front of the doors of the upper deck.

"You can put your stuff wherever you can find room," he told her dispassionately. "We'll go after the rest of your clothes tomorrow."

"Will we?" she murmured. "You and whose army?"

She faced him fully then, aware of the tension whipping between them.

He shrugged out of his jacket as he turned to her, tossing it over her suitcase. He stared back at her, his gaze vividly hot as his fingers went to the buttons of his shirt.

"I don't need an army, Marey." His lips pulled back from his teeth in an elemental snarl. "Stop baiting me. You know you're going to be here, at least for a while. Why not stop fighting it, and me, and we'll see where the hell this thing is going."

She drew in a short, quick breath.

"It shouldn't go anywhere," she snapped back. "Vince is insane, Sax. Do you enjoy placing yourself in danger?"

"The most danger I intend to face is that hot little pussy creaming between your thighs," he snarled back, jerking the shirt from his broad shoulders as his words left her knees trembling.

If her pussy hadn't been creaming before, it was now. Thick and hot, the juices seared the sensitive folds as her clit began to throb in an erratic, erotic rhythm. Her breasts became swollen, her nipples poking against her sweater, and she was certain every inch of her body was flushed from the heat rising inside her.

"Well, you're as direct as always." She crossed her arms over her breasts, facing him with a frown.

"I've learned to be, with you." His hands went to the waistband of his slacks, his fingers loosening the clasp of his belt with a rough movement.

"Sax." She swallowed tightly as the belt opened and his hands worked at the fastening. "Slow down."

He paused, staring back at her with hungry demand.

"I heeded that plea three years ago," he said coldly. "I won't this time, Marey. The time for games is long past."

But he didn't remove his pants. He came toward her instead, towering over her, making her feel weak, helpless. But protected. For such a large man, Sax had a way of turning her inside out and making her feel more feminine than any other man ever had.

"Look at you," he sighed as he came abreast of her, staring down at her with sensual demand. "So small and perfect, your eyes darkening with arousal. Every time you look at me, I watch that, watch your eyes get dark and hungry for me. Do you know how hard that's been to resist? How much I've wanted to throw you over my shoulder and take you away someplace where objections don't exist? Where the world disappears around us and there's nothing but me and you?"

Oh, now that really wasn't fair. She felt the breath suspend in her lungs as her womb convulsed in longing. To hear that sexy, deep voice saying something so wickedly hot that it had her trembling in need.

How long had it been since she had known a man's touch? Three years since Sax's kiss. Years before that. She had held herself aloof, no matter the loneliness or the sense of isolation. It had been easier to deal with the deprivation than the rages she knew Vince was capable of.

She stared up at him, helpless, weak with the needs thundering through her as he reached out, his hands gripping the hem of her sweater.

"I'm going to taste every inch of your body," he whispered as he drew the material over her midriff. "I'm going to eat you like candy, Marey, and listen to you scream for more."

He was going to have her screaming for more before he even got her shirt off at this rate.

"Sax." Her hands fluttered helplessly as the sweater cleared her swollen, unbound breasts.

No bra. She hadn't had time for one.

"Hell, I could come in my pants just looking at you, Marey," he sighed as his hand gripped first one wrist then the other, lifting her arms so he could pull the sweater over her head.

She was bare to him now, her breasts heaving, her nipples aching in response to the heated look in his eyes. His hands smoothed down her uplifted arms, drawing them down until her hands rested on his broad shoulders.

She trembled, shuddered in driving response as his hands lowered, cupping her full breasts, lifting them in his palms as his thumbs and forefingers tweaked the tender, responsive nipples.

She arched, gasping for breath as heat struck from the hard tips to the center of her womb. Her pussy rippled, the slick juices flowing in a rich stream to coat and prepare her for his penetration.

"Take my shirt off," he whispered. "Come on, baby. Show me you need this as much as I do."

She stared up at him nervously.

"I'm…" She licked her lips in hesitation. "I'm not good at this, Sax."

Her fingers flexed against his chest as she stared up at him, imploring. Vince hadn't been her first lover, but his abuse had all but destroyed her confidence. She was terrified of disappointing him.

Shame coursed through her. She had known it would be like this. He would expect her to participate, to know what to do, to know how to love him in turn. Her throat thickened with rage and tears as she realized she didn't know, had no idea how to touch him, how to pleasure him.

"It has nothing to do with how good you are at something, Marey." His voice was dark, deep, as he shrugged the shirt from his shoulders, her fingers touching impossibly warm teak flesh then.

She trembled at the feel of him. Strong and heated, the muscles of his chest bunching beneath her touch as her lips moved along his chest.

"Just touch me," he crooned gently, weaving a spell of sensuality around her that was impossible to resist. "I've dreamed of it, your hands on my flesh, your lips, your tongue, touching and stroking me with your hunger. Show me how hungry you are for me."

Hungry? She was starved. She could feel her hand soaking in the feel of him, sending the sensation to parts of her body that shouldn't even be considered erogenous zones.

As she stared up him, she licked her lips, her gaze centering on his. Perfectly, sensually full, they looked warm, inviting. She needed his kiss. She whimpered with the need, suddenly overwhelmed with the thought of touching and being touched. God, she needed him to touch her. Just a kiss. One small, light touch of his lips…

His head lowered, but there was nothing light in the possession he took of her. He groaned, a rough, desperate sound as his lips covered hers, his tongue stroking against the seam until she parted for him, gave him permission to raid the warm depths of her mouth.

One arm went around her, clasping her to him as her hand roamed over his chest, his steel-hard abdomen. He might work at a desk, but his body was in perfect shape, muscular and hard. So hard.

She moved against him, feeling the wedge of his cock behind his slacks, against her lower stomach. She trembled, pressing closer, her head falling back in surrender, her body sliding against his as her tongue reached out timidly to his.

Racing, desperate, clawing lust bit into her with a demon's razor-sharp bite. She arched, sizzling heat blooming in her belly and streaking to her clit, her pussy, her engorged breasts. Out of control, her hands slid up his chest, his strong neck, gripping the back of his head as his hands arched her closer, lifting her until he could grind the thick erection against the pad of her cunt.

She cried out, shaking in the grip of an arousal she had never known before. Never, even in the darkest dark, when dreams so erotic, so sensual attacked her, had she known such a powerful, driving need as what she felt now.

"Easy, sweetheart." His lips moved from hers, his hands holding her still when she would have followed, would have begged for more.

When he refused the caress, her lips moved to his chest. Sleek, tough skin over powerful muscles. Her tongue stroked over the dark flesh, her hands moving from his head to his abdomen. She wanted him naked, wanted him hot and blistering with desire as she was. It was killing her, the sudden, powerful sensations sweeping through her.

"There you go, baby." His deep, crooning voice urged her in her madness.

And it was madness. She was setting herself up for a fall, a small weak portion of her mind warned her. This was destruction. It was a fall from which there would be no recovering.

Her lips moved to his abdomen, close, so close to the opened waistband of his pants. And beyond. Beyond lay the object of her desperation.

She nipped at his tight flesh as his fingers threaded in her hair.

"Loosen my pants, Marey. Release my cock, baby. I'm dying to feel your hands on me. Soft, silken hands. Do you know how often I've dreamed of watching your hands stroke me?"

She could feel the pressure burning in her clit as he urged her on.

Her hands trembled, fumbled with the tab of his zipper, but finally managed to work it over the straining erection. She heard him moan as her fingers brushed the tightly stretched cotton of his boxer briefs as her eyes opened, widened as she glimpsed the impressive length of him beneath the material.

His fingers tightened in her hair.

"Do it, baby," he growled, his voice resonating with the same painful hunger whipping through her body. "Release my cock. Touch me, before I go crazy here."

She pulled the elastic waistband down, pushing at it as it cleared his thighs, freeing the dark length of his erection to her touch. She touched him timidly, amazed at the feeling of satin warmth, and beneath it, iron-hard strength. Thick veins ridged the length of his cock as the pulse of blood pounded at the flesh.

The head was flared, a perfect mushroom shape designed for pleasure, damp with pre-come and throbbing imperatively. Closing her eyes, Marey allowed her tongue to peek out, to wash over the crest, tasting the salty male essence of him as he moaned roughly.

"There you go." His breathing was rough, his voice deeper. "Let me feel that soft little tongue. Do you know it feels like hot silk?"

She licked over the head again, moaning herself at the taste of him. She wanted him, wanted more, she wanted to consume him.

Chapter Six

Sax knew he was walking a thin, fragile line with Marey. Her sexual confidence, as Ella had warned him, was extremely low. Nearly untried, hesitant, frightened, but so naturally sensual she was blowing his mind as she licked and probed at the tight, desperate flesh of his cock.

He wanted to push inside her mouth, wanted to fuck her lips and feel her sucking at him hungrily. But not yet. He had to let her take him as she needed him, explore and make him insane with the hot bite of lust.

His fingers tightened in her hair as her lips finally began to join the play. She sipped at the head of his cock, caressing him with feather soft strokes he was certain were designed to strip him of control. She was killing him, lick by slow, luscious lick.

"Oh hell. Yes. God, yes." The words were torn from him as her lips finally, blessedly, wrapped around the straining head of his cock and sucked him in.

Heat lashed at him, whipping through his shaft, tightening his scrotum and sending electrical impulses of sheer sensual pleasure streaking up his spine. He held her head, keeping her in position, holding her that she could only suck him deeper, but never fully release him.

She was moaning around the flesh stuffing her mouth, her tongue lashing at it as she sucked at him.

"Damn, your mouth is paradise," he growled. "All silky and wet and hot. Suck it, baby. Suck my dick, sweetheart."

He couldn't stop the words from pouring from his lips. Each phrase made her hotter, made her mouth tighten on him, her little tongue to go wild along the underside of the bulging head.

"That's a good girl," he crooned to her, closing his eyes, his head falling back on his shoulders as she sucked him like a little sex goddess. "Damn, Marey, that's so good. So damned good it's all I can do to hold back, baby."

He could feel the tightening in his balls, feel his release gathering, threatening to break the fragile control he was fighting so hard for. He wouldn't come in her mouth, not yet, not like this. When he filled her with his semen, it would be in a far more satisfying place than her sweet, hot little mouth. At least, he hoped it would.

"Enough." His voice was a rasping sound of desperation as his fingers pulled at her hair in warning, intending to draw her back.

A sharp moan echoed around the stiff flesh she suckled as he pulled the strands. Her fingers clenched tighter at his straining thighs as her back arched.

Sax grimaced tightly, tugging at her hair again.

She whimpered, the sound one of dazed, intense pleasure. So he pulled harder.

Big mistake.

Her mouth moved on him, shuttling up and down, sucking him voraciously as her little tongue stroked and probed and pushed him further over the line. Her hands wrapped around the base of his cock, holding it steady, stroking in time to her mouth above as he pulled her hair again.

Slick wet heat engulfed him nearly to her throat. She was taking more of him, ravenous now. "Marey, baby. I'll come down your throat," he warned her desperately. "Let up, sweetheart, or you're going to get every drop of it."

She stroked him more intently than ever, her mouth consuming him as he bucked against her, fucking past her lips as his hands pulled at her hair, relishing the unbidden, kittenish little mewls of pleasure that erupted from her throat.

He hadn't meant to take her like this first, he thought despairingly as he felt his balls tighten further, the tingling at the base of his spine intensifying. But it was paradise. Paradise and torment at once, and he was helpless against her. For now.

He held her steady, his hands exerting pressure on her hair as he deepened his strokes, driving into her suckling lips, his body tightening, sensitizing…

"Son of a bitch. Suck it, baby. Suck my dick, Marey. Take it all."

He felt the first hard pulse of semen as it shot from the head of his cock, splattering against the back of her throat as she began to swallow, moaning and twisting against him as he buried in deeper and gave her all he had. Harsh, rapid jets of seed spewing into her mouth, only to be caught by her hungry little tongue and consumed until he had nothing left to give.

He pulled back from her then, ignoring the soft cry of regret as his cock pulled free of her lips with a hollow little "pop".

"Come here." He urged her to straighten as his hands went to the metal snap of her jeans. "Kick your shoes off for me, baby."

He was pushing the waistband over her hips, going to his knees and burying his face in the soft flesh of her stomach as she shuddered in his grip.

"Your mouth is destructive," he whispered before allowing his tongue to dip out and probe at the shallow indention of her navel as she struggled out of her sneakers. Then he was pushing her jeans to her ankles, lifting her feet free and opening his eyes to stare up at her.

"You were a very naughty little girl," he drawled as his hand stroked up her leg to curl around the curve of a buttock. "Do you know what naughty little girls get?"

Her eyes darkened further, almost black now as he caressed her ass.

She shook her head sharply, her lips parted as she fought to draw in air. She looked dazed, almost uncomprehending as he licked at the damp, rounded flesh of her belly.

"They get spanked," he whispered then, watching her eyes, her expression.

Curiosity and trepidation filled both.

God, he couldn't believe how innocent she was, so sweetly untried that it would be the same as taking a virgin. Something he had never dreamed would turn him on until now.

He rose slowly to his feet, pulling her to the bed and sitting down as he stared back at her.

"I'm going to spank you," he told her, relishing the very idea of it. "I'm going to make your ass and your pussy burn so bright you're going to scream for me to take you. To fuck you until you can't breathe for coming."

"I will now," she gasped, her engorged, hard-tipped breasts rising and falling sharply.

His cock jerked at her rough declaration.

He glanced at the crotch of her panties. A silky thong that left her ass bare and clearly showed the dampness seeping from her pussy. He was going to bury his mouth there and see if it was possible to lick her dry. His mouth watered at the thought.

"You will anyway." He pulled her to him, drawing her down across his knees as she shuddered, the soft curves of her ass clenching.

Stretched over his lap, her head hanging down, her feet lifted from the ground, his hand smoothed over the soft, creamy perfection of her ass. He lifted the little band of fabric from the cleft of her butt, grimacing in raging lust as he parted the cheeks of her ass and glimpsed the small, delicate entrance to her anus.

Tempting. Tight. His cock clenched at the memory of being buried there.

He returned the material to its resting place, smoothed his hand over her butt then lifted it for the first soft blow.

She flinched, crying out at the first small smack. Not pain, he could tell by the arch of her sweet backside that it wasn't pain. Or at least, not a pain she didn't want to experience again.

The erotic, sensual burn on her butt was driving her crazy. She could feel her flesh heating, absorbing each small smack as it tingled and ached for more. She had never known anything so sexual, so completely naughty as being bent over Sax's knee, her ass burning from each erotic blow.

"You flush so pretty," he praised her, his voice dark and rough as another burning caress was applied to her rear. "A soft beautiful little blush." She shivered, jerking and crying out as he landed another soft blow.

It wasn't painful. It heated her flesh by degrees and sent sensations whipping through her body with lightning fast precision. Each little smack heralded a sharp, burgeoning ache in her pussy, making her juices flow from the ache deep inside. Her clit was swollen, throbbing, desperate for his touch.

"So pretty, Marey." His hand smoothed her buttock a second before he smacked it again.

She writhed on his knees, pressing her pussy into his thigh and whimpering with the rising demand vibrating there. She was burning. Each well-aimed, carefully timed smack to her rear only increased the flames.

"Sax, please..." she finally wailed as the next, firmer tap sent her senses careening. She jerked, shuddering as a burning lash flayed her clit and sent fiery fingers of sensation to attack her womb.

Her pussy was soaked. She could feel the juices clinging to her flesh, dampening her panties. Fire burned her from her ass to her cunt, making her writhe with a lust she hadn't thought was possible.

Before she could gasp, he lifted her, turning her in his arms and depositing her on the bed as he came over her. His cock stood out from his body like a flesh and blood lance, the tapered head glistening with pre-come.

His lips came down on hers again. A hard, deep kiss that had her moaning, twisting beneath him as her hands gripped his shoulders and her hips lifted to him.

"Not yet," he growled, his voice rough as his lips moved to her cheek, her neck. "Not yet, Marey. I've waited too long for this, I have no intention of rushing it."

"Sax, you're burning me alive," she whimpered.

It wasn't supposed to be this good. How was she supposed to survive losing something that felt this good, and he had even taken her yet.

"You'll burn brighter before I've finished," he warned her, the dominance in his tone making her shiver in anticipation.

His hands cupped her breasts then, lifting them to his lips. She watched, spellbound, as his tongue curled around the stiff peak of her nipple, licking at it, sending lightning-bright sensation shooting to her clit.

She convulsed with the pleasure, shuddering beneath him as he sucked the tender tip into his mouth, rasping it gently with his teeth before sucking it firmly. Her head twisted on the mattress as she fought to breathe. Arousal pulsed through her body like a hard electrical current, sensitizing her nerve endings, whipping through her bloodstream and driving her closer to an edge of pleasure she could never have imagined.

"Damn, you're exquisite," he growled as his lips began to roam lower.

He spread her thighs wide as he licked and kissed his way over her midriff, her abdomen, growing steadily closer to the steamy pussy covered by little more than a scrap of silk.

Silk that a second later ripped beneath his hands.

Excitement burst through her bloodstream, anticipation electrified her flesh.

She stared down her body, watching as he pushed her legs apart a second before he licked his lips and lowered his head.

The first firm, broad lick of his tongue through the drenched slit of her pussy nearly threw her over the edge into climax. She shuddered in the grip of pleasure, crying out hoarsely as she lifted her hips, begging for that final stroke that would throw her over the edge.

"Not yet." His voice was raw, carnal lust. "I'm going to taste you first, Marey. Every soft, slick, sweet inch of this delectable pussy is mine now. And I promise you'll never forget it."

She screamed a second later as his tongue plunged inside her. There were no gentle preliminaries, no warning. She was empty, then she was filled, his tongue stroking inside her as his hands gripped her buttocks and lifted her to his mouth.

He sucked at the juices that flowed from her, hummed his approval of her taste and her response against her clit until she was begging, screaming. She was dying in need of him.

"Please, Sax." Her hands gripped the comforter with desperate hands. "Please now. I can't stand it any longer."

He moaned against her flesh, his tongue suddenly flaying her clit, lashing at it with devilish greed as the pleasure grew and grew toward the explosion that would rip through her and destroy her mind. Her eyes widened, her lips opened to scream but all that emerged was a hoarse, brittle cry as her orgasm built, exploded through her with a force that left her convulsing, her muscles locking in desperate sensation as he came over her.

"You're not finished yet, Marey."

She felt the broad head of his cock press against the tender opening of her pussy, and while the spasms of her climax echoed through the clenching flesh, felt him begin to push inside her.

"Damn." He grimaced almost painfully as she arched, a throttled scream tearing from her throat as fiery pleasure-pain assaulted the muscles of her pussy as he began to stretch them open. "You're so fucking tight, baby."

She couldn't stand it. She couldn't survive it. She felt every inch of his erection as it tunneled inside her, stretching apart unused muscles, stroking nerve endings she didn't know she possessed.

The previous climax wasn't given time to die away or to abate before he began building the next one. Marey stared up at him, her eyes locked with his, bemusement whipping through her as she gasped, tried to beg but could only cry out as he shifted against her and wedged tighter and deeper inside her.

"You feel like wet silk. Hot, tight wet silk." His voice was a hoarse rumble as he breathed roughly above her, but his words…his words had her pussy convulsing around him as more of her juices eased his way.

Retreat, reenter. Retreat, reenter. Pulsing, throbbing strokes opened her tender flesh as he thrust his cock inside her. In and out, probing, deepening, wringing gasping screams from her throat as each stroke drove her higher.

"Oh, baby," he whispered as he lowered his head, kissing her lips, her neck. "Do you know how good this feels? Your pussy tightening around me, milking me like an erotic little mouth, sucking me in even as it tries to force me out."

His voice was so deep, so rough it was like a physical caress, stroking over her, inside her.

She bucked against him, driving him deeper as they both moaned in rapture.

"Hold on to me, sweetheart," he whispered at her ear then. "I'm going to take all of you now. Every. Sweet. Fucking. Inch."

She screamed as he drove inside her the last few inches, filling her to the hilt with heat and hardness, with fiery pleasure and the rasp of pain. One hand held her hip as the other lifted her closer to his chest as he began to move.

This wasn't fucking. She didn't know what it was, how she was supposed to describe it, but this wasn't what she had done with her ex-husband. This was primal, elemental. She hung on to his shoulders, her nails biting into his flesh as each stroke seared her cunt and set her clit on fire.

She moved beneath him, pushing against each thrust, driving him deeper inside her as she writhed on the impalement.

"Yes," he hissed at her ear. "Fuck me back, baby."

His hips rotated, his pelvis stroking against her clit as a white, bright light began to glow at the edge of her vision. She couldn't stand it. She couldn't breathe, she wouldn't survive the pleasure.

"Fuck me," he snarled at her ear again as he began to fuck her harder, driving inside her, pushing her higher as she slammed her hips back at him.

"Sax. Sax, please…oh God… Sax, it's too good…too good…" She felt the crescendo rising inside her. Her womb tightened, her clit began to pound with a steady hard throb until she exploded.

She felt herself come apart in his arms, over and over again. It wasn't a single, terrifying explosion, but multitudes of them washing over her, convulsing her entire body beneath him as a strangled cry wailed from her throat.

Another hard thrust as she heard him groan, his head lowering, his hips driving his cock deeper, harder, and she felt the first torrential explosion of his semen inside her. Each hard blast of his release had her shuddering in renewed pleasure as it echoed within her own climax.

It seemed to last forever, and yet it ended too soon. She collapsed beneath him, fighting to breathe, drowsiness weighing at her limbs as she felt him move, and moaned at the feel of his cock sliding free of her as he fell beside her.

His arms came around her, hard, warm. Protective.

"I'm tired," she sighed, snuggling against him as her eyes fluttered closed.

"Sleep, baby," she heard him whisper gently. "Sleep right here. Where you belong."

Chapter Seven

Sax sat at the edge of the bed hours later, staring down at Marey as she slept. His mind was a morass of thoughts and emotions. Finally, he had her here, where he wanted her, had wanted her for years.

The sheet was pulled to her hips, revealing the delicate lines of her back. Her dark blonde hair fell over her neck and shoulders and framed her profile like a silken cloud.

Her unique looks could never be described as beautiful, they were too strong, too stubborn for such a term. His lips quirked in a grin as he considered the stubborn part. Her expression often reflected the inner part of her, willful and determined, but it was subtle. A quality many people often missed because they were unaware of what they were looking at.

But Sax knew. He had seen it in her the first time he met her, just before her divorce. He had seen the misery in her eyes, but her determination to hide it from her friends. When she thought no one was looking, weariness and resignation would draw her shoulders down before she would resolutely straighten them.

For years after the divorce, despite the hell he knew her ex-husband had put her through, she had maintained a dignity that he could do nothing but admire. And a body that drove him crazy to possess.

He loved her. Despite the fact that she had run from him, that she had denied him at every turn, the need for her wouldn't ease. It only grew stronger, deeper. He had her, for now, but he was smart enough to know that keeping her wouldn't be as easy and getting her into his bed had been. He would have to keep her off balance, keep her body humming, her mind immersed in her sensuality until she knew she couldn't survive without him.

He knew what she hid from herself. He saw it in her eyes, in her voice, in the hunger in her expression. He had her heart, she just had to realize it. And getting Marey to realize what she didn't want to see would be his hardest battle.

He drew the blanket further over her back before rising from the bed and heading for the shower. He had waited, watched, knowing the day would come when Marey would drop her shields and allow him the chance he needed to break into her heart. He was in there now, though he was certain she would deny it to herself as long as she could.

He also knew something else about Marey, something she had revealed hours before. She loved the sensual dominance he could give her. She liked the fiery pleasure-pain and walking that fine line of carnal intensity. He would push her, he couldn't give her time to think, to consider the evolving relationship he could see coming. If he did, she would run. And he couldn't allow her to run. He wouldn't allow her to run.

"When you get ready, I need to run in to the office for a few hours," Sax announced as Marey sat silently after breakfast, fortifying herself with caffeine, wondering how she was going to manage to escape this new situation.

Sex with Sax was incredible. Too incredible.

"Go ahead." She took the final sip of her coffee. "I'll get ready and you can drop me off at a hotel."

The tension that filled the room was like a punch in the gut. She raised her eyes, staring back at him as he watched her silently, his eyes narrowed on her.

"Stay a few days," he finally suggested casually, as though it didn't matter either way, as though there was no risk in such an action. "At least until they've picked Vince up, Marey. You aren't safe in a hotel. You're safe with me."

She breathed out wearily, pushing her fingers through her still damp hair as she sat back in her chair and watched him directly.

"And if Vince decides to blame you for the fact that I'm here, rather than where he can get to me?" she asked him defensively. "What then, Sax? He's not sane. He won't go after you with his fists as he does me. He could come after you with a gun."

A savage smile tightened his lips.

"I would look forward to it, Marey," he snarled. "Unlike you, I know how to deal with bastards like that. He won't get to me easily, I promise you that."

Were all men insane? Or just the ones she knew?

She closed her eyes as she clenched her teeth and held back a furious growl.

"And what makes you think you're invincible all of a sudden?" she snapped, coming to her feet, ignoring the glint in his eyes as they dropped to her bare legs beneath the long hem of one of his T-shirts.

"I don't think I'm invincible, Marey," he assured her, his voice deepening, thickening with lust as he watched her. "But I know the type of man Vince is. A bullet isn't personal enough, it doesn't prove his strength, and that's what's important to him, proving his superiority."

In that, he was right. Vince couldn't tolerate believing an opponent could be physically superior to him. He didn't own guns, he owned fists and knives.

"And I'm supposed to just accept the fact that you're placing yourself in his path," she snapped belligerently. "I don't think so, Sax. I don't need these problems."

"Do you think he can beat me, Marey?" Genuine amusement reflected in his expression then. "Are you afraid your man can't protect you?"

"You aren't my man," she muttered, using the only defense she could come up with. "And right now, you're acting like a little boy playing one-upmanship."

"One-upmanship is not a child's game," he informed her with a slow, sexy smile. "It's a man's game. Want me to show you?"

Oh man, the sound of his voice, the look in those dark eyes. Her pussy was suddenly humming in need, creaming furiously to the pure sexuality there.

"That's okay." She scuttled quickly out of his way, watching him warily now. He could turn her knees to mush and her resistance to no more than a passing thought. There wasn't a chance in hell she was going to let him touch her. "You go on to the office. I can just lounge around here. Use the hot tub." Call a cab and find a good hotel.

He tilted his head questioningly. "If you walk out of here now, we'll never know what could have been, Marey. Is that what you really want?"

Was it? No, she didn't want that, but neither did she want to see Sax pay for her mistakes.

She drew in a harsh breath. "After they catch Vince—"

He was shaking his head before the words were out of her mouth.

"I don't want a woman who can't trust me to protect her." He crossed his arms over his chest, staring down at her somberly. There was no anger, no fury, just pure male stubbornness.

Marey stared back at him, bemused. He should be furious, not calm. In hindsight, she realized she had more or less given the impression she didn't trust him to protect her. She hadn't meant to. She had never felt that way. But his male pride should have at least been pricked. There should have been anger, a snarl, snapping sarcasm. Something besides somber intensity, steadiness.

Her hands clenched in the material of the T-shirt as she fought to come to grips with this new brand of male species. Who knew they could be so damned hard to figure out?

"I trust you to protect me," she finally answered, clearing her throat nervously. "It has nothing to do with that. I'm used to protecting myself, Sax."

She had been doing it for a long time. She might have messed up a time or two, but for the most part, she thought she'd done a fairly good job.

"And Vince is determined to hurt you, no matter the cost to himself," he told her quietly. "You know you can't fight him, Marey, you've seen that. He tried to kill you."

"I don't need you to stand in front of me." She turned away from him, furious herself now as she paced to the sliding glass doors that led to the deck. "Dammit, Sax, why do you think I've stayed away from you? Why do you think I've lived like a nun in that damned fortress Father built, and forgot I was woman all these years? He's crazy. He could try to kill someone."

"Yes, he could," he snapped, but not in anger, more in frustration. "And that someone could be you. Because he knows you're not strong enough to fight back. Until the sheriff apprehends him and the courts put him away for good, you need to stay safe. I can keep you safe."

He said the last sentence as he moved behind her, pulling her against his much taller body, his strong, warm body, as she fought the weakness that filled hers. He made her weak, made her want to lean on him, trust him. How insane was that? She knew better than to trust anyone.

"If you walk away now, Marey, it's forever." He lowered his head, pressing a kiss to her hair as his eyes met hers in the glass. "Now, are you going to the office with me, or do you want me to take you to that hotel?"

She stared back at him, their gazes locked in the glass of the sliding doors, and frowned fiercely.

"You are going to piss me off," she finally snapped.

Surprise flared in his eyes. Surprise and arousal.

"Baby, that's a given," he chuckled. "Now, make up your mind and let's get out of here. I have work waiting."

Chapter Eight

Sax watched from beneath his lashes as Marey lounged on the couch on the other side of the room, calmly flipping through a magazine as he worked on the reports he needed to finish up for the day.

She was driving him crazy. She was as calm and placid as a mountain lake right now, waiting on him, as though it was nothing unusual to have little or nothing to fill her day. He knew she was an editor for a small publishing company, one that published extremely erotic content. She hadn't been the one to reveal the information though, it had been Ella who had dropped that little bomb months before.

Was that how she had learned to sit so silently, immersing herself in whatever she was reading? Or had she learned patience and silence while caring for her ill parents so many years ago?

There was so much about her that he needed to know. So many ways he wanted to learn everything possible about this intriguing woman.

"Bored?" he asked curiously.

She glanced up, her gaze a bit distant as it met his.

"No." She shook her head. "I have company."

She lifted the edge of the magazine before returning her attention to the article she was reading. It wasn't fluff. The news magazine was one of his favorites actually.

He shifted in his chair, attempting to ease the uncomfortable weight of his throbbing erection.

"Do you need to run by your house before we head back to mine?" he asked her then. "Pick anything up?"

She glanced up again. "No. I should have enough for a few days."

Her attention went back to the magazine. It made him crazy. Made him horny. She was as calm and relaxed as a summer's day, and just as damned hot. He knew how hot she could get, how wet and sweet.

"How long has it been since you've had a lover?" he asked her then, shifting to relieve the discomfort of his hard-on.

He watched her tense before she looked back at him, narrow-eyed and suspicious, but hot.

She glanced at her watch mockingly.

"Eight hours maybe?" She went back to the magazine.

Sax observed her for long moments. She looked cool as hell, but he could see the altered breathing, the heavy rise and fall of her breasts. She was aroused. Just that fast. Her nipples were pressing tight against her shirt, her face flushed just enough to testify to her heat.

"Before that," he bit out between clenched teeth, waiting, his erection throbbing in agony.

She flipped the magazine closed and turned to him defensively, her gray eyes sparkling in defiance.

"Exactly what do you want to know, Sax?" she asked him. "And why all the questions?"

God he loved it when her eyes went hot like that. Anger and passion and complete female stubbornness mixed with arousal. It was invigorating, energizing. It was making him so fucking horny he couldn't breathe.

"Does everything have to be a test?" he growled back, coming out of his chair and stalking across the room. "Maybe there are just things I want to know about you."

"You should pretty much know everything by now," she shot back, staring up at him as he towered over her. She didn't jump to her feet to even out the distance or to assert her own control. She kept her seat, though she leaned back against the couch to keep the arch of her neck at a more comfortable angle. "It's not as though we've just met."

"And the more I think about it, the less I know," he told her, frustration rising within him.

"And how many lovers I may or may not have had is important?" She arched her brow mockingly. "Fine, Sax, until you, there's been no one since my divorce. Before my marriage there were two. I'm sexually inexperienced but not stupid. Anything else?"

"What the hell do you do all day besides flip through magazines and edit romances?" His cock was steel-hard and driving him crazy with the need to fuck.

She smiled slowly, her eyelids drifting lower, giving her a mysterious, sensual look.

"Play with my favorite toys and fantasize about you," she drawled. "What do you do when you're home alone?"

The little liar. He could see the devilry in her gaze, the deliberate teasing in the way her tongue stroked slowly over her full, lower lip.

"Jack off and imagine your ass burning red," he snarled, reaching down and pulling her to her feet. "I won't let you hide from me forever, Marey."

"But I'm not hiding anymore, Sax," she reminded him, her hands moving up his chest, over his shoulders. "I'm right here where you can see me."

God, she was a temptation. A sweet, beautiful little keg of dynamite standing placidly in his arms. For now.

She shifted against him then, her lower stomach pressing against the hard ridge of his cock as a light flush of arousal stained her cheeks.

"Are you finished working?"

His fingers burrowed in the soft weight of her hair as he held her still, watching the heat flame in her eyes.

"I'm finished," he growled as he pulled at the silk he held, watching her eyelids drift lower as sensual weakness consumed her.

"We could go back to the house." Her hands moved from his shoulders to his waist, gripping the flesh there as his head lowered to her cheek.

"I won't make it to the house," he told her roughly. "I want you here. Now."

A low, aroused laugh came from her throat as she tilted her head back, allowing his lips to caress her neck.

"Trojans and their office sex. I've heard about that."

"You hear too damned much. Those women have loose lips." He nipped at her neck, imagining her stretched out on the leather sofa, naked and filled with his dick.

She gasped as his hands moved to her breasts, cupping the delicate weight, his thumb and forefinger testing the hardness of her nipple through the soft silk blouse she wore. He was dying to get it in his mouth, to feel the sensitive nub growing harder as he sucked at it.

"You know too much about things you shouldn't." He nipped at her neck, feeling her shudder from the erotic little pain he delivered.

"Hmm, have to get my jollies somewhere," she moaned as he licked at the soft flesh he had nipped.

Oh, he could give her jollies, he thought with a grimace of building lust, more jollies than she could have imagined.

As his lips moved to hers, taking her in a kiss that had them both moaning at the heated pleasure of it, his hands went to the small buttons of her shirt. He wanted her naked, wanted her wet, wild and screaming out her pleasure.

"You need to lock the door," she gasped as the sides of her blouse fell apart and his lips wandered down her neck.

Her breasts were swollen, flushed, her hard little nipples poking against the lace of her bra as his lips drew closer.

"Hmm. Live dangerously," he murmured as he licked over the delicate curves. "Consider it a jolly."

Chapter Nine

Consider it a jolly? She was fucking going to go through the roof as it was.

"You're crazy." She could feel the fires building in her body, the heat attacking her pussy like an inferno gone wild.

"Am I?" He drew the shirt from her shoulders, dropping it to the floor as his fingers moved to the clasp of her silk slacks. "It's closing time, but anyone could still walk in. A lot of the Club's members come in to my office, Marey. They wouldn't touch you, but they would watch, see your little pussy flared around my cock, hear your cries as I go in hard, deep, and push you over the edge."

She trembled, her eyes closing at the insidious images he was provoking.

"Have you ever been watched, baby?" Her pants dropped to her ankles, revealing the white lace thong she wore beneath them. "Seen the arousal in another man's face as your lover pumps into you? And I would. I would give them a show. I would show them how sweet and tight your cunt grips me, draw out and let them see the slick, syrupy juices that flow from you before I'd push back in, and let them hear your screams."

Oh God. This was just nasty. Depraved. It was killing her. She had never, ever done anything like that. But she had to admit, Terrie and Ella had piqued her curiosity, made her wonder if it could truly be as good as they claimed it was to be part of Sax's sexual lifestyle.

"How..." She fought the moan that would have been more a scream as his hands gripped the cheeks of her ass and he pulled her closer to him. "How can you share like that? Why aren't you jealous?"

"Because I want your pleasure. All of it. I want to see the surprise and the sensual agony twisting your features, and know I'm a part of it. I want to see you screaming, begging, every inch of your body caressed and pleasured. But we'll both know who you belong to, Marey," he whispered. "Won't we?"

His lips lowered to her breast, his gaze still locked with hers as his tongue curled around the elongated nipple, sensitizing it further, sending currents of pleasure ripping into her womb.

Who she belonged to? She knew who she belonged to, and it terrified her. Marey shuddered as pleasure burned through every cell of her body and the truth of her own sensuality and emotions burned through her mind.

She had waited for this. Longed for this. Even before she knew the sexual lifestyle Sax embraced and what a relationship with him would mean. She had put her own sexuality on hold, waiting, knowing the day would come when she would have this chance, this brief time to be the woman she had always longed to be in his arms.

As his lips created havoc and mind-destroying pleasure with her nipples, Marey's hands moved to his shirt. Her fingers slipped the buttons free, her hands pushed the material from his broad shoulders. She needed to touch him, to feel him. She needed to memorize every rough indrawn breath, every groan that came from his chest, so she would have the memory later, when the man was gone.

Her hands smoothed over his bare chest, down the tight planes of his abdomen, to his slacks. She made short work of opening his slacks as his lips sipped at her nipples and his hands roamed over her back and shoulders. She needed him naked, close to her, warming her.

"Come here." He pulled her to the couch, easing her upon it until she was stretched out and staring up at him with dazed need.

God, she ached. The sensual pain was destroying her. She had never, at any time in her life, been as aroused as she was now.

"I could eat you forever," he whispered as he knelt on the floor, slowly pulling the thong from her body, his hands spreading her thighs, positioning her until her pussy rested at the edge of the cushions. "You have the sweetest pussy I've ever tasted, Marey."

His lips lowered to her as she watched, his expression tight with lust, his dark eyes glowing with it as his tongue extended and swiped slowly through the shallow, bare slit of her pussy.

Marey jerked, flinching at the pleasure of his heated tongue licking her, caressing her waxed folds with hungry intent. He wasn't in a hurry. He parted the inner lips with his thumbs and explored the valley with destructive leisure as she tensed and fought to rein in her own pressing need for orgasm.

Her hands went to her breasts, her fingers plucking at her nipples as she watched him, entranced by the sight of him, so big and broad between her splayed thighs, as he made a sensual meal of the heated juices that spilled from her pussy.

His eyes flared at the sight of her pleasuring her breasts. It sent a sharp biting thrill shooting through her body to realize it had pushed his arousal higher. She fought to ignore the emotional impact, the chinks developing in the shields she had raised against him. She wanted to enjoy, to allow every fantasy she had ever had of him, life.

Her breath hitched as his tongue circled her clit, his lips surrounding it to suck at it gently as tremors of ecstasy began to ripple through her womb. Then his hand moved, his fingers sliding through rich feminine cream, easing it lower as he massaged the tiny entrance to her anus.

Her eyes closed. She couldn't watch him, couldn't let him see what it was doing to her. He prepared her slowly, drawing her juices back, pressing the pad of his finger into the small opening as she bit her lip and tried to hold back the pleas and cries that would have spilled from them.

"You're so tight," he groaned, his voice a hard rumble in his chest. "So sweet and hot. But I want you hotter. So hot, that you have to have more."

She wanted more now. The small, tiny little bites of sensation weren't enough. She needed more.

"Do you like that?" His finger slid in deeper, massaging the sensitive nerve endings just inside the entrance, making her tighten on him, then relax. She needed more.

"Sax..." She was breathing hard, heavy. "More. Please."

She heard a growl, a hungry male sound of pleasure as he slid in further, his lips moving on her clit again, building the pleasure inside her to a lava-hot intensity. She couldn't bear it. She whimpered, her hips writhing, pressing closer, impaling herself further on the broad finger penetrating her ass.

Each surging, burning fork of pleasure that struck her drove her higher. She was panting, pleading, mewling sounds of need falling from her lips as she felt herself nearing the edge.

"Go over for me, baby," he whispered roughly as his lips surrounded her clit, one hard finger penetrated her gripping pussy, while the one that teased her anus slid in, sending fire scorching through her body, pleasure tearing through her senses until she erupted, shuddering and screaming out her pleasure as her orgasm exploded through her.

He didn't give her time to come down, for the vibrations to ease away. He rose between her thighs, his cock jutting toward her, thick and hard as her gaze centered on it.

He pressed the erect flesh against the bare folds of her pussy as Marey gasped, watching as the flared crest pushed in, disappearing inside as flames began consume her. He held her legs over his arms, holding them apart, watching as she watched, filling her slowly as she began to tremble.

"Sax. It's so good," she cried out, her voice barely more than a low gasp as the pleasure began to consume her once again. "It's so good...so hard..." Her back arched as she panted for breath, using her inner muscles to caress and milk the iron-hard flesh as it impaled her.

"And you're so soft," he growled. "So soft and tight you steal my mind, Marey."

He pushed into her, stretching her slowly, filling her pussy with the incredible heat and pleasure that she knew she would only find with Sax.

Her gaze stayed centered on his dark cock as he impaled her. Moving inside her slow and easy, working in and out until finally, every inch buried inside her, stealing her breath.

Control was, for both of them, a thing of the past then. Sax didn't take her gently, though he never hurt her. He held her firmly in place, his hips moving hard and fast, his cock jackhammering inside her with a frantic, almost desperate pace as the pleasure began to build, to whip through her in blistering bolts of sensation that had her screaming, her head falling back against the couch as she arched to him.

It was too good. Too hard. Too much pleasure.

"Harder," she screamed out as her orgasm began to peak, the slamming of his erection inside her stroking nerve endings too sensitive, too responsive, for her control to handle. "Harder, Sax. Fuck me harder."

He groaned, the sound rough and primal as the thrusts increased, the heavy pressure building in her pussy, her womb, her soul...

She exploded, screaming out his name as she felt him drive in deep, felt the flexing of his cock, then the scalding release of his seed as it began to jet inside her, prolonging her own orgasm, driving it higher, hotter.

She collapsed minutes later, fighting to breathe, to make sense of the incredible lethargy and sense of peace that suddenly filled her. As though this was where she was meant to be.

That evening, wrapped in a towel and carrying a bottle of chilled wine, Marey joined the five Trojan wives in Sax's hot tub. The impromptu meeting had been arranged before they left the office. As they were leaving, James had invited them to ride back with him and Ella in the company limo. With a knowing grin, he had informed Sax that Ella was becoming impatient to visit with Marey, and putting her off was evidently causing him a few sleepless nights.

Tess, Cole's wife, was stretched out on one end of the ten-seat tub, eyes closed as she smiled at something Terrie, Jess' wife, said beside her. Ella, married to Jess' twin brother James, sat on the far end beside Tally, the only woman lucky enough—or was that courageous enough?—to be in a relationship with the twins, Lucian and Devril Conover. Kimberly, Jared Raddington's wife, sipped at her wine as she watched everyone else. She was the quietest of the five women, but no less important within the small group.

"You're taking long enough, Marey," Ella smirked as Marey dropped her towel and eased naked into the bubbling water.

She snorted at her friend's comment as she poured a glass of wine and sat the bottle on the deck behind her.

"Doesn't it bother the rest of you when those men close themselves off like that?" she asked, referring to the fact that the seven men were now closed in Sax's office, discussing only God knew what.

It bothered her. Made her nervous, especially considering the fact that her lover was one of them.

"Yeah, maybe the rest of them are giving Sax advice," Ella drawled. "You know, on how to spank stubborn women."

"Naw, that's a treat," Tess countered with a laugh. "They're in there convincing him of the merits of abstinence. Punishment lies in doing without, not getting extra. Ask Cole, he's learned that fact several times."

"Yeah, right," Terrie snorted at that one. "Come on, Tess, 'fess up. What's your best holdout time? An hour?"

"Almost," Tess laughed back. "Or until he pulls out the toys."

"Oh God. I shouldn't have to listen to this." Ella covered her ears in mock horror. "That's my daughter."

"Prude," Tess chuckled.

"Not anymore, Tess," Terrie pointed out with a laugh. "James and Sax reformed her."

Ella's blush covered her upper chest, neck and face as she splashed water back at her friend.

Marey glanced at Kimberly then, seeing the flush that filled her face, the way her eyes lowered. Ella had admitted it had been damned near impossible to talk Kimberly into joining the group, because of her past exploits with Sax at the Club.

"Sax as a reformer," Marey drawled. "Now that one is hard to imagine."

She ducked as Ella splashed water at her, before chuckling easily. It was odd, being amongst this group, all of them together at once. She had avoided the larger gatherings over the past year, unwilling and unable to bear the frank discussions she knew arose within them.

"Of course he is, Marey," Tally entered the joviality then. "He's reforming you. I bet he's already choosing prospective seconds now. Maybe that's what all the secrecy is all about."

Her tilted eyes sparkled with amusement and fondness as Marey shot her a dark look.

"It occurs to me, that the five of you are finding much too much amusement in this," she announced haughtily. "Maybe I'll reform Sax."

Laughter erupted around her at her comment.

"Yeah, I can see that one happening," Ella toasted her with her wineglass. "Let me know when it works, hon, and we'll all enjoy our fun and games in your memory as we make a note to keep our men away from yours. If you reform the Trojans, we might all have to hurt you."

Marey rolled her eyes, shaking her head at the knowledge that her friends relished the occasional threesomes their husbands provided, and the more extreme sexuality they possessed.

"I can't see Sax reforming," Kimberly spoke then as though forcing herself to face a problem head-on. "Any more than the others would."

"Sax definitely does seem to enjoy the screams he inspires," Ella chuckled. "Are you screaming yet, Marey?"

"Remind me to kill you, Ella," Marey growled affectionately. "How do the five of you do this? Sit and discuss this? Jess had sex with Tessa, but I'll be damned, Terrie, if it bothers you in the least. Lucian had fun and games with Terrie. The five of you should be mortal enemies."

"Yeah, and Sax played really nice with me and Kimberly," Ella pointed out with a smirk. "But you still love us."

"I'm still debating your worth, Ella," Marey gave her friend a mock snarl. "I didn't say I wasn't just as perverted as the rest of you, I'm just pointing out how damned odd we are."

"No odder than the men of that Club," Kimberly pointed out then, accepting the refill of her wineglass from Ella. "I've never seen so many men gather in one place, and actually get along. They don't stress over their women fucking around, and they don't get pissed over the games. I've actually heard them discussing positions and how loud it would make the women scream." She rolled her eyes. "They're worse than us."

"How many are in that damned club now?" Tess opened her eyes for that one.

Kimberly, though she no longer had limited membership after her marriage, had been one of the few women allowed the freedom to come and go within the mysterious estate that housed The Club.

"The last I heard, there were more than fifty members." Kimberly shrugged. "Though, I would say twenty regulars."

According to Ella, they had stopped pressing the other woman for names months before.

"Yeah, Kimberly was their practice piece," Tally laughed as the other woman flushed crimson.

"It amazes me no one has murdered you yet," Kimberly growled, narrowing her eyes on the other woman. "That was snide, Tally."

"Naw, that was Tally's jealousy," Marey assured the other woman with a slight wink. "She's still pissed you were able to get in and she wasn't."

Tally sniffed arrogantly. "I would have, of course, been a perfect choice," she declared, surveying her nails with an air of offended pride.

"Sure you would have," Terrie drawled. "If they wanted to follow your orders and obey your unwritten, unvoiced little rules. You were supposed to submit, Tally," she reminded her with a laugh. "Not them."

"So Lucian and Devril keep having to remind me," she sighed, though the wicked glint in her eyes gave lie to her put-upon tone of voice. "Maybe I can get them to remind me again tonight. I did point out that exceptionally designed paddle we found on the internet."

Laughter filled the tub again as wineglasses were refilled and the conversation began to dissolve into hilarity.

"Hey, what happened to Sax's car?" Tally suddenly asked, her question creating a ripple effect that had silence filling the tub.

"There's nothing wrong with the car." Marey frowned. "Why?"

"The sheriff's office was towing it off as Lucian and I left the office. I was just curious... Ouch, Ella, why the hell did you pinch me?"

"Because you don't play dumb nearly well enough," Ella snapped, her eyes glinting in anger as she set her glass on the deck behind her. "Let's hope we've all had enough to last us for a while because I bet we get cut off for a long time after this one."

Marey's eyes narrowed as her heart began to beat furiously in her chest. She turned to Kimberly. She was now part of Delacourte's security team and would know more than any of the rest of the ladies.

"I like my job, Marey," she sighed. "Don't make me jeopardize it. But I promise you, everything is under control."

"Vince," she whispered. "He did something to the car."

"I think I overheard someone mentioning a damaged brake line and possible deterioration before the car reached the cliffs." Tally was on a roll, and her own anger showing now. "She's not a child, she deserves the truth."

"I bet Lucian and Devril don't spank you for a week," Ella muttered.

"You and James lied to me." Marey turned on Ella, fury flaming inside her. "You were going along with it, Ella?"

Ella stared back at her unapologetically.

"For now," she admitted defensively. "Dammit, Marey, you're ready to run from Sax at the least excuse. I wasn't about to see you get an excuse. I don't want to see you dead."

"You'd rather see Sax dead?" she yelled back, jumping to her feet as she stumbled from the hot tub, pulling the towel around her as Ella joined her. "What do you think that would do to me, Ella?"

"Well, no one is dead this way," Ella shouted back as she knotted the towel between her breasts. "You're so stubborn, Marey, you'd cut your own nose off to spite your face. Sax can protect you."

"I don't need his protection or yours," Marey spat furiously. "Damn you, Ella, you had no right to lie to me."

"Why not?" she snapped. "You lie to yourself all the damned time. It shouldn't bother you so fucking bad when someone else tries to do no more than protect you from your own foolishness."

"I'm here aren't I?" Marey nearly screamed. "I'm sleeping in his damned bed and he's fucking me regularly. Isn't that what you wanted?"

"More to the point, it's what you want and deny yourself with any and every excuse," Ella accused her, crossing her arms over her breasts, her expression mulish, defiant. "I just wanted to make certain you didn't come up with a new excuse."

"It was none of your business..."

"The hell it wasn't. Do you think we enjoyed sitting in that goddamned hospital room with you after he nearly killed you?" Ella yelled, her own voice hoarse with her anger. "Get a clue here, Marey, he wants you dead."

"Get a clue here, Ella, you're a nosey bitch," Marey snarled.

"And you're a stubborn bitch." Ella was nearly in her face now, nose to nose, her face flushed in anger. "And if you try to walk out on Sax over this I'm going to beat you myself."

"Oh, be careful, baby, you might make me hot," Marey mocked her heatedly. "Wouldn't that be a new stroke of pleasure for the bastards?"

"Ewww. They're going to get all pissy and gross now," Tess announced to one and all. "Someone go find Sax and James to cool them down."

"Shut up, Tess." They both turned on her, snarling furiously before turning back to each other.

"Well, I can see we left you ladies alone too long," Sax spoke from the sliding doors, his voice calm, a shade mocking as Marey turned to him slowly.

His arms were crossed over his broad chest, his teeth flashing in a mocking smile as the others stood behind him, watching the scene outside with varying expressions of disapproval.

Her eyes narrowed on him before she looked to each one in turn.

"Remember me telling you that you were going to piss me off?" she asked him then, her voice sarcastically sweet.

His brows lifted slowly.

"Consider me pissed off."

She swept into the house, shaking with rage and fear. Fear uppermost. It crawled through her system, twisting her stomach in knots that threatened to send her to the bathroom heaving.

Vince wouldn't stop, she knew. He was proving it. And dear God, she didn't know if she could bear losing Sax.

Chapter Ten

"This is a mistake, Marey, please don't do this." The driver pulled the limo into the parking lot of the hotel as Ella voiced yet another plea that she return to Sax's.

"I have to think," she muttered, staring out the window into the brightly lit interior of the hotel lobby.

"Vince isn't sane…"

"I know that, Ella," Marey sighed tiredly.

"Sax loves you, Marey…"

"Ella." James voice was low, soothing. "Sax and Marey have to fight this out themselves."

Marey looked over at James, the concern on his face, the worry, before she looked back to Ella.

"I love you, you old harpy," she said softly. "And I know he cares. I just have to figure out what I'm doing here. I can't do that with him hovering over me. I'll be careful though, I promise."

Ella sighed regretfully. "Fine. And I love you too. Even if your decisions do suck sometimes."

"Most of the time," Marey admitted with a sigh, already missing Sax, uncertain if the decision she had made in anger was one should stick to now that the rage was dimming.

"We can take you back, Marey," James offered, his voice gentle.

"No." She drew in a deep breath as the driver opened the door and stood aside patiently.

She hugged Ella quickly.

"I'll call you tomorrow."

She jumped from the car before she could change her mind, striding purposely into the hotel, refusing to look back.

"You know, if stubborn had a name, it would be Marey."

Marey froze in the act of securing the hotel door and turned slowly.

Sax.

Well, this explained why James had the chauffer drive around aimlessly while Ella argued with Marey.

"Boy, when they say Trojans stick together, they mean it," she snorted. "How much did you have to bribe the concierge to arrange this one?"

The hotel was the best in the city, security had always been exemplary.

"Delacourte/Conover holds an account here," he informed her, his voice cool. "The owner also happens to be a member of The Club."

She snorted at that. She should have figured that one out on her own.

She stood silently, her hands fisting in the loose material of her dress as she stared back at him.

He stood in the center of the room, his feet braced apart, his head tilted as he watched her, his eyes dark and brooding.

"If you're finished being pissed, we can go back to the house now," he said patiently.

Her teeth snapped together angrily.

"Can you get any more arrogant?" she snapped. "Maybe I don't want to go back."

"And maybe you like to lie to both of us too damned much," he suggested silkily, moving to her, slow, relaxed, his steps stalking.

She wasn't going to run from him, she promised herself. She wouldn't give him the satisfaction. Or was that, deny herself the satisfaction? She was as sick as Ella and the others.

"You know, Marey," he whispered, his voice soft, dangerous. "It occurs to me that somewhere, somehow, you're going to have to trust someone. Trust starts here and now. Bend over on the bed."

She gaped back at him.

"Excuse me?"

He shook his head slowly. "Excuses are over. Bend over, baby. Now..."

Running from him wasn't going to work. She had admitted that while she was arguing with Ella. It was useless. He was her weakness, the one she feared most, and was most helpless against. She moved slowly to the bed, licking her lips nervously at the determined, dominant glint in his eyes. Her pussy was heating, dampening, her breasts swelling in anticipation. Perv, she accused herself. But she moved to the bed, gave him one last nervous glance then bent over slowly.

"There's a good girl." Marey knelt on the bed, her rear in the air as Sax slid the last inches of a butt plug slowly into her ass nearly half an hour later.

She was stretched, burning. Her hands were clenched in the comforter as she fought to breathe through the sensations, to think past the dazed sexuality that filled her.

"You're going to wear that until we get home," he whispered as his hand smoothed along the curves of her butt. "Then I'm going to fuck you. While your ass is filled with that plug, and you'll be ready for me, Marey. So wet and so ready that when I slide inside your tight cunt you won't be able to stop screaming."

She believed it. She was going to scream now.

"Come on, stand up for me."

He helped her from the bed, drawing her up until she faced him, swaying, the muscles of her ass clenching around the fiery width of the dildo penetrating her.

She stared up at him, trembling, increasingly aware of the stuffed depths of her rear, and the aching emptiness of her pussy.

"Ready?" He held out his hand for her, a small smile quirking his lips.

"I don't know if I can walk." She swallowed tightly, attempting to still the tremors racking her body.

"Yeah, you can." His hand smoothed over her rear. "Slow and easy. And let it feel good."

She snorted sarcastically. "I'm going to get off just walking, Sax. This is cruel and unusual treatment."

"No, you won't. You'll just wish you could." He chuckled as he drew her to the door. "And just think how good it's going to feel when we get home."

"Have you ever been raped, Sax?" she asked conversationally then, almost missing the surprise that crossed his face as she picked up her purse and headed for the door, a hard breath exhaling from her chest as pleasure tore through her.

"No," he chuckled. "I can't say as I have."

"Expect it," she warned him with a snap as he opened the door for her and she swept from the room. "Soon."

Raping Sax was going to be delayed.

"What the hell is he doing here?" Marey snapped out with a groan as they pulled into the tree-shaded driveway of Sax's home late that evening beside a black Mercedes and the brooding, dark-haired man standing beside it.

He straightened as Sax stopped the rental car, his arms unfolding from across his chest as he shoved them in his pants pockets instead. Daniel Conover was as well known to Marey as Tally's lovers, Lucian and Devril. He was a top-notch private investigator, and a pricey one as well. He was also part of the exclusive little club Sax belonged to if the woman was to be believed. And Marey knew her well enough to know she wouldn't lie about it.

And he wasn't too hard on the eyes. Thick black hair, intense gray eyes and a brooding expression that made more than one woman sigh in longing. He was a bad boy, wild and dangerous, and you could see it in his face.

Her pussy was blazing, her ass was on fire and every nerve and cell in her body was screaming out for release. She didn't want to wait. She wanted Sax in the house, naked and fucking her. She didn't want to socialize. No matter how easy the company was to look at.

"I've hired him to find your ex-husband."

Marey gnashed her teeth. "We'll argue over that one later. Get rid of him, Sax. I'm dying here."

"As soon as possible," he promised, opening his door and moving around the front of the car to open her door.

He helped her out of the car as a sharp, indrawn breath hissed between her teeth. She clenched the muscles of her anus, feeling her juices leak from her pussy, burning her clit and sending ripples of incredible hunger convulsing through her vagina.

"Hurry." She felt like snarling. She wasn't in the mood to be polite. To anyone.

His hand cupped her hip as he closed the door and led her to the house.

"Come on in, Daniel," he invited, causing Marey to elbow him in his tight abdomen.

She wanted to be fucked. She didn't want company.

Sax punched the security code quickly on the control panel, which automatically unlocked the door for him to swing it open. Lights flipped on inside the house, casting a gentle, soft glow through the large living room.

"Daniel, you know Marey Dumont." Sax introduced them as he headed for the bar at the side of the room. "Would you like a drink, Daniel?"

A drink? He was staying long enough for a drink?

Marey cast the other man a glare from beneath her lowered lashes. In return, she got a slow, wicked smile and she was going to ignore what that did to her overly aroused body, she assured herself.

"Hello, Ms. Dumont." He nodded, his deep voice a rumbling in his chest as he watched her closely. "You're looking lovely as ever."

"Good to see you, Daniel." She nodded briefly before turning to Sax. "I'll wait on you upstairs..."

She turned to leave the room. If she didn't get the hell away from him, she was not going to control herself.

"Marey." His voice stopped her as she turned from him. Turning back slowly, she watched him with narrow-eyed warning. "Daniel might need to ask you some questions. You should stay." His voice hardened.

Okay, she hated bossy men, but the sound of his voice, the warning implicit in it, had her pussy clenching spasmodically.

She licked her lips quickly, fighting to control her breathing as she faced him, aware of Daniel watching the scene. She bared her teeth at him, ignoring the flare of amusement in his eyes as she did so.

Daniel was a Trojan. For a moment, her knees weakened at the suspicion and the arousal that overwhelmed her at the thought. Sax was moving faster than she had anticipated if he had planned this.

She breathed in deeply. She had waited years for this. She had known the day she pulled into the parking lot of that damned motel what would happen if she ever went to Sax's bed. This would be part of it, she had known. The sharing. And she wanted it.

For a moment, she wondered if she should have felt shame. It wasn't every relationship that began with the understanding that there would often be more to the sexual depth than was considered decent. If so, then she guessed she was shameless. She had known for years that Sax was more sexual, more dominant than other men. She had gone to that motel knowing, knowing it would never end with one night, knowing that eventually, she'd be part of the lifestyle she knew he led, if she managed to hold onto him long enough to experience it.

She ignored the little voice in the back of her head that warned her this was more than sex. The part of her heart that weakened, softened, and laughed gently at her refusal to look beyond the sexual, or to delve deeper into the fact that it was a lifestyle she would have never embraced with another man.

She would eventually walk away. Most likely sooner than later, simply because she knew she couldn't bear the fear, day in and day out, that he would leave her. That the day would come that he would wake up, bored by her, having realized it was only the sex holding them together rather than any emotion on his part. Though she had to admit, he played the loving suitor quite well.

"In that case, I'll have a glass of wine if you don't mind." She tried to relax, to still the trembling in her hands, in her body as she met his gaze.

A slow smile shaped his full lips as he nodded slowly.

Walking slowly, swallowing tightly, she moved to the couch and sat down. Sweet mercy. Her muscles clenched, convulsed around the thick plug as she moved. She wasn't going to survive this.

She watched as Sax handed Daniel his whisky on ice then moved to her with the wine he had poured. She needed something to still the nerves rising inside her, and the depraved images running through her mind.

"Does your ex-husband have any computer skills, Ms. Dumont?" Daniel sat in the chair across from her, his gray eyes watching her curiously, knowingly.

"Not that I'm aware of." She accepted the wine from Sax, forcing her attention on the questions as he sat beside her. Close. Reminding her of how well they seemed to fit together.

"Any friends who do?" Daniel leaned back in his chair, crossing his ankle over the opposite knee. "Your security company's computers were hacked into night before last. We think this is how he managed to get the security codes. He didn't break the system."

Geez, she was supposed to think right now?

"Vince's friends rarely called or came to the house." She concentrated on trying to control her breathing, but it wasn't easy when Daniel flicked a glance to her breasts. Her nipples were standing out, hard and tight and getting worse as Sax began to stroke her neck with his fingers.

"Do you remember any of his friends? Names, anything?"

She breathed in deeply. "We were barely married a year, Daniel. And I can't remember the few people he did introduce me to."

She could barely remember her own name right now.

Sax's fingers drifted to her collarbone, then the upper edge of her breast.

Marey lifted the wine to her lips and took a heavy drink. Her hand was trembling and she couldn't stop it.

"Daniel, maybe questioning Marey should be done later," Sax said gently.

Daniel shifted in his chair, his gaze going to her breasts as Sax slid the first button of her shirt free. Her head fell back against his shoulder, weakness filling her. She was going to do it. God, she couldn't believe she was actually living the fantasy that had filled her dreams for so long.

"Sax, if this is solo event, you better let me know now," Daniel half groaned as Sax caressed the upper mounds of her breasts.

"Is it a solo event, Marey?" Sax whispered, taking her wineglass as his finger glanced over her nipple, causing her to jerk in reaction.

"I knew what I was getting into." She breathed in harshly as Daniel stood to his feet, moving slowly to the couch, his eyes lowered sensually as Sax moved her until she was stretched out, her head on his opposite shoulder.

"Yes, you did know, didn't you, baby?" he crooned. "Were you looking forward to it?"

"I was looking forward to you," she whispered, unable to lie to herself or to him. "All of you… Oh God!"

Her entire body convulsed from no more than Daniel loosening the belt of her slacks and sliding the button that held it together free.

"You're beautiful aroused," Sax whispered as his fingers flicked the buttons of her blouse open. "But I want to see you insane with it. There's a pleasure that women find, only when taken like this, Marey. A pleasure we only find in seeing you experience it. One that makes us as high as it does you."

"High?" she gasped as Daniel lifted her, sliding her pants over her hips as he removed them, sending her senses reeling, her nerve endings flaming in response. "Sax, this is passing 'high'."

Her blouse fell away from her breasts as her pants slid from her body. The plug in her ass felt like an erotic wedge, burning her with the knowledge of what was to come as her panties slid as easily from her body as her pants had.

Minutes later, she was naked, staring up at the two men who had quickly disrobed, their fingers wrapped around their straining cocks, two sets of hungry eyes—one gray, one chocolate brown—watching her intently. She wasn't willing to lie there and wait. Rising, she turned on the couch, her hand reaching out for the bronzed length of Sax's cock, her mouth opening as he pressed the wide head to her lips.

She sucked him in hungrily, tasting male heat and desire as Daniel moved to her side.

"Easy, baby." Sax pulled back from her, ignoring her protesting cry as his cock slipped from her mouth.

She wasn't going to protest too hard though. Instantly, Daniel's lips covered the straining peak of one breast as Sax knelt at the arm of the couch and similarly captured the other.

Oh God. Her hands tangled in Daniel's hair, clasped Sax's smooth head.

This was paradise. Their lips tugging on her breasts, sucking her deep, tongues flaying her nipples as their hands roved over her body. She was being consumed, devoured. She shuddered in their grip, her head falling back as she whimpered with the storm rising within her.

"Sax..." His name escaped her lips, though she was certain she couldn't breathe, let alone form words. "Sax..."

She wanted to say so much, and yet the words wouldn't come. Wanted to whisper whatever that emotion was burning in her soul, yet she couldn't make sense of it.

"So sweet." His lips trailed from her nipple, down her torso as he lifted her, propping one knee on the cushion to allow his tongue freedom to dance over her swollen, saturated pussy.

He circled her clit, licked at it, breathed over it, until she was straining against him, begging for more. Heated, calloused fingertips trailed up her thigh until they were parting the trembling folds, one finger working its way inside her burning vagina.

She pushed against it, moaning, begging for more as Sax covered her clit with his lips and sucked it into the fiery heat of his mouth.

"Sax, damn you," she cried out, twisting, thrashing in their grip as lips, tongues and fingers drove her on a spiraling ride she wasn't certain she could survive.

The lash of his tongue on her clit had her straining, begging for her orgasm. The firm, suckling pressure at her nipple sent arcs of near violent sensation shooting to her womb as the finger filling her pussy worked in and out, stroking her ever closer to what she knew would be a destructive climax.

Then just as quickly, both were gone.

She screeched hoarsely, reaching for them, only to have Sax return her to her previous position as he once again filled her mouth with his cock.

Daniel knelt behind her, his lips smoothing over the curves of her ass as his fingers moved to the cleft, gripping the base of the plug and turning it slowly.

She cried out around the erection filling her mouth, sucking it firmly, her tongue lashing at it as Daniel began to torment the filled tunnel of her ass. She ached. She whimpered with the pain, her hips moving, backing against him as he drew the flared end back then impaled her slowly with it again.

Sax moved until he stood at the arm of the couch, forcing her to brace her upper body over the thick cushion to maintain the deep penetration of her mouth. His cock stretched her lips, his hands burrowed in her hair, holding her still as he thrust in and out easily.

Behind her, Daniel slowly removed the plug as Marey screamed at the sensations the action invoked. She was going to come. Oh God, she was going to come from no more than the erotic pain of the thick bulb blistering the small ring of muscles it passed. Almost, she was almost there.

Her nails bit into the cushion of the couch as the impending release slowly drifted away, leaving her to growl furiously. She needed that release, desperately.

"Damn, Sax, she's wet." His fingers slid through the drenched folds of her pussy.

"Wet and wild," Sax whispered, staring down at her as she raised her eyes to his, her mouth filled with his cock as she moaned in excitement.

She worked her mouth on him as much as the hands in her hair allowed, but as she felt the cooling sensation of lubrication gel being applied to the stretched entrance to her ass, she stilled.

She watched Sax, seeing his expression tighten as he watched Daniel slowly stretch and lubricate her ass. His face was twisted with arousal, but something more. Something undefined as Daniel moved and the head of his cock nudged against her.

His eyes came to hers again, the dark color flaring with emotion, pleasure. Pride. Then she couldn't see, couldn't hear anything but her own strangled screams as she felt the thick cock easing inside her.

Sax eased back, pulling his cock from her mouth, though he continued to hold her head up, to watch her as Daniel slowly worked his cock up her ass.

"Sax. Sax…Oh God…it burns…" Hard hands held her hips as she bucked against the penetration, desperate to force more of the hard flesh inside her. "Make it stop…"

She was screaming, arching, her pussy so hot, so wet now she could feel the excess dampening her thighs.

"So pretty." His thumbs smoothed over her cheeks as she stared up at him imploring, feeling every bulging inch of

Daniel's cock as it slowly filled her. "Let it go, Marey," he whispered. "Just let the pleasure control. Not you."

She tried to shake her head. She couldn't allow that. If she did, she might not survive never having it again.

"You will," he crooned, glancing past her as Daniel groaned roughly. "You're tight, Marey, he's having to work his dick inside you. Do you know how good that feels, having to move so slow and easy? Can you feel it, Marey? The edge between pleasure and pain. It's the same for Daniel, working his cock up your ass as you tighten on him, wondering which sensation is stronger and dying for more."

She tried to shake her head. She needed him to just shut the hell up. She couldn't fight him and these sensations.

"Look at me, Marey." His voice hardened as her eyes closed. They opened again slowly. "Look at me. He's almost filling you, just a few more inches, baby. He's going to work that tight ass open then fuck you slow and easy. And I'm going to watch your face, sweetheart. Watch you fly over the edge while you scream."

Scream? She couldn't breathe, how was she supposed to scream?

All she could do was concentrate on the rising tension in her body, feeling Daniel slide in those inches until he was seated inside her to the hilt, filling her with every inch of cock.

And it wasn't enough. She whimpered, shaking, staring up at him, terrified to ask for what she needed. If she did, how would she maintain her distance from him?

Behind her, she felt Daniel's hands grip the curve of her buttocks, pulling them further apart as she watched Sax glance behind her. Daniel pulled back then, causing her to clench her teeth tight, to hold back a scream as he began to work his cock in and out. Long slow, deep thrusts and retreats, shafting her rear with measured thrusts as she felt the pleasure building inside her. Pleasure, pain, fire and ice. The alternating sensations shuddered along her nerve endings as each stroke of Daniel's erection inside her pushed her past the point of control.

She needed more.

She strained against Sax's hold on her face, needing to bury her face in the pillowed armrest, to chant her needs in silence so he couldn't hear.

He smiled down at her tightly, his lips pulling back from his teeth, his teak dark face twisted in pleasure as he watched her, his gaze going from her face to the point where Daniel was fucking her ass with diabolically slow strokes.

"Sax…" she whimpered his name, unable to hold back the unspoken plea raging through her body. "Please…"

"Please what, baby?" His hands held her face steady. "Tell me what you want, Marey. All you have to do is ask me for it. That's all. Anything you want. It's yours."

She wasn't going to make it. She moaned at the knowledge that he had known her better than she knew herself. She couldn't deny it, the pleasure, the edge of pain, or her need for him.

"More…" she mouthed silently.

His thumb smoothed over her lips.

"I have to hear you, baby," he groaned, compassion and more reflecting in his gaze.

She didn't want to see that *more*. That emotion she couldn't admit to, even to herself.

Behind her, Daniel continued to move, each stroke breaking her control further. She was full, yet she was empty. She needed more, needed that something that would push her over the edge and send her screaming into climax.

"Fuck me," she demanded roughly, driving back on Daniel's cock as his hold slackened.

Instantly, a light, reproving smack was delivered to the curve of her buttock.

Sax chuckled as she jerked, snarled and drove back again. Another smack sounded on the opposite cheek. It was making her crazy. How the hell was she supposed to survive this, to hold on to any part of her heart if he kept forcing her to relinquish so much to him?

"Sax, fuck me." She tossed her head, jerking from his hold, tossing her head in demand. "Damn you, fuck me now."

Chapter Eleven

"Easy, sweetheart. We're going to do this slow and easy..."

Together, Daniel and Sax had eased her up, keeping her impaled on the cock penetrating her ass as Sax stretched out on the couch beneath them. Her legs spread, knees bent as together they began to lower her.

How they kept her suspended in such a way, she didn't know and she didn't care. All she knew was finally, finally, Sax's cock was tucking against the folds of her pussy, pressing against the weeping entrance as she was lowered by slow degrees.

Daniel's erection throbbed in her ass, filling her so full that she feared Sax would never be able to work his inside her convulsing pussy. But slowly, by smooth, thick degrees, he began to fill her, working in and out as Daniel had done, forcing her muscles to stretch, her cream to flow faster and slicken his way until he slid into the very depths of her.

Her head lay against his chest, her arms around his neck, and she swore she wasn't crying as she listened to his crooning words.

"So good, baby...hot and sweet...so fucking tight... That's it, love, take all of me now. All of me, Marey..."

He had all of her.

"Sax." She was dazed, weak, despite the fires erupting from nerve ending to nerve ending and the pleasure-pain consuming her.

"That's okay, love," he whispered. "Just lay there. We'll do the rest."

They began moving then. Perfect, practiced moves that drove Sax's cock deep in her pussy as Daniel retreated from her rear, only to then have Sax retreat as Daniel pumped inside her ass. At first, their movements were slow and easy, allowing her to accustom herself to the fullness, the hunger. Allowing the inferno building from the dual penetration to destroy her mind.

She couldn't just lay against him, she fought the arms that held her close, her hips writhing, struggling to increase the strength of the thrusts as the sensations began to grow, to build, to tear through her body until every inch of her flesh was sensitized, pulsing, waiting…

When it came, she screamed. The words that escaped didn't matter, the tears ran down her cheeks unheeded, all that mattered was the release exploding through her, deep, brutal detonations that convulsed her quaking pussy and sent her cream spilling past the cock shuttling hard and deep inside her. She was consumed by it, destroyed by it, barely able to understand that the men filling her were finding their own release as well, pumping her body full of hot semen, sending another series of contractions ripping through her.

Finally, she collapsed wearily on Sax's chest, her body still shuddering almost violently as she felt Daniel ease slowly from her rear, his hand sliding over the curves gently as Sax whispered soothing nonsense at her ear.

"I'm going to shower, buddy," she heard Daniel breathe out roughly. "Should I stay or go after I'm done?"

"Hang around," Sax grunted. "We need to talk."

The words drifted around her as she lay against Sax, feeling him ease from her, holding her close as he lifted himself from the couch then swung her in his arms.

She was only distantly aware of the trip upstairs, or of how he washed her tenderly before tucking her into his bed.

She curled beneath the blankets, into his pillow and let sleep overtake her.

"Did that a little fast didn't you, Sax?" Daniel walked into the kitchen later, dressed, toweling his hair dry as he watched Sax quietly.

Sax glanced up from the sandwiches he was making, grimacing at his friend's comment.

"I have to keep her off balance," he admitted with a sigh. "She runs scared as hell when she has time to consider things. Until Vince is in custody, I'm walking a fine line."

Daniel snorted. "She's crazy about you. We've known it for years. She runs if she just thinks you'll be in the vicinity. Her face flushes if your name is mentioned, and according to Tally, toys can be a girl's best friend and all hers are named Sax."

Sax grunted rudely. "So I was told."

Ella had been a font of information lately where Marey was concerned. That bit of information he could have done without though.

"Vince has disappeared, Sax," Daniel said wearily as he took his seat at the small breakfast table, accepting the saucer that held his sandwich and the bottle of beer Sax handed him. "I have several men on his trail, but nothing has come up yet. The sheriff is scratching his head too. We're tracking whoever hacked the security company's computers. It was a good job, but they messed at a pivotal point. Sheriff found Vince's prints all over your car though. He definitely did the tampering on the brakes. We'll find him, but I don't know how soon."

Sax breathed out roughly. "She's scared of him," he growled. "Marey's not scared of much. She has a backbone of steel, but Vince scares her."

Daniel shifted uncomfortably. "You read the report you hired me to put together three years ago, man. He's not sane. He played a good game to get her. A lonely rich woman. She spent her life taking care of her ill parents, putting her own on hold. They die, she's ripe for the picking. Vince picked. You're lucky she was smart enough to get rid of him before he killed her."

"I want him found." Sax took his seat, keeping his voice calm despite the fury rising inside him. "He damned near killed her at that motel and the next time, she might not be so lucky. Find him, Daniel, I don't care how many men it takes or how much it costs. I want him gone."

Daniel stared back at him broodingly.

"Gone how?" he asked carefully.

Sax lifted his gaze, staring back at his friend coldly.

"However it takes."

Chapter Twelve

Marey awoke slowly the next morning, her eyes fluttering open, the dark beams of Sax's ceiling the first thing she saw. Sax slept deeply beside her, his arm lying over her hips, his head lying next to hers as he kept her tucked close to his body.

He had awakened her in the early morning hours for a hot shower, washing her carefully, gently, before drying her and tucking her back into bed before crawling in beside her.

He had taken care of her.

She frowned deeply up at the ceiling, wondering if there had ever been a time when anyone had taken such care of her. She couldn't remember it if there had. Perhaps as a child her parents had, but if so, she had been so young that those memories had been lost over time.

She had cared for them since she was a teenager. First her mother, who had conceived her only child in middle-age then contracted cancer when Marey turned thirteen. She had fought it for ten years, but she had been weak. So weak that her heart had given out before the renewed cancer had taken her.

A year later, her father had a stroke that had left him bedridden.

She could have hired someone to care for him. She could have deposited him in a nice little nursing home and resumed her life. But she loved her father. With his gentle smile and soft voice and his remorse that her life had been spent caring for him and her mother rather than being the woman she should have been.

There had been no regrets. But there had been no time for relationships. She had known her father would be gone within a short time, and she hadn't been willing to desert him, to leave him to strangers to care for him any more than she had to.

But she had found an escape. From the pain and the depression of watching her parents dying in front of her eyes, Marey had found an escape in the books she loved. First as a reader, then as an editor. She had worked the past six years as an editor for an erotic book publisher. The books were blistering, incredibly hot. And for a while they had eased the dark, sexual fantasies that haunted her. After her father's death...

She breathed in deeply. What a fool she had been. She had married the first man to ask her no more than a few months after having met him. Within weeks the rages had started. Within six months he was hitting her. It had been a horrible blow to her confidence. Within weeks of the divorce, she had learned that Vince had no intentions of letting her go. If he even suspected she was interested in another man, accidents began to happen.

She didn't know if she could live if something happened to Sax because of her. To this point, Vince had always struck at her, but she knew Vince had never felt truly threatened that she would find someone else to share her life, or her money with.

It was all about the money and the power he thought it would bring him.

"If you don't stop thinking so hard, I'm going to have to fuck you again," Sax mumbled at her ear, his deep voice rumbling in his chest with morning drowsiness.

A smile quirked her lips.

"You play dirty pool," she told him quietly. "Sometimes I have to think, Sax. This is one of those times."

He grunted mockingly. "I don't like how you think sometimes, have I mentioned that?"

He pushed the sheet away from her body before his hand flattened against her belly, his lips smoothing over her shoulder. She stared down at the rich coffee tone of his skin contrasting so exotically with her pale skin.

"Now, I would have never guessed that," she countered, allowing the amusement to weigh heavily in her voice. "You've surprised me, Sax."

He chuckled, a low sexy sound that had her womb clenching in response.

"You're a smart-ass first thing in the morning." He stroked her stomach slowly, his fingertips lightly drawing over her flesh, sending soft, though destructive sensations washing over her nerve endings.

It wasn't so much sexual as it was caring…loving. She tried to steer clear of that. She couldn't let daydreams get mixed up with reality. She had made that mistake once before.

He cared. She was certain he cared for her. Sax was often a brutally honest person, he rarely pulled his punches with anyone. But for three years he had moved on the outer edges of her life, always there, always watching her. He had never, not at any time, unleashed his infamous biting sarcasm on her. He had never looked at her with the brutal icy-eyed gaze she had seen him give others. He had never done anything but treat her with the utmost consideration and heated hunger.

Yes. He cared. And perhaps he could have loved, if she was strong enough to be as brave as she had needed to be three years before.

"Yeah, Ella calls me a smart-ass often," she finally answered, her gaze going back to the ceiling as she smiled fondly, thinking of her friend. "Actually, I think her favorite insult is bitch."

"Not hardly." His fingers strummed over her hip. "Smart-ass I'll accept though. Now what has you so solemn this morning?"

She could feel his erection against her thigh, but there seemed to be no haste in him to relieve his arousal. He touched her gently, easily. The caresses as calming as they were arousing.

"Just stuff," she sighed. "I was shameless last night, wasn't I?"

She heard the note of pride in her voice and almost winced.

"You were indeed shameless," he chuckled. "And wet and wild. So fucking hot you were incredible."

She turned back to him.

"Why do you share, Sax?" she asked him then. "You've said it's for the women's pleasure, but that doesn't make sense."

"Why not?" He propped his head on his hand as he levered up, watching her curiously. "Do you think I don't find pleasure in it, Marey?"

"I wouldn't find pleasure in seeing another woman touch you." She frowned at that thought. She would feel murderous.

"And you won't ever have to," he promised. "But you can't deny you enjoyed what happened last night with Daniel. That you haven't thought of it, looked forward to it. I heard it in your voice, saw it in your eyes and your response. Why did you enjoy it?"

"Because I'm a pervert," she snorted sarcastically. "Now your excuse?"

He laughed, a smile curving those sexy lips as he stared down at her reprovingly.

"Shame on you," he growled. "You're not a pervert. You're a very sexy, very sexual woman. That edge of the forbidden is exciting though, isn't it? Makes the pleasure higher, hotter. Maybe that's why we like it. I don't know. But it's something I wouldn't want to do without. Seeing you like that, embraced between myself and Daniel, your eyes dazed, your face flushed, pleasure swamping every particle of your being is addictive. It's a high, baby, only unlike any other I've ever known."

"Beats drugs, huh?" She rolled her eyes expressively.

His grin kicked in again, his chocolate brown eyes watching her closely, warmly.

She was so lost, she thought. She had lost her damned heart to this man so long ago and now she faced losing him.

"I love you, you know." He said the words so simply, so matter-of-factly that for a moment, she was certain she hadn't heard him correctly.

"Boy, you really like to play dirty pool," she snapped then, anger, helplessness washing over her. "You couldn't at least wait until this was settled? Until Vince was caught and I could make sense of any of this?"

She jumped from the bed, casting him a furious glare as she jerked the shirt she was using for a gown from the small chair beside the bed and pulled it on. He was lying back on the pillows, watching her somberly, his eyes piercing her, filling her with guilt.

"I like things clear," he amended calmly. "Don't play dumb, baby. You knew this was more than an affair when you went into it."

There he was, just lying back in the bed, his erection tenting the sheet, staring back at her in that calm, solemn way of his. What the hell was she supposed to say? To do?

"I can't even think about this." She pushed her fingers through her hair in irritation. "I won't think about this. Not until Vince..."

"This excuse is getting old." His voice never changed inflection but it still hardened, grew deeper. "It's like you pull it around you whenever you can't face what's growing between us. It's a crutch."

"That isn't true," she snapped back defensively. "He's dangerous..."

"Because you refused to stop him when his violence escalated." She flinched at the calm accusation, staring back at him furiously.

"It doesn't matter why it happened." She breathed in deeply, fighting to make sense of the clash of emotions rising inside her now. "I can't make decisions about the future now."

"I'm not asking you to make decisions, Marey." His smile was a wolf's snarl, predatory, confident.

Rising from the bed, completely unashamed of his nudity and the erection jutting from between his thighs, he stalked toward her.

"It doesn't take a decision." Gripping the neckline of the T-shirt with both hands, he tugged forcefully, ripping it down the front as she stared back at him in shock, gasping in arousal. "It doesn't take anything from you, baby. I'm not asking for anything. I don't have to ask. I know what's mine and I know how to claim it."

He pulled her to him, a strong, forceful movement as he gripped her hips. His head lowered, his lips covering hers, possessively, dominantly.

She couldn't hold back her moan. There was nothing like Sax's kiss or the way he held her to him. He seemed to surround her, his heat and his strength protecting her even as his kiss ravished her senses.

She couldn't fight him. There was no fight in her. She could only grab his shoulders, hold on tight and absorb him into the very depths of her soul. There was nothing so hot, so tempting, so completely overwhelming as Sax's embrace.

As his lips moved on hers, gentle and sure one moment, hard and possessive the next, Marey moaned in rapturous pleasure, her hands clenching on his shoulders, rubbing her body against him, loving the way his hands stroked her back, drew the remnants of the T-shirt from her body, and sipped at her lips with hungry demand.

This was what she had run from for three years. As insane as it sounded, and inconceivable as it was, she could feel him sweeping not just through her heart, but through her soul.

"I know how to love my woman," he whispered as his lips slid from her lips to her ear. "I know how to protect her, and I know how to hold her. And I will hold you, Marey."

He pulled her back to the bed, lifting her against him as he lay back, staring up at her with heavy-lidded sensuality as he cupped her buttocks in his hands, moving her until she straddled his hips, lifting her until the head of his cock seared the sensitive opening of her pussy.

"Ride me," he growled, arousal thickening his voice as his hand raised to her heaving breasts, his head lifting to allow his tongue to lick at her hard, distended nipples.

Marey whimpered at the sensuality of having the control, staring down at him, his body reclining beneath hers, his cock hot and erect, waiting to pierce the willing depths of her pussy.

She lifted up, her breath hitching as she moved against him, whimpering as his cock began to penetrate the slick, heated entrance to her hungry pussy. Her head fell back as she took him slowly, working the hard flesh inside her by increments, driving herself crazy with the incredible sensations streaking through her body. She loved it. Loved feeling his cock stretch her, burn her.

His hands were on her breasts, fingers tweaking her nipples as she rode him with long, slow strokes, fighting the need to rush, to drive herself to madness on the thick stalk of flesh filling her.

"There you go, baby," he whispered as he tensed, obviously holding himself back as he allowed her to take her pleasure as she needed.

Her juices were flowing between them, the sounds of wet, suckling flesh echoing around her, driving her arousal higher. His hands, warm and slightly calloused, rasped her nipples as his voice crooned in that rough, deep baritone and sent her mind spiraling with her pleasure.

Her pace increased, their moans mingling as the intensity and the heat grew. She could feel her womb tightening, fingers of fire racing through her pussy. She was going to come…

"Sax. Harder. Oh God, fuck me…" She couldn't gain the force she needed, the rhythm he used to power into her and throw her over the edge.

She shook, shuddered, fought her own weakness and pleasure in her drive for ecstasy.

His hands moved from her breasts to her hips. They held her still, his fingers clenching there as he began to move. He drove his cock inside her with enough power and force to cause her to arch in his arms, a strangled scream leaving her throat as her orgasm began to race through her body.

She convulsed above him, her thighs tightening, her hands clenching into the muscles of his chest as she felt herself come apart around him. His strangled groan met her scream as he drove in one last time, tensed further and then found his own release. Hard, rapid jets of semen burning her, the feel of the silky fluid flooding her, throwing her higher.

The aftershocks seemed to last forever. She shuddered through them as he drew her to his heaving chest, his lips pressing to her forehead, his hands stroking over her back. Soothing her. Easing her down from the almost painful heights of pleasure.

"Can you walk away, Marey?" he asked her then, his voice gentle, understanding. "No matter the risks, can you really walk away?"

Chapter Thirteen

Could she walk away?

Later that evening, Marey stepped onto the back deck of Sax's home and eased into the hot tub bubbling merrily in the corner.

The hot water wrapped around her, the massaging pulse of the jets beating against her weary muscles. Sax was insatiable. She ached in places she had no idea she could ache. But for the first time in years, her body was relaxed, even if her mind wasn't.

He was right, she couldn't walk away. He terrified her. Loving him terrified her. And not because of what she was scared Vince would do, though that was a worrisome aspect. No, he terrified her because she knew she had already given him so much of herself. If she stayed, if she accepted this relationship for what it was, then he would own her soul.

She had been alone for most of her life, even before her parents' deaths. Sharing it with someone determined to take such an active role wasn't easy to accept. Sax wouldn't go his way as she went hers. He was a possessive man, not controlling, but possessive all the same.

He would expect to share her life, not just exist within it.

She leaned her head wearily against the rim of the tub and breathed out roughly.

She loved him. She had always known she loved him, but she hadn't known how much until he began to fill her life.

"I'm going upstairs to finish up a few reports." Sax stood at the glass sliding door, chest bare, his teeth gleaming in his dark face as he watched her with a wicked glint in his eye. "Need anything before I go up?"

Marey chuckled at his suggestive tone. "I think you've more than taken care of anything I could have needed," she assured him. "I'm just going to lay here and relax for a while. You go work."

He moved to the deck, kneeling behind her and pressing a kiss to the top of her head.

"Just yell if you need me," he whispered warmly. "I'll leave the bedroom window open just in case."

"Mmm." She closed her eyes as his kiss moved to the shell of her ear, his tongue lapping at it heatedly. "Get out of here. You're insatiable."

He laughed at that, a male sound of pleasure and pride as he rose to his feet and walked back to the door.

"I'll be back down in about an hour," he promised. "Don't overheat."

"With you upstairs, there's no danger of that," she laughed back at him, watching as he flashed her a wicked grin and turned away.

She closed her eyes, fighting the need to call him back.

"I love you, Sax," she whispered, knowing he was gone, unable to hold back the words any longer.

What the hell was she going to do with him? She couldn't let him go. She couldn't walk away. He fulfilled too many parts of her soul. He fulfilled her, period. Laughed with her, loved her, touched her with such passion and hunger that she knew she would never be the same again.

"Well, you look comfortable enough, bitch!"

No.

Her eyes flew open, fear and disbelief clamoring through her as she met Vince's furious gaze.

"You really have lost your mind," she said, amazed at his daring. She had pretty much caught on to the fact that Vince wasn't too bright, but this was ridiculous. "Vince, Sax will kill you if he catches you here. Don't you realize that?"

His brown hair was still kept shaggy short, but stood on end, unkempt and dirty. His brown eyes narrowed in hatred, his fists clenched. The faded denim shirt he wore was streaked with dirt, his jeans ripped at the knees.

"The son of a bitch," Vince snarled. "He's too busy playing his computer geek games upstairs. And you're not going to scream, are you, Marey?" he sneered. "Little Miss Too Much Pride. I heard you screaming for him, though, didn't I, you little whore? Him and that bastard he put up your ass!"

She flinched at the fury rising in his voice.

Drawing in a deep breath, she tensed. Sax would be down soon, he rarely left her long while he worked upstairs, checking on her often. Being naked and at the mercy of a man she knew wouldn't hesitate to kill her with his bare hands was a frightening prospect.

"How did you evade the sheriff?" she asked him, hoping to buy some time, to distract him just long enough for Sax to make his way downstairs.

His thin lips twisted in disgust as a dark, brick flush rose under his skin, barely noticeable in the dim light of the deck. It wasn't a good sign.

"I can't believe you actually had the nerve to file charges." The low, evil chuckle that came from his lips had her shuddering in terror. "That was very bad of you, Marey, you should have taken your punishment and kept your stupid mouth shut."

"You nearly killed me, Vince," she snapped, refusing to let him see her fear. "And you tried to frame Sax for it."

"He shouldn't have been sniffing around you," he snarled. "What makes him think he can take what belongs to another man? He's a trespasser and you're a whore, always watching him, eating him with your eyes. Did you think that just because you forced that divorce that it changed anything,

Marey? The vows were until death do us part." His lips curled in a feral sneer. "And only death will part us!"

She was rising from the hot tub, a scream on her lips as he tensed to jump for her, knowing her time had run out. As she turned, Daniel rushed from the house, his hard hands gripping her as he pushed her against the side of the house. Sax rushed past them, leapt the distance of the tub, tackling Vince as he moved to run.

Eyes wide, she watched as Daniel quickly followed. His voice rose as he informed Sax of all the legal ramifications of murder. Not that Sax seemed inclined to listen as his hands tightened around Vince's throat, a snarl of fury twisting his lips.

It was over quickly, too quickly for her to process the fact that Vince was unconscious on the deck, and she was still standing naked in the cool fall air, staring back at Sax in amazement as he rose from the deck.

"I should paddle your ass," he yelled, staring at her over the churning water of the tub. Furious. His eyes were blazing, anger contorting his expression as she watched him in amazement. "What in the living hell possessed you, woman, to sit and bait him like that? To just sit there, calmly talking to him in a tub of water knowing fucking good and well he was capable of drowning you?"

Screaming. He was screaming at her, his body so tense, so tight, she wondered if something would break.

"I knew you would save me," she whispered, blinking back at him in surprise. "I knew you wouldn't let him hurt me."

Shock filled his face then. "I wasn't here!" He wiped his hands furiously over his slick head as he yelled again. "How the hell was I supposed to save you?"

"But you did, Sax," she pointed out. "I knew you would be here. I knew you would be..."

Tears filled her eyes as she stared back at him.

"You don't leave me alone, Sax," she said softly. "You're always close, touching me, embracing me, needing me. How can anyone have a chance to hurt me when you love me so well?"

A heavy frown darkened his brow. "That is not getting you out of trouble," he assured her through gritted teeth as he stomped around the hot tub, jerking her in his arms and holding her rapidly chilling body close to his warmth. "But God help me, Marey, the next time you do anything so stupid, I'm going to paddle your ass."

A tearful smile crossed her lips as she tilted her head, her hand reaching up to touch the dark features of his face, the sensual curve of his lip.

"I love you, Sax," she whispered. "I was going to tell you that tonight, while you held me, while you loved me. I've always loved you."

A hard breath shuddered through his chest as he buried his head in her hair, his arms tightening around her.

"I'm definitely spanking you," he groaned. "God baby, I love you. So much you terrified the hell out of me sitting there talking to that bastard so calmly, knowing how easily he could hurt you."

"Knowing you would be there," she said against his chest as he lifted her into his arms while Daniel called the sheriff.

"You're cold," he growled. "You didn't even bring a robe out."

"So warm me." She burrowed against his chest, her arms wrapping around his neck, her head resting naturally on his shoulder. "Warm me, Sax…"

Chapter Fourteen

"Somehow, Vince managed to hire an ex-employee of the security firm to hack into their computers for the code to Marey's house," Daniel reported the next morning after the sheriff and his deputies had arrested Vince, taken their statements and then left them in peace.

Marey was sitting tiredly on the couch, bleary-eyed, certain she had never been so exhausted in her life as she listened to what Daniel had come to the house the night before to tell them.

Neither she nor Vince had heard the car pull up at the front of the house, but Sax had. Just as he had heard Vince through the opened bedroom window seconds before. Moving carefully, he had let Daniel in, then together they had contained Vince. A few broken bones were the least of her ex-husband's problems now.

"What will they do with the hacker?" Marey asked, fearing the moment when Daniel would leave and she would have to face Sax alone. She was suddenly terrified. Not of him, but of herself.

When he had jumped across the hot tub, the rage that had filled him had been palpable. He would have killed Vince if Daniel hadn't stopped him.

Son of a bitch, I'll fucking kill you for touching her. Vince's eyes had been bugging from his head, his face turning purple. *Do you understand me? My fucking woman, you low-life motherfucker!*

His woman. Conviction, determination, commitment had filled every hoarse word, every finger that tightened on Vince's throat before Daniel managed to pull him away.

"They'll arrest him." Daniel watched her closely, but not near as close as Sax was watching her.

She nodded, lowering her head again as she stared at the floor, her arms wrapped around her chest.

"I'm going to head out of here, Sax," Daniel announced then. "I still have to stop at the sheriff's office and take care of some more paperwork. I'll call you later."

"Thanks again, Daniel." Sax moved across her line of vision, his powerful legs moving slowly across the floor.

"I can see myself out," Daniel said. "Take care of your woman. The night has been hard on her."

Marey shuddered.

Seconds later, the front door closed, leaving her alone with Sax.

Silence filled the house.

Emotions rose within her with a force that had her shaking in their grip.

"Marey." Sax knelt before her, his broad hand lifting her chin as he stared back at her somberly.

Oh God. He shouldn't look at her like that, she thought. His expression so tender, loving. She had fought so hard not to believe in happily-every-afters, in warmth and love. How was she supposed to protect her heart?

But she knew, had known for days that such protection was a long time past.

She felt a tear slip down her cheek.

"Everyone I really love leaves me," she said. "I didn't love Vince, and I knew it. I barely cared, but I was so damned tired of being alone." Her breath hitched in her throat as he continued to watch her, his dark face intent, his expression filled with love. "When I met you," she continued. "I couldn't believe. If I believed, I would have had to face how I've hidden for so long. The coward I've been." She pulled away from him as a sob shook her.

"Marey, don't do this to yourself," he whispered. "We can talk about this later. After you've rested."

"I won't have the courage then," she cried painfully, moving away from him as she rose to her feet, tightening her arms around her chest as she turned her back on him. "You don't understand. You were right. All along. Vince was a crutch. An excuse to keep you away." She turned back to him, staring back at him, refusing to hide any longer. "I had to keep you away, Sax."

"Why?" He pushed his hands into the pockets of his slacks as he stared back at her, his brown eyes wary.

"Because you could hurt me," she whispered. "And I knew it. You could rip the heart from my chest, and you terrified me because of it. Because Sax, in a matter of months, as you tried to make me laugh, to talk me into your bed and your life, I fell in love with you. And I didn't know what to do with that love. Or how to handle it if you ever walked away from me... Or if you were taken from me..."

She thought of her father, his patient resolve, his gentleness and the hole his and her mother's deaths left in her life. She had spent her own life caring for them, putting it on hold, forgetting her dreams, her needs in the face of theirs.

"I can't promise I won't die, Marey," he whispered, and in the rough tone, what she heard, she heard with her heart, not her ears. Hopes, dreams... "All I can promise you is that while I live, as long as I draw breath, I'll love you. And I'll pleasure you with everything I have."

His arms wrapped around her then, his hands smoothing up her back as she clutched at him, tears flowing freely from her eyes, sobs tearing at her chest.

"I love you," she cried out, her hands clutching at his shoulders as he lifted her, moving until he was sprawled into the chair Daniel had vacated, drawing her over him, her thighs clasping his while his hands tore at her robe.

"Feel me, Marey," he groaned, throwing the robe to the floor before he shifted, his hands tearing at his pants as hers ripped at the buttons that held his shirt together.

Naked. She needed him as naked as she was, bodies, hearts and souls bare to one another. Embracing each other.

When he surged into her, her head fell to his shoulder, her arms wrapping around his neck as his circled her back. He moved into her powerfully, thrusting hard and deep as she undulated against him, driving him deeper, gasping, crying out as he whispered his love, his lips moving over her shoulder, her neck, his tongue stroking trails of moist flames as his arms tightened around her, holding her still as he began to drive inside her harder.

Waves of pleasure suffused her, overtook her. Perspiration built along her body as she fought to breathe, to reach the peak of rapture that she knew she could find only in Sax's arms.

The closer she came, the more she could feel opening inside her soul. She cried into his shoulder, gasping her love, her need, her regret that she had waited so long to accept what she had known was in his heart.

"Hold me, Marey," he growled at her ear. "Just hold me, baby."

He was moving stronger now, his cock pushing to the very depths of her, burying to the hilt over and over again, impaling sensitive nerve-ridden tissue as his love had impaled her soul.

She was held, just as she held. Her pussy clenched around his erection, tightening as the bands of pleasure began to explode. Her arms held him to her, his held her as well.

Her strangled cries echoed around them as her orgasm finally erupted. Unlike any other, it swept her reality, sizzled through her body, and left her shuddering in his arms as his hoarse shout filled her ears and she felt his release explode inside her.

Embracing. Embraced. And for the first time in her life, free.

SHAMELESS

Trademarks Acknowledgement

The author acknowledges the trademarked status and trademark owners of the following wordmarks mentioned in this work of fiction:

Velcro: Velcro Industries B.V.

Prologue

Courtney lay silently, a frown on her face as she stared at the dimly lit ceiling above the bed. Cool air wafted across her body, drying the fine sheen of perspiration that had built there over the past hour. Her hand strummed idly against her stomach, her index finger flicking against the emerald belly ring that pierced the flesh above her navel.

The feel of her nails rasping over her flesh was a pleasant sensation. In many ways, more pleasant than the experienced caresses of the man who lay beside her. Not that he hadn't tried, not that she hadn't tried, but satisfaction lingered just out of reach, an ethereal promise that she knew would remain unfulfilled for a while yet.

Doubts assailed her in that moment, as well as a lingering regret. She hadn't imagined this as her first sexual experience. She had envisioned an event much more earth-shattering, one that would fulfill not just her sexual desires, but those that filled her heart as well. Unfortunately, there were sacrifices to be made for the dream she had carried in her heart for so long. Her virginity was one of those sacrifices.

She breathed in carefully, deeply, restraining the weakening emotion that assailed her at the thought of what could come. She wasn't leaving her country or her home without knowing exactly what she was doing. She had studied her objective, learned every facet of his character possible and planned each move out carefully. She couldn't fail. Too much was at stake to fail. Her future, her very heart and the dreams she had carried since childhood now lay on the line.

"Well. I can honestly say you are my one failure, darling." Sebastian DeLorents leaned casually on his side as he interrupted her musings, his voice filled with amusement.

She turned her head, a smile quirking her lips as she stared back at perhaps her dearest friend on this Earth. Bastian had led her through many of her most important adventures and helped her ensure that her father never suspected that his little princess was perhaps a tad bit more reckless than he would have wished. Dane Mattlaw believed his perfect, innocent daughter was unwary of the world, unknowing of the darker side of life that could be found outside the walls of the estate he had raised her in. He had no idea of the free spirit, the reckless, outrageous woman his daughter had become.

She wasn't trying to be cruel in keeping him in the dark. She just knew how he worried, how he fought to always protect her from any harm that could come her way. He wasn't overbearing, merely overprotective in a very fatherly way. And she understood the reasons why, had lived those reasons for three long, nightmarish years at her grandparents' home in Spain when she was a child.

But she wasn't a child any longer.

"Don't take it personally." She turned to him, heedless of her nudity, staring back at his darkly handsome face, the well-muscled, powerful body, the wicked glint in his black eyes. "I told you, I was saving myself for another, Bastian. I had only to get rid of that pesky shield of virginity to set my plans in motion."

He grimaced, though she knew he accepted it good-naturedly. She hadn't deceived him. She had been aboveboard, honest. She couldn't lie to Bastian, the very thought was abhorrent. Besides, he had wicked ways of getting even with those who crossed him. She wasn't frightened of him, but she had a healthy respect for the code of honor to which he adhered.

She reached out, trailing her fingers along his cheek as his arms came around her, pulling her close against his body. There was no sexual tension, no arousal. The friendship they had formed throughout her life was a comforting, supportive relationship that had given her the courage to go after her greatest dream. He had given her a memory to treasure, if not one of satisfaction, this night. He had tenderly, lovingly taken that last barrier to womanhood and given her the freedom to chase after her final dream.

"I will miss you, *la luz más, querida." My little light.* He had called her that for years. He kissed the top of her head as he sighed heavily. "You keep the world brighter."

A soft laugh escaped her at that. "You mean I give you a reasonable shield between you and the calculating mommas and baby girls snapping at your heels. Come on, Bastian, you need to settle down someday."

She followed as he rolled to his back, groaning lightly as she propped herself against his chest, staring down at him as laughter welled within her.

Her Bastian was one of the finest-looking men Spain and England had ever beheld. He was a product of a Spanish aristocrat and an American mother, the pure blue blood of his ancestors diluted by the hated American sludge. At least, this was his grandfather's point of view.

For Courtney, it was the opposite. Her mother was the youngest daughter of one of Spain's oldest bloodlines. Her father, though, was pure blond American mutt, as he referred to himself. An Army man, tall, strong, dominant enough to stand up to the combined disapproval of Marguerita Catherine Santiago Rodriquez's maternal and paternal families.

Thankfully, Courtney had not been required to spend a vast amount of time around her Spanish relatives. Marguerita had been unfortunate enough that during her relationship with Dane, her family had learned of her lifestyle, and had nearly destroyed her with their efforts to "save" her. Escaping them and the life they would have confined her to had not been easy.

Courtney had been seven when her mother had taken her to visit her relatives, and the three years they had been confined there had been hell. Thankfully, her father had finally seen through the lies her mother's family had told him of their deaths and had rescued them both. It was a time her parents never forgot. Her mother had once told her that it served to remind them both of how fragile life can be, and that they should never take a single day for granted. It was a lesson Courtney had taken to heart.

"The calculating mommas are becoming wearisome," he grunted reflectively, interrupting her thoughts. "Perhaps I should follow you to America. I'm certain I could help you with the mayhem you wish to create there."

His smile was pure devilry. She rarely saw him so relaxed, playful. Bastian rarely relaxed enough to become playful. Which was a truly a shame, because when Bastian cared enough to play, he was an incredibly sexy sight to behold.

"Perhaps this is something you should do," she agreed laughingly. "But give me time to capture him first. He won't be an easy conquest, Bastian. And I could always fail."

Such an option was something she fought against. She couldn't fail. She had dreamed of him for too many years, had yearned for him with a strength that refused to allow her any rest.

"Failure is not a part of your destiny, *querida,*" he assured as her as he lifted his head, bussing an affectionate kiss on her lips before lifting her from his chest and rising from the bed. "You'll succeed, just as you've always told me you would."

She rolled to her back, lying against the pillows as she watched him pace to the wide windows of the bedroom and stare out over the city pensively. He seemed distant, reflective, as though some part of the evening weighed heavily on his shoulders.

"Are you upset with me, Bastian?" she asked then, wondering if perhaps she had asked too much of the friendship they had shared for so long.

He turned back to her, a slow, gentle smile on his lips.

"Never," he assured her, his dark eyes watching her with a glimmer of his earlier amusement. "You, my dear, are like a breath of fresh air among the swine. I shall miss you though."

He scratched lazily at the planes of his chest before his hand ran along his abdomen to rub absently as the heavy sac between his thighs. He was an impressive man, in all ways. But he wasn't Ian. Bastian was her dearest friend, but Ian was her heart. He had been for nearly a decade. Before she had even known what the odd, unfamiliar feelings were that rose inside her, she had known they belonged to Ian.

Moving from the bed, she walked to him, settling into his embrace and rubbing her cheek against his chest as his hands smoothed down her back.

"I will always be near," she promised him sincerely. "You work too hard, Bastian, and play too little. Should you require amusement, you have the numbers where I'll be. Be sure to call me often."

He chuckled. "Definitely. I shall require updates, little one. Now get dressed." He patted her lightly on the bare expanse of her rear as he pushed her to the bathroom. "Your plane leaves within hours and you wouldn't want to miss it. I believe your dear Ian is due to meet you?"

Excitement rose inside her. Instantly, her body became sensitive, her nipples hardening as the tender muscles of her pussy began to throb in hunger. It was like this each time she thought of him, her arousal would build within her body, making her weak with longing, with hunger. How surprised Ian would be when he learned the true reason for her visit to America, and her intentions. She was going to seduce the unseducible. She was going to capture the most elusive prey in the world. The heart of the most cynical, jaded male she had ever known. A man who had sworn to possess no heart, no tender emotions.

She was going to claim Ian as her own.

"Perhaps you should visit while I am there, Bastian." She moved quickly for the shower. "We would have a wonderful time in America. And Ian's club is rumored to be one of the most exclusive and entertaining among the sharing clubs in the world. It's not as though it is not a pleasure you greatly enjoy." She cast him an impish smile over her shoulder as she grabbed up the overnight bag at the bottom of the bed.

Bastian was perhaps much like Ian. Open only to those closest to him, his sexuality running deep and hot. He wasn't a man known to deny himself any pleasure that he deemed appropriate. He was a true sensualist, one of the few men who cared little for the opinion of those around him, and only for the personal code of honor he held.

"Perhaps soon." He shrugged, but his expression was thoughtful. "Perhaps soon."

* * * * *

Ian Sinclair fought to breathe deeply as he rolled from the limp, exhausted form that had been sandwiched between him and her husband. Kimberly Raddington was like a flame, searing them with a sexual heat as she clenched around the cocks invading her slender body, screaming for more, pleading with Jared for release and fighting to drive them both deeper inside her.

Now, hours later, she moaned tiredly as Jared shifted her between them, allowing the rest they had denied her through the night. Long, flame-red hair flowed over her back to fall to her side, caressing Ian's arm where he lay beside her. Reminding him too much of darker, silkier locks. Of a woman he knew he could never possess.

He stared down at the bright silk, a smile playing about his mouth as she grumbled grouchily at her husband's movements beside her.

Ian patted her rear affectionately as she settled back down, his gaze lingering on the blushing flesh. He had spanked her until her silken ass had flushed as red as her hair, and still she had screamed, begged for more. They had used her well into the midnight hour, and she had drained both men more than once, leaving them nearly as exhausted now as she was.

"You stayin'?" Jared asked as he yawned tiredly, cuddling close to Kimberly's sleeping form as he stared over her shoulder at Ian.

Ian glanced at the bedside clock and grimaced wearily.

"Not tonight." He didn't want to shower and leave. The effort seemed monumental, but he had no choice. "I have to meet Courtney's plane in a few hours and take her back to the house. I may be back tomorrow though."

The relationship he shared with Jared and Kimberly was a unique one for him. He had never formed close ties with one of the members of his club, and never with one of the women that he played a third to. But Jared and Kimberly were different. Kimberly's natural affection had touched him, made him realize there was perhaps more to sex than the act itself. The itch that needed to be scratched.

Unfortunately, she also reminded him too much of someone else. The realization, when it had hit him months before, had sent a chill chasing through him. But it hadn't eased the arousal that filled him each time he spent the night with the couple. It had, perhaps, made it stronger.

Ian was a man uncomfortable with weakness. He had made certain over the years that his heart remained free of entanglements and that his soul was his own. He had learned early the value of keeping his emotions to himself and of steeling his heart against the women who entered his life. But

Kimberly had touched him, had wormed her way into his emotions before he realized it, or, unfortunately, realized why.

"That's Dane Mattlaw's daughter, right?" Jared watched him in concern. "You're keeping her at the house? Think that's smart?"

"No." Ian knew it wasn't smart. If he remembered anything about Courtney Mattlaw it was her reckless, wild nature. Dane never seemed to see the wildness that glittered in his precious daughter's eyes, but Ian had. And it made him more than a little uncomfortable. It spurred a response in him that made him feel like a dirty old man.

Hell, she had been too damned young for the hard-on that filled his pants the first time he saw the heat in her gaze as she watched him.

What kind of pervert lusted after a seventeen-year-old? It was perverted. Depraved. Even worse than what he knew he was. Sharing a lover was a far sight less despicable than getting the hardest erection he had ever experienced in his life, for a child. And had Dane known, he would have castrated him. Courtney was his baby. His precious little jewel. If he even suspected that Ian's thoughts were less than pure about the girl, then Ian was dead.

"What's up, Ian?" Jared's gaze was sharp, suspicious as he stared over Kimberly's sleeping body.

His dick, that's what was up. He sat up on the bed, jerking his pants from the floor and pulling them over his legs as he kept his back to his friend.

Where the hell was his shirt? He looked around the room, his lips twisting humorously as he spied it half under the bed. Kimberly had been desperate to get them undressed by time they got her to the bedroom.

He bent, jerking it from the floor and pulling it roughly over his shoulders, buttoning it, leaving the tails hanging free to hide the erection pushing against his jeans.

"Not a damned thing," he finally answered. "I'm stuck babysitting Dane's brat for God knows how long, because he doesn't want his precious baby in America alone. She's twenty-four years old, for God's sake. I doubt she needs a chaperone anymore."

He raked his fingers through his hair, casting Jared a furious look at the thought.

"Where is the man's common sense? Does he think The Club is some lily-white establishment catering to male virgins? What the hell is he doing sending his daughter to me of all people?"

He had been very careful of Courtney in the past years, visiting her parent's estate in England rather than having them visit him. Staying for only short visits, and limiting his time in her company. As she grew from the child he had carried from a virtual prison during the darkness of night, to a young woman whose very presence lit up a room, he had realized how dangerous she could be to him.

He turned away, shaking his head at the situation he found himself in. He searched for his socks, finding one in the corner of the bedroom, the other under the bed. Dammit, Kimberly was going to have to pay more attention to where she threw his clothing.

"Dane's not a stupid man." Jared yawned again, obviously dismissing the subject. "He knows you'll take care of her."

Yeah. Flat on her fucking back with her feet around her ears while his cock plowed into her. That was how he was going to end up taking care of her if he wasn't extremely careful.

As far as he was concerned, Dane had lost his fucking mind.

"You would think so," he grunted at the comment. "You would definitely think so."

* * * * *

Lord save him!

Ian leaned against the wall of the airport waiting area and watched as Courtney made her way from the escalator and looked around the crowded terminal with a slight frown on her face. She hadn't caught a glimpse of him yet, for which he was extremely thankful. It gave him a moment to catch his breath.

How could he have forgotten how damned pretty she was? Her long, dark brown hair was left loose to flow down her back, nearly to her hips, her expressive face was currently holding a slight pout as the sight of him continued to elude her, and her tall, slender body was a wet dream walking.

Dressed in below the hip jeans, and a blouse cut too high for comfort, there was enough flesh displayed to make his mouth go dry, not to mention the dirty old men passing by her, sneaking looks at the silken, glistening flesh she had bared.

And winking shamelessly at her navel was an emerald in the shape of a cat's eye, glistening against the dark flesh of her belly. It was enough to make a grown man whimper. Despite the provocative clothing and the sensual grace with which she moved, innocence still seemed to shroud her. A cheeky smirk curved her lips, chocolate brown eyes gleamed with joy, curiosity, and a love of life. She was like a breath of fresh air blowing through the stale atmosphere of the airport lounge.

A grunt of laughter escaped his throat.

He had been getting hard for her since she was seventeen years old. Who was the dirty old man? He was eleven years older than she was and old enough to know better, now, seven years later. But his cock had no conscience. It was hard, straining beneath his jeans, and throbbing in hunger.

"Ian..." He watched as a wide smile curved her lips and pleasure lit her dark eyes as she finally spotted him.

Striding quickly across the room, her full breasts bounced—damn, she was obviously not wearing a bra. The emerald that pierced her belly button winked erotically and had his tongue aching to lick and probe at the little indention it called attention to.

She was the most tempting thing he had seen in his life. A temptation he didn't need.

"About time you got here, brat." He opened his arms to her, closing his eyes as she threw herself into his embrace, her arms wrapping around his neck as he lifted her from her feet and hugged her tight, relishing the feel of her in his arms. She was going to be a pain in the neck, but she was one of the few people in the world that he cared anything for. One of the few who truly cared for him.

It had been more than a year since he had seen her last. For just that reason. He didn't want to hurt her, but more importantly, he hadn't wanted that caring affection they shared harmed. The joy she showed when he was around lit up the dark places in his soul. Letting that go would be a wound to his heart he knew would never heal.

The hunger growing by the year was becoming uncomfortable enough to stress the control he prided himself on so deeply though. He was now forced to confront the seductive little baggage whether he wanted to or not.

"Ian, you are as handsome as ever," she exclaimed as he set her back on her feet, staring up at him with those mysterious brown eyes and wicked humor.

"And you're as pretty as sunrise." He shook his head at the truth of his own statement. She was as fresh, as innocent as dawn.

She smiled up at him, her hands still gripping his shoulders, her hips pressed into his thighs. And that wicked, hungry light in her eyes assured him she had felt the hard-on raging beneath the cloth.

He shook his head mockingly.

"You're a bad girl, Courtney." He moved her back. "Your father should have spanked you more when you were a child."

Her laughter was low, filled with heat. "So Mother keeps telling him. Perhaps you should spank me, Ian. Since it appears you are the one being affected. I might like having you spank me."

The thought of it nearly had his eyes glazing in lust. And she damned well knew it if her expression was anything to go by.

She watched him beneath lowered eyelids, her thick lashes shadowing her cheeks as she damped her lips with a flick of her hot little tongue. His cock jerked, his lust howled out in hunger.

"Come on, wench." He shook his head at her blatant flirtation, leading the way from the reception area to the limo outside. "Where's your luggage?"

"You see it." She indicated the carryon duffel bag at her feet as she picked it up and moved behind him. "It was time to go clothes shopping, so I thought I'd pick up the essentials while I was here. Why travel with tons of bags if you don't have to?"

Ian took the bag from her as she came up beside him, nearly skipping to keep up with his stride.

"Has nothing to do with that shopping bug you picked up from your mother," he grunted at the information as he fought the laughter welling in his chest. Her mother, Marguerita, could shop for days and never tire.

"Of course not," she assured him with mocking emphasis. "I needed new clothes. A girl has to look presentable, Ian."

He glanced at the clothing she wore now. "Buy something that fits this time," he suggested, unable to keep from grinning at her free-spirited laughter. "Your father should lock you in a padded room, Courtney. You're a menace."

She pouted teasingly. "But you love me, Ian, you know you do." She looped her arm through his, pressing close to his side as they exited the airport. "Just think of how dull and boring this winter would be without me. I came to heat things up for you, and you aren't showing the least amount of thankfulness."

Thankfulness wasn't exactly the way he would describe it, he agreed silently.

The limo waited just outside the doors, its warm interior protection against the cold on her tender flesh. Why it should bother him, when it didn't bother her, he wasn't certain. Maybe he was hoping it was the cold that had her nipples pressing hard and tight against her shirt. If it wasn't, he was in a hell of a lot of trouble here.

"You didn't even bring a coat," he growled as his driver whisked the door open and helped her in immediately.

"Who needs a coat?" She burrowed into the warm leather as he stepped in and the door closed behind him. "I could just cuddle up to you. You stay hot."

She had no idea.

She flashed him a saucy smile as she began to play with the controls set against the opposite side. Within seconds, the tinted privacy window rose between them and the driver.

Ian watched her curiously. It was obvious the little minx had something on her mind. He waited patiently, watching as she leaned back in her seat, then turned, leaning her side against the leather back as she stared back at him silently.

He lifted a brow inquisitively. "You needed privacy?"

"Well, you never know when it might come in handy." She was openly laughing at him now. "How far are we from the house?"

His gaze narrowed on her. "Half an hour, maybe."

She turned to face him, laying her cheek against the back of the seat.

"I hate these late flights. Why is it, you can spend the night dancing and never tire before dawn. But take a flight that lands at three in the morning and you're wasted?"

"Try meeting one at three in the morning," he chuckled. "You dragged me from my warm bed, Courtney. Shame on you."

"Not to mention the warm body likely sharing it."

Her moue of displeasure was ignored.

"Your room is already prepared and waiting for you at the house," he promised her. "You can fall right into bed the minute we arrive. Tomorrow, I'll arrange for Stan to be at your disposal with the car. You can shop to your heart's content."

"Are you…coming with me?" She batted her eyes innocently.

Her sexy little innuendos were going to get her spanked. Unfortunately he had a feeling if he got his hands on her ass, discipline would be the last thing on his mind.

"I think I can do without the shopping trip." He grimaced at the thought of it. "I'll see if my housekeeper's daughter is free if you like. She can help you become acquainted with the city, and show you the best stores. You'll like Ivy. She's as much a menace as you are."

"Have you fucked her?"

The question had him pausing, his gaze sharpening on her now. He wished he had kept the careful distance he had started with. If he had, he might not have noticed the hard little nipples poking against her vest-style blouse, the white cotton doing little to hide the dark points from his gaze. There was no mistaking the arousal in her eyes, but he had been trying to ignore that.

"Is that any of your business, Courtney?" he asked her then, his voice gentle. He had no desire to hurt her feelings.

"Of course it is." Her smile was faintly mocking. "I don't want to go shopping with someone who's already shared your bed, Ian. If I wanted to do that, I would have brought one of my maids with me."

He arched his brow in surprise at the thread of anger he heard in her voice, as well as the fact that she knew who he played with while he visited. Well, he may as well strike fucking her maids if he visited her father's estate again. And that was a shame. Dane insisted on hiring women whose coloring complemented his daughter and wife. There had been a few who resembled Courtney so closely he could even fool himself for brief moments.

"No, Courtney, I haven't fucked Ivy," he answered her coolly, fighting for a show of strength in the face of a possessiveness toward him that did nothing to soften his cock. "Any other questions."

A vivid smile shaped her lips. "None. I just wanted to be certain. I would hate to be jealous of a potential friend."

Aforementioned cock throbbed.

Damn her, he was aching to his back teeth to fuck her and she dared to sit there teasing him? He had done everything he could to avoid her for the past year, going out of his way to refuse Dane's invitations, whereas he had accepted them eagerly in the past. He had fantasized about her, dreamed about her. Jacked off to her image. And now, he was going to have to deny himself. Denial wasn't something he did well.

He watched her gaze flicker to his lap and grimaced at the fact he wasn't exactly hiding his arousal.

"You're going to get into more trouble than you can handle, Courtney." Ignoring the situation wasn't going to solve the problem.

"Am I?" Were her nipples harder? Were they pressing tighter against the cloth of her blouse? He knew his mouth was watering, hungering for a taste of them.

He smiled with an edge of mockery, more toward himself than toward her.

He wasn't exactly used to denying himself anything he wanted sexually. As the owner of The Club, the exclusive men's club that catered to dominant males whose tastes ran to the extreme, Ian was considered one of the most carnal of the group.

"Courtney," he sighed her name warningly.

She grimaced at the tone of his voice. "I'm not a child, Ian. Even though you persist in trying to treat me like one."

She edged closer. The scent of her, peaches and sweet female flesh, wrapped around him.

"You're acting like one," he accused her, attempting to find some distance, some defense against the hunger raging in his loins as she slid across the seat, too close, too warm and willing.

"Am I?" she whispered sensually. "Or perhaps I'm tired of watching you fuck my maids and moan my name as your head falls back and you climax to a vision only you can see. Evidently, a vision of me."

She was leaning close to him now, watching him knowingly, leaving him no room to deny the obvious.

And what was the point? It wasn't that he didn't want her, that he didn't crave the taste of her. It was her innocence, her connection to him. How could he destroy the purity he saw in her gaze? The trust her father placed in him. His connection to her was so much more than his connection to anyone else in his life. He cared for Courtney. Cared for her in ways he had never cared for anyone.

He hadn't anticipated this, he realized. He should have. In hindsight, he knew he should have expected it from her. He had seen the attraction grow within her, just as it had grown within him. His experience hadn't helped him to ignore it, or destroy it. It was a hunger, a fascination he knew could destroy them all. And he cared too much for her to allow that.

"You are so beautiful," he whispered, lifting his hand to touch her face, to marvel at the silken feel of her flesh. "So fresh and so innocent." He allowed his voice to harden in warning. "Don't push me, Courtney, to destroy that innocence. You won't like me much afterwards, and losing your affection would hurt me more than you know."

She stared up at him, her dark eyes filled with myriad emotions as he watched her process not just what he was saying, but what he wasn't. In the meantime, he seemed unable, unwilling to stop his fingers from drifting down the smooth column of her throat just to feel the warmth and the hard pulse of blood beneath her flesh.

"You want me," she stated, her voice soft, aching with need. And in that moment, he wanted her even more.

"I want you until I burn with it," he admitted bitterly. "Until I nearly denied your father's request to allow you to stay here. But I want more than you could ever give, baby. What I want from you could well destroy you."

Something flashed in her eyes then. Some unnamed satisfaction that had his gut clenching in surging hunger.

"Would it? You forget who my parents are, Ian. You forget, I've watched you for years, having sex with my maids. And you weren't alone with them. I'm very well aware of what you are, and what you may want from me."

His cock was going to burst straight from his pants. Its engorged width throbbed, ached, demanded that he fuck her here and now and responsibilities be damned. Yes, she was her parent's child, and he knew well the sexuality that Dane and Marguerita shared. Her father wasn't one of the leading members of The Club for nothing.

"I'm not a game you can play, Courtney." His thumb smoothed over her pouty lips as his body tightened to the point of pain with his need. She was so young, so fucking innocent, like a breath of pure, sweet air in his life. There was a special type of hell that waited for men perverse enough to corrupt such innocence. His soul was already stained once, he wanted nothing more to mar it.

Son of a bitch, arousal had never been this hard to deny in his life though. The hunger pulsed, bewitched, tempted him as nothing else ever had in his life.

"Then it's a good thing I'm not trying to play a game, isn't it?" she asked him softly. "And what makes you so certain I'm a virgin? That's something only I and my gynecologist knows for certain. He's not telling... And there's only one other way to find out..." Her wicked look sent his pulse soaring.

"And no friends." Ian had learned that lesson the hard way. The best way to lose a treasured friend was to take her to bed. The complications became astounding.

No virgins. No friends. No strings. No emotion. It was a recipe for loneliness, yet also the solution to avoiding the mistakes of the past. There were nights that loneliness ate him alive, but that was far better than the alternative.

He pulled his hand back, glancing past the window as they pulled into the long driveway that led to his home.

The three-story mansion was nearly a hundred years old, built by his grandfather, created as a home for his family. It was Ian's father and several of his friends who had created The Club, and based it in the back wing of the mansion.

"Spoilsport." The teasing pout in her voice he could handle. The naked arousal, the ever-deepening hunger touched too much of him, struck too close to a past he wanted only to forget. And it tempted him too much. She tempted him more than anything or anyone ever had in his life.

"Brat." He glanced at her, smiling fondly, wishing, not for the first time, that life were different. "Come on, let's get you to your room. Next time you decide to visit, Courtney, an earlier flight might be best..."

Control, he reminded himself as he escorted her into the house and up to her room. All he had to do was remember his control, and everything would work out well. She would leave in a week or so, her innocence and affection for him still intact. And if the loneliness dragged at him, darkened his life or left him regrets, then he would remind himself that at least her smile still charmed the world, rather than being dimmed forever.

Chapter One

One Week Later

If Courtney had a dream, it was Ian. From the time she had first thrown herself into his arms at age ten, ignoring his stiff surprise, his uncomfortable reaction, she had known no one else would do for her.

At first, the dream had been simple. Ian laughing with her, having a tea at her dainty little iron table, smiling at her with that crooked smile that made her feel as though he truly wasn't certain why he was amused by her.

As she grew older, her needs had grown with her. The boys of her age lacked excitement, they lacked sophistication.

They weren't Ian.

She had continued with her girlish crush, though the dreams had grown hotter, more erotic as she grew older and developed her own unique, individual personality. Wild and reckless, she had fallen into an older crowd of friends and learned the facts of life much sooner than she imagined her father could have ever guessed.

By the time she was seventeen, she knew of most every sex act and had seen many of them performed. And she fantasized of Ian. His lips covering a nipple, drawing on it hungrily, or buried between her thighs, his tongue licking her with ravenous greed. His cock... She closed her eyes, her breath catching in her throat as she pushed the sheet from her, her fingers trailing to the center of her body and the swollen heat of her pussy.

On his last visit to her father's estate, she had caught sight of that perfect stalk of flesh. Thick and heavily veined, the crest a dark purple, tapered and glistening with cream as he bored into the housemaid who had shared his bed that night. The small sucking sounds created from the act had her clenching her thighs as her own juices began to flow.

Now, her fingers slid through the thick, syrupy proof of her lust, circling the swollen bud of her clit as she imagined him touching her as he had the maid, fucking her with hard, deep strokes that would surely have her screaming from the tight fit of his erection inside her snug pussy.

She whispered a moan at the thought of him there, between her thighs, tempting her, teasing her, making her beg. And more. So much more. He would push every sexual boundary known to man and most women. He would make her body sing with pleasure, make her blood boil with the heat and desire that had simmered within her for years. He would give her the freedom, the courage to allow the wildness inside her free. To give the tempting fantasies life as the heat flamed through her. He would do more than allow her to be the sexual being she knew she was. He would encourage it.

She bit her lip, the sudden vision of her body, slim and delicate, sandwiched between him and one of the men she had seen going into the back entrance of the house. He would hold her tight, his hands clenched on her hips as he filled her pussy, holding her still as another touched her, pulled her buttocks apart, slid his erection along the crease of her ass until his cock was buried in the small hole there.

She bucked to her own touch, gasping at the fantasy of his expression. Seeing the pleasure, the wildness in his blue eyes, the flushed, eager lust on his face as she cried out for him.

Her pussy gushed, cream flowing to her thighs as her fingers pressed inside her weeping vagina, her palm rasping against her clit as her hips bucked involuntarily.

More. She pressed two fingers inside the hungry tunnel, tossed her head and began to thrust mindlessly. She needed… She ached to the point that she wondered if she could survive the arousal without release soon.

Frustration echoed in her guttural moan as the elusive climax teased her, just out of reach. So close… She was so close. She lifted her other hand to her swollen breast, her fingers pinching at her nipple, pulling at it roughly as the small streak of pain shot from her nipple to her clit, making it throb with impossible desperation. How was she to survive this?

Her fingers were moving harshly inside the clenching depths of her cunt, her palm grinding against her clit, yet still, to no avail. The hunger grew, striking with devastating need through every cell of her body, while fulfillment remained just out of reach.

A wild, needy groan tore from her throat as she collapsed against the bed in exhaustion long minutes later. The cream frothed between her thighs, so wickedly hot she felt each bone and muscle was on fire from the longing inside her. Yet, she lay there, frustrated, unable to climax, and burning with anger.

"Damn man." She pushed herself from the bed, grimacing at the untidy state of the silk sheets she had slept between.

She kicked the comforter out of her way as she stalked to the closet and opened it furiously. She was tired of waiting. She had played nice for a week now. The perfect little houseguest, never overstepping her boundaries, flirting to no avail, and wandering about the huge mansion in complete boredom as he made himself scarce.

She pouted as she pulled a short skirt from the closet and matched it with a small top. The stark white, barely decent skirt flared from the low hip band, covering the curves of her ass and swishing sensually along her upper thighs. It bared the flesh of her stomach from the snug, high hem of her white Grecian-style top to only inches above the throbbing, swollen tissue of her clit.

The emerald belly ring winked wickedly at her navel, a glittering earthy teardrop against her dark flesh. She shook her head, running her fingers through the wavy length of her long, dark hair before flipping it over her shoulder, a small shiver chasing up her spine as the curling ends caressed her lower back.

She felt decadent, sexy and wild. And she looked it.

"Take that, Mr. Sinclair," she whispered with a sensual little smile as she pushed her feet into the white stiletto heels.

She was tired of trying to be good. Of feeling her way among the strangers he introduced her to, yet paying close attention to those he steered her away from. She knew the women he would prefer she not associate with. Tally Conover, Kimberly Raddington especially, and Tessa Andrews and her mother Ella Wyman. Wives of now married Trojans, she had been told by one chatty little guest at the latest party she had attended. The Trojans, of course, being the nickname given to the men who frequented The Club.

Ivy, the daughter of Ian's housemaid, had been at first hesitant to discuss The Club, its members or their wives. It had taken a vow of utmost secrecy and several drinks to get the information out of the woman. That those wives Ian steered her away from were considered the most adventurous, daring women to have ever married one of the men.

They were habitually tormenting Ian by sneaking into the club, attempting their matchmaking wiles on the single members and generally causing havoc whenever the opportunity presented itself. It was Ivy's opinion they did so merely to tempt the overly dominant personalities of their husbands.

Those were the women Courtney wanted to talk to. The ones who knew Ian, who were intimate with the Trojans, their lifestyles and the rumors. But first—she moved carefully down the spiral staircase, listening for signs of movement as she stepped into the foyer and headed to the back of the house—she wanted to see The Club itself.

She had noticed the vehicles arriving earlier, parking along the back of the estate near the rear entrance that led to the rooms reserved for The Club's membership. Ian had left explicit orders that the far wing was off-limits to her, and that she should confine herself to the main portion of the house.

Yes. She would do such a thing, she thought with an inelegant, little snort.

She moved quietly to the back of the foyer, to the door beneath the stairs. Turning the knob, she opened it carefully before stepping inside. The hall was well lit, carpeted with a thick, rich cream carpet that muffled the sound of her steps as she headed along the corridor.

She refused to sneak. She squared her shoulders, raised her head and moved along the hallway with the supreme confidence of someone who knows where she belongs. She belonged here. And if Ian were behind those closed double doors ahead, then she would fight anyone who dared attempt to deter her.

She opened the doors without a care, stepping into the marble foyer that held the entrance to the back of the house. As she closed it behind her, Matthew Harding, who had been introduced at a recent party, stepped from a small office at the side of the room.

His hazel eyes immediately darkened as his dark brows snapped into a frown. He was well over six feet tall, broad, muscular. He was ex-military, she guessed. He held his shoulders back, his body straight and ready to move at a moment's notice.

"Hello, Matthew." She allowed a small, devilish smile to tilt her lips as she moved confidently for the set of doors that she assumed led to The Club's main rooms.

"Miss Mattlaw." He stepped quickly in front of the doors. "Have you lost your way, ma'am?"

She lifted a brow as he blocked the doors, her eyes narrowing enough to allow him a warning that she wouldn't be barred from the rooms.

"No, I haven't." Ice tipped her voice. "I know exactly where I want to go."

He crossed his arms over his chest, frowning deeper.

"These rooms are off-limits to you, ma'am. I think you were already informed that the back of the house is no place for you to be. If you wish to visit, then Mr. Sinclair will have to accompany you."

Luck was a mercurial suitor. Some days she had it in spades, others, it eluded her entirely. This evening, it seemed to be on its best behavior. The doors opened wide, causing his attention to fracture and give her the opening she needed to slip into the room.

She glanced behind her, smiling innocently at the irate butler and the more than surprised club member as he stared back at her.

She stepped inside the ornately decorated room, her gaze flickering over the heavy chairs and dark tables. It reminded her quite a bit of her father's study. Shelves lined the inner wall, stacked with books and erotic statuettes. A fireplace flickered merrily on one end of the room, while banks of windows looked out on a heated pool and Jacuzzi.

Several seating arrangements were scattered about the ballroom-sized room, as well as tables and areas of privacy. The bar graced the far end with a wealth of bottles lined up along the wall.

Ahh, yes. This was where she needed to be. She paused at the mahogany bar, glancing over her shoulder to meet the astounded gazes of the dozen or so men now watching her before turning back to the bartender.

"Club members only."

She nearly sighed as the burly, savage-featured bartender watched her with chilling politeness. Men were such aggravating creatures at times.

"Perhaps I'm a guest?" She lifted a brow mockingly.

His lips twitched but of course, the smile did not make its appearance. Ian must be instructing them on how to make her life miserable, she decided.

"It's a men's club, Miss Mattlaw," he said coolly before flickering a suggestive glance at the gentleman sitting two stools down, or perhaps hinting at a fellow conspirator.

She turned to survey the other man. Wicked, wicked blue eyes were filled with laughter, while thick black hair framed an outrageously handsome face.

"Ian is such an old fuddy-duddy." She rolled her eyes with practiced charm. "Could I convince you to buy me a drink? It seems he's already effectively tied my hands where such matters are concerned."

A black brow lifted slowly as his gaze flickered to her wrists. "Not yet he hasn't," he said before turning to Thom. "Give the lady a drink."

Thom grimaced good-naturedly. "Long as it's your ass rather than mine, Cole." He turned back to her then. "Hurry with your order, darlin'. My guess is that Matthew has already called Ian. I'll give him a flat five more minutes before he arrives."

"Jack on the rocks then," she sighed, propping her chin in her hand as she leaned against the bar, well aware the skirt was edging indecent on the backs of her thighs.

The drink was delivered within seconds.

Turning, Courtney lifted the drink to her lips and stared back at the gazes trained on her. A subtle salute, a curl of her lips, before she took a healthy swallow of the fine whisky.

The bite and burn tore into her belly, causing her to close her eyes at the sensations it evoked. A pleasure, a pain. She hummed her enjoyment, feeling the room heat up drastically as several curses whispered through the room.

"Ian isn't going to happy to see you here, Miss Mattlaw," Cole, her savior, informed her humorously.

Courtney opened her eyes, turning to slant him a curious look. He was wearing a wedding band. A thick, obvious stamp of ownership. Trojans might share their women, but they never touched other females. He was safe.

"Perhaps Ian's pleasure in this small area isn't high on my list of priorities," she suggested archly.

Suspicion filled the dark blue eyes. "What areas interest you?"

"In Ian's pleasure?" she asked curiously. "Why would you care?"

"Ian's a friend." He shrugged muscled shoulders carelessly. "And you don't appear to be the sweet little virgin he warned us all against."

Her brows snapped into a frown. "He warned you against me? In what manner?"

"In the manner that if they touch you." He nodded to the men still watching curiously. "They don't just lose membership, they lose vital body parts."

He was laughing. It was obvious he found it all highly entertaining.

"And he did such a thing for what reason?" Not that she had any designs on the other men, but the fact that he would do so irked her feminine pride.

"Virgins are endangered species," he lowered his voice, though it still vibrated with laughter.

"Virgin?" She threw back the rest of her drink before smacking it back to the bar. "I would have never guessed Ian was a virgin. My, my, who was that I saw fucking the housemaids while he stayed on the estate? I should discuss this with him. Rumors can be so cruel."

Chuckles echoed through the room.

"I gather the virgin isn't you?" He sat back in his stool, watching her intently as his hand drummed idly, silently against the bar.

Slowly, she spread her arms, well aware of the wickedness of the outfit and the soft sheen of silky bare flesh.

"I hardly think so." She smiled slowly. "Virginity is such a chore. One is never allowed to have any fun when her daddy believes such a heinous thing. But, when Daddy is happy, life is much better."

"So what Daddy doesn't know, doesn't affect the little non-virgin's life?" he asked with a hint of mockery.

"Exactly." She shot Thom a disgruntled look as she turned from Cole. "You are not a very effective bartender. My glass is still empty."

Thom looked to Cole, as though asking permission. What happened to Trojans being dominant, alpha, take-charge men? She was about to become very disappointed in them.

Courtney barely restrained her exasperated sigh.

"My glass is empty, Thom," she reminded him.

"Yeah, and Ian's most likely on his way," he grunted. "You've had your limit, ma'am."

She would have pouted if she thought it would do her any good. Instead, she allowed a small smile to cross her lips, the one that should have warned him that her day was coming.

"Fine. Ian has a perfectly outfitted bar upstairs. I merely assumed the company was much more interesting here. I heard the Trojans were a bit more adventurous than it appears they are."

"Being adventurous and having a death wish are two different things," Cole reminded her as she stood from the stool and stepped down from the small dais the bar sat upon before turning for the door.

She watched suspiciously as one of the men at the table closest to her pushed his bottle of whisky across the table in invitation. He lounged back in his chair, lazily relaxed, his black eyes curious as he watched her.

Now there was one willing to break the rules, she thought admiringly. It was too bad that for this first confrontation with Ian, it was much better that no other males be involved.

Too bad Thom and Cole weren't as forthright.

What had ever made her think that the men in his club would dare go against Ian's orders? He was as dangerous to cross as her father was, and she knew it. What was it about her that she seemed surrounded by overprotective males? Did she seem so innocent? She didn't feel innocent. She felt frustrated and on edge and purely pissed that the only emotion she seemed to be able to inspire in Ian was his blasted protectiveness.

She ignored the silent offer of the whisky. It wasn't the drink she wanted. She turned and headed for the closed double doors, intent on perhaps trying a different venue to tempt her prey. There had to be a way. As she took her first step, the doors were flung open with a controlled, subtle display of power and anger. They didn't bounce against the wall, but the crack of wood meeting wood echoed around the room.

And there was Ian.

She drew in a deep breath, fighting to ignore the gut punch of arousal that suddenly clenched the muscles of her belly and left her fighting for breath. She could feel tiny, invisible fingers of sensation chasing over her flesh, tightening on her breasts until they became swollen, her nipples tight and hot.

He wasn't exactly handsome, not as Cole was. He looked like he would be more comfortable in jeans and a sweatshirt than the silk slacks and white Egyptian cotton shirt he wore. His long, dark brown hair fell below his shirt collar, tied back at the nape of his neck, giving him a reckless, dangerous appearance right off.

His blue eyes were narrowed, glittering angrily behind those generously lashed eyelids. She felt her pussy convulse, her cream immediately preparing her for him. Her clit became engorged, throbbing heatedly as she caught his gaze and saw, for the briefest moment, a wild, burning surge of arousal.

This what she wanted. This was the Ian she fantasized about. Now, what the hell was she supposed to do?

Chapter Two

Instantly. In a second, Ian's dick was steel-hard and throbbing with a lust he had never imagined possible. He could feel hunger pulsing in every pore of his skin, his body tightening, his mouth watering for the taste of her.

Masses of long, dark hair flowing nearly to her hips, framing a delicate, aristocratic face, wide dark eyes, high cheekbones, lips that trembled. She didn't wear so much as a speck of makeup, but he'd be damned if she needed it. The fresh, natural innocence that glowed beneath her flesh gave her an ethereal, sensual beauty that had his loins tied in so many knots he wondered how he was breathing.

And there she stood, in the middle of his club, her nipples poking against the white fabric of her snug top, her dark brown eyes partially covered by lowered lids but shining, as though some inner light brightened the beautiful orbs. Surrounding her were nearly a dozen of the most dominant men to possess membership in the club. Not counting the married Cole.

Khalid, the half-Saudi illegitimate son of a sheik watched her from a table nearby. His black eyes were naked with lust, his expression curious, as the sexual tension seemed to shoot sky-high within the room. Fueled by the center of attention, the delicate little morsel dressed like a dream, and obviously, heatedly, unashamedly aroused.

She was what they all dreamed of. Unabashedly aware of her surroundings and the men watching her, aroused, eager to be touched. And yes she was eager. It glittered in her eyes, just as the pebble-hard tips of her breasts proclaimed it. She would give to him. She would scream for him and beg for more. She would fight him when he needed it, give in eagerly when he hungered for it.

She would destroy him.

Ian forced himself to pull the fragmented remains of his anger around him. Nothing was going to ease the hard-on pounding between his thighs, but maybe, if he was very, very lucky, he could control a situation that threatened his sanity.

"You were told this area of the house was off-limits." His voice was rough, the guttural tone surprising him.

He watched as her cheeks flushed before his gaze flickered down to watch her abdomen convulse.

"I'm told a lot of things that I ignore, Ian." Composed, husky, filled with hunger. He heard it all in her voice and it made him impossibly harder. There was no anger in her, only a bit of humor, a lot of arousal.

Son of a bitch. He was going to explode if he wasn't careful. The rueful suggestiveness in her voice had every man in the room shifting in his chair, obviously as hard as he was. How long had it been since he had seen such natural sensuality? Such supreme confidence in a woman and her effect on the male sex?

He forced himself to move, to walk to her, to keep from throwing her across a table just to see if she was wearing panties under that tiny skirt. He had a feeling she wasn't. Did she shave or wax? he wondered. If she were his, she would be bare, pierced, screaming as his dick stretched her wide.

He gritted his teeth, forcing back the thoughts. Dane would fucking kill him. And rightly so. There was little enough innocence left in the world, he would be damned if he would be the cause of so much as a single virgin losing hers. And she was a virgin. Innocence shrouded her, glowed from inside her despite her sensuality. There was no possibility that she was anything less.

"You don't ignore the rules here, Courtney." Touching her was going to be hell. "They're here for a reason. Get back to the main part of the house. Now."

Her brows snapped into a frown as the flush on her cheeks deepened.

"Do I look like a child to you?" She waved her hand down her upper body as she cocked a hip and faced him in challenge. "Excuse me, Ian, but I haven't been a child for quite a while, and I don't appreciate being spoken to as though I were one."

His hands itched. They fucking itched to feel the soft, sweet flesh of her well-rounded ass burning beneath them. Damn her, he had never, ever wanted to possess anything as desperately as he wanted to possess Courtney now.

"You know what this club is, Courtney." He crossed his arms over his chest, fighting to instill derision, censure in his voice. "How would your father feel if he saw you here?"

"How many times has he visited?" She smiled knowingly. "I know my parent's lifestyle, Ian. Just as I know my father is indeed a member of your very elite establishment. As I have already explained to you, I am not a child."

"You are not a member of this club," he snapped then. "Members only, Courtney, for a reason. Now get your ass out of here."

"So, how does one go about receiving membership?" She seemed to ignore the harshness of his voice. Even her eyes hadn't dimmed, nor sparkled with pain or anger. As though the cruel words hadn't even registered. "I will assume some of your women are allowed in here?"

"Our women." He smiled tightly. "You do not belong to any man here. You are exempt."

Her eyes narrowed, though the smile that tipped her lips was almost frightening. Knowing. As old and as knowledgeable as Eve herself. She licked her lips slowly, her gaze flickering around the room.

"Then I need a patron of sorts?" she asked softly. "I think that could be arranged."

Like hell.

Touching her was the worst mistake possible, but every damned man in the room was ready to stand up and offer their services. His gaze hardened as he followed her look, warning them all. It didn't sit well with any of them.

"Such force," she murmured in amusement, aptly deciphering his look. "Very well, Ian. I'll leave your very lovely club and return to the main portion of the house. It's obvious I'll find no entertainment here…" She paused before staring back at him, her look direct, determined. "But there are other places I'm certain I'll be welcome."

She moved around him slowly, obviously not in the least intimidated by either his anger or the tension pulsing between them. Sexual tension, so fucking hot his skin prickled with it.

He turned, watching her leave, the swish of her skirt just beneath the rounded globes of her ass, her luscious legs moving with an inborn, natural grace. She passed through the doorway, looking neither right nor left, nor glancing behind her. She knew every man in the room was watching her, she didn't have to check to be certain. Finally, blessedly, Matthew closed the doors, leaving him to face the condemning stares of the men now watching him.

"Virgins are off-limits," he snapped, reinforcing his past rule. "Especially this one. Most especially this one."

"And what makes you so certain she's a virgin?" The argument came from the one person he hadn't expected to speak up.

Cole Andrews lounged lazily on the barstool, a drink cradled in his hand as he watched Ian closely.

"Does it matter?" he snapped.

Cole shrugged. "Not to me, but it might to the others." He indicated the men now watching with single-minded focus. "The rules don't give you a right to select the women they choose to share. Just because she's the daughter of a friend doesn't make her exempt."

Ian clenched his fists, fighting the need pounding through him. Damn Cole to hell and back, he had no idea just how much Ian wished he could make her exempt.

"Her virginity makes her exempt," he snarled, hating it, despising that veil of innocence that held him from her. If he were a lesser man, he would allow one of the others to have her, to bring her in, then take her. It would ease the lust, but not his conscience. He had known her too long, helped Dane protect her too many times. He wouldn't be party to seeing that light inside her extinguished. Not him, and not those within this room.

"She's not a virgin." Cole's confident conclusion had heat swirling through Ian's body, pooling in his dick and torturing him with the demand that he go to her, fuck her, pound the hunger out of his system.

"And you know this how?" he snarled. "Should Tessa be making an appointment with her lawyer?"

Cole laughed. A low, amused sound that grated on Ian's nerves.

"You're a fool, Ian." He shook his head slowly. "That girl is no more a virgin than Tess is. But you do what you want to. I'm sure, that as she said, she'll find entertainment elsewhere. Beautiful women like that have no hardship finding what they need."

He lifted his glass, tossing back the last of his drink as he rose from his stool and moved to leave the room.

"Too bad she only got aroused when you walked in the room," he said as he passed Ian. "That's one woman who shouldn't be wasted on a cynical prick such as yourself. Maybe Tess can try her hand at matchmaking…"

Maybe Tess could try her hand at matchmaking…

He didn't bloody well think so, Ian snarled silently as he stalked up the main staircase, turning down the hall to Courtney's bedroom. The little vixen was pushing him, and she knew it, she was doing it deliberately. He wasn't a fool. He had watched the subtle signs she had put off for the past week, the heat in her dark, sexy eyes, the way her body seemed to soften, and arousal flushed her face.

He could feel that same heat growing in his body, a hard, steady simmer that he feared would boil out of control with the least provocation. She had no idea what she was tempting. She couldn't understand the sexuality that drove him, the need he had to dominate—sexually—any female he bedded. It wasn't just a need, it was a hunger, a driving, lascivious greed he had no intention of denying himself.

He clenched his teeth at the thought of her, so small and rounded, screaming in pleasure and pain as he spread the perfect curves of her ass and watched his cock invade that sweet, tiny hole. Or holding her thighs wide, her mouth filled with his dick as he watched another take her, fill her. Sharing her, seeing pleasure suffuse her body as she was driven past any limits she could have imagined.

Damn her. He wouldn't take her. Not him.

He deliberately chose women who knew well the games they were facing. Women with experience, who knew the trick to taking two men at once, or accepting the more depraved hungers that drove the men who inhabited the club he ran. Courtney couldn't know, she couldn't understand. The sweet innocence that glowed from some inner core and lit every cell of her body couldn't have survived such wicked knowledge.

As he reached her door, he curled his lip at the thought of knocking. The hunger rushing through him fueling the anger of self-denial had him opening the panel forcibly and stepping into the room.

"Your entrances leave something to be desired, Ian." She faced him, as pretty as an angel, all that beautiful dark hair flowing around her back and shoulders as she turned from the closet, a soft white jacket trailing from her fingers as she faced him in that siren's outfit she wore.

Dear God, could anything be more tempting than all the bare, perfect flesh she was displaying?

Ian crossed his arms over his chest, fighting for control as he frowned down at her, using his most intimidating scowl as he fought to regulate his breathing. His cock was already a lost cause. It was fully engorged and throbbing in demand.

Her gaze flickered down, heated, glowed with hunger.

Son of a bitch.

"Stop tempting me, Courtney," he snapped furiously, surprised at the roughness of his voice as he fought to keep from shaking her. "You don't want what you'll get."

She propped a slender, graceful hand on her cocked hip, her eyes languorous, her cheeks flushed.

"And who decided that?" she asked him with an arched brow. "You know, Ian, I really prefer to make my own choices, rather than having them made for me. Perhaps you should remember that before you work yourself into a fury."

Patient, amused. Her voice stroked his senses as her accent seemed to give the tone an almost lilting quality. It was driving him mad. How would she sound screaming his name? Begging for his dick?

"Stay out of The Club." He refused to argue with her, to tempt his self-control further. "It's no place for you."

"Shove your club, Ian." The haughty tone and cool mocking expression had his blood boiling. "I don't need it to entertain myself."

"Your entertainment?" He felt like pulling at his own hair. What the hell was he supposed to do with this woman? "And exactly what kind of entertainment are you looking for, you little minx? Are you out to get fucked? Or just out to see how crazy you can make me?"

Her lashes drifted over her eyes, giving her a sleepy, lust-filled look that had his balls tightening as she strolled closer. Stopping within a breath of him, she stared up at him, her little pink tongue running slowly over lips, making his mouth water.

"How crazy could I make you, Ian?" she asked him then, her breathing escalating, her hard nipples nearly brushing his chest. Damn, he wanted to feel them—in his mouth, between his fingers, burning into his flesh.

Oh, she could make him crazy, he thought silently. Too crazy.

"Crazy enough to call your father and inform him it's time you headed home," he growled, nearly biting his own tongue.

She laughed. A low, devilish sound that sent flames licking over his body.

"Poor Ian, you must truly be desperate to threaten me with Daddy." Knowledge, as ancient as sin itself, echoed in her voice. "I haven't been under Daddy's thumb for many years. Your only chance is throwing me out, period. Perhaps finding a patron wouldn't be so hard under such circumstances."

"Are you so desperate for a sugar daddy, Courtney?" he snarled. "Doesn't Dane provide you with enough?"

A smile curved her lips. "Daddy can't get me into your bed, Ian, otherwise I would have tried that route already. I refuse to lie about the reason I'm here any longer." She laid her hand against his chest. He watched her breath catch, the way she swallowed tightly as pleasure tore through him. From such a small touch. How would he survive feeling her, bare flesh to bare flesh, burning beneath him?

"I won't take you to my bed, Courtney." He hated the words that slipped past his lips, hated the fact that he couldn't allow himself to possess her.

She lifted her shoulder in an elegant shrug. "Then another will. Perhaps the nice Middle Eastern gentleman. He seemed to have promise…"

Khalid. Ian fought back his instinctive response, and it wasn't anger.

He gripped her arm when she would have slipped past him.

"Don't make decisions you'll regret, little girl," he warned her harshly. "You're too young to know or to understand what he'll ask of you. And it's nothing compared to what I would demand."

"Or perhaps, nothing compared to what I would demand," she said then, causing his blood pressure to escalate, his cock to harden to impossible degrees. He felt as though the thickening shaft would rupture from the hunger filling it. "But—" She shrugged again as she moved away from him. "As you have decided to deny yourself as well as me, I will leave you in peace, Ian. But I refuse to lay here and masturbate to sate the needs. I will see what other entertainment your fair city has to offer me."

She swept from the room as he turned slowly, watching the little skirt swish around her upper thighs, nearly baring her ass as she left the room. His eyes narrowed as he clenched his fists, leashing the almost violent response rising inside him.

She was pushing him. Pushing him too far, straining what little control he had left.

What the hell was it about her? Why did she tempt a part of him that no other woman had ever touched, even Kimberly? Why did she make him hunger for things that he couldn't even put a name to? And why the fuck was he letting her do it?

Chapter Three

She was shaking inside. She was nearly shaking on the outside.

Courtney could feel the nervous energy racing through her body, pulsing nearly as furiously as the arousal flaming across her nerve endings. Her pussy felt swollen, intensely sensitive, her clit rasping against the silk of her thong as she walked sedately down the stairs and headed for the front door.

Not that she had any true plans for the night. She would allow Ian's chauffeur to drive her to a few clubs, perhaps dance a few hours as she drowned her sorrows and her arousal in a few stiff drinks, since Ian wasn't volunteering his stiff cock.

And how stiff it looked beneath his slacks. Thick and long, mouthwateringly tempting. She wanted nothing more than to go to her knees and release the engorged flesh to her hungry mouth. She could almost feel it, so hard and thick her lips would feel bruised, so hot she would feel blistered. And she wanted it. Longed for it.

As she reached the foyer, she was aware of Ian moving down the steps behind her, almost stalking her as though she were his prey. A shiver worked up her spine, part trepidation, part satisfaction. Finally, his reserve was faltering. If she had known that visiting The Club would bring such a reaction, she would have done so the first week.

The ringing of the doorbell had her pausing as she shrugged on the short, thin leather jacket that matched the outfit she wore. She watched, curious, as the house butler, Jason, moved from the sitting room, casting her a cool look as he gripped the doorknob and opened the double doors.

Courtney felt the immediate tension that filled the room as Ian stepped from the stairs. She was between them, the man she longed for, and the mysterious, devilishly handsome Saudi.

"Well, my luck knows no bounds this night." The stranger stepped into the foyer, tall, nearly as tall as Ian's six feet three inches, his black eyes blazing with lust.

Where it had done little to affect her earlier, that look, when paired with the flames she could feel licking over her flesh from Ian's gaze…she nearly lost the strength in her knees. Dear heaven, they had yet to even touch her, but she could feel the need to, the lust racing around them.

"Prince Khalid el Hamid Mustafa," the butler announced his presence, his voice an irritating buzz to her side.

Courtney turned, surrounded by testosterone, until her gaze met Ian's. What she saw there was nearly more than she could bear without begging for his touch. She turned back quickly, her lips curving into a smile as she met the Saudi's wicked look.

"Khalid, you weren't invited up here," Ian sniped rudely as the butler closed the doors behind the other man.

"I need an invitation?" Khalid lifted a brow curiously, his gaze trained on her. "I wasn't aware of that. And you haven't introduced me to your lovely guest, Ian."

Oh, she could just imagine the anger rising inside Ian now. She flicked a glance his way, seeing the stiff set of his shoulders, the flat line of his mouth. But his eyes were burning, not with anger, but with arousal.

"Courtney Marguerita Mattlaw. Prince Khalid el Hamid Mustafa," he introduced them, with no pretense to civility.

"A most beautiful name, for a most beautiful young woman," the Prince murmured as he accepted her hand, bending his head gracefully to place a dark kiss on the sensitive flesh of her wrist. "And a most bold young woman as well."

She allowed her expression to smooth to one of amused patience as she saw the laughter in his gaze, the quick, hidden glance behind her before those dark eyes seemed to flash a hidden message her way. A co-conspirator? It appeared she might well need the help.

Besides, causing trouble was so much more fun when one had help.

"Bold?" she questioned him flirtatiously. "And what would lead you to such a conclusion?"

"It is not every young woman who would dare breach the walls of a club such as the one Ian heads. I would definitely describe such a woman as bold."

"I believe I would use the word…adventurous rather than bold," she amended his description. "Bold implies a less permanent trait. Adventurous is more genetic." She glanced at Ian once again, wondering if he caught the suggestive implication.

Sweet mercy, blue eyes could burn, they could glow with lust, and he was proof of it.

"Adventurous it is," Khalid agreed. "I wondered, as our less than charming host has thrown you from The Club, if you would perhaps grace me with your presence for dinner tonight? My chauffeur is waiting outside, the limo cozy and warm. I believe I could perhaps help relieve the incredible boredom that must be filling your day, trapped as you are with our less than adventurous Mr. Sinclair."

Laughter trembled on her lips, though she held it back valiantly. She was certain the description of less than adventurous was a grave insult to the man she knew Ian was. But it tempted her sense of humor, her sense of daring to push him further. He had all but ignored her this week pretending there was no attraction, no need flaring between them. She wasn't about to allow this advantage to slip through her fingers.

"What a lovely offer." She smiled slowly, flirtatiously. "And one I'll gratefully accept, Prince Mustafa."

"Khalid, please." He grimaced at the title. "Ian and his butler persist in tacking the title to the name. An illegitimate prince is not much of a prince at all. Especially one who prefers the wicked temptations of the West, rather than his father's beliefs."

"And some men are a prince, whether born to it, or deserving it," she praised his offer of escape in glowing words. "I'm ready to leave whenever you are."

His hand moved to her back, riding dangerously low on her hips, his fingers nearly cupping the curve of her ass as he steered her to the door. She allowed the muscles there to clench, the tingling arousal electrifying her as she felt Ian's gaze on her rear.

"Courtney." Ian's voice stopped them as they neared the door.

Turning slowly, she met the brilliant heat emanating from his gaze.

"Yes, Ian?" Maintaining the cool façade, the appearance of control was the hardest endeavor she had met in her life. Ian's gaze melted her, sent flames searing her pussy and electrifying her clitoris. She could orgasm from that look alone, she believed.

"There are some paths that once taken, you can never turn back," he warned her, his voice dark, filled with intent as his eyes raked over the obvious arousal that tightened her nipples and flushed her face.

The look burned her, had the blood singing through her veins, desire pulsing in a drumbeat of desperate arousal in the depths of her pussy and the sensitive, swollen knot of her clit.

"And some paths are sought after, Ian," she answered him, her voice just as low, throbbing in answer to the unvoiced desire. "Just as others are destined."

She turned from him, a superhuman effort, thankful for the support of Khalid's hand at her back as he led her outside. Cold winter air slapped her in the face, but did little to ease the heat burning through her body as he led her quickly to the limo that waited just below the steps to the house.

The chauffeur opened the door quickly, allowing her to slide into the warmth of the interior as Khalid followed at a more leisurely pace. Courtney was aware of him watching her, amusement lingering in his gaze as she breathed in roughly. Leaving the house was the hardest thing she had ever done. She wanted nothing more than to stay, to rub against Ian like a spoiled cat and feel his hands stroking over her body.

"He'll be waiting when you return." Khalid's voice was low, suggestive.

Courtney glanced over him, noticing the casual grace and inborn arrogance that surrounded him like a shield. His thick black hair fell to his shoulders, framing his dark, aristocratic features. High cheekbones, a straight, hawkish nose, sensual, full lips. Those lips were almost candy, she thought. They would tempt most women to unknown daring in an attempt to taste them. Most women. But not her, not without Ian.

"Then perhaps we should let him wait a while," she suggested with a smile, though careful to keep the width of the seat between them. "I believe he could use the time to consider his options."

His brow arched mockingly. "You're playing with fire, sweetheart. I've never seen Ian deny himself before. It's obvious the strain is wearing on him. Should his control snap, you could be the one paying the price."

"Or reaping the benefits," she retorted confidently. "Ian would never hurt me, Prince Mustafa. No matter how tempted he may be." And she had no doubt he was tempted by now.

He settled more comfortably in his seat, his black eyes filled with laughter as his lips curved into a smile.

"Do you know the beast you are tempting then?" he asked her carefully. "Ian won't necessarily be a gentle lover. None of us who inhabit The Club truly are. Our tastes run to the extreme, Ms. Mattlaw, are you prepared for that?"

"The Trojans." She restrained her smile as she turned in her seat, crossing her legs as she watched him carefully. "I've very well aware of the sort of lover Ian will be, Khalid."

His eyes roved over her upper body slowly.

"You're unaroused now that he is no longer in your presence. It is Ian you hunger for. But if you tempt him to your bed, you will find he will not come alone." It was a warning, a statement of intent. He intended to be there with them.

"And I look forward to it," she assured him. "Never doubt that I'm not aware of what Ian will ask of me, or the fact that I don't desire it myself. But only with Ian, Prince Mustafa. Never without him."

She had no desire to be touched, held, caressed, without him. It was one of the clues that helped her to unravel the frightening feelings she had known as she entered adulthood. Each time he had visited she had watched him, found ways to learn what she could of him. He made her feel things that for years she had been unable to understand. Brought desires and hungers that had been difficult to make sense of. And the fantasies. Even now, the thought of them made her shift in uncomfortable desire. Such fantasies she had of him.

"He will share you." He had no intention of covering a truth he evidently believed she was unaware of.

She smiled, a slow curve of her lips meant to assure him that she knew well what was coming.

"When I was twenty-two, I happened to have need of my maid for some reason," she recounted with a shrug, not clearly remembering now why she needed the young woman. "There were several maids who traveled with me, each resembled me strongly. That night, when I went searching for her, I happened to oversee and hear as Ian instructed her lover in taking her." She licked her suddenly dry lips. He had mistakenly called the maid by the name Courtney as she listened. Unconsciously revealing his own hunger. "I knew then that only Ian could fulfill what I needed as well. This is my chance, Prince Mustafa. A chance to convince Ian of this as well."

Even now the memory of that night tormented her.

Spread her ass slowly. Make her anticipate what's to come... Slow and easy, boy, fuck that ass slow and easy, let her feel every stroke... Suck my dick, Courtney, suck it, baby. Deep...

Had he realized he was whispering her name? Courtney wondered. Had he known his voice throbbed with lust as he whispered her name?

"He could break your heart." His gaze was suddenly serious, concerned. "You're in love with him."

"Of course I am," she agreed with a soft laugh. "Why else would I be here? Do you think that if it were only sex I required that I would tolerate such a frustrating male temperament? I could find the sex anywhere, Prince Mustafa. The sex, without Ian, leaves little to be desired."

"I'll join him," he told her then, leaning closer, his black eyes suddenly intent, determined. "Do you hear me, girl? When he turns that pretty ass up and spanks it until it burns, I intend to be there. Just as I intend to fuck you. And not only for one night. Ian is perhaps the most sexual, the most intent of any of The Club's members. He will share you often, and share you well. He will leave you screaming until you're hoarse, begging until you no longer know why you're pleading. He will lead you into a pleasure that borders exquisite pain. Are you certain this is something you can endure?"

She rolled her eyes at the concern in his voice. The overprotectiveness she was inspiring in the men around her was becoming stifling.

"Why is everyone so certain I am unaware of what I'm seeking?" she asked him, growing weary of the warnings.

"Perhaps, because of the innocence that shines so sweetly from those dark brown eyes," he suggested. "You have the appearance of a precocious schoolgirl. A man's greatest sexual fantasy, his most frightening reality. Pair that with a woman fully grown and one who appears willing to fulfill every fantasy, and you would terrify even the most perverted hedonist. You, my dear, could bring Ian to his knees. And for a man as dominant, as intent on his freedom as I know Ian is, you are a weakness he can ill afford. You arouse protectiveness, in the same depths that you arouse lust. Be careful that your heart isn't broken."

* * * * *

"Marguerita, what the hell has happened to Courtney?" Dane was not at home, which was a damned good thing because Ian was ready to blister his ears. What the hell did the other man think he was doing, sending his daughter here? Here? To the same house where the now infamous Trojans met. To the same house filled with a club of depraved, perverted men who wanted nothing more than to devour her, inch by gorgeous, lovely inch.

"Courtney?" Marguerita's soft voice held equal amounts confusion and amusement. "Why, Ian, I thought she was with you. Has she left your protection?"

His protection? What protection? He was her daddy's worst nightmare. Didn't they know that? Since when had Dane and Marguerita lost their ever-lovin' minds?

"She's out of control," he snapped, pacing the foyer as he glanced at the grandfather clock that tick-tocked the time with an irritating cadence. "She slipped into The Club. She's driving the members crazy. What happened to the sweet little girl I used to know?"

He raked his fingers through his hair, grimacing as he remembering the seventeen year old with knowing eyes and a glimmer of hunger. No, sweet had never described Courtney. He had just wished it had.

"Did you ever know her, Ian?" Marguerita asked then, taking him aback by the seriousness of her voice. "Courtney, despite Dane's perception of her, is no longer a child. If you can't deal with this, then perhaps she should return. At least here, those who know her, accept her for who she is."

He stilled then, his body tensing at the censure in her voice.

"What do you mean by that?"

She sighed heavily. "I owe you a great debt, Ian. Had it not been for you, those years that Dane and I were separated, then I fear I would have lost him forever."

"What does that have to do with anything?" he gritted out, remembering those years that he had trailed Dane, wondering if his friend would live to see another day. The reported deaths of his lover and child by her family had nearly destroyed Dane. For close to three years until he had sobered up enough to suspect the truth, he had been a madman.

"Courtney is much like her father," Marguerita said then, her voice a soft warning. "She is just as dedicated and loyal to those she loves as Dane ever was. But much like Dane, and in many ways like myself, Courtney's needs are different than others."

He felt the breath halt in his throat. Marguerita couldn't be saying what he thought she was, it wasn't possible.

"She's twenty-four years old. A virgin…"

"She's twenty-four years old, but I highly doubt she's still a virgin. And Dane may like to bury his head in the sand where his daughter is concerned, but I do not. Courtney has spent the last two years trying her wings, slipping easily from her pappa's sight and learning the ways of the world. The two of you too easily discount the woman my daughter has become. And I would not have expected it of you, Ian."

"And why's that?" he snapped. "I've known her since she was a child."

"Because you've been getting hard for her since she was a teenager," Marguerita chuckled knowingly. "If you do not want Courtney, then the best thing you can do is send her home. But be careful of her heart, Ian. She is bold and adventurous. But she is still yet a woman. And one who cares deeply."

The implicit permission he sensed in taking Courtney to his bed staggered her.

"You're giving her to me?" He blinked at the wall across from him, shock and surprise filling him.

"Giving her to you?" Marguerita mused with a soft laugh. "I would not say this exactly. It is up to Courtney who she belongs to and who she does not. I am merely attempting to warn you of her intentions. I do not wish to see my daughter hurt. If you have no desire for her, then she is better off not within your care."

"You know what I am," he growled.

"As you know whose daughter she is." He could almost see the delicate shrug of the woman's slender shoulders. "How many women did you and my husband share during the years I was forced to another's bed? Dane has been quite honest with me concerning that time in his life. Just as he has told me, quite explicitly, how sexual you can become with your females, either alone, or while sharing them. Just as you know well Dane's preference. We have had a third in our marriage since the first week of our relationship. It is a pleasure we both greatly enjoy. I doubt sincerely my daughter would be scarred by your hungers, my friend."

His hand tightened on the receiver. Yes, he knew well the lifestyle Dane and Marguerita enjoyed. He hadn't participated himself, not with them, but he knew Marguerita, as delicate and small as she was, was married to a man who could accept nothing less than the most intense pleasures he could bring to her.

"Dane would kill me." He grimaced, knowing it wasn't going to make a difference.

"Dane is no hypocrite, as you well know. He will accept his daughter's choices, even if it means accepting she is a woman, rather than a child."

Ian snorted. Dane wasn't the only one hiding his head in the sand if she truly believed that.

"Marguerita, you should tell Dane exactly what she's up to and have him drag her ass home," he sighed wearily, watching the clock tick away a mere minute.

"It would be much easier to send her home if you do not want her," Marguerita laughed, a lilting sound that had him grimacing at the knowing tone.

"I don't have the strength," he finally whispered. "I'm about to make the most incredible mistake of my life, and I think I'm going to blame you for it. You're an evil woman."

"Ahh, so Dane tells me often." She didn't sound in the least apologetic. "Please give Courtney my love. Care for her, Ian. A young woman's adventures should always be made with one understanding of her tender heart. This I trust you in."

She disconnected, leaving Ian drifting in a sea of desire so intense it cut into his loins, and a confusion so thick it threatened to smother him. It bothered him that Marguerita had known his lust for Courtney during those first years. Seventeen, prone to hug and touch and rub against him like a little cat. He had fucked her maid raw the week he had stayed there. Several years later, it had been worse. He could still remember awakening, reaching for her, locked in dreams so erotic they were torture.

Snarling silently, he punched in another number, waiting impatiently for the phone to connect.

"Khalid." The bastard answered the phone on the fifth ring, his voice lazy, filled with sensuality.

"Bring her home. Now." If he had to go looking for her, he might well get them all arrested.

"I see." Khalid's voice was a low, deep growl. "I will take care of this."

Ian disconnected before moving to the living room to wait. Leaning back on the couch, he loosened his pants, pulling his engorged cock free and grimacing as his fingers tightened on the torturously hard flesh.

He stared down at the ruddy flesh, the thick, violently colored crest as it swelled and pulsed within his grip. He was a large man, and he well knew it. Courtney was small, the shape of her legs, the curve of her rear, the contours of her shapely little cunt beneath her clothing assured him that her sweet little tunnel would be tight, snug.

He groaned at the thought of it, stroking his desperate flesh as his eyes closed in such need it was nearly pain. He would show her tonight the needs that tormented him. He wouldn't begin easy. He wouldn't allow her to dismiss the knowledge she already had.

There was something about watching a woman, holding her as another touched her, watching the agonized pleasure that transformed her features, that he could never explain to himself. Their screams of need, eyes wild, body glistening with perspiration as they fought to understand the different sensations two men could bring them. Or watching another touch her as he fucked her. Able to lose himself in the feel of a tight pussy or ass and knowing that the other male would pleasure her as she needed to reach the highest peaks of ecstasy.

Driving her crazy.

His fingers stroked over his cock, imagining her lips surrounding him, sucking him deep as she tried to scream around the thick stalk because even as she pleasured, she was being pleasured.

He was different. All the members of the Club were different. It was a difference Ian had fought for years, one he had agonized over and finally accepted. Either something was missing within him, or something was much too strong. Because the thought of holding her to him, his cock buried deep inside her as Khalid touched her, tweaked her hard nipples or filled her as well, had pre-come spilling from his dick and lubricating his fingers as his thighs tightened, his hips arching to his hand.

Her mouth. He wanted her mouth wrapped around the head of his erection, sucking it hot and deep as her slender fingers stroked the shaft. He would bury his hands in her hair, feel her screams vibrating on his cock as Khalid prepared her for further play.

He clenched his teeth, tightening his fingers on the bulging head as he imagined holding her open, fitting himself between the soft folds of flesh between her thighs and filling her. Slow. He would push in so slow, holding her still as she fought to accept him, the satin tissue of her pussy gripping him, straining to stretch around his width.

He would take her first. He would fill her, fuck her until she screamed in climax and begged for mercy before he would allow another to have her. First, she would belong to him. He would mark every sweet inch of her body with his touch and make certain she always remembered who she belonged to. Make certain it was imprinted into her very soul, that she was his first.

His.

He erupted. A hoarse groan filled the room as his release jetted from his cock, shuddered through his body and left him gasping for breath at the very thought of her accepting him, screaming his name. Silky streams of semen filled his hand, splattered onto his shirt but did nothing to lessen his hunger. Only Courtney could ease that pain, and tonight, she would sate it, or he would end up fucking her to death in the attempt.

Chapter Four

Courtney knew when Khalid hung up the phone in the middle of dinner that it had been Ian on the other end. Khalid didn't inform her of that fact, he did no more than resume eating his meal, as charming and wicked as ever. Regaling her of the years he spent in his father's land, and many of the adventures he found there. As well as the harem his father had gifted him.

He was an interesting companion and reminded her much of Sebastian. Courtney imagined Khalid and Sebastian would be the best of friends should they ever meet.

"Are you finished?" he asked as she pushed her plate away, having barely touched the excellently prepared salmon she had ordered. It wasn't food she was hungry for.

"I believe I am," she sighed as she finished the wine and watched him curiously. "That was Ian on the phone, was it not?"

His lips quirked as his black eyes met hers ruefully.

"He sounds a bit more intense than I've ever known him to be. He of course demanded your return. Now, I believe he said."

The self-satisfied smile that curved his lips assured her that he was enjoying the thought of defying his friend.

Forcibly, she restrained a cry of glee. So perhaps it wasn't so mature, but the excitement radiating through her now was tremendous.

Khalid leaned back in his seat, lifting his wineglass to sip at it casually as he watched her.

"You aren't demanding that we return," he stated the obvious.

"Not because it isn't what I prefer," she assured him with a wide smile. "I'd run straight to his arms if I thought it would accomplish my goal."

"And your goal is?" His brows lifted in inquiry.

She tilted her head, dropping the amusement she had adopted for the evening and allowing the determination she could feel in her soul to reflect on her face. She could feel it building in her day by day, the assurance that she was indeed right. That she had chosen wisely, and that the battle she had set for herself would end in success.

"I want his heart," she finally said softly. "As you said earlier, I love him."

He blinked once. She had a feeling few people could surprise Khalid, but it appeared she had done so. The cynical, handsome son of a prince was staring at her as though she had suddenly morphed into an alien being.

"Interesting." He leaned forward, bracing his arms on the table as he watched her. "You are, of course, aware that Ian believes he has no heart. How do you capture what a man believes he does not possess?"

She was aware of the sad curve of her own lips at the thought of Ian and the heart he believed he did not have. There was a haunted light in Ian's eyes, a dark, almost hidden shadow of pain that she wanted nothing more than to wipe away. As naïve as she knew it sounded, she wanted to fill his life with light, with love. She wanted to see that special gleam in his gaze, such as her father had with her mother. That smile, secretive, almost bemused, that graced his lips each time her mother was near. She wanted that for Ian.

"You help him find it. One step at a time." She could only pray that the steps she was making were the correct ones. She could only follow her heart and her woman's intuition and hope she wasn't making any drastic mistakes.

"And you think you can change him because of this love of yours?" He was looking at her with equal parts pity and amusement. "Reform him so to speak?"

"Not hardly." Some men should be placed in pens and taken out for breeding purposes only, she thought. They had no understanding of women, or of how adaptable their love truly was. "Love doesn't seek to change what already is, Khalid. It seeks only to be a part of it. Thankfully for Ian, I look forward to being a part of the life he lives and the sexuality that is a part of him. I don't seek to change him."

Once again, his gaze became confused, as though he couldn't quite figure out what she was talking about.

"You'll see," she assured him with a smile. "I will succeed, Khalid. I've known since I was a child that I belonged to Ian. I just have to convince him of this now." She rose to her feet to stare down at him questioningly. "Shall we go?"

He shook his head, but followed suit. "Of course." He moved around the table, his hand settling in the small of her back as he led her from the restaurant to the waiting limo.

Courtney could feel the blood pounding through her body as they rode back to Ian's estate. He would realize of course, how she was manipulating the situation. Ian was no fool. Just as he would realize that once she knew how to push him, she wouldn't let up. It was a dangerous game she was playing, and she was well aware of it. Ian was a man, full grown and in his prime. She was but an amateur and she knew that well. But, a very determined amateur, she assured herself with a flare of satisfaction.

"That smile is frightening, Courtney," Khalid mused with a chuckle as he led her to the waiting limo. "I believe I may well decide to feel quite sorry for my good friend Ian, rather than the little chick I feared he would devour. In this case, I believe the chick has teeth and the wolf may well be rendered helpless."

The thought of succeeding in her goal was nearly as arousing as the thought of Ian awaiting her, demanding her return.

She could feel her breasts, swollen and sensitive as they pressed against the fabric of her top, her nipples rasping against the material and sending sharp, heated sparks of longing shooting through her nerve endings, straight to her engorged clit. And that small mass of nerves was demanding relief. A relief she had never known, never found on her own, just as she had failed with Sebastian.

"I want him with every cell of my body, Khalid," she whispered longingly. "I've wanted him like this since I was little more than a child. Before I ever knew what sexual heat could be, or how intense it could become, I have felt this for Ian."

His hooded gaze raked over her breasts as he sat in the seat across from her, his dark gaze hot and filled with lust.

"I've shared women with Ian before, little chick. He won't go easy on you." She heard the warning in his voice.

"It isn't easy I wish," she breathed hungrily, shifting on the leather, her thighs tightening at the thought that soon, very, very soon she would face Ian once again. Perhaps a hungrier Ian. One who had given up the battle to keep her from his bed.

Khalid's expression became more sensual, heavy with desire as his eyes glittered with intent, though he said nothing more. She could see his thoughts though, the lust that built slowly during the drive, the erection that thickened beneath his pants.

She drew in a slow, deep breath as the limo pulled in front of the steps that led to the house. She waited patiently until the chauffeur opened the door, helping her from the backseat as Khalid followed.

Her heart was racing in her chest, her juices collecting between her thighs and slickening the swollen folds of her pussy as the butler opened the door. Warmth spilled from the house as they stepped inside, sexual tension immediately whipping around them as Ian stepped from the receiving room to the side.

His eyes were wild. The Irish blue glittered beneath thick black lashes as his gaze went first to Khalid, then to her.

"Good evening, Ian," Khalid was the first to speak, his voice thickening as his hand slid from her back to the curve of her hip. "As you can see, I've delivered her safe and sound."

"So you have," Ian growled as he gestured to the butler to leave.

The other man nodded and retreated toward the back of the house.

"I believe it must surely be my bedtime." Courtney ignored the racing of her blood and the arousal destroying her.

She turned and smiled back at Khalid as she reached up and kissed his cheek lingeringly. "I had a very pleasant evening."

"No more than I, sweet one," he said, his voice dark with lust. "I will look forward to seeing you again soon."

"Ian." She turned back to him, ignoring the dangerous stillness of his body. "Goodnight. Perhaps I'll see you in the morning."

"I think not." He surprised her.

He moved quickly, standing before her, tall and broad and aroused as he stared down at her, blocking her way to the stairs.

Courtney lifted a brow mockingly. "It is rather late, Ian."

She was aware of Khalid watching the byplay with hot interest.

"Did he touch you?" There was no jealousy in his voice, but rather avid hunger.

"And would you care?" she asked him with a smile, a deliberately sensual curve of her lips, rather like the one she had seen her mother giving her father when teasing him unbearably.

She watched his eyes darken. His gaze flickered to Khalid.

"Did you touch her?"

"She belongs to you," Khalid said softly then. "I know the rules of The Club, Ian. Even those unspoken."

Fire bit into her nipples as Ian's gaze flickered to them.

"Such games you play," she said with a sigh. "I thought you were a bit more honest about your desires, Ian. Such whimsies do not become you."

She frowned as she moved to the side to pass by him. He was there again, shifting to keep her in front in of him.

"I've wondered this evening," he said, his hands reaching out to slide the shoulders of her jacket from her. "If you are as brave, as courageous in your desires as you appear to be. Are you, Courtney?"

"It would appear more so than you, Ian." She shrugged the jacket off herself, allowing it to fall to the floor at her feet as he gripped her arms, less than gently, turning her quickly and half-carrying her into the living/receiving room he had vacated moments before.

* * * * *

Courtney had no idea what happed to Khalid. To be perfectly honest, at that moment, she really didn't care. Others had no place in this first confrontation between her and Ian. No audience was needed in this first, subtle battle that would decide if she would become special to him, or merely the little girl who forced him to take her to his bed despite his best intentions.

He was fighting sheer habit, that she knew. His friendship with her father changed the rules for her, made taking her more difficult for him. She had to win this first confrontation, prove to him that she was more, that she was different from the others. It wasn't his lifestyle that drew her to him, as it was with the other lovers who had sought him out. It was Ian, his touch, his heart, that drew her. The rest was merely a sweet little fringe benefit.

She twisted out of his grip inside the room, swinging around to face him as he stared at her with dark, glittering eyes.

"What now?" She propped her hands on her hips as she watched him, allowing a daring smile to shape her lips, a challenge, one that said she didn't believe he would follow through with whatever wicked thoughts were racing through his mind. And they were wicked. She could see it in the heavy sensuality that tightened his expression, the way his eyes narrowed on her.

That look speared straight to her pussy, causing the cream gathering in her vagina to ease slowly along the bare folds beyond.

"What do you think?" Ah yes, he was angry. She could see the anger pulsing inside him, mixing with the arousal, pushing his boundaries, testing his control.

She lifted her shoulder negligently. "I have no clue, Ian. Should I strip for you?" She spread her arms wide. "Or should I go to my knees for you? I've not truly researched the proper rules of a submissive, as it's not the role I intend to really play, so perhaps you should tell me what is expected of me next."

Her arms fell to her sides then as she stared back at him questioningly. Not that she expected much of a fair answer from him. If she knew anything about angry men, it was that they would cut their noses off to spite their faces. They were stubborn, arrogant, and more likely to deny the obvious than to admit to it. Such stubborn creatures, she sighed regretfully.

"You think being such a naughty little girl is cute, don't you, Courtney."

Oh shit. How had he picked on one of her favorite fantasies so damned fast? It was one that often left her wakening, damp with perspiration, her thighs quivering with the need for release, the cheeks of her ass clenching in remembered heat as she dreamed of his palm landing heavily on her rear.

"Am I being naughty, Ian?" The fingers of one hand moved to the small emerald ring piercing her navel as she played with it with studied laziness. "I thought I was quite well behaved. Of course, you always have the option of punishing me. Would you like to punish me?" She deliberately adopted a softer, more innocent tone as she allowed her eyes to widen in mock surprise. "Spank me," she breathed seductively. "Spank me so good."

His gaze glittered, wilder, hotter.

"You think you know me," he growled then. "You think your soft little dreams are safe with me and this is all a game you can play. It's not a game, Courtney. This isn't a sexual taste for me, it's a lifestyle, and what I demand of you will be nothing compared to what you think you know."

"Have I acted as though I were playing a game?" She arched a brow mockingly. "I know more about you than you could ever believe, Ian. I'm very well aware of the fact that it isn't a game." Her heart and life were very serious matters to her. "My question is, are you?"

"Are you still a virgin?" It was a question she had expected.

"Only in your dreams." Her gaze flicked to his fists as they clenched in the pockets of his slacks, stretching the material over the thick erection beneath. "Do you dream of that, Ian? Of taking my innocence? Of being the first? Had I known that, I wouldn't have been so eager to rid myself of it."

But she knew better. She knew Ian well enough, and had overheard her parents discussing him enough to know he would have never been comfortable taking her virginity. He would have regretted it, and she didn't want that for him, or for herself.

"Never," he snapped. "If I wanted a bloody virgin I could find one any day."

"But not a bloody virgin named Courtney," she reminded him sweetly. "You may have missed out on the shield of purity but there is still much you can teach me. Wouldn't you like to instruct me, Ian?" She moved closer, deliberately teasing him, taunting him. "To teach me your pleasures? To leave me screaming in shock and desire? You may not be the first to touch me, but you will be the first to possess me, perhaps."

He grabbed her shoulders, his grip snug, almost tight as he pushed her to the nearby chair before stepping away. The strength and dominance in the act was enough to weaken her knees. The implications of his weakening control had her blood singing in exhilaration.

"Bend over the chair," he fairly snarled. "Before this goes any further, I'll know for certain. Trust me, Courtney, you don't want me to take you if you are."

"Oh really, Ian…"

"Now!" The crack of his voice had her shuddering. Dominant, harsh, riding the edge of control. But not out of control. He was determined to hold part of himself back, to maintain a distance with her that she knew she would never survive.

Inside, she was trembling violently, fighting not to beg for his kiss, his touch, for so much more than she knew he was willing to give at the moment. She would have gladly bent over him for him, if it were more than an experiment, a furious test that he felt she would fail.

"I do not think so, Ian," she snapped right back at him instead. "I am not a puppet for you to command, nor am I a toy for you to tease and taunt as you please. I could get better than this from a gigolo on any street corner."

She turned on her heel and strode to the door, anger tightening her body. Not even a kiss. He had not even kissed her, caressed her, given her so much as indication that he desired more than just the pussy that he believed still yet maintained its purity. Bastard. She would be damned if she would bend over for him.

"Walk out that door, Courtney, and you may as well forget sharing my bed, at any time."

"As though your bed is what I am after," she snorted as she paused, turning back to him, knowing well the lights from the foyer now bathed her body. "Poor Ian. The highest of all Trojans. The master of The Club, dominant extraordinaire. How sad it is that you would allow something as trifling as the suspicion of virginity to stand between you and the hunger I know eats at you. Eats at me. I do not care to submit to your desire, but never will I submit to your self-inflicted fury that you may want something more than your asinine rules. Go fuck someone willing to bend over and stare at the wall as you satisfy your inane curiosity. I deserve more, and I will be damned if I will accept less."

She swept through the doorway, grabbing her jacket where it still lay on the marble floor and striding quickly up the stairs. Trepidation rode at her heels as she felt his gaze following her, knew that she was only pushing him further. It wasn't a choice she could manipulate. She knew Ian would have to be pushed past his very rigid self-control and forced to admit that she was different. If she submitted as any other woman would to him, then she would become little more than one among many who had paraded through his bedroom. She was unique. She belonged solely and completely to him, and he must be forced to admit to this. Her own satisfaction, her very future demanded it.

She had no more than reached the upper landing when she felt him behind her. Tall and hot, overpoweringly sexual as his hands gripped her waist, turning her, pushing her forcibly against the wall a second before his lips possessed hers with a dominant, powerful force that left her knees shaking.

There was no warning, no seeking permission. This wasn't a man asking for submission, it was a man demanding it. Unwilling to accept anything less. And Courtney found herself helpless in the face of it. Her head fell back into the hand that cupped it, his fingers tangling in her thick hair as he held her in place. Her lips opened, a fractured moan escaping as pleasure surged through every cell of her body. Electric, intense sensation exploded in the pit of her stomach, suffusing her in a wash of pre-orgasmic bliss.

How could the touch of another's lips bring such pleasure?

Her hands gripped his shoulders, moving frantically over the fine fabric of his shirt before sliding into his hair, gripping the strands, her fingers kneading his scalp as she fought to get closer, to deepen a kiss that already reached to her very soul.

Oh God, he was consuming her.

His tongue licked at hers, twined with it, his head tilting until he could devour her deeper as his hands began to rove over her body. Hands slightly calloused, fingers rasping as he pushed her top over her breasts to allow his fingers free rein on the sensitive swollen mounds.

She would have screamed if she had the breath left in her chest. The pleasure was fiery, destructive, weakening her muscles as she arched into the touch, her hands clenching tighter in his hair as his fingers plucked at her nipples. He pulled at the hard tips until she mewled in frustrated desire, her pussy spasming with need, the hot wash of her cream easing from her vagina to further slicken the bare folds beyond.

Courtney could feel flames licking over her flesh as he suddenly tore his lips free of hers, leaving her fighting to catch her breath as his lips moved along her arched neck, down further, until she felt them cover one violently sensitive nipple.

"*Qué usted hace a mí…?*" She shuddered as she slipped into her mother's language. "What do you do to me, Ian?" She could barely breathe, let alone think to remember which language to use.

Her head fell back against the wall, her senses trained on each touch Ian bestowed to her flesh. His fingers wrapped around the swollen mound of her breast, flexing, testing the weight and feel of her as the deep suckling motions of his mouth sent wicked shards of sensation shooting through her.

He was sinfully sexual, nipping at her nipple as the fingers of his other hand played with the opposite peak. Every touch, every moved designed to destroy her sanity, to make her pliable. Submissive.

She struggled past the dazed mists filling her head, a small part of her recognizing, in much amusement, the tactics he was employing on her. As though she were one of the countless women he had bedded over the years. To drown her in sensuality, to capture her senses and hold them captive until he was finished. Until he had drawn every measure of pleasure from her body, leaving her weak and exhausted. Unable to make any demands on his heart, because she was insensible with the sensations he had filled her with.

And he was so close to his goal. The pleasure was like a whirlwind, engulfing her, pushing her deeper into the abyss of sexuality that opened wide within her.

It would be a battle.

Her hands moved from his hair, her nails raking against his neck as they moved beneath the collar of his shirt.

He shivered. She felt the telltale tremor as her womb convulsed in response. His hand clenched at her hip, the other in her hair, a muttered growl echoing from his throat.

It was a warning.

She fought to catch her breath, her head lowering against his, her lips at his ear as his hand moved from her hip to her thigh, just below the end of the short, flirty skirt she wore.

"I'm so wet, Ian," she gasped against his ear, her teeth nipping at the lobe as she tilted her hips to him.

"Shut up." His lips moved over her reddened nipple, the spike-hard tip so sensitive now that the caress of his breath against it was nearly painful.

His hand paused on her thigh as he fought for breath.

Her hands slid to the front of his shirt, her fingers gripping the material before she tore it apart, hearing the sound of buttons scattering as satisfaction surged through her.

Ian raised his head, staring back at her as his blue eyes darkened, the flushed features of his face intent, sexual. His fingers tightened on her thigh.

"I've been dying to taste you." Her lips lowered to his neck, her tongue swiping over the rapid pulse that beat just beneath the flesh. "Can I taste you, Ian?"

She had no intention of being gentle. It wasn't gentleness she wanted, it was Ian, all his hunger, all his sexuality, and she would give him nothing less in return. Her teeth scraped over his collarbone, her tongue flickered rapidly over his flat, hard male nipple before she nipped at it playfully.

"Damn you, Courtney." He sounded less than pleased with the hard shudder that raced through his body.

She bent her knees, her fingers moving to the waistband of his slacks.

Her mouth watered.

The hard wedge of his cock was just before her eyes, hidden by nothing more than the fabric of his clothing.

The belt was disposed of quickly, despite her shaking hands.

As her finger slid the metal clasp of his slacks free, her head tilted back, her eyes locking with his. She gripped the tab of the zipper, licked her lips and pulled it down slowly.

Ian watched carefully, seeing the daring in Courtney's eyes, the challenge in her expression as she slowly released the zipper of his pants, pulling apart the material before hooking her hands in the band of his underwear briefs and releasing his straining cock.

Her hands were like silken flames. It was all he could do to stay still, to endure her teasing, taunting gaze, her soft fingers wrapping around his dick, stroking it, threatening the self-control that had always been so much a part of him.

He wasn't about to give in to her dare.

He wasn't about to give her the desire he could see raging in her eyes. The desire to break him. She wanted everything he had turned his back on years before. She wanted something he could never be again.

"So hard," she whispered, her lips tilting mockingly. He didn't know if she meant his cock or him in particular.

He watched her silently, wondering how far she dared to go. How far she would carry this charade she had begun. Innocence gleamed in her dark eyes, pure, sweet, it made his heart clench, his chest tighten at the sight of it. No woman so soft, with a gaze so pure, could be the temptress she was pretending to be.

Then she licked her lips. A slow, sensual glide of her silken pink tongue over full, pouty lips. His cock jerked in her grip as a bolt of lust whipped through his system. Fiery. Control-threatening.

Ian grimaced at the lightning-fast surge of pleasure, then clenched his teeth with furious determination as her tongue touched the head of his cock, swirled around it.

"Fuck!" She consumed him.

Her lips opened over the broad crest, surrounding it in a blistering, agonizing pleasure so overwhelming he wasn't certain he wouldn't spill his seed then. Now.

And she had no mercy.

As though his single lapse had been all she needed to turn from innocence to sinful bold lust in one fell swoop. Her eyes darkened to nearly black, her mouth opened and the head of his cock disappeared into the moist, rich depths of her mouth.

"Damn you, Courtney." He heard the strangled, hungry sound of his own voice and would have winced at the depth of desire it revealed, if he had the strength to do anything other than hold back his release.

His hands went to her hair, his fingers clenching on the long silken strands as he felt her hold him snugly in the dark, heated cavern. And he watched.

Watched as his cock slid back, sliding along the moist curves of her lips as her tongue stroked him heatedly. Watched as he pressed back in, feeling her taste him, consume him as his strokes became deeper, stronger.

It was the most sensual, erotic thing he had ever seen.

Why? How could a woman that he would almost swear was a virgin, affect him to this depth?

"Suck it, baby," he groaned roughly, his thighs tightening as his balls ached with the need for release. "Suck me deep, sweetheart."

He could only watch as she took him deeper, the head of his cock touching her throat, the ultra-sensitive flesh absorbing her ragged moans as he stretched her lips wide, reddened them, and gave her a carnal, sinful appearance.

And that tongue.

It was like a lashing flame, licking, flickering beneath the sensitive head, rubbing, stroking…

"Fuck yeah. Suck my dick, Courtney." His knees were weak, sensations flooding his body that he would have never expected.

The pleasure was so intense. Too intense. It was destructive.

"So pretty... That sweet mouth stretched so tight... Oh hell yes, lick my cock, darlin', lick it like candy..."

She was killing him.

She drew back then, fighting his hold on her hair, her tongue curling over the flushed, bulging tip before it popped free of her mouth. He pushed back. She pulled away, straightening slowly as her tongue ran over her swollen lips.

"Goodnight, Ian," she whispered then, the shocking words spearing straight to his gut as he watched her with brooding, simmering lust. The hunger rising inside him was nearly violent. Strong enough, intense enough, to terrify him.

And there she stood, confidence simmering in her eyes, anger lighting them.

"What more do you want?" He felt like howling in raging hunger.

A sad little smile tipped her lips, reddened from the light fucking he had given them.

"I want it all." Her answer shocked him. "Everything, Ian. Haven't you figured that out yet?"

Chapter Five

The bedroom door opened less than two minutes after Courtney closed it behind her, Ian stepping into the room and closing it with a barely leashed control that had shivers chasing up her spine.

"Are you wanting me to rape you, Courtney?" He leaned against the panel, crossing his arms over his torn shirt as he watched her with blazing eyes. "Didn't your mother ever teach you better than to tease a man in such a fashion?"

She lifted her shoulder negligently as she pulled the snug top from her body and tossed it to the wide chest at the end of her bed.

Soft light spilled from the bedside lamps, emphasizing the heavy dark furniture and the brooding expression of the man watching her.

"I won't lie to you." She released the button to her skirt and let it fall to the floor as she stepped from her shoes. "I didn't come here to fuck you, Ian. I came here to belong to you. There's a difference. I'm not one of your submissive little one-night stands."

His eyes flared, darkened to a midnight blue as his expression became savage, intense. There was hunger there, more hunger than Courtney had ever seen reflected in a man's face. But there was also denial, wariness.

"Then you shouldn't push your way into my bed," he snapped. "There's only one type of woman who joins me there, Courtney. It's not tender little innocents with stars in their eyes."

She pushed back the flare of pain his statement brought.

She knew better of course. Oh, not that that wasn't exactly the type of woman he used. But he wanted more. She had seen it in his eyes as his cock sank to her throat. She had watched the emotions raging there, and knew that he hid from himself as well as her.

"Keep your bed, Ian." She pretended to be unaware of the lust blazing from his eyes as she walked, nearly naked now, to the chest of drawers and pulled a short, midnight silk gown from the top drawer. "I am not a one-night stand, in any man's bed. Especially yours." She pulled the gown over her head, shimmying out of her thong panties as the hem fell over her hips.

If she wasn't mistaken, the temperature in the room shot up by several degrees. She could feel the heat moving in the air around her, caressing the sensitive nerve endings still rioting from Ian's touch.

"You knew when you began this harebrained campaign what you were getting into, Courtney," he snapped. "You know me, perhaps better than most..."

"Better than anyone," she injected coolly, facing him squarely now. "Don't fool yourself, Ian. I know you too well. And this is why you're terrified of taking me into your bed. You know I'll not be a one-night stand. Once you have me, you'll only want more."

"You're not exactly potato chips, Court," he grunted, his lips tilting mockingly.

"For you, I'll be a drug." She lowered her voice, struggling to control her breathing, the harsh beat of her heart. "One you'll only become more addicted to each time you experience it. Because that's what you are to me, Ian. A drug. Addictive. I can't get you out of my mind, nor my heart..."

"It's a crush, Courtney," he whispered gently then, moving across the room slowly, his expression so tender it made her want to weep. "An immature obsession."

There it was. In the only way he could allow himself to feel anything for her. As though she were a child in need of a pat on the head.

"Oh, get over yourself, Ian." She tried to whirl away from him. She couldn't allow him to touch her, not now, not while he was trying to convince himself she was still a child. "I've never had a crush on you…"

"You've always had a crush on me." The confidence in his voice raked over her patience. "When you were sixteen, you watched me as though I were a god."

"When I was sixteen, I would sneak into the closet of your bedroom and watch you and my bodyguard fuck my maid," she informed him blithely. "I've done this for the past several years, Ian. I'm tired of watching."

He hid his shock well. He merely stared back at her, unblinking, his eyes nearly black as hunger flared within them.

"You watched?"

"Oh yes, indeed I did," she assured him. "And each time I watched your cock pleasuring another woman I knew what I wanted. Who I wanted. I'm not a fool. And I'm not too homely to attract enough attention to keep my bed filled if this is what I want. I didn't have to come to you. I could have stayed in England and fucked until hell froze over. But I came here, to you."

His jaw clenched.

"You're a fool, Courtney."

"And I agree with you, wholeheartedly," she bit out, moving across the room before turning back to face him. "I should just pack my bags and head home. I'm certain I could get fucked just easily there as I can in your bed. Hell, easier. And with just as little emotion."

He pushed his fingers roughly through his thick hair, glaring back at her.

"You're pushing me, baby. So help me, you are. And God knows I don't want to hurt you."

But he was excited. She could see it in his eyes, in the bulge of his pants. He was so excited by the thought of taking her, taming her, that he could barely control it.

She had lost control months, years before.

"Are you certain you don't feel a need to hurt me, Ian?" she asked him then.

"I feel a need to spank your ass until it glows," he finally growled, his hands fisting as he pushed them into the pockets of his slacks.

She let her eyelids lower, let her own hunger flow from her as the ass in question began to tingle.

"Spank me," she whispered then. "I bet you've imagined it, Ian. Putting me over your knee, and spanking my bare ass as I beg you prettily not to. Shall I call you Uncle Ian as I do so? Have you ever imagined that? Please, Uncle Ian, don't spank me."

She was tempting him, taunting him, and she knew it. She could possibly be pushing him past a boundary that she was perhaps not ready for quite yet. But she couldn't seem to stop herself.

A firestorm erupted in his body, through his senses.

Please, Uncle Ian, don't spank me.

The words should have disgusted him. But they turned him on, made his lust burn higher, hotter than ever before. He could feel his cock pressing against his slacks, fighting for freedom as his gaze locked on her all too innocent expression. Sweet, pure, her face, her eyes, reflected the wonder of a fucking teenager. But that was not the body of a teenager. The full, swollen breasts, their hard tips pressing against the dark blue silk, pleading for his touch. That was a woman's body. A woman's response.

A woman who liked to play very dangerous games.

He moved toward her. A step. Two.

But the innocence was still there.

God help them both if she was a virgin.

"You want to play games, sweetheart." He kept his voice low, just barely affectionate.

"I like playing games, Uncle Ian." She blinked innocently as she licked her lips in anticipation. "Are you going to teach me some new ones?"

He reached out, smoothing her hair back behind her shoulders.

"Such long, pretty hair," he whispered, rubbing the strands between his fingers and luxuriating in its silken texture before he gripped a thick swath, holding it in his fist as he pulled her head back slowly.

She was breathing hard, her breasts rising and falling sharply as her dark eyes began to daze. A flush brightened her cheeks as her lips parted almost pleadingly, her eyelids lowering with drowsy sensuality.

He lowered his head, tasting the honey sweetness of those lips. They parted further for him, a whispered moan breathed against his as he caught her lower lip, licking at it sensually.

"Such a bad girl," he whispered against the curves, watching her eyes closer, the dilation of her pupils, the sensual, sexual greed that filled them.

But she was on overload. He could see it in her eyes, her response, hear it in the breathy little cries that left her lips. She thought herself so adept at hiding how innocent she truly was, that he would never know the difference. But he knew. And it broke his heart.

"I could be." She smiled as she answered, her hands braced against his abdomen, her fingers curling into the warmth she found there. "I can be a very bad girl if you want me to be, Ian."

Want? That was a rather mild term for what he was feeling right now.

He could feel his balls knotting with overwhelming need, his cock throbbing, engorged with a hunger that swept through every portion of his body. Before he could consider his own actions, before she had time to protest, he used the grip he had on her hair to hold her to him as he turned her quickly around, pushing her last few steps to the wall, pressing her against it.

Her gasping little moan was nearly his undoing. Her response to him, uninhibited without the usual rituals of weakening a woman's defenses, was addictive. She was pliant, her responses unplanned, unrehearsed. Her pleasure, no matter how he touched her, astounded him.

He smoothed his hand over her buttock, feeling the muscles clench in response. She was naked beneath the dark silk and he knew it, knew it and wanted nothing more than to taste it, to drown himself in her response.

The silk moved along her flesh, creating a cool barrier between his hand and her flesh as he smoothed his fingers over her buttocks. Reaching the hem, he began to lift it slowly, his head lowering until his lips rested against her ear.

"How wet are you, Courtney?" He nearly flinched at the rough, ragged sound of his own voice. "How much does the thought of learning my games turn you on?"

He pressed his fingers between her thighs, groaning at the hot, slick dampness he found there. There were no shielding curls surrounding the swollen flesh. Only the blistering sweet juices coating sensitive folds.

She jerked in his arms as his fingers circled the small entrance to her pussy. The wet heat scorched his fingers as he gathered it around them, sliding back, his touch light, teasing as he then circled the tight, closed entrance to her anus.

"Are you a virgin here, Courtney?" He shuddered himself at the thought. "This virginity I could easily take."

She was panting, mewling cries exiting her throat as he pressed against the flexing muscles.

"Talk to me, Courtney," he crooned at her ear as he worked his fingertip into the ultra-hot entrance. "Do you feel how tight you are there, baby? How hot? Imagine how my dick is going to feel, pressing into it, filling it."

She had never been taken there. He could sense it, feel it. The opening rippled around his fingertip like the flutter of tiny birds' wings. She had no idea how to relax, how to open for him.

He grimaced tightly. She would scream when he took her there. Her head would fall back, her eyes would widen, daze, and she would beg. Beg because the pleasure and the pain would fight for supremacy and send her hurling through sensations she could never imagine otherwise.

He wanted to be the man to give her that adventure. To watch as the ultimate trust was extended to him. In exchange, he would begin giving her the ultimate in pleasure.

It was going to happen. He could feel it pulsing in his veins, throbbing in his cock. There was no way to keep her out of his bed. No way in hell he could keep his hands off her now. If he wasn't very, very careful, she could become the ultimate addiction.

"Tease." Her gasping accusation had a smile tugging at his lips as he moved his hand back, allowing his fingers to slide in the soft warmth of her juices beyond.

"I've been accused of many things," he mused as he rubbed at the small opening to her pussy, feeling the silken heat of her juices trickle from it. "But never teasing…"

He pushed the teasing, taunting finger deep inside her in one smooth thrust. Instantly, fiery damp heat enveloped his finger as tight muscles clenched around the digit. She was incredibly, overwhelmingly tight, spasming around his finger until he could feel every ripple, every fluttering response in the velvety heat of her cunt embracing him.

Gasping cries poured from her throat as she arched, legs tightening, back bowing as he felt the cream of her response soak his finger before running along his palm.

"Do you like that, baby?" He nibbled at her neck as she shuddered against him. "Damn you're tight, Courtney. So tight, it might take all night to work my cock inside you."

The thought of it, of being held so snug, so heatedly inside her soft pussy was making him mad with hunger. Heat poured from her vagina, coalescing into a vivid humidity filled with the scent of her arousal.

"I'm going to fuck you, baby," he whispered at her ear, feeling the spasms of response to his words shudder through her cunt. "I'm going to push my cock so deep inside you, you'll wonder if you'll ever be free of me."

"I don't want to be free..." Her gasping cries were nearly his undoing. "God, Ian. Please do it again."

His arm curled around her waist, holding her steady as his fingertip found the ultra-sensitive bundle of nerves high in the back of her pussy. He stroked it gently, gritting his teeth as tremors of sensation began to rack her slender body. Her pussy clenched around his finger, her hips jerking against him as she tightened to near breaking point against him.

He could feel the desperation rising within her.

She was dying to climax.

He could feel it, hear it in the pleading sounds now filling the air around them.

"Ian, I'm begging you..." she cried out then, panting for air, fighting for release. "Please, Ian, let me come, I've waited too long to come..."

He stilled, ignoring her frantic cries as her hips bucked against his.

"You've never come?" He closed his eyes in defeat, fighting the suspicion, the knowledge that he might not have her virginity, but he would have her innocence all the same.

"Never." Her cry was one of desperation. "And if you don't finish this, Ian, so help me, I just might kill you."

She was so close. Courtney could feel the building tension in her pussy, the tightening of her womb, the tingles of electric pleasure moving up her spine as Ian continued to stroke and torment that secret place inside her cunt that she had no hope of reaching herself.

She had read about it. But had never been able to find just the right spot, with just the right touch to induce the levels of sensation Ian was building within her.

Her nails clawed at the wall as she felt his fingertip caress the sensitive area, felt the desperate, raging hunger rising higher than it ever had before. Perspiration built between her breasts, along her brow. She could feel a million different sensations racing just beneath her flesh, fueling her pleasure as the blood raced through her veins.

She could feel Ian behind her, solid, muscular, the heat of his body searing into her back as his hand parted her thighs, his finger parted the muscles of her pussy.

"More, Ian." She couldn't contain the wild gasp that escaped her lips. "Please more."

She moved against his hand, lifting herself on tiptoes before lowering again, creating the barest amount of friction against the clenching muscles gripping his finger as it invaded her cunt.

"Easy, baby," he crooned at her ear, his voice dark, velvety rough. "Just let it feel good for now. Let it build, Courtney."

She whimpered at the gentleness in his voice. It wasn't his gentleness she needed. Never that.

"Are you going to spank me now, Uncle Ian?" She could barely focus enough to speak. "I've been very naughty."

He tightened behind her, his breathing growing heavier at her ear.

"Don't tempt me, little girl," he growled as the arm loosened around her stomach to allow his hand to move to the curve of one swollen breast.

Her nipple ached, it was so hard and tight.

"Do I tempt you?" Her back arched as he cupped the supple weight of her breast, his fingers unerringly finding the thrusting tip.

"You tempt me," he admitted roughly. "Too much."

His fingers tightened on her nipple, pulling at the tender tip as his finger moved slowly within her pussy. The tiny bit of friction had the blood racing through her system, her juices rushing from her cunt as she clenched on his finger, fighting for release.

Finally. After years of useless, hopeless masturbation, erotic dreams, and a hunger that had nearly drove her crazy. Finally, she was within sight of a measure of satisfaction. Nothing else mattered now. Only the climax, the release and Ian's touch.

He chuckled in amusement, his voice low as he whispered, "Do you think it's going to be that easy."

Before she could stop him, before she could do more than cry out in longing, his finger moved from her inner core, his hand raising as he pulled her back against his chest and slid the syrup-laden finger over her lower lip.

She tasted herself as pleasure punched her womb, stealing her breath.

She licked at his retreating finger, her tongue swiping over her lip as he groaned, a low, hungry sound, at her ear.

"Now there's a good girl," he whispered in approval as he moved her back.

The world tilted around her. Her hands reached out as he turned her quickly, pulling her over his lap as he sat on the mattress of the bed and pushed her gown over her hips before lifting it free of her body.

His hand landed on her rear.

There was no warning. No asking permission. Just a blazing sudden heat that had her writhing across his legs.

"Stay still." His hand landed again, causing her rear to flex in response.

Heat surged through her ass to her pussy. She could feel the dampness trickling to her thighs as she heard the bedside table open.

She bit her lip, knowing what he would find there. The tube of lubrication. The butt plug she had never found the opportunity or the courage to actually use. Why suffer more than she had already? If her fingers thrusting into her own pussy did nothing to relieve the horrible hunger, how would a plug up her ass bring her any more satisfaction?

"Ah, you are a naughty little girl, aren't you, Courtney?"

She felt him moving, heard the cap to the tube flip open.

"These come with such wondrous little inventions," he crooned as one hand parted the cheeks of her rear. "Don't you just love the little insertion tubes? This way, I just pierce your little ass with it..." She felt like screaming at the sensation of the cool penetration inside her rear. "And squeeze..."

The lubrication filled her rectum, sizzling inside her as she conjured images of what was to come.

"This way, working that butt plug up your little ass is going to be so much more fun. No preparation, Courtney. No easing those tight muscles. This way, you deal with the pain as well as the pleasure as I work it inside you. And that's nothing compared to what's coming as it inflates."

His hand landed on her ass again.

Courtney twisted in his grip, crying out at the incredible, mind-numbing sensations the spanking incited within her body.

She was depraved, she knew. She had accepted that long ago.

The feel of his hand landing on her ass, knowing it was Ian, imagining the look on his face, the narrow-eyed steely determination and fierce eroticism she had glimpsed there when he had performed these acts as she secretly watched.

Now he was touching her.

Spanking her.

The erotic slaps were destroying her senses as her bottom began to burn in tandem with the burning ache deep inside her cunt. With each little slap the electric heat whipped through her ass, to her pussy, to her clit. The swollen bud began to tingle, to ripple with sensation as she tightened, feeling the oddest pleasure, a deep building tension tightening it further…

"Not yet…" His hand lifted, the pressure easing as he gave the firm order.

"Damn you, Ian. This isn't fair," she cried out, attempting to rise from his lap, to push him to the bed and force him to ease the painful ache churning in her pussy.

"I said stay still." His voice hardened, sending a shiver of trepidation down her spine as his hand landed again, a bit harder, definitely in warning, on her heated rear.

She stilled.

"Ian…" She felt the tip of the plug, the low vibrating caress from the tip as it was placed at the entrance to her ass.

"This toy was created for a reason, baby," he assured her, his voice becoming sensual, crooning, erotic. She could almost orgasm to his voice alone. "It's made to penetrate and insert easily…" He suited action to words.

The slender, tapered device began to penetrate the untried entrance, stretching the nerve-laden tissue with a burning bite more erotic than the light spanking she had received moments before.

He worked the plug easily inside her as she bucked in his hold, unable to stay still, the pleasure ripping through her with such destructive results that she was certain she must be dreaming of his touch rather than actually feeling it.

And she knew there was much more to come.

The plug was unique, hard to find and bought because of its design. Tapered, slender, it was made to insert easily. A small pump then attached to the base of the plug to inflate it within the anus, to stretch it slowly.

"Damn, this is pretty." His voice was raspy as she whimpered in excruciating pleasure. "Watching your pretty ass part for the plug, knowing your soft little cries are about to become screams of pleasure..."

The first cry escaped her lips as the length slid fully inside her, the base anchoring tight at the entrance.

"You took it so easily," he praised her heatedly. "You're such a bad little girl, Courtney."

His hand landed on her ass again in a light smack.

The vibrating caress inside her ass, the feel of his hand burning her flesh was nearly too much.

"Ian, sweet God, you're killing me." Her ass clenched around the buzzing little toy, feeling the harsh pleasure of the light spanking, the waves of sexual intensity and building hunger beginning to overwhelm her senses.

"Not yet..." He was breathing roughly, she could hear it in his voice as she felt him attaching the small pump to the slender air-line at the base of the plug.

She felt the slow increasing fullness inside her rectum, the stretching of virgin muscles, the fiery bite of pleasure blending pain that sent ever-increasing strikes of electric-laden sensation spearing through her nerve endings.

She could feel her juices flowing from her pussy, wetting the folds of her cunt further, slickening her thighs and making her clit pound with the need for relief. And still, the fullness increased. The fiery sensations built, blooming in her ass and spreading out as nerve endings began to transmit the pleasure-pain through the rest of her body.

"Easy, baby," Ian crooned as Courtney realized she was twisting in his lap, attempting to lift her rear closer, to force him to complete the agonizingly slow adjustments of the width growing within her.

"Ian, I don't think I can stand it..." she gasped, her voice strangled as tears filled her eyes. "Please, Ian. Let me come. I can't bear it."

Her clit was tortured. The mass of nerve endings felt like an open wound, the intense ache went so deep. Her pussy wept in hunger, her womb clenching with spasmodic tremors as he pushed her to the very edge of her sanity, and refused to let her fly over the precipice.

"You're perfect, Courtney, do you know that?" he whispered, his voice dark, deep as the plug swelled further. "Few women enjoy the inflatable plugs, or the constant burn it produces."

And it did burn.

She craved more, but the swelling stopped, leaving her suspended, filled, too close to the edge of bliss to bear the pain of it.

"But even more." He lifted her, turning her until she tumbled to the bed, staring up at him in dazed desperation as he began to undress. "Even more is how tight it's going to make your pussy. It's going to take me all damned night just to work my cock inside you, you'll be so fucking tight, baby. And then we'll see how naughty you can really get."

He shed his shirt from his shoulders as the words finally penetrated her brain. He had no idea just how naughty she could be.

Her hands moved then, cupping her breasts, her fingers pulling at her torturously tight nipples as his hands moved to the waistband of his slacks.

Moaning helplessly at the pleasure, she let her fingers trail down her stomach, her abdomen, finally allowing them to slide through the glaze of moisture that filled the narrow slit as he stripped the material from his legs.

His cock stood out from his body, angry, throbbing in need, the thick head glistening with moisture as she parted the lips of her pussy for him. Her legs bent, spreading for him as she lifted her hips to allow her fingers to pierce her cunt.

Ian's hand fell to his cock, his fingers wrapping around it, stroking it as he watched her. The expression on his face was pure hunger. His eyes were wild, glittering in his flushed face as she pushed her fingers slowly inside the ultra-tight entrance.

She could feel the degree to which the plug had made the channel even tighter than before. She jerked at the feel of her own fingers penetrating her pussy, moaning at the incredible pleasure as they stroked over the sensitive tissue. With each penetration of her fingers, Ian's eyes darkened, his gaze intensifying, becoming wilder as she fucked herself closer to orgasm than she had ever gone before.

"Enough." He knelt on the bed, his fingers catching her wrist as she felt the fire blooming in the pit of her stomach.

She was so close.

Too close to be stopped.

But he was as well. She could see it, sense it. His expression was tight with lust, a fire raging in his gaze that burned her, exhilarated her. She could feel the heat burning in him, raging. A heat she had never seen in his face when she spied upon him at her father's estate. He had always been calm. Cool. In control. He had directed the sexual situations, reveled in that, but controlled them. She had never seen him burn as he was burning now.

That control was quickly disintegrating.

"No, Ian, damn you. I'm too close..." She jerked against his hold, fighting to return her fingers to the aching, desperate flesh of her pussy.

"Yes, you are," he whispered, coming over her, catching her wrists in his hands and anchoring them over her head as she struggled against him. "You're so close, Courtney, so wet and hot. And so fucking tight you're going to scream when my cock sinks inside you."

She shuddered at the roughness of his voice, fighting to breathe, to maintain a semblance of sanity as she felt his legs part hers further as he came over her. Bracing his weight on his elbows, he transferred her wrists to one hand, the other lowering to her hip.

"Is this what you want, Courtney?" His lips touched hers, his eyes stared into hers.

The intense blue of his gaze was nearly a shock this close up. They were brilliant, blazing with lust, with the struggle to maintain his control.

The head of his cock parted the soaked folds of her cunt, lodging at the entrance to her weeping pussy. Breathing in deeply, Courtney struggled against the pleasure that demanded her submission, demanded she give in to him, that she no longer tease, no longer tempt. But she knew Ian. And she knew this first battle in the war they were waging against each other, could well decide the future she was fighting so hard for.

"I want you," she whispered. "All of you, Ian." Her tongue licked over his lips, as her hips lifted closer, feeling the head of his cock begin to stretch her.

"All of me?" He smiled, the curve of his lips tight with the effort to maintain his control. "Let's see how much you can take, baby. Then we'll see if you want it all."

His hips flexed.

The buzzing in her anus was driving her crazy, but the slow, rhythmic press and retreat of his cock into the entrance of her pussy began to replace the burning pleasure in her ass.

She cried out his name, gasping, nearly incoherent with the sensations as she felt him slowly making his way inside her. The anal plug filled her, Ian overfilled her. Retreat and thrust, retreat and thrust, stretching her as her cries turned to screams, her pleas to wordless, incoherent gasps as the pleasure and pain combined. Teasing. Taunting. Each stroke went deeper inside her, fueling the already flaming pulses of hunger erupting inside her.

She could feel every inch of his heavily veined cock invading her pussy as her fists curled, her wrists still locked in his as a heavy sheen of sweat covered his face, his chest. His breath was sawing in and out of his chest, the fight for control apparent in the baring of his teeth.

"You feel so good, Ian," she whispered against his lips, her fingers curling against his hold in her need to touch him. "So hot and hard. Like heated steel." She lifted against him, a moan rippling from her chest at the caress of his cock, barely penetrating her. "Take me, Ian. Take all of me."

His eyes narrowed. They blazed.

"When I watched you," she panted in excitement. "With my maids. I would watch you take them, so slow, so easy, as they screamed beneath you. And I heard you…" She saved her closest secret for the most important battle. "I heard you cry my name as you fucked them."

He jerked against her. Fury flared in his eyes, his muscles tightening with his anger, his lust, as he stared back at her. His hips flexed, his cock forcing inside her with a hard, sharp thrust, burying him in another scant inch before his control reasserted itself. Barely.

She smiled slowly.

"I dare you to fuck me," she taunted him then, gasping at the sensations tearing through her.

"I swear to God, I'm going to gag you." He retreated, pushed back, but the tension was growing. The threads of his control unraveling.

She licked her lips, tightened the muscles of her vagina and moaned in nearing rapture.

"Gag me," she cried hoarsely. "Let me scream, Ian. I need to scream for you. God, please, I'm fucking dying for you."

Her head thrashed as he retreated again before moving back, forcing more of the straining width of his erection inside her. His expression was tight, savage, his breathing harsh as perspiration dripped from his brow and a savage grimace tightened his lips.

"More..." She could barely form the words. "So close...Ian... Please. Let me come. Let me finally come..."

"No, damn you..." His voice was rife with tortured hunger.

"Fuck me, Ian. Fuck me hard. Make me scream for you... Just for you..."

His head lowered to her neck, a curse ripping from his throat as he suddenly surged inside her. Hard. Deep. Filling every portion of her pussy as the control he prided himself so deeply on, broke.

Nothing could have prepared Courtney for what was to come.

His hips began to move with a powerful flex of his muscles as he began to fuck her, shafting inside the tender channel with strokes that parted, stretched and burned the delicate tissue of her cunt.

His hold on her was tight, his hand gripping her hip, the other leaving her wrists to burrow in her hair, pulling at it, kneading her scalp with exciting tingles of sensation as she felt his cock thrusting strong and deep, rasping the delicate tissue already tormented by the vibration of the plug in her ass.

The dual sensations were hedonistic. The most sensual experience she could have imagined.

"Lift your legs. Wrap them around me." His hand slid to her thigh as she obeyed the hoarse direction.

His cock went deeper, her pussy became tighter.

She chanted his name as her arms curled around his neck and she hung on for dear life. With each hard thrust into the clenching channel, he sent a wildfire of pleasure-pain coursing through her body as she arched to him.

"God, yes," she moaned, nearly insane with the sensations pouring through her senses. "Fuck me, Ian. Fuck me harder."

Each stroke, though hard and deep, was measured, controlled. She had thought she had stripped him of his restraint, but it was still there, he was still torturing her, tormenting her with the orgasm that pulsed just out of reach.

"My game," he growled as his lips moved to her neck, his teeth scraping, nipping at the sensitive flesh. "My way, Courtney."

He surged to his knees, pulling her legs further, gripping them, spreading them as his gaze went to the center of her body.

"Look," he commanded her roughly. "Watch as I fuck you, baby. See how tight and wet your sweet pussy is."

Dazed, consumed with need, her gaze dropped along her body as she cried out at the eroticism of what she saw. Her hips were elevated by the position of her legs, the glistening bare flesh of her cunt in full view as his cock slowly retreated.

The dark, bulging flesh gleamed with a thick coat of her juices as the moist sound of his retreat echoed around her. Then he was sliding in again. Slowly. So very slowly.

"Feel it, Courtney," he snarled then. "How tight your cunt is. My cock is filling you, stretching you. Does it burn, baby?"

She screamed at the pleasure-pain, her hands clenching in the sheets as she bucked against him.

"Is this what you want, sweetheart," he growled as he retreated again. A second later he thrust into her, hard, fast.

"Yes!" She screamed her answer. "More."

"More, baby?" The abrupt stretching, the sensation of being overfilled, the rasp of his heavily veined cock over nerve endings so sensitized they were nearly painful, was stealing her mind.

Every cell of her body pulsed in the need for orgasm.

"More." She arched as he surged inside her again, before crying out brokenly as he retreated.

"I can give you more, baby," he crooned, his voice harsh as he slammed inside her again.

The blend of pleasure and pain increased, wrapping around her, blending together in a force that sent the tension building in her womb, her clit, her aching pussy, to an explosion that had her screaming his name, wailing her pleasure. The muscles of her pussy tightened further, the strokes of his cock creating greater friction, sending another powerful blinding orgasm ripping through her.

She bucked beneath him, shuddering, violent tremors of release echoing through her nervous system as she felt him tense above her, a muttered oath escaping his lips as the sudden, fiery blasts of his semen began to spurt into the rippling depths of her pussy.

Satiation slowly began to fill her as Ian collapsed over her, breathing harshly, his cock still trapped snugly within her. The harsh, shuddering effects of her release began to ease, and languor began to overtake her.

"I knew you could make me come," she whispered drowsily as he slowly pulled from her and collapsed on the bed beside her.

Her eyes opened drowsily, a smile tugging at her lips as he turned her to her side, his fingers releasing the inflation of the plug still filling her rear and disengaging the vibration before tugging it easily from her tender rear.

"Sleep now," he whispered as he rose from the bed, staring down at her, his eyes no longer wild, no longer filled with the raging hunger, but still gleaming with lust. "While you can."

She watched as he moved to the bathroom, listened as water ran. Minutes later he returned, returned the toy to its drawer and thankfully, moved back to the bed beside her.

Cuddling against him, she let sleep take her. Finally.

Chapter Six

Well, that hadn't exactly gone as he had planned.

Ian had a feeling it had gone exactly as Courtney had planned though. The scheming little witch.

A smile threatened to tug at his mouth as he acknowledged the fact that she had done as no other woman had managed in more years than he cared to remember. She had made him lose control.

He should be angry at her, hell, he should be angrier with himself. He hadn't even remembered to don a condom.

He grimaced at the thought of that added, forgotten protection. He knew she was on birth control, but that was no excuse. He rarely allowed himself the freedom of sex without a condom. Kimberly had been the first in recent memory. And now Courtney.

He sighed wearily, turning from the sight of her sleeping form and pacing to the window to stare into the night with a frown.

His flesh prickled with the memory of the pleasure he had found in releasing his own control. It was a bittersweet memory, tinged with regret. If he was going to carry through with this abrupt change in the relationship he shared with Courtney, then he was going to have to be very careful. A hell of a lot more careful than he had been thus far.

The woman was enough to make a saint crazy, he admitted to himself. From the moment she had walked through the door to his home she had tempted, teased and pushed her way past his defenses.

Any other woman would have been out on her ass weeks before. But this was Courtney. And he had admitted that some part of him had known exactly what she was up to when her father had called, expressing her desire to visit for a while. He had known and he had allowed her to arrive anyway.

This rested on no one's head but his own.

What now?

He rubbed his hand over his face as he snorted mockingly.

Dane would of course kill him. It was just a matter of time before the other man found out that Ian was fucking his sweet, precious little girl. And Ian couldn't even blame him. If he had a daughter, he'd lock her in her room until she was a dried-up old prune to keep her from entering the life he lived.

For the first time since he had entered the sexual, carnal atmosphere of sharing his women, Ian felt a pang of remorse. Remorse because he knew he could never truly be happy, sexually, without the excesses he had come to enjoy. And because he knew innocence such as Courtney's could never survive within it.

Sighing wearily, he picked his pants from the floor and pulled them on over his underwear quickly before fastening them. Jerking his shirt over his shoulders seconds later, he strode to the door and opened it silently before leaving Courtney's room.

It was too late to go back, and he knew it. Hell, he didn't want to go back. Fucking her had been more pleasure than he had imagined it could be. Seeing her uninhibited response had spiked his arousal further. The challenge she presented kicked his sexuality into overdrive.

She had won this round.

He had lost control.

He smiled coldly as he entered his own room and headed for the shower. The next round would be his though. She thought emotion was the basis for sex. For her, it always would be. He had learned years ago though, to never allow emotion to interfere with the sensual side he possessed. The potential for pain was just too great.

He could enjoy a woman, pleasure one and be pleasured by them. His sex drive was, at times, all-consuming. It was his greatest hunger. And somehow, Courtney had managed to tap into an area of that sexuality that he had been unaware of. His affection for her and his knowledge of her innocence was a heady aphrodisiac for some unknown reason. He couldn't figure out why, had never been able to understand why she could make him so hard, so damned fast and so hungry for her that even his fantasies became filled with her.

As the hot, soothing water of the shower pelted over his skin, he closed his eyes, remembering her hands, her mouth, the wickedness in her eyes. There was so much he could show her, so many ways to pleasure that he could teach her, without stealing the innocent joy he saw in her gaze. He didn't have to share her. There was no need to dim that purity with his more extreme desires.

For a moment, the memory of her dark, laughter-filled brown eyes was replaced with hazel, staring sightlessly, accusingly up at him.

His jaw clenched.

Opening his eyes he hurriedly finished the quick shower before drying and padding back to his bed. He wanted nothing more than to join Courtney in her bed. To pull the warmth of her body close and hold her as he slept.

He threw himself into his own bed instead, growling at the thought of the many ways he would never get any sleep if he did anything so foolish.

Yet, as he stared up at the ceiling, a frown creasing his brow, he found himself fighting the urge to do just that, rather than to sleep.

You're so depraved, Ian. I sold my soul into hell to be your woman. To what end? This is my end.

The words haunted him. Written words signed in blood.

Yes. He was depraved. He was well aware of the extremity of his tastes, and he had made certain his lovers were well aware of it as well. He had never pretended to be anything other than what he was. Yet, it seemed he paid daily for one mistake, for allowing his emotions to cloud the sex and failing to see the danger his lifestyle could pose to another.

She had been young. Hell, he had been young.

Her name had been Melissa. Melissa Gaines. And she had killed herself because of him, because of his hungers, his depravities. Because he had taken an innocent and introduced her to the lifestyle that had drawn him so fiercely.

He had wanted to please her. Had wanted to show her all the pleasures he knew could await her. Hell, he had thought he had loved her. He had swiftly learned the difference between a woman of experience and one too innocent to call a halt to what she saw as nothing more than a game to secure his heart.

He had shared her. He had touched her, glorying in her cries of pleasure, her pleas for more, whispering his praise, drawing her to him as her orgasms shuddered through her body. And he had thought nothing else could be as good. That he couldn't love any woman as much as he loved Melissa. Until he walked into his apartment the next day to find her lifeless body, her accusation written on a single sheet of paper beside her.

It hadn't mattered that she had a history of psychiatric problems, or that he had been unaware of them. Even her father's forgiveness and his tearful explanations of his daughter's weaknesses hadn't stemmed the guilt. She had died because she couldn't handle what he had asked of her. Because she had wanted his love so desperately that she would do something that she couldn't live with in the cold light of day.

And he had sworn it would never happen again.

Innocence would never suffer at his hands again.

And here was Courtney. So damned innocent he couldn't believe she wasn't a virgin. So daring, wickedly so, yet as soft and new as dawn. She was as different as day from night to Melissa. Yet, she served as a cold reminder to the mistakes of the past.

* * * * *

One would think, that with the extremely explosive orgasm the night before, and the fact that she had finally managed to push Ian that final step into a physical relationship, that she would feel some sort of satisfaction.

She felt only remorse.

Courtney sat silently in the bleak, winter-shrouded garden, perched on the top of the cement table that a summer growth of greenery would have hidden from view. Now, it sat like a lonely sentinel in a garden that was presently sleeping the short, dreary cold days away.

Her feet were propped on the curved bench below it, one arm lying across her knees as she propped the elbow of the other on her leg and braced her chin within it to stare across the silent gardens into the pine forest beyond.

The thick cashmere sweater she wore and snug jeans protected her from the outside cold, but it was the chilly foreboding within her that caused her to shiver.

She had been such a child, thinking herself grown up enough to seduce a man such as Ian. Believing she could walk in, and one step at a time, find something he wanted no woman to touch. Believing that she could somehow touch his heart as easily as she could touch his body.

Not that she had expected it to be easy. She hadn't.

And it wasn't as though her heart had given up on Ian. That was impossible.

She was young, true. But she knew her heart, just as she knew that her body responded to no one as it did to him. Which left her between a rock and a hard place, so to speak.

Ian would keep the relationship purely physical now. He would use her own inexperience against her, just as he had the night before, to keep his control. It wasn't possible to wage this battle on an equal footing.

She breathed out wearily, shaking her head at the mess she had found herself in. She should have anticipated this. Her mother had warned her that Ian would not be as easy to conquer as she had convinced herself he would be.

"Ms. Mattlaw, you have a call..." the house butler, Jason, spoke behind her, interrupting her morose thoughts as she turned to him.

He extended the cordless phone to her, nodding coolly before turning and retreating.

"Hello?" She frowned as she raised the receiver to her ear.

"Courtney, it's Tally Conover." The smooth cultured voice spoke with lazy amusement. "We didn't get to talk much during your introduction party. I'm Lucian and Devril's wife."

"I remember you. Ian was quite insistent on pulling me away from your group." Courtney smiled at the memory of Ian's harassed expression.

"I heard you still had quite a bit of shopping to complete," the other woman drawled. "I'm at loose ends today and thought I would invite you to join me as I hit the stores. With the parties coming up in the next few months, I find myself in need of new shoes, and perhaps a dress or two."

And a bit of gossip to finish out the trip, Courtney read between the lines quite well.

"Sounds good. Where should I meet you?"

Tally chuckled knowingly. "Jason will inform Ian I called you, so I may as well pick you up myself. How about around eleven? We could stop for lunch, and then begin shopping in earnest. We might even extend the trip to dinner if you like. We could invite Terrie Wyman and a few others and have a real girls' night out."

"Why do I get the feeling I should bring the barbeque sauce," Courtney responded with an edge of self-mockery.

"No darling, they baste you in your own juices at a roast. I promise, you'll survive the outing," Tally assured her, her laughter filled with friendly mockery. "So, are we on?"

"Of course," Courtney responded, as though there had been no doubt. "I wouldn't miss it for the world."

There as a small stretch of silence, then a light chuckle.

"I think you'll fit in well, Courtney. I'll pick you up in about an hour and a half then. Bring plenty of credit cards and wear comfortable shoes. I haven't been shopping in weeks."

The line disconnected as Courtney moved from the tabletop and began to walk back to the house. Tally Conover, who claimed to be married to both Conover twins and rumored to, at the very least, hold both men in the very palm of her hand. The gossip Courtney had heard regarding the other woman was vivid to say the least. The jealousy she had heard in the voices of the supposedly decent women who had sneered contemptuously, had been rife.

As she stepped back into the house, Ian's butler materialized from another room, glancing at the phone she carried questioningly. The man had to be a robot.

"Jason, could you inform Ian I'll be out for the day." She handed him the phone as she headed to the stairs. "And possibly this evening as well."

"Of course, Miss Mattlaw," he responded coolly. "Shall I tell him where you'll be?"

She stopped at the first step and turned back to the butler with a frown. Why the hell would Ian care?

"That's not necessary," she said coolly. "I'm certain I'm old enough to go out alone now. I'll have my cell phone with me if he needs me though."

He inclined his head once again, his expression composed, reflecting little if any emotion.

"I will relay your message then."

Courtney had the oddest desire to snort derisively at his arrogance. As though she were somehow putting him, or Ian, out with her plans. Devil take them both, she was tired of wandering around this bloody mansion waiting on Ian to find a few spare moments to spend with her. And after last night, she wasn't even certain she wanted to see him.

After giving her that long-awaited orgasm, leaving her voice hoarse from her own screams, and leaving her body tender from his lust, he dared to sleep elsewhere, to not even be there when she awakened. As far as she was concerned, there was little chance that he even cared if she returned before morning.

Stubborn man. He was so intent to show her how little it mattered, how little she would matter as his lover, that he was cutting his own nose off to spite his face. And it was a game she wasn't willing to play.

Entering her bedroom, she strode to the closet. The sweater and jeans were perfect for a day in the garden, but shopping required clothing more suited to the adventure. Something easily taken off, to make way for changes. Low-heeled shoes rather than the high-heeled, half-boots she now wore.

As she reached into the closet for the below knee-length, button-up cotton sweater dress she chose, the bedroom door was pushed opened rather forcefully, to clash against the wall. Turning, she frowned at Ian, as he stood framed in the doorway.

"Your entrances leave much to be desired," she stated mockingly.

"Where the hell do you think you're going with Tally Conover?" His expression was borderline angry.

"Shopping," she answered him with a shrug as she laid the dress over the back of the nearby chair before stooping to retrieve the low-heeled walking shoes she had bought to go with it.

"Tally never just goes shopping." He snorted. "Shopping to her is seeing how much trouble she and those other women can create in one day."

"Excellent." She flashed him a brilliant smile as she straightened and set the shoes on the floor beside the chair. "Sounds like the type of company I enjoy. Life would be rather boring otherwise, Ian."

"Not for you." He closed the door behind him, watching her broodingly. "You create enough havoc on your own. You don't need any help."

She allowed a sense of pleasure and pride to infuse her expression.

"Thank you, Ian. That's one of the nicest compliments I've received today. Now, I really need to get ready."

A quick frown furrowed his brows.

"How long does it take to get ready to go shopping?"

"I'll be pressed for time the way it is," she sighed. "Tally will be here in an hour and a half."

Actually, it took her no time to get ready, but she would be damned if she was ready to deal with Ian right now. He looked much too dark, too sexy for her peace of mind. Especially after last night.

"I would prefer that you didn't go." His expression filled with chilly disapproval.

"Why? Because Tally is married to two of the Trojans? What, you thought I hadn't heard the gossip on your married members?" She laughed at the faint surprise in his expression. "It's been a little over a week, Ian. I learned who was who, married when, and fucked where, during those two dismally boring parties you insisted I attend those first few days. I would guess I'm acquainted with the better portion of your club memberships through hearsay. By the way, is it really true that Khalid has a harem?"

His eyes closed briefly as he pushed his fingers through his dark, loose hair.

"Trouble waiting to happen," he muttered as his eyes opened and he pinned her with a fierce stare. "After last night, I thought we could have lunch..."

"Why?" She propped her hand on her hip as she faced him squarely. "You set the rules this morning, Ian. You couldn't even share the bed you fucked me in. I was remiss, I guess, in learning the rules before pressing myself into your life. I was under the impression lovers slept together."

He crossed his arms over his chest. "I know you're upset—"

Why now, she just couldn't have him thinking she was upset, could she? She gave him a mental, mocking roll of her eyes.

"Actually I'm not." She smiled lightly. "Merely adjusting. We can discuss this after dark perhaps. I'm certain the cold light of day makes things rather uncomfortable for you. It's so much harder to hide from the truth then. I'll make it easy on you and we'll discuss it tonight. If I'm home in time."

"Why wouldn't you be?" His voice lowered almost dangerously.

"Tally mentioned dinner with friends." There wasn't a chance in hell she was going to let him intimidate her. "I may be late returning."

That bit of information didn't seem to please him very well. *Good,* she thought.

"Good Lord, the fate of the known universe is in danger," he growled then. "Did she happen to mention the friends involved?"

He sounded rather serious. How cute. And how very interesting.

"Only one, actually. Terrie, I believe. I'm certain the known universe is in no danger from us though."

"You don't know Tally," he grunted. "Stay here. We could spend the time together."

She shook her head as she turned and walked across the room to the dresser.

"We can talk later, Ian," she said as she pulled a drawer free and collected a thong and matching bra. "I'm not ready to discuss your horrid manners at this time. I'd prefer to relax for a while."

"My horrid manners?" There was definitely a tone of offense there. "How the hell were my manners horrid? What's gotten into you?"

She turned back to him, sighing deeply.

"You left my bed within ten minutes of believing I was asleep." She counted off a finger. "You didn't just leave my bed, you returned to your own." She counted off another. "This morning, I awoke alone, without even an invitation to join you for breakfast." The third finger went down. "And when I sought you out, Jason informed me, quite bluntly, that you were too busy to be bothered. Now go back to whatever required your attention and leave me be to get ready. At the moment, shopping is definitely preferable to being in your company."

Well now, he didn't appear to care much for that little announcement.

His eyes darkened, glittering with lust as his expression became decidedly carnal. Now wasn't this interesting?

"You are the one who sought out my company," he growled. "If you intend to leave for the entire fucking day, then you can at least be pleasant about it." He advanced on her, his eyelids lowering, not exactly narrowing, but giving him a hungry, wicked look.

Her own response was immediate, and not welcome as far as she was concerned. Her breasts became instantly swollen, her nipples rasping against the soft material of the sweater as her pussy began to heat.

"I did not seek out your company," she informed him imperiously. "I have left you alone this morning, Ian. And your dominance is not appreciated at this moment. Save it for a time when it might be."

A smile curled his lip as she frowned back at him.

"My dominance is a twenty-four/seven kind of thing, Courtney," he informed her darkly, stopping within inches of her as he stared down at her. "You're right, you were very remiss in not reminding me to discuss the rules with you. I assumed you knew that when you informed me so confidently of how well you knew me."

Before she could avoid him, before she could prepare herself, his arm lifted, his hands tangling in her long hair to pull her head back.

The sheer dominance of the move had her nerve endings instantly screaming in response. Perverts that those nerve endings could be. They were depraved. There was now no doubt about it.

Chapter Seven

Courtney fought for breath as Ian's head lowered, his lips heavy with passion as they neared hers.

"Take off your pants," he ordered roughly. "You may go out to plan the destruction of the world as I know it, but I'll be damned if you won't go without a reminder of me."

He licked at her lips then, a teasing reminder of the pleasure he could bring her with them as her hands moved to the snap of her jeans.

"This is completely Neanderthal," she rasped, despite the fact that her lust was rising with each breath she took, simply because of it.

"What's your bitch?" He nipped at her lips. "I bet it's making you wet, Courtney. I bet that pretty pussy is so slick and hot it's all you can do to bear it."

His point was?

"That is not the issue, Ian. My pussy stays wet for you. It has no common sense in that regard," she groaned, wishing he would just kiss her and get it the hell over with. She could feel the horrible, mind-destroying arousal beginning to climb as her clit became more swollen, her nipples tightening with fiery need.

She was hopeless.

A creature of complete hunger, ready and willing to do his bidding. Ahh, but the life of a sex slave, she thought with some humor.

"Get the pants off, Courtney," he growled as she deliberately took her time. "Then we'll see what kind of game we can come up with to amuse ourselves until Tally arrives."

Oh, that was going to be a hard one. She trembled at the idea.

"My boots," she whispered. "The jeans will catch..."

He released her slowly, moving back no more than a foot as he stared down at her, his expression determined, dominant.

"Undress. All the way."

She licked her lips slowly. Turning, she moved to the oak chest at the bottom of the bed, propped a foot on it and slid the zipper down on the half-boot before removing it and repeating with the second boot.

Her jeans were at her thighs, showing her ass, and she knew he was looking.

Straightening, she shimmied slowly out the jeans before lifting the hem of the sweater and pulling it over her head. And Ian had been busy as well. The white silk shirt lay in a puddle on the floor, his shoes, socks and slacks scattered along with it.

Tall and imposing, he exuded male confidence and lust. Of course, the engorged length of his rather impressive cock wasn't hurting the image any.

"Lean against the bedpost. Reach behind you and grip it, and don't take your hands down, Courtney, or I'll tie them in place. Then you may not make lunch with Tally for days."

She moved to do as he bid, watching as he gripped his erection, stroking it unselfconsciously as he watched her.

"Spread your legs," he ordered her as she reached up, gripping the tall post of the heavy wood bed.

She spread her legs, whimpering at the shocking arousal beginning to surge through her. She could feel the juices leaking from her pussy, coating the bare lips and trickling to her thighs.

She fought to breathe as he knelt before her, his hand still wrapped around his cock as her mouth watered to taste it. She could have sucked him clear to her throat and swallowed him down she wanted it so bad.

"Stay very still, baby," he whispered as he pushed her thighs further apart. "Very still. Otherwise, you may be very, very late for your luncheon appointment."

Oh yeah, and she really cared about that one right now.

"Oh my God, Ian…" She jerked, her fingers clenching on the thick wood post as one broad finger ran through the sensitized slit of her pussy.

No more than that, and her nerve endings were sizzling.

"Like that, baby?" he crooned gently, his breath wafting across her heated flesh, a caress nearly as destructive as the touch of his finger.

"I love it," she gasped, arching closer as she felt his fingers spreading her, opening her to the cool air of the room.

Then he was there, his mouth hot, his tongue a demon as it slowly, too fucking slowly, circled her straining clit. Her head fell back against the post, her eyes staring sightlessly toward the ceiling as whimpering moans fell from her lips.

"You taste so good," he whispered before his lips enclosed the straining bud, suckling lightly at the tortured mass of nerves as she cried out hoarsely.

"You are a demon, Ian," she accused him roughly. "You know I'm dying for you to fuck me. Why do you torture me this way?"

He hummed against her flesh, his tongue lapping around her clit as he sucked at the dewy flesh. He didn't deign to answer her, merely continued to torture her. It was an exquisite agony, sending flames rushing through her blood, sparking along her nerve endings.

Mewling whimpers of pleasure escaped her lips as she felt his tongue rasping against the delicate tissue, echoed around her as she shuddered, her knees weakening with the continued assault on her senses.

He lapped at her. Sucked at her clit. Lifted her leg and braced it on the low chest to the side of them before he thrust his tongue into the greedy depths of her sheath, sending her to her tiptoes with the force of pleasure slamming into her.

At the same time, one thick finger slid into the depths, stretching her, opening muscles already sensitized from the night before. She fought for her orgasm, her body tightening, reaching desperately for that free-fall of pleasure that lingered just out her grasp. She clawed at the post, arching, pressing her pussy tighter against his mouth, screaming with flaming lust as she felt his finger fuck inside her in a rapid series of thrusts that sent her hurling through the vortex of sensation as it exploded around her.

Color burst behind her closed eyes, vivid colors of passion that streaked around her, burst through her nerve endings and shattered her senses.

Almost instantly she felt the mattress beneath her breasts, cushioning her as her legs were pressed apart and the fiery, broad length of Ian's cock began to work inside her with short, desperate strokes. He stabbed into her, his breathing rough as he came over her, one hand clenched at her hip, the other sliding beneath her body to plump one swollen breast.

"You're so fucking tight." His voice was rabid with lust now. "So hot and tight you make me want to howl with the need to be inside you."

She tilted her hips higher, screaming out at the whiplash of pleasure and pain as he held her in place. She could feel the sensitive tissue of her sheath rippling around him, sucking him in, tightening on the fiery heat of the intrusion before caressing it with convulsive spasms of another nearing orgasm.

"More," she screamed out her need. He was going too slow, working inside her when she wanted to be taken, possessed. "Harder. Fuck me, Ian. Fuck me hard and deep before I die of the need."

She could feel it eating at her, the need tearing at her womb, clawing at her senses as she fought for the next release, the hard, cataclysmic explosions she knew would shape her, define her, would somehow ease the violent hunger he awoke within her.

Perspiration dripped from her body, from his. A rain of passion as she felt him pause, buried only halfway inside her, retreating, then suddenly, shockingly, filling her. Her hands tore at the comforter as she felt his fingers tightening on her nipple, pumping it, pushing her closer as the strokes inside her sex began to gain in speed and desperation.

Her breath sawed from her chest, rasping moans breaking past her lips, pleas…desperation…

"Fuck me!" She screamed out her hunger as she felt the conflagration building in her womb. "Oh God. Ian. Ian. Please…"

He fucked her harder. Faster. Slamming inside her with a power she could not have anticipated as she felt her body dissolving beneath him. Flesh and bone became liquid, pliant, melting, exploding as the orgasm began to rush through her. She didn't explode in release, she didn't come. She melted and became him. On and on the soul-deep merging whipped around her as she tightened on his burrowing cock, her juices flowing between, melding them together, wiping her senses and replacing them with Ian.

With Ian…

Escape.

The word bloomed in Ian's mind, his very being, as he felt the scalding violence of his release as it erupted from his cock. Something happened, changed. As he held her tight beneath him, heard the greedy need in her voice, felt it in the tight ripple of her pussy and felt her orgasm, he felt something rip inside him.

A knowledge.

No woman had ever surrendered so easily to him.

No one had ever opened that part of him he kept so carefully hidden. That he hid even from himself. And now it tore open. He felt it. Felt his soul rip in half and something, some dark, forbidden emotion began to flow from him, into her. Began to build inside him until nothing was enough, until he hungered even as he became sated. Until he needed even as he was given.

Until nothing, no one existed but Courtney and the ravaging needs building inside his own soul.

It wasn't enough. He could still feel her beneath him, her pussy contracting around his cock, sucking at it, eager for more even as she fought to catch her breath. She was wilder than the wind, hotter than the deepest pits of a volcano and as pure as the deepest reaches of the ocean. And so much a part of him he could feel her reaching out to him, binding him, locking a part of his soul to hers.

"It's sex," he growled at her ear then, furious, savage, fighting to reclaim what no one else had ever possessed. "Do you understand me, Courtney? It's sex. No more. No less."

Her pussy rippled around his dick, stroking it, keeping him hard when he should have been satisfied, should have been sated. Keeping him on the edge of a hunger he couldn't hide from.

"Mmm." The sound was drowsy, yet filled with hunger. "Whatever you say, Ian. Whatever it is, can we do it again?"

He forced himself to retreat. With every measure of strength inside him he forced himself to pull his hard flesh free of the fist-tight grip she had on him, grimacing in pleasure, in regret as the broad head popped free.

Tearing himself from her was harder. He wanted to scream as he moved, every cell in his body aching to return to her, to feel the soft touch of her flesh against his. As though the electrical currents flowing between them were being ripped apart, the pain sliced at his flesh.

"I have work to do." It was impossible to contain the fury building within him. "You have lunch."

He could feel her. He could fucking feel her rolling over on the bed, her gaze caressing his back as he jerked his pants from the floor and quickly dressed. Goddamn, he had to get away from her. He had to break whatever the bloody hell was suddenly binding them together, and he had to break it quickly. Before it went much further.

She didn't speak. She just fucking watched him.

He glanced back at her, fury pulsing through his body at the soft, welling emotion in those deep brown eyes. Eyes that ensnared him, that made him feel. Damn her to bloody fucking hell, if he wanted to feel this, he would have sought her out. She wouldn't have had to come to him.

"It's just sex," he snarled again, the anger pumping through his veins, thickening his blood, forcing his heart to race to keep it flowing through his veins.

"Yes, Ian. It's just sex," she agreed, too softly, too easily and with too much goddamned emotion in her voice.

"And don't forget it." He jerked the shirt over his shoulders before bending to collect his shoes and socks. "Never fucking forget it."

"Never, Ian." She sounded satisfied, not sated, but her voice echoed with pleasure.

Clenching his teeth against the surging forces rising within him, he turned and stomped from her room, striding quickly to his own.

It was just sex…

He pushed his fingers roughly through his hair at the thought. If it was just sex, if it were nothing more than he had known with all the women before him, then why did he crave her touch now, more than he had before he went to her? Why did he hunger for something that had no name, no definition? Something that now ate at his soul and he knew would never again allow him any peace.

If it was just sex, then why in the hell was his soul screaming that it was more…

So much more…

* * * * *

The last thing Courtney wanted to do was leave Ian and have lunch, go shopping or try to be civil in any way, shape or form. She wanted to race after Ian, wanted to scream at him, demand that he stop hiding from her just when she could feel him reaching out to her.

But she showered, dressed, and when she left her room she restrained from slamming the bedroom door and cursing violently.

Ian, of course, was no place to be found.

Hiding.

Coward.

She wanted to rage with him, rage at him. She didn't want to leave and give him the opportunity to build even more defenses against her. She wanted to hold him, feel again that merging she had known could exist between them. The completion that had, for endless seconds, rushed through her senses and left her shuddering in the aftermath.

"I think we need drinks before lunch," Tally Conover commented as Courtney joined her in the foyer, her gaze sharp, her expression thoughtful. "And we definitely need to talk to Kimberly."

Courtney barely refrained from glaring at her.

"Come along, dear, girls' day out. Do you need to inform Ian you may be late?"

"I'll need to be late?" Her fingers clenched on her purse as she fought to make herself follow the other woman to the door the butler held open politely.

"Please inform Ian that Ms. Mattlaw may be severely late returning tonight," she informed him imperiously. "I'm certain he'll understand why."

Courtney hoped to hell he did, because she didn't.

Her senses were overloaded. She had no business venturing out into the real world right now, and she knew it.

"This might not be a good idea," she sighed as she stepped into Tally's sporty little Jaguar. "Perhaps we should go shopping some other time."

"I agree with you one hundred percent." She might agree, but the amusement in her voice assured Courtney that the other woman had no intention of canceling whatever plans were in the making.

"I think a nice quiet lunch at my home, with a few friends, and plenty of drinks are in order. What do you say?"

Courtney turned to stare at her as tires screamed in protest at the quick application of gas she gave the vehicle. She jerked in the seat, frowning at the thought of whiplash.

"Will we get there in one piece?" She winced as Tally shot onto the main street, barely glancing at oncoming traffic as she did so.

"Of course we will," Tally laughed with a natural, sharp humor.

Courtney shook her head, an unwilling smile tugging at her lips. She knew she liked the other woman for a reason, and she was beginning to learn why. She knew how to drive right, just to start with.

"I'm going to make a guess here," Tally suddenly stated. "Ian has, in some way, made a complete ass of his Trojan self and you haven't regained your balance yet. When they do that, the only thing you can do is drown your sorrows in liquor and friendship and plan his downfall to the last detail. How close am I?"

Too close.

"Are they all alike?" She sighed, bemoaning the fact that she assumed Ian was somehow different from the others.

"Hell no," Tally laughed. "They are as unique as they can get. But Ian is the hardest. The one least affected, from what I gather, by any emotion. Even Kimberly despairs of him. Did you know he's often the third in her marriage with Jared Raddington?"

Damn, and she had liked Kimberly too.

"She'll join us for lunch. I'm certain she'll have some ideas on how to bring him to his knees."

"He's fucked her and you want me to meet her?" Perhaps Tally wasn't as intuitive as she was beginning to think.

The other woman's lips curled in a smile of satisfaction. "Don't worry, you'll love Kimberly. And you'll learn we have to stick together, or else they'll drive us insane. And trust me, there's no way to avoid her or get out of liking her. Jared is as close to Ian as anyone has ever managed."

Courtney frowned. "Let me guess, you're the troublemaker of the group?"

"How did you guess?" An almost feline smile of accomplishment crossed her features, giving the unique planes and angles a decidedly wicked cast. "Now, settle back and relax. Ian will know you're with me and that will make him crazy. He knows me. And he knows exactly what we'll be plotting. We have to keep him off-guard, otherwise you'll not have a chance at bringing him down."

Courtney wanted to shake her head, to somehow jerk herself back to reality rather than this strange conversation she was having.

"Who says I need help?"

Tally snorted. "Your eyes say it all, darling. And the fact that Ian left a meeting with Devril and Lucian to make you scream loud enough to bring down the rafters and echo into the office was clue enough. They called me, of course."

Courtney blinked back at her as she automatically braced herself at the next turn.

"They called you?"

"Of course." She shrugged. "We've been waiting for this for months. Ever since Ian learned you were visiting he's been like a bear with a sore paw every time it was mentioned. You mean something to him, Courtney, but he's fighting it. Ian could easily cut his own nose off to spite his face. His friends aren't willing to watch that happen."

There was an edge of warning in her voice. "And neither are you, I assume?" That question was filled with more than casual curiosity.

Courtney narrowed her gaze on Tally, reading more now than a friendly invitation to anything. This was a carefully thought-out outing, with Tally Conover in the lead.

"So what was your plan?" She sat back in her seat, watching as Tally shot her a knowing look before she turned her attention back to the road.

"Ian's fall, of course." Tally shrugged. "Let's just say that Ian deserves to be toppled from his little seat of icy splendor. He should be as tortured and as tormented as he claims our husbands are. Now, when he taunts them into their little adventures to torture and torment us, he'll think twice about it."

"What will you do when you can no longer plot Ian's downfall?" Courtney suddenly laughed. She had a feeling Ian had given the women she was about to become very close friends with, just a bit of hell.

Tally flicked her a glance rife with mocking enjoyment. "We have a list, darling. His name wasn't exactly the last one on it."

Now that sounded like fun.

"So today is a plotting session so to speak?" she ventured with no lack of amusement.

"That's a good description." Tally nodded, obviously restraining her glee. "A plotting session. The first of many."

There wasn't a chance in hell Courtney was going to miss out on this.

"Then let the games begin," she laughed, suddenly more optimistic than she had been before leaving the house.

These women knew Ian, if nothing else, through their husbands. They would have the information she needed to hold the advantage she gained today. And right now, Courtney knew, she needed every advantage she could steal from him.

"She has left with Ms. Conover, sir. Should I have her followed?"

Ian stood silently before the wide windows of his office, his hands shoved in the pockets of his slacks as he frowned out at the dreary, cold day.

"Don't bother, Jason," he sighed. "Tally would know they were being followed and she would cause as much of a fuss as possible."

"If I may say so, sir. Ms. Mattlaw is proving to be a bit of a wildcard. I believe letting her out unattended could turn into a catastrophe."

Ian snorted at the understatement.

"Catastrophe would be a mild word if she learned she was being watched. As long as she's with Tally, she's reasonably safe."

He was aware of Jason's bafflement at the initial order of the security measures he had placed Courtney. He had been unable to help himself. The past was a demon he couldn't seem to shake, no matter how hard he tried.

"Was her safety in question, sir?" Jason's tone was concerned now.

Ian sighed wearily, pinching the bridge of his nose as he closed his eyes and pushed back the need to find her, to order her back to the mansion.

"Her safety is not in question, Jason." At least not yet. Not from anyone other than himself and his desires.

"Very well, sir." Confusion radiated from the butler. "Shall I inform the Misters Conover, Wyman and Mr. Andrews that you will resume the meeting soon? They have expressed some question as to whether or not the previous business discussions have been concluded."

He shook his head, turning back to the butler slowly.

"They're in The Club?"

"Yes, sir."

"I'll join them there. Please let me know when Ms. Mattlaw returns."

"I'm certain the sound of the commotion will reach your ears before I can scurry to your location," Jason harrumphed.

"I'm certain you're right." An unwilling smile tugged at his lips at the thought. "But make the attempt in any case."

"Yes, sir." Jason inclined his head before turning smartly and leaving the room, returning it once again to the oppressive silence which had filled it before his arrival.

You're so depraved, Ian. I sold my soul into hell to be your woman. To what end? This is my end.

Once again, written words seared his memory.

He couldn't control the need, the hunger. It was eating him alive, as it never had before.

He could see it, he could almost feel it.

Courtney's sexual appetite was strong, blistering in its heat. He could see her, her eyes dazed, pleasure consuming her as her lips opened in a scream, sandwiched between him and Khalid.

The half-Saudi would complement her passions, his patience. His control would match Ian's as they drove her past any boundary of pleasure she could have known.

He wanted to play with her. He wanted to watch her writhe on the bed, retrained, pleading, gasping for release as he and Khalid drove her past any restraint, any conscious control. He wanted, fuck, he needed—hungered—to see her reach that point where she climaxed from not more than a breath against her clit, a lick to her nipple. Where her body was so sensitized, so aroused, so perfectly attuned to the pleasure they could bring, that when they pierced her snug channels, the orgasms would roll through her, a continual progression of release that would stroke, milk, convulse around their burrowing cocks.

The need was overshadowed only by the memory of the last woman who had loved him. It was a pleasure he had wanted her to know as well.

He hung his head, breathing in roughly as his shoulders bunched with tension.

He had taken many women to his bed, experienced women, women who sought nothing more than that peak and went eagerly, too eagerly, toward it. He had thought that would be enough. It wasn't.

Courtney would fight it. She would beg, scream, curse his control and attempt to break it, whether she knew the end result or not. It was a part of her nature. She would never give him that part of herself without a fight, without a challenge to his dominance.

"Are you finished moping yet?"

Ian turned slowly to meet Cole's mocking gaze.

Of all those who surrounded Ian in his day-to-day life, Cole alone knew the truth of what held Ian back. He had been there, in those horrifying days after Melissa's death.

"You're out of line, Cole." His jaw clenched with anger as he read the mocking condescension in the other man's gaze.

"Am I, Ian?" He shook his head, entering the office as he closed the door behind him. "She's a wild woman. Maybe even more than you, with all your experience, could ever hope to tame. She's your match. Everyone sees it but you."

"She's an innocent," he breathed out roughly.

"She's not Melissa, Ian. Melissa was broken, inside. You couldn't have anticipated that. You couldn't see through her lies and her games because you hadn't known her through the bad times. You had no idea that she was less than the person she showed you. You know Courtney."

And he knew she was as wild as the wind. That she had always been impossible to peg, or to constrain. Even as a child she had been like a whirlwind, rushing around the estate, creating havoc, drawing smiles and unrestrained laughter. From the moment she turned sixteen she had tried to tempt him. God, according to her, she had watched him.

"Maybe I don't need to share Courtney." He pushed back his own attempts to justify what he wanted.

Cole snorted as he threw himself into one of the leather chairs in front of the desk Ian was striding to.

"Yeah, and maybe the sun doesn't need to rise tomorrow." He scratched at his jaw thoughtfully. "You might not need it, but I bet she does."

Ian's eyes narrowed. "You're out of the running."

"Thank God," Cole grunted. "Tessa's the only wild woman I can handle. If she doesn't fuck me into an early grave it will be a miracle."

Ian dropped into his chair, slouching into the thickly padded back as he propped his feet on the desk and leaned his head back to stare at the ceiling morosely.

Such inaction was against his nature. He had kept his involvements at a certain level for a reason, to allow himself the full immersion of his senses into his sexuality when the opportunity arose.

He was a businessman, running not just The Club, but also overseeing the various businesses his father had left him, as well as the multitude of other interests. His life was often fast-paced, filled with on-demand questions, answers, and lightning-fast business reflexes. He thrived on it. Craved it. But the stress level often became tremendous.

It was then that Ian found his sexuality rose to the fore. He began to hunger, to need the excesses he found such enjoyment in. In all honesty, he would have found relief for that by now, if it had been any other woman. He had dated the innocents, hell, he had even bedded several women whom he had known were not cut out for the life he lived. And he had always, without fail, found his ultimate satisfaction, the relief of the building stress, the loneliness, the need to just fucking give, when he was helping to send a lover to the very pinnacles of ecstasy.

It was where he hungered to send Courtney.

It was beginning to torture him, to torment him. He was beginning to fear he couldn't hold out much longer.

"Let's make a little bet." Cole's voice drew him back from his own musings.

"What kind of bet?" Ian narrowed his eyes on his longtime friend.

"Ten thousand says she pushes you into it. That she does something that shatters all that careful control you're forcing on yourself, and before you know it, you'll have her tied and blindfolded, screaming for mercy while you and a third work her over. Another ten says you choose Khalid."

Ian snorted. Khalid was a given. None of the other Trojans, save for Cole, understood that particular kink.

Hell, the first was a given. He was fucked and he knew it. The only question was how much longer he could possibly hold out. He was actually beginning to pray that Dane got a clue and arrived quickly.

"Go to hell."

"Bet still stands. Club rules. I set the challenge, it's up to you to make or break it. Time allowances." Cole narrowed his eyes thoughtfully. "I'll make it easy for you. A week."

Could he hold out a week? Sure he could. A week would be easy. Especially after the phone call to Dane that he intended to make. Ian wasn't above admitting he was drowning in a puddle of his own making.

"A week," he agreed as Cole rose to his feet, a mocking smile tilting his lips.

"Damn. I have to come to The Club more often. This could get amusing," he snickered as he moved to the door. "Good luck, buddy. And no padding your own bet. I wouldn't be pleased."

"Meaning?" Ian rose slowly to his own feet.

"Meaning. If you call Dane, all bets are off, and I make certain your sweet little innocent learns some amazing home truths. Tess is good at having loose lips when the need arises." Cole turned back and saluted him, mocking. "'Night, Ian."

Ian's fists clenched. If the son of a bitch weren't his best friend, he would kill him.

Chapter Eight

Ian was pacing the floor at midnight when Courtney hadn't returned to the house. At one o clock, he was cursing and nursing a stiff whisky. At two in the morning he had enough. He knew Tally too well. She was an instigator and determined to torture and torment the men she knew. She drove her husbands crazy at the office, and when they could take no more she conspired with the other women to make their husbands' lives hell.

She was continually thinking of ways sneak into The Club without Devril or Lucian, and even worse, she was sneaking the other women in. Forget about just *asking,* the woman thought she had to play fucking commando.

At three that morning, the limo pulled into the driveway in front of the Conover mansion. Every light in the lower level of the house appeared to be on as Ian strode up the front steps. As the butler opened the door, a scowl on his taciturn face, Ian could hear the pulsing beat of Depeche Mode pounding through the house.

"Sir. Misters Conover have retired to that attic, I believe, for the safety of their eardrums." It was evident Devril and Lucian had left the brawny ex-bouncer, Tim, to keep an eye out for the mayhem developing.

"I'll collect Ms. Mattlaw." He was forced to raise his voice by several levels as he stepped into the house and headed for the family room.

As he stepped to the doorway, he stopped in horror.

Dear God, they were all there.

Tally Conover, Tess Andrews, Ella and Terrie Wyman, Kimberly… He swallowed tightly as he watched the women toasting each other as they lay sprawled on the floor, more than a few empty bottles of wine thrown to the side. Within seconds they polished off the glasses they had just toasted each other with.

Courtney was drunk.

She polished off the wine then sprawled on her back, obviously speaking, though he doubted anyone could hear her.

He strode to the other side of the room and flipped the power switch to the CD player quickly.

"...and then he'll be putty in your hands..." Kimberly Raddington was laughing with glee as she leaned close to a wide-eyed Courtney, her voice echoing eerily in the near-silent room.

They all seemed to freeze. Six pairs of eyes turned slowly to him as Courtney breathed out in exaggerated patience.

"Told you he would come looking for me." The precise accent in her voice warned him that she was going to be less than cooperative. The frown that creased her brow was further proof.

"Ian, darling, that is my CD player." Tally stayed on the floor, though her voice was less than pleased. "And Depeche Mode should never be shut off with such force."

She sounded imperious. Furious. Too damned bad.

He rubbed at his brow wearily before staring across the room to where Courtney was struggling to come to her feet.

Her long, dark hair flowed around her shoulders, caressing her arms and trailing across one breast as she straightened to her full height. She was barefoot, her toenails shimmering beneath the bright overhead light. The soft cotton dress draped over her full breasts and caressed her hips before falling in a cloud of soft material to just below her thighs.

It was almost scandalous.

And she was damned cute.

The thought slammed into his chest with the force of a sledgehammer.

She *was* cute. Soft and sweet, and so desirable it was all he could do to maintain his fragile control. He wanted to smile at her. His heart seemed to melt at the sight and that terrified the hell out of him.

"Hi, Ian." Her smile was wide, her dark eyes gleaming with slumberous amusement. "Did you miss me?"

"Horribly." His lips twisted with an edge of self-mockery as he advanced on her. "The stores delivered your clothing this evening. I think you've emptied them for a while. Are you ready to come home now?"

She bit her lip, her expression softening as he realized what he had said. *Home.* Dammit, she was making herself too much a part of his life.

"Well, if you need me bad enough to collect me yourself, then I guess I'm ready to go." She stared around the room with some confusion as the other women sat up. "Anyone seen my shoes?"

For some reason, this produced another round of snickers and giggles from the other women.

Minutes later, her shoes were located under a chair. Five feminine rears were pointed in the air as the other women decided she might need help pulling them free. Ian was standing across the room, his head tilted, watching them with no small amount of confusion when he heard an exasperated sigh behind him.

Turning, he faced Devril and Lucian Conover.

"Thank you." Lucian's expression was morose as he stared back at Ian. "That damned music was driving me crazy."

"At least the music drowned them out." Devril motioned to the women as Courtney collapsed into the chair and wiggled her petite feet into the low-heeled shoes. "The things I heard out of their mouths will give me nightmares for years to come."

"Who knew Tally had such a bloodthirsty streak?" Lucian shook his head, staring at the woman with a pensive expression.

That comment and the look on the other man's face assured Ian that Lucian's "bloodthirsty" wife must have been giving Courtney pointers on making *his* life hell. Just what he needed.

"I'm ready," Courtney announced as she came to her feet, wobbling a bit before finally standing straight.

She walked carefully across the room, her gaze becoming drowsy, sensual as she neared him. His dick grew harder.

"Good luck," Lucian muttered as she neared. "Remember, Tally has been giving her advice. That's never a good thing."

Ian shook his head, his arms enfolding the slight form that nuzzled against his chest. He was aware of Lucian and Devril's surprise as he enfolded her close to his chest, just as he was well aware of the sense of balance, of warmth it brought him.

"Come on, vixen." He wasn't about to trust her to walk the distance to the limo on her own.

Ignoring the other two men he picked her up in his arms, his lips quirking in amusement, as she seemed to hum in pleasure, her arms encircling his neck.

"I like you carrying me, Ian," she murmured against his ear as he strode for the front door. "My legs get shaky around you, have I mentioned that?" she mused as the butler opened the door and he strode in the cold night air.

Courtney, completely unfazed, just burrowed closer, her nose tucking into his neck as the chauffeur quickly opened the door.

"You are going to be the death of me, Courtney." He stooped, stepping into the limo with his burden and sitting back in the leather comfort of the seats as he pressed the button that raised the privacy window between the front and the back.

He was so hard, so damned horny he thought his cock might well burst from his pants. And if Courtney's sensual little murmur of approval as she felt the hard length of his erection against her rear was any indication, the ride home could be one fraught with frustration. Because there was no way there was time to lay her back and have his way with her.

"When are you going to fuck my ass, Ian?" She wiggled against his lap as the breath slammed from his chest.

"I'm going to spank your ass," he growled, unable to stop himself from allowing his hand to smooth up her leg, sliding beneath the soft weight of the dress.

And he was smiling. In the dim light he felt the curl of his lips, the laughter in his chest and it amazed him. He should have been enraged that she would stay out so late plotting to make him insane. Instead, all he truly felt was a strange sense of joy that she was back in his arms.

"That would be foreplay," she giggled playfully as his hand caressed the sensitive flesh behind her knee.

"So it would be." He grunted to cover his laughter.

The dark confines allowed him the freedom to release a small measure of the surprising happiness she seemed to fill him with at the oddest moments. What was it about her? He should have been raging, furious at her for her manipulations, her scheming determination to get her way with him. Instead, he could do nothing but allow the little minx her way and stand back and watch in bemusement as everything inside him reached out for her.

"Hmm. We need to take a very long limo ride one night, Ian." She leaned back in his arms, her eyes gleaming beneath her lowered lashes. "I could get so naughty in the back of this car."

"Really?" He lifted a brow.

"Really," she sighed. "We could get naked and have wild flaming sex as we traveled. The night we rode home from the airport, I wanted nothing more than to kneel before you and take your cock into my mouth. Would you have been surprised?"

Surprised? He would have had a stroke. He still might.

"We could have so much fun." She leaned forward, nipping his ear as his hand clenched at her thigh, spreading her legs as he felt his breathing escalate. The woman was going to drive him insane.

"There's no time for these games, Courtney," he groaned as her tongue stroked along his neck. "We're nearly to the house…"

"I could come just rubbing against you I bet," she sighed against his ear. "Just the sound of your voice stroking me. Talk dirty to me, Ian. Make me come for you."

Her voice was teasing, her body wasn't.

His fingers skimmed over the crotch of her panties to find them hot, wet. Her juices were plastering the silk to the bare curves of her pussy and tempting him beyond endurance. The hard catch of her breath as his fingers stroked over the material had his jaw clenching as he fought for strength.

She would come so easily for him, he knew. She would unravel in his arms, spill her sweet cream around his cock and scream his name.

"When I get you home, I might not make it to the bedroom, Courtney. You're in danger of being fucked on the stairs."

"Mm." She wiggled in his lap. "However you must do it, Ian. As long you're inside me. I feel so empty. I need you inside me."

His eyes closed at the emotion he heard in her voice. He had a feeling she had more in mind than just his cock filling her.

She snuggled against his chest again, her head resting against his shoulder as her hair fell like a ribbon of silk over his arm to the seat. His hand buried in the mass, something inside him clenching painfully.

Now he knew why he had kept his relationships purely superficial. Why he never allowed himself to get close to the women he took to his bed. Because he knew the dangers inherent in letting himself feel again.

Unfortunately, Courtney was asking for nothing. She never had. From the first moment he had seen her as a young child, she had moved into his reluctant heart with her open smile and generosity. She had been a child. He thought himself safe loving her. Hell, he needed someone to love, and she had asked for now more from him than a smile at that time. He had never imagined the changes that time would bring.

As she lay against him, Ian rested his chin against her head, his hand still stroking the soft flesh of her inner thigh, so near, and yet so far from the heat he craved. His eyes closed as the silence wrapped around them, the intimacy of the moment weaving through his soul.

"I love you, Ian."

Her voice was soft, the words slipping out as she relaxed against him, sliding into sleep with all the innocence and trust of a child.

His teeth clenched as a shattering sense of hunger overwhelmed him. As though the words had opened something inside him, torn it loose and left him grasping for a tenuous hold on his rapidly slipping control.

I love you, Ian…

The words drifted around him, echoing through his senses and leaving him with a hollow ache he couldn't make sense of, one he knew he couldn't live with.

Love. A child's dream. A young girl's fantasy. But Ian was a man, no longer a child, and without a drop of innocence left within him. And love, he knew, could hold no part in his life.

Chapter Nine

Courtney groaned miserably as she came awake the next afternoon, her eyes fluttering open in the dim light of the room. And it shouldn't be dim. Her bedroom faced the afternoon sun, the filmy curtains doing little to hold it at bay as it spilled into the room.

Opening her eyes further, she gazed across the expanse of a huge bed, into the cool dim room as an unconscious smile tugged her lips. She was in Ian's bed. Not that he was there with her, but he had been.

Her hand reached out to smooth over the pillow beside hers, the slight indention in it assuring her had slept beside her.

Had he held her as she slept?

She moaned miserably. What the hell was she thinking the previous night to drink so much? She had known she couldn't stay awake. Wine was more effective than any sleeping pill where she was concerned. Her foolishness had caused her to miss a night she would have given anything to remember.

The feel of his arms holding her. If he had held her.

She stared pensively around the masculine room. Heavy dark furniture emphasized the dimness of the room and added to its air of protective comfort. Here, Ian had surrounded himself with furniture of comfort. The chest and dresser and wardrobe were definitely antiques and beautifully preserved. The rolltop desk on the far side of the room looked a bit incongruous with the laptop that sat on its polished surface.

And the bed. She stared at the heavy foot posts, rising a good foot from the mattress. It was huge, obviously custom-made and superbly comfortable. She could lie there for hours. Ian's scent wrapped around her, his blankets warming her, his bed cushioning her. Everything she needed was here, except Ian.

She settled deeper into the warmth of the bed as she stared at the glow of the sun's warmth behind the heavy drapes. Last night had been informative. Not just in the information she had learned about Ian, but things she had learned about herself. She had believed she would be uncomfortable having to actually acknowledge any female Ian had fucked within a relationship. But where Kimberly Raddington had been concerned, there had been no jealousy.

The woman was warm, friendly, and so obviously in love with her husband that Courtney had quickly gotten over any ill feelings toward her. Yes, Ian had touched her, often. He had been the third in her marriage for many months now. But it had ended the night Courtney had arrived. He hadn't been back since, and the most encouraging bit of news the other woman had dropped, was that Ian had informed her and her husband Jared, that they would need to find another third to fulfill the balance they both sought in their sexual relationship.

But Ian still hadn't made any moves to complete his relationship with her. She bit her lip in indecision as she tried to figure that one out. She knew he wanted to. Knew he ached to do it. She could feel the tension whipping through the air each time another male came around them. She could also feel the tension rising in Ian. When he touched her, he was so obviously restraining himself, tamping down the wild lust she ached for.

She had thought just getting him into her bed would be enough. That the rest would automatically follow. She was finding out it wasn't.

"Hangover?"

Her head swung around quickly to the bathroom door. Her heart rate picked up, her mouth drying out at the sight of him. He had obviously just completed his shower. His shoulders gleamed with a slight dampness, as did his silky midnight hair.

"I wasn't drunk," she informed him with what little pride she could dredge up as her gaze drifted lower, to the impressive erection straining forward from his body.

"Hmm..." He moved then, walking slowly toward her as she sat up in the bed.

He looked wild. Untamed.

"No headache?" His voice throbbed with lust.

She shook her head slowly, flicking her tongue over her dry lips as her position placed her at the perfect level to greet his hard-on with a moist morning salutation.

"I waited all damned night for you to wake up," he growled then, his hand reaching out to spear through the tangled mass of hair at the side of her head. "I need you, Courtney."

He hadn't said he wanted her. He hadn't said he was going to fuck her. He said he needed her. Everything inside her clenched in hope, even as her lips opened, a ragged moan passing them as the broad head of his cock entered.

Her tongue swiped against the ultra-soft underside as the hardened flesh jerked against it. His hands clenched in her hair as she braced one hand on the mattress beneath her, the fingers of the other curling around the thick base.

"Good girl," he whispered, his voice tight with lust as she took as much of his erection as she dared into the dark confines of her mouth. "You have the sweetest mouth, baby. So soft and hot, like silk and fire."

Her pussy throbbed at the words as she stared up at him, seeing the narrowed intensity of his gaze, the fiery hunger of his lust.

She tightened her lips around him, suckling at him slowly, easily, moaning at the clean male taste of his dark flesh.

"How pretty." His voice was a heated caress to her senses. "Seeing your mouth stretched open by my cock, your pretty face all flushed and hungry. You're pushing me, baby. Pushing me further than you want to." He jerked against her as her hand stroked along the shaft until she came to that taut sac below. "Fuck yeah. There's a good girl."

She palmed his balls, her lips sucking noisily at his erection as he wrapped his fingers far enough along the thick stalk to keep from choking her as his thrusts began to increase.

Courtney whimpered in painful arousal as she tightened her thighs against the ache in her pussy.

"Do you know what I'm going to do to you this morning, Courtney?" he asked her, his voice rough as he drove his cock into her mouth. "I'm going to fuck your pretty mouth first. Watch your eyes go all dark and round as I spill my come down your throat. And you're going to take it, aren't you, baby? Take it and love it."

God yes. She wanted it. She hungered for him. All of him.

"When I'm finished, I'm going to fuck your ass, Courtney." He sounded tormented now, tortured. "I've tried not to, sweetheart. God knows I have. But I need it."

She sucked his cock deeper, her rear tingling at the thought, the blood rushing through her system as she began to moan at the anticipation. This was what she needed, what she had longed for. Ian, hungry, intent on satisfying the hungers that raged through them both. Dominant. Fierce.

He chuckled, the sound stark and filled with lust.

"You like the thought of that, don't you, sweetheart? My cock digging into your ass, stretching you, making you scream from the sensation. Is that what you want?"

Yes! She screamed the word silently as she took him deeper, to her throat, so hungry now for the taste of him that the need was ravenous, out of control.

"You don't have to watch another suck me anymore, Courtney. It's all yours for now, darling." He was moving faster, his cock hardening as she licked, sucked, the sounds of her pleasure, of his, echoing around her.

He reached down, moving her fingers from where they caressed his balls, and curling them in place about his shaft as he moved his hand to her head. Both hands were now tangled in her hair, holding her in place as he began to fuck her mouth harder, faster.

Courtney could feel the warnings of his release then, the pulse and throb of the head as it glanced the entrance to her throat, the surge of blood through the thick veins against her tongue, the near bruising hardness.

"Harder," he ordered roughly, his fingers tightening in her hair, tugging at the strands and sending fiery streaks of sensation spearing through her head. "Suck it harder, baby. I'm going to come. Fuck, Courtney…yes, baby…suck it, baby… I'm going to come…"

He tensed, driving the erection into her mouth with several hard, shallow thrusts before he threw his head back and she felt his semen began to erupt from his cock. Fierce, a touch of salty male perfection and dark lust, the taste of him was addictive as it filled her mouth, the hard pulses of his release dragging fractured moans of pleasure from him as she consumed him.

She held onto the fierce male flesh as long as he allowed it, her mouth moving easily on him, drawing each drop of his semen from the tip of his cock until he moved back, pulling free from her with a reluctant moan.

His lips quirked. A bittersweet smile as he held her head in place, staring down at her.

"When I let you go, I want you in the center of the bed, on your stomach, your arms and legs spread. Will you do this for me, Courtney?"

She would walk through fire for him.

She nodded slowly.

"I won't go easy on you." His voice lowered, throbbed with greedy lust. "Understand that now, if you do this, I won't go easy. I'm too hungry…"

"Ian, I won't break." She slid her hands slowly up his thighs, her lips moving to the tight, hard planes of his stomach. "Whatever you want, it's yours."

His abdomen clenched as she spoke.

"Just this." His hands tightened in her hair, his body tightening further. "Everything I can give you, no matter what."

Everything *I* can give you. He had emphasized that. Alone. Just him. When she knew they both craved so much more.

"Do as I said." He moved back from her then, releasing her as he moved away from her. "Center of the bed."

She did as he ordered, feeling him jerk the sheet and comforter out of the way as she lay on her stomach in the very center as he prepared the bed. The pillows were thrown to the floor, and seconds later the rattle of chains took her breath away.

"I'm going to restrain you." He wrapped a padded cuff around one wrist and secured the Velcro closure. "There's plenty of slack in the chains for now."

He moved to her ankle and secured the restraint there, before repeating it on the other side. Seconds later, she was held to the bed by the chains. They were thick enough to hold her in place, yet not so thick as to be cumbersome.

"Excellent." He patted her bottom before moving from her line of vision.

The sound of a drawer opening had her senses sharpening, her breathing escalating as she heard him return to the bed.

"I'm going to blindfold you."

She gasped as the dark cloth slid over her eyes and was quickly tied in the back.

"Your other senses become sharper, more clear when you can't see your surroundings," he whispered. "Every touch, every sound, is amplified. It makes the anticipation climb higher, the sensations striking harder through your flesh." He tied it quickly behind her head. "You have no idea how hard it makes me, Courtney, seeing you like this, laid out for whatever I desire, unable to fight the pleasure. Knowing you'll be lost among the sensations I can give you."

She whimpered at the sound of his voice, the anticipation rising within it as she fought to find a glimmer of light within the sudden darkness surrounding her.

"Ian!" A sharp exclamation of surprise left her lips as his hand landed heavily on her rear.

He chuckled in response.

"Are you paying attention, baby?"

"Duh!" She snorted at the question, the cheek of her ass tingling with fiery pleasure.

Her pussy was growing wetter by the second, and she swore her nipples were poking holes in the mattress.

"Come here." The bed dipped beside her as she felt his arm slide beneath her, lifting her until she rested on her hands and knees. Just barely. She had to strain to stay in place as the chains tightened and she felt him lay beside her, his hair stroking the sensitive flesh of her arm as his head moved beneath her.

"Perfect," he whispered, his breath heated and moist, caressing her nipple a second before his tongue curled around it.

Courtney jerked, crying in out in surprise as the pleasure nearly sent her careening into a release of her own.

He licked slowly, his tongue rasping the hard peak for long seconds. Then his mouth surrounded her, drawing on her tightly, near painful shards of pleasure streaking from her nipple to her womb with each sucking motion of his mouth.

Her head tossed, the pleasure wrapping around her, extreme, near painful in its intensity. Then just as quickly, it was gone.

She could hear him breathing, the sound harsh as she strained to hear him.

"Such a good little girl," he whispered, moving up beneath her body as she shook with blind tremors of anticipation. "Give me your lips, Courtney. Kiss me, baby."

She lowered her head frantically then, searching, finding his lips as the hunger overwhelmed her. Lips and tongues fought to get closer, to eat at the passion rising hot and fierce between them. No, not passion. But something much more fierce, more elemental. It became more than desire, more than hunger as she bucked in his embrace, her nipples rasping over his chest, her lips held and controlled by his as his tongue tasted every dewy inch of her mouth and tongue.

"No. Don't," she cried out as he broke the contact, searching frantically for his lips.

He found hers instead. Sipping. Nipping. He refused to take her fully, to give her the hard, dominant force of the kiss she pleaded for.

Courtney groaned in frustration as he moved again, pulling from beneath her, forcing her to hold herself in place as his hands stroked along her body. He palmed her breasts, his fingers flicking at the hard nipples.

"I could suck at those tight little tips all day," he whispered at her shoulder. "But there's so much more to explore, Courtney. So many ways I need to pleasure you."

So many ways she wanted to be pleasured.

"Stay still." She felt him moving to her rear, his hand stroking over it gently. "First, we get you ready."

"Oh God. Ian…"

She could feel him stretching out on the bed, his damp hair caressing her thigh as his head moved between her legs.

"Stay still." He slapped her ass as she moved to lower her pussy to his mouth.

Courtney bit her lip, straightening, panting for breath as one hand curved along her buttocks, spreading the cheeks slowly as the other moved closer.

Every muscle she possessed began to scream in pleasure as she felt the narrow tip of the lubricating tube began to slide slowly inside the tight entrance of her ass.

"Relax..." His breath caressed her clit, causing her to jerk in reaction.

She could feel her juices gathering, dripping along the lips of her pussy as he murmured his appreciation. His tongue—was it his tongue?—swiped over the drenched folds, gathering the creamy excess as it lingered on her flesh. He never truly touched her, but made her mad for more even as she felt the nozzle sliding deeper inside her.

"We're just going to play a little bit," he whispered, his breath searing the folds. "I'm going to fuck you nice and slow as I spread the lubrication inside you. And while I'm doing that, I'm going to do this..."

The nozzle slid back, spreading the cooling gel as his tongue swiped through the narrow, cream-laden slit of her cunt before wrapping around her clit. She would have come off the bed from the sensations if the restraints weren't holding her in place. She shuddered, a hoarse scream leaving her lips as the pleasure tore through her with the force of lightning, searing every nerve ending she possessed before he drew back and slid the nozzle deep inside her ass again, causing her to buck against the pleasure of the penetration.

"Mmm... Your juices are dripping from your pussy, Courtney. I don't even have to touch you to taste the sweetness."

Tremors raced up her spine as the muscles of her anus clenched on the nozzle. He moved it again, drawing back as she tightened, expecting the feel of his tongue. It never came. The nozzle slid inside her again as he began to fuck her with slow, easy strokes, squeezing small amounts of the lubrication inside her as he moved.

"Ian…please…again…" She was nearly sobbing from the need.

"What, baby?" His breath stroked her clit. "Tell me what you want."

"Lick me." She had no shame. "Lick my pussy, Ian. Please."

Slow, barely touching her, his tongue swabbed over the swollen folds as she moaned in frustration.

"Like that?"

She bucked, lowering her hips, only to receive another smack to her rear in payment.

"Stay still," he ordered firmly.

"Ian, this is cruel," she wailed, her head hanging between her arms as she fought to stay upright. "I need more."

The nozzle slid in again, a hard, fiery thrust through the slick recess as her back arched. At the same time, his tongue plunged inside her weeping pussy, flickering, licking, caressing the inner muscles as a strangled scream of pleasure tore from her throat.

"No. Damn you, Ian…" she begged as he retreated once again.

Courtney fought to breathe, to hold onto her sanity as her hips lowered, trying to follow his wicked tongue. Sharp smacks to her rear only added to the pleasure, as did the smooth, short strokes of the lubricating nozzle in her anus. She writhed, fighting the darkness surrounding her, the hunger eating her alive as his tongue licked, his teeth nipped, but never in the spots she needed, never as she needed.

"This isn't fair," she screamed, clenching on the nozzle as it retreated again. "Ian, I swear. I swear you're killing me."

She could feel her juices running from her cunt, the channel weeping in an agony of pleasure as her womb spasmed with the need for release.

"Damn, your pussy is so hot, baby," he growled, his tongue licking at her again, his hand delivering another heated, pleasure-giving blow to her ass as she fought once again to grind the needy flesh into his mouth.

"Eat it," she panted, feeling the perspiration gather along her body as one broad hand lifted her hips from his face, his tongue licking around the silken folds of her pussy. "Fuck me with your tongue, Ian. Please. Oh God, have mercy on me."

He chuckled at her plea, slowly easing back from her as she screamed in rage.

"Be quiet." The strike to her rear was harder. Hotter. "Keep begging, Courtney, and I'll gag you. Would you like me to gag you?"

Tears dampened the silken cloth over her eyes as she shook her head desperately.

"Good girl." He pulled her hips back into position as he pulled the nozzle from her ass. "Now, stay still."

She did as he ordered, shaking, in agony as she fought the hard pulsating sensations racking her body. Her clit was so sensitive that even the air around it was a torment. Her ass ached, not from the small slaps, but from the need to be filled. Every nerve ending in her body was heightened, throbbing, begging for his touch.

"I'm placing a dildo harness on your hips. It will go around your thighs, and will hold the vibrator I have inside you." Smooth leather straps were worked around her hips, her thighs. "Don't beg me for mercy, Courtney," he whispered then. "In this, I have none. You wanted to be here, in my bed, beneath my body. Unless you're begging me to stop, then I won't hear you. Do you understand?"

"Yes!" As long as he got the fuck on with it.

"Easy now. I'm going to push the vibrator inside you and anchor it in. If it's uncomfortable, let me know."

Her back arched as she felt her muscles separating, felt the warm width of the device beginning to fill her. It was thick, supple, moving inside her with slow strokes as Ian eased it into her drenched pussy, filling her by slow, agonizing inches.

"There we go." She could feel it nudging at her cervix, not touching, but she was filled, stretched, on fire and dammit, she needed more.

"Fuck me, Ian," she cried desperately, clenching on the device as she felt him tucking something against her clit. It swelled to meet the embrace of whatever device rose from the vibrator to encircle it.

"Shhh." He kissed the cheek of her ass gently. "The vibrator is a Rabbit, Courtney, I'm sure you've heard of it." She felt him tighten another portion of the harness, something that covered the mound of her pussy and tightened at the side of her thighs.

A sob escaped her lips. She had heard of it, knew he was going to tease her until she lost her sanity.

"I thought you had," he crooned, panting as his hands smoothed over her damp thighs. "I'm turning it on now…"

She jerked, wailing as the slow, gentle rhythm began to fill her. The dildo rotated inside her, the beads in the shaft pulsed against her sensitive entrance, and the ears that wrapped around her clit began to hum a seductive cadence. A mind-destroying cadence because the speed was barely enough to feel, just enough to torture.

Tremors of response began to quake through her body as his tongue painted over the cheek of her rear then, moving to the narrow crevice where he licked tenderly, his hands holding her in place as she began to jerk against the rising sensations building inside her.

The device was driving her insane.

"Fuck me..." Her head tossed as she lost strength in her arms, her upper body falling to the bed as she felt him rise behind her.

Two fingers tucked at the entrance to her ass, working slowly, parting her, filling her easily as she pressed outward, relishing the additional sensation. But it wasn't enough. She bit her lip, holding back her screams as she felt a third finger join the others.

Yes. The tight stretch had fire blooming in her rear, streaking to her cunt. Pleasure, hard, destructive, painful pleasure, began to whip through her as his fingers pressed in deeper, stretching her, preparing her for the much greater width of his cock.

Seconds later, they slid free. She tensed, mewling cries echoing around her as she felt his cock tuck at the small opening.

"The ultimate trust, Courtney," he whispered behind her. "And the ultimate pleasure. Are you ready for me?"

She felt him opening her as the speed on the devilish vibrator began to hum faster, harder. The dildo filling her worked at the muscles of her pussy, the beads shattered her senses as the little ears stroked her clit and Ian began to fill her ass.

She was screaming. Maybe she needed the gag after all. Hoarse, agonized screams of pleasure left her throat as she felt him sliding inside her, short, firm strokes of his cock opening the near virgin channel for the thick cock possessing it.

Pleasure and pain, hard, brilliant arcs of sensation began to spear inside her as her back bowed beneath the impulses. She could feel each fiery inch taking her, stroking nerve endings she never could have imagined existed, stroking them, heating them, until with one last powerful thrust, he forced his hard flesh to the hilt inside her.

The Rabbit began to hum and move harder inside her.

Ian began to fuck her with slow, long strokes, groaning behind her as his hands clenched at her hips and Courtney began to lose her mind to the sensations whipping through her. Did it hurt? Or was the pleasure merely agonizing? There was no answer, no way to answer as his thrusts began to increase powerfully in synchronization with the destructive effects of the vibrator driving her insane.

Harder. Faster. She could feel his cock shafting her ass with the same power he had used to fuck her pussy as her orgasm began to build. Her womb convulsed, her pussy tightening around the rapid whirls of the fake cock inside her as the muscles of her ass began to clench, to milk the erection filling her rear.

Combined, it was too much, and it yet, it wasn't enough.

She began to shudder as she felt her clit swell within the ears of the device, felt her nerve endings begin to react to the sensory overload. Bright, jarring colors filled the darkness behind her closed eyes as the brutal explosion erupted inside her.

Behind her, Ian's harsh cry was heard, but she couldn't understand it, could barely make sense of his cock pounding inside her, filling her with the fiery pulses of his seed as the world collapsed inside her mind, and refused to stop. One explosion after another, on and on as violent, convulsive shudders racked her, spasming through her muscles and sending her senses rocketing with each orgasm until she could do nothing but collapse beneath him, jerking in his grip as the vibrator suddenly stilled within her and exhaustion swamped her.

Aftershocks, hard quaking shudders shook her body as she felt Ian slowly withdraw from her rear. She moaned at the sensation of her tight muscles gripping him, lust threatening to flare inside her once again as he finally slid free of her grip.

She lay still, her muscles limp as he began to release her from the harness about her hips, sliding the dildo free as a shaky moan left her lips.

"Shhh..." His voice was velvet-soft, gentle as he eased her.

Seconds later, he released the restraints then pulled her into his arms as he dragged the comforter that had somehow been thrown to the floor, back over them.

"Let me hold you now," he whispered, drawing her against his chest as she cuddled close, drifting in a haze of remembered pleasure. "Just let me hold you..."

Chapter Ten

"We have several applications for membership within The Club unanswered. Khalid's recommendation for the DEA agent Gray Powell and Cole's for Mr. Armitage from Texas. We've also had several requests from Senator Sizemore, though to be honest, I believe he would be a poor choice. My investigations thus far on him lead me to believe he may be more a danger to The Club than anything else..."

Ian sat back in the leather chair, watching the club's investigator from across the wide expanse of his office desk as he gave his report on the three men currently under consideration for membership.

Accepting married members had never been an issue. The Club wasn't a brothel, nor did it supply women to the men who accepted membership. It was, quite simply, a place where they were assured of finding men who shared their tastes, their lifestyles and the various problems caused by both. A support network.

Despite the rumors currently making their way within Squire Point of a few local members, the broader base hadn't been compromised. Yet. The influx of sudden queries for membership was worrisome.

"Cut the Senator from the list." It was a decision he had made weeks before, though he had followed through with the investigation merely to substantiate his own suspicions. "Continue with Powell and Armitage. If they pass the final screening we'll issue the introductory letter and see if they're willing to meet the initial Club fees."

The investigator, Cameron Falladay, nodded his head sharply, sending the mass of long, black hair rippling around his shoulders. He didn't look much like an investigator, which was one of the reasons he was so effective.

He looked more like a biker, ready to rumble at a moment's notice. Amused dark green eyes were shielded by thick black lashes in a face that was saved from being pretty, only by the wicked slash of a scar across one cheek. Tall and well-honed, he moved with deceptive laziness. He was lethal, one of the most dangerous men in Ian's employ.

"Jesse reported back on your houseguest a few moments ago as well," Cam leaned back in his chair then, his gaze reflective. "She's currently having lunch with the Sexy Six..." The current nickname for the small group of wives who had banded together had Ian wincing. "There's trouble brewing there." As if he didn't already know that. "This makes three days in a row, with Khalid joining them yesterday."

Ian masked his irritation.

"She's under control." Ian waved the report away as though it were of little consequence, despite the fact it had his cock tightening in frustration. "Keep Jesse on her."

Cam nodded briefly before making an entry into the small notebook he carried for the meetings.

"Ms. Hampstead arrived a few hours ago. She's had Matthew prepare her room for a week's stay." Alyssa Hampstead was the only female member of the group since Kimberly Raddington had dropped her membership. "There are also several of the out-of-town members present. Should I have security added to the inner doors of the Club to keep Ms. Mattlaw from the main portion?"

Ian's lips quirked at the thought.

"Do that and she would get in or die trying," he growled, as he rubbed at the tension in his neck. "We'll leave Matthew in charge for now. I'll handle her if she actually manages to get back in. She's not so much a security concern as she is one for the peace of mind. That woman would drive a saint to curse."

Cam chuckled at that. "She's a wild one all right. There's no way she would get along with the other six if she weren't."

Ian shook his head at the thought. Yes, she was wild, as untamed as any woman he had ever known. But so fucking innocent it made him want to scream in denial.

"If that's all, I'll get back to the fun stuff." Cam rose to his feet, staring back at Ian in amusement. "Armitage is having a nice little party at his ranch this weekend. I managed to get an invitation to accompany one of the guests. I'll see what pans out there before giving my final report."

Ian watched Cameron turn and leave the room, closing his eyes as the door closed behind the other man.

It had been three days since he had allowed her in his bed. He had expected to be uncomfortable, unable to sleep with her curled around him like a damned kitten. Instead, he was sleeping better than he had in...longer than he could remember.

Her response to him was never-ending. Adventurous, as wild as the wind and willing to try any position, any sex toy he used on her. The hours spent pleasuring her was ecstasy and hell in the same heartbeat.

Ecstasy, because she met him stroke for stroke, relishing in every touch, every adventure they entered. And hell because he knew he couldn't take that final step.

Rising from his chair in a rush of energy, he paced to the windows, staring into the garden as he pushed his hands into the pockets of his slacks. No matter how often he took her, or how, that edge of innocence she possessed remained. It was an added turn-on, almost addictive to see the shocking pleasure in her rapt expression. And still, the lust burned. It burned to the point that no matter how many times he took her, he still craved her. And she still met him with a hunger of her own.

And each time the need to share her grew.

Even his dreams tormented him. Dreams of seeing her, pressed between him and Khalid, blindfolded, restrained, helpless against each touch, each stroke of her body as she begged for more. Screamed. Pleaded… His cock jerked fiercely at the image as a strangled groan left his throat.

Because the ending of those dreams were always the same. Courtney lying in his bed, her eyes staring sightlessly at the ceiling, the damned note Melissa had written so many years ago by her side. The haunting image had his gut clenching in fear even as his balls tightened in hunger. Damn her, she had him torn in so many different directions he didn't know which way to turn anymore.

Damn, what was it about her? He shook his head as he turned and moved back to his chair before throwing himself in it. He propped his elbows on the desk and ran his fingers through his hair before gripping the back of his neck tightly.

She thought she loved him. Innocent dreams and sexual heat shimmered in her eyes every time she looked at him. He should have called Dane the minute he saw that he wouldn't be able to deny her. The other man would have been furious, he would have made certain Courtney was never in Ian's company again, but the friendship would have survived, and in a few years, Courtney would have gotten over her infatuation.

Instead, he had broken.

A muttered curse left his lips, because despite knowing they were both going to hurt, that the relationship he had shared with her and her family was now forever scarred, he couldn't stop. The more he had her, the more he craved her touch, the more he craved, period.

"Now you look like a man approaching the end of his control…"

The dark amusement in the accented voice had Ian's head rising, his eyes narrowing as Khalid stepped into the room.

The half-Saudi sauntered across the room, his dark face creased in a mocking smile as he took the chair Cam had recently vacated.

"You look tired, Ian," he snickered. "Too many late nights?"

Ian grunted at the suggestion before straightening back in his chair.

"What can I help you with, Khalid?"

Khalid chuckled, his dark eyes filled with amusement.

"Nothing much." Broad shoulders shrugged lazily. "I saw Courtney with the Sexy Six an hour or so ago, and thought I would warn you that there was a definite air of conspiracy at their table. I do believe, my friend, they are plotting against you."

Ian sighed roughly. "They are always plotting against me," he growled. "They were born to torture and torment men, Khalid. Pray you don't come within their sights in this lifetime."

Khalid's laughter was filled with a bit more anticipation than made Ian comfortable.

"They are an imaginative lot, my friend." His teeth flashed against his dark skin as his eyes filled with laughter. "A man could only be so lucky as to have such women plotting for his future."

Ian groaned silently.

"What the hell do you want, Khalid? You may live a life of ease, but I, unfortunately, need to work to keep things going here."

"Ah yes." Khalid nodded. "Tracking stocks, merging companies, maneuvering political factions and such is a great hardship."

Ian could only shake his head. The other man was evidently conspiring with Courtney and Tally's crew to drive him insane. He leaned back in his chair, staring back at his friend broodingly as he rested his arms against the padded rests of the chair. He might as well become comfortable.

Khalid grimaced at the obvious air of patronizing patience.

"Very well." He shrugged as though whatever game he was attempting had lost its fascination. "Have you chosen your third yet?"

It was expected. Ian had known that eventually one of The Club's members, most likely Khalid, would question the fact that thus far, no one had been invited into the relationship he shared with Courtney.

Tension tightened his body as he fought the need to do just as was expected of him. He was...whatever the hell he was, he sighed wearily.

"There will be no third, Khalid."

The announcement had the other man's expression going blank in shock.

"No third?" He shook his head, his shaggy black hair rippling about his shoulders. "I don't understand, Ian." He stared back at Ian as though he feared he were having problems with his more than excellent grasp of English.

"You understand perfectly." He throttled the anger building in his gut. "There will be no third. Courtney will tire of this game soon and realize it's no more than infatuation, curiosity. When she does…" He swallowed back his bitterness. "When she does, there will be nothing for her to regret."

Khalid's eyes narrowed, suspicion flaring.

"Ahh, I see," he intoned softly, regret flashing in his eyes as he rose to his feet then. "Should you change your mind, my friend, I hope you would consider my request that I be your third."

"I won't be changing my mind."

Khalid's lips quirked at the announcement, as though amused by the statement.

"Very well. I will not keep you then." He nodded respectfully. "I wish you a very productive day, Ian. Should you need me, you know I am at your disposal."

"You as well, Khalid." Ian stood to his feet, watching as the other man left the room, closing the door gently behind him.

"Fuck!" He cursed fiercely as he threw himself back in his chair, wiping his hands over his face as he stared up at the ceiling.

Unfortunately, it wasn't the white ceiling he saw. It was Courtney, her head thrown back in pleasure, her lips opened in a scream of release as he and Khalid pushed her past the boundaries of any pleasure she could have conceived.

He could feel the need for it, searing his senses, fueling his frustration, his hunger. He could only pray he could manage to hold onto his control until she came to her senses.

Unfortunately, he had a feeling that coming to his senses was going to be his greatest hurdle.

Khalid stepped into the back of his limo, barely giving the chauffeur-bodyguard a chance to close the door before he hit the speed dial on his cell phone.

"Yes, darling." Tally's smooth, amused voice came through with questioning emphasis.

She was a lively one, he had to give her that. She had yet to focus one of her torturous matchmaking schemes his way, but he was enjoying being part of the conspiracy. It was much less nerve-racking than being the one conspired against.

"He says he has no intention of taking a third," he relayed the information, keeping his voice free of the amusement that curled his lips. "I do believe the shadows of Melissa haunt this little scheme of yours, sweetheart."

She was silent, obviously weighing his analysis.

No one ever spoke of Ian's past, but most of The Club's members were well aware of it. The membership was a close support network, many of them had known each other since young adulthood, gravitating to The Club with the advice of their fathers, several of whom were members as well at that time.

Melissa Gaines had, quite honestly, been a nutcase. Ian had adored her though, the zealous infatuation of young manhood transferring to the woman he believed was his perfect match.

"Suggestions?" Not that Tally needed any, but he knew she was thinking. He wished he was there to watch the process. The few times he had watched her plot, it had been a masterpiece of skillful, dark design. She would have made an excellent ruler.

Khalid grinned as he thought of Courtney then. She was younger than Tally, but rapidly gaining her own ground in the feminine arts.

"I am but a man," he sighed morosely, mockingly. "Who am I, my dear, to opinionate on the grand designs of such feminine works?"

Besides, it was so much fun to watch these women as they plotted and planned. The sight of it was amusing as well as vastly educational.

"In other words, you're keeping your ass out of the fire." Tally snorted. "Fine. See if I show any mercy when I find your weak spot."

"But Tally, sweetest, I am such a simple man. My weak spots lay bare to your gaze. Go gently with me." He leaned back in the butter-soft leather of the seat and let satisfaction fill him.

Of course, they both knew the game. He had no intention of allowing her to find his weak spots. Such folly could break a man.

"Yeah, you know I will," she drawled. He expected nothing less than complete mercilessness where she was concerned. "Thanks for the information, Khalid. I'm certain we can find a way to use it."

"I have no doubt, my dear." He disconnected the call before pocketing the cell phone and staring at the dark glass that separated him from his driver. A frown tightened his brow.

Ian was, of course, in love with the little spitfire-in-training, Courtney. It had been so readily apparent that he had nearly felt sorry for the other man. How horrible to love so deeply, and to be so very unaware of the exact nature of the torment that raged inside him.

Considering the job Melissa Gaines had done on Ian years before, though, one could forgive him for his denial now. At least for a short time.

Khalid sighed in self-satisfaction as a smile tipped his lips. Poor man. Better to love many, than to love one. In that, at least, there was always consolation should a relationship fall through.

He had no doubt Courtney would prevail. Ian was quickly reaching the end of his patience, and his control. Soon, it would happen. And when it did, Khalid intended to be there. There were few women who would present a challenge such as the one Courtney would present when the final game played out.

Despite her love of the pleasure, of Ian's touch, she would fight the ultimate dominance, the complete submission of her senses to the two of them. And that instinctive fight, the delicate, subtle precision of undermining her defenses would be a joy to be part of.

Shameless she was, but she had no idea of how shameless she could ultimately become.

Chapter Eleven

"Ian, wake up." Cheerful, full of energy and clashing with the bone-deep sleep he had been immersed in, Ian opened one bleary eye to stare back at Courtney's shining face.

The bedside lamp was on. Obviously. Its glare was about to blind him as he peeked over her shoulder to stare at the clock.

"Go back to sleep," he muttered, closing his eyes as he groaned at his body's refusal to accept that she had actually woken him after the hours he had spent exhausting them both.

Exhausting her wasn't easy.

Surely to hell he wasn't getting old.

He would have shuddered at the thought if he actually had the energy.

"Ian, come on, wake up..." Playful, undeniable, her voice had his eyes blinking open in resignation at he stared up at her.

She was leaning over him, her hair flowing down around her face, creating an intimate, seductive curtain as her dark eyes, her very awake dark eyes, gleamed with joy.

His dick twitched in interest despite his body's exhaustion.

"I'm awake." His hand smoothed up her thigh, heading for the soft flesh between her thighs. Perhaps a quickie would satisfy her until he could wake up.

"Stop that." She laughed, pushing his hand away as he sighed in resignation. "Guess what?"

Guess? It was fucking midnight. He wasn't supposed to be awake right now, let alone guessing anything. He started to remind her sharply of that, but the soft glow of her eyes, the gentle smile on her lips, stopped him. It would be criminal to kill such a look of joy with a sharp word.

"I can't guess. I'm asleep," he finally grumped, a grin tugging at his lips as her slender fingers raced over his side in a retaliatory tickle.

"Come on, grouch." The feminine amusement, softly voiced and filled with wonder, had him staring up at her, willing to guess whatever the hell she wanted. "Guess what's happening right now?"

"Hmm." His hand moved to tangle in the hair at the side of her face. "You're pussy's getting wet?"

"No." She rolled her eyes at him, but she was having fun. Strangely enough, so was he. It had to be the sleep deprivation. "Guess again."

A smile tugged harder at his lips. "My dick's getting hard."

"That wasn't a guess." Her throaty laughter had a chuckle blooming in his chest. "That's a continual state."

"When I'm awake anyway," he reminded her, a drowsy sensuality flowing around them. He could feel the hunger for it, but it wasn't imperative, it wasn't a driving need as it had been previously. It was just there, connecting them.

Intimacy.

It wasn't sensuality, so much as intimacy.

The thought of that should have terrified him to the bottom of his bachelor's soul. Instead, the lazy, drowsy atmosphere allowed it to seep into him, to fill him.

"Come on. I'll give you a better hint," she whispered, leaning close to feather her lips over his. "What's it doing outside? Right now?"

He thought a minute.

"No..." His eyes closed on a groan, though the chuckle slipped free. "No way, you little minx. I am not going outside in the freezing cold at midnight."

He was warm. The blankets were pulled over them, Courtney was snuggled close to his side, and he was not leaving his bed.

"But Ian..." He opened his eyes and groaned again at the wonder in her face. "It's snowing, Ian. We could slip down to the hot tub and watch it snow while we cuddle in the hot water."

Cuddle? In the water?

He shivered at the thought of it.

"Courtney, you have to drag your ass out of that hot water into the cold air eventually," he reminded her, knowing he couldn't refuse the playful pout shaping her lips.

"I'll warm you back up." She batted her eyes innocently at him. "Come on, Ian. Let's go play in the snow. It will be like our own little world."

"We have our own little world here," he growled, snuggling closer to her as he pressed his face between her breasts. "Stay with me and I'll fuck you instead."

"Go out to the hot tub with me. We could sneak out through the Club. No one would be there now, and that way, you won't get cold," she teased against his hair. "I'll sit on the rim, surrounded by the snow and let you show me how much you like the new wax job I got yesterday."

He perked up at that. He hadn't taken the time to worship her soft pussy, as he had wanted to earlier in the night. Somehow, there was never enough time to do all the things he wanted to once he got her responsive little body beneath him.

"You're going to drag me out of my warm bed, aren't you?" he muttered before licking at the stiff nipple to his side.

She laughed softly, moving back from him, her eyes and her smile, her very expression one of luminescence. She was like an angel, staring down at him with an air or wonder and soft light.

"Come play in the snow with me, Ian. Let's make beautiful memories."

And how could he resist?

He wasn't entirely certain how he allowed her to draw him from the bed. He helped her put on one of this thick robes, satisfied it would keep her reasonably warm on the short distance from The Club's door to the heated tub. Pulling one on himself, he halfway convinced himself that he must surely be dreaming now. Only in his dreams would he would be sneaking through his own house, into the deserted Club and onto the back deck with the little minx who had wormed her way into his life.

As they moved through the dark corridor leading to the Club's inner door, he had his arm wrapped snug around her, holding her to his side as she seemed to shimmer with the joy that reflected in her soft voice.

"You live such a staid life for a Trojan," she teased as he keyed in the security code to unlock the door that kept her barred from the inner rooms. "Really, Ian, locking me out isn't kind."

"Safer." He chuckled at her tone. "You're a menace, Court. I feel it's my duty to protect my own kind."

Her small hand smacked at his chest.

"Oh, that was just cruel," she pouted. "Good comeback, but cruel."

"Score one for Ian?" He lifted a brow teasingly as she stared up at him.

"Score one for Ian." Her soft giggle touched his heart.

Yes, he had to be dreaming, because only in a dream could the past evaporate as it had now.

"Come on, minx." He opened the doors into the bar, glancing around the dimly lit area and seeing it empty before leading her to the French doors on the other side of the room. "I can't believe I'm going out in the cold to get wet and then try to get back to our room. We'll be ice cubes before we make it. They'll find us tomorrow, frozen..." He faked a shudder as he led her quickly out the door onto the heated deck.

She laughed. The intimate sound of it, soft, as delicate as the mist surrounding the hot tub, had him smiling and he wasn't even certain why.

"Come on, grouch." She shed the robe with no sign of discomfort as she stood beneath the heavy snowfall, her face raised to allow the soft fluff to caress her face. "Feel it, Ian, it's like a fantasy." She turned back to him, her hair shielding her upper body, framing the delicate features of her face.

He could feel his chest expanding, feel the wonder of *her* burning within it. She amazed him, drove him crazy, made him so fucking hot he thought at times he would melt from the conflagration.

How could he possibly get cold? Siberia would be a rainforest with her in it.

"Aren't you coming?" Her voice was still whisper-soft, encouraging him in the madness she created.

He found himself untying the belt of the robe and quickly removing it, allowing it to drop in unconcern on the damp heated cement beneath their feet as he moved to the steamy water.

He stepped in, feeling the rush of the water caress his lower legs as he held his hand to her. A vivid smile crossed her face, and in the soft light of the full moon above he saw the flash of eternal dreams in her eyes.

"You're beautiful, Courtney," he whispered as she stepped into the water with him, the snowflakes drifting down to melt on her flushed cheeks, her soft lips.

Pleasure flashed in her eyes as she stared up at him, looking for all the world like one of the fairies in the prints his mother loved before her death.

His own precious fairy.

He touched her cheek, lowered his lips to hers and whispered suggestively, "Now tell me about that wax job?"

Courtney stepped into the front doors of Ian's mansion just before the sun was setting over the mountains surrounding it the next evening. She was reflective as she closed the door behind her, brooding over the fact that it seemed Melissa Gaines, and something that had happened almost fifteen years before, still had the power to hold Ian's heart so deeply.

She had thought she was making inroads the night before as they laughed and made love in the hot tub long into the midnight hours. But this morning he had been his usual brooding self, if a little grumpier than usual.

Had he truly loved the woman? Surely not. If he had, then he couldn't be so certain that love didn't exist, could he?

Truth was the man was going to make her completely insane. She shared his bed, spent hours upon hours each night in the throes of the most exciting pleasure she could have imagined, but it wasn't enough. Not for Ian, and not for her either.

She could feel the restlessness building in him, and it only caused hers to intensify.

"Your coat, Miss Mattlaw…"

She jerked in surprise as Jason materialized by her side.

"Stop sneaking up on me." She lightened the startled snap with a laugh. "That's creepy."

"You were obviously very deep in thought, ma'am."

The robot.

She allowed him to help her with removing the black jacket she had worn with her jeans that afternoon as she stared about the foyer.

"Is Ian in this evening?"

"Mr. Sinclair is away presently," he informed her. "He asked me to let you know that he would return later this evening."

She nodded slowly. "Very well." The house was quiet, too damned quiet. And she was sick of being a good girl. Ian kept a very close eye on her when he was home, careful to keep her from The Club at all costs.

A wicked smile curved her lips as the butler moved through the foyer to the back of the house. Removing her cell phone from her small purse, she dialed Khalid's number and waited as it rang. Once.

"Well, my favorite girl is calling," he answered, a smile in his voice.

"Hello, Khalid." She kept her voice low, in case anyone dared to attempt to listen. "Where are you?" She allowed a vein of teasing wheedling to enter her voice.

A chuckle came over the line.

"Where you aren't allowed to be." His voice was equally as low.

"But I want to be." She pouted prettily, watching the doors leading from the foyer suspiciously. "Get me in. We'll have dinner. A drink. Play some cards…"

"…Make Ian insane." He didn't sound a bit frightened of the prospect. She liked Khalid in that way—he was one of the few men that Ian didn't intimidate.

She shrugged negligently. "He's away at present. He may never know. But that bulldog of his, Matthew, is so mean to me, Khalid. Surely you could help me." She used her best, most pathetic little voice that normally inspired complete devotion.

Khalid laughed.

"You are such a bad girl." He kept his voice low. "I might have heard, in passing, that Matthew has to leave in about forty minutes to pick up another member at the airport. I suppose I could slip out and unlock that pesky door he's taken to securing while he's gone."

Excitement filled her veins.

"The minute he leaves, give me a call. I'm certain he'll check my whereabouts before he dares to depart." She snorted. "He's worse than Father's guard dogs."

Khalid chuckled knowingly.

"I'll be certain to let you know," he promised. "Dress pretty for us though, it's not often we're blessed with such lovely company. And it may well come in handy when Ian finds you here. He's partial, I believe, to the sight of that little belly ring."

Evidently, he wasn't the only one.

"I'll be certain to dress appropriately."

She disconnected the phone before rushing up the stairs, determined to make the best of this opportunity that had fallen her way. Ian had kept the Club completely out of bounds to her since he had taken her to his bed. Come to think of it, he had kept any sort of temptation into the darker side of his passions far out of her reach.

That darker side was what had drawn her to him as she matured. The infatuation of childhood had grown, strengthened, as had her assurance that Ian could meet the darker side of her own hungers. The ones that tormented her in the dead of night, even as she slept in his arms.

She loved him, regardless of his attempt to hold back. If she had thought for a moment he was doing so because that need wasn't a part of their relationship then she would have let it go from the beginning. But she could *feel* it. She always had. As though a part of her soul was connected to his, binding them, fueling the sexuality and the hunger. And those darker urges were a part of it.

"Some men and women are born with deeper hungers, with a need to explore all facets of their sexuality," her mother had explained when Courtney had gone to her, questioning the needs that tormented her, despite her innocence. "When the time is right, when you've found the man you can trust with that intimacy, Courtney, then the pleasure and that sharing is something that has no shame, no limits, and no second thoughts. But only if it's right for you, and for him..."

There was no shame, no limits, no second thoughts. She would be more than willing to allow Ian to guide her through the learning process, to help her navigate the needs that tormented her.

And she knew he would relish the job. She could see it in his eyes, feel it in his touch. He grew more aroused with the thought of it, and each time he used the toys to play out the fantasies that tormented them both, the tension went higher as he grew more aroused.

After slamming the bedroom door behind her, she strode quickly to the closet and pulled out the outfit she had bought with this night in mind. The skirt was incredibly short, snug and indecent fiery-red. Red looked good on her.

The top was a button-up, vest-type that left her belly button bare and would allow the emerald to wink suggestively as the light hit the emerald that dangled from its tiny gold ring.

She stripped to bare skin as she rushed to the shower. She lathered, shaved, rinsed, dried and lotioned every part of her body until it shimmered with life. Her hair was pulled to the side and braided loosely, the nearly black strands a stark contrast for the red outfit.

Then she dressed.

Matching thong, no bra. She pulled on the skirt, adjusting the snug material at her hips and again just below her ass. The vest ended way above her belly button, flashing an indecent amount of flesh between the two, then she pushed her feet into matching spiked heels seconds before her cell phone beeped demandingly.

Checking the incoming number, she flipped the receiver open before bringing it to her ear.

"Your timing is perfect." She smiled as Khalid's light chuckle came through the line.

"I'll be waiting you at the doors, dearest," he informed her smoothly. "My best guess is, we have perhaps an hour before Ian returns home and finds out where you are. Are you certain you're prepared for the consequences?"

She rolled her eyes. That wasn't even worth answering.

She disconnected, tossed the phone to the bed and moved quickly for her door once again. If she could have skipped in the slender heels, she would have. This was it. She could feel it burning through her body. Ian was already strung as tightly as her father's guitar strings, all it would take was a nudge to push him over.

She knew she should feel guilty for manipulating him so. That she should fear the repercussions, and in many ways, she did. But she knew Ian. To the very bottom of her soul she knew him. If she allowed him to continue as he was, he would only convince himself further that she couldn't possibly know what love was, and that there was no chance she could handle his appetites.

He was so stubborn. So certain that she needed to be protected. It wasn't his protection she needed, it was his love. His acceptance.

Shaking her head, she slipped along the foyer until she came to the inner door that led to The Club. Opening it carefully, she moved into the dimly lit hall and made her way to the door that Ian had ordered be kept securely locked against her.

She turned the doorknob carefully, excitement surging through her as she opened the door.

"Ian will no doubt punish you terribly for this," Khalid drawled from where he was leaning against the wall beside the doorway. "I can only hope he allows me to help." His gaze became brooding. "I'm going to enjoy paddling your ass, Courtney."

She flashed him a brilliant smile, her hand lifting to play with the braid that fell over her shoulder, affecting an innocent expression despite the sexual intensity thrumming through her.

"Should I call you 'Uncle', too?"

She almost laughed at the glazed, sexual intensity that filled his eyes. Sometimes, men could be so simple.

"You are wickedly shameless," he finally sighed with a wry expression. "Every man's greatest fantasy and worst nightmare. Beware, Courtney, bad girls often get spanked."

"Hmm, spank me, Uncle Khalid?" She laughed as he shook his head at her, though his eyes gleamed with amusement.

"Come along, vixen." He placed his hand against the bare flesh of her back and guided her to the open doors of The Club. "I have purchased the finest bottle of whisky that Ian stocks, and I promise Thom will keep you in ice until Ian arrives."

From the sound of his voice, he was eagerly awaiting Ian's arrival. But then again, so was she.

They entered the main room of The Club as nearly a dozen pairs of eyes turned and looked their way. Surprisingly enough, there was another woman present, one Courtney knew quite well.

"Courtney Mattlaw, your father would have a stroke." Alyssa Hampstead came to her feet as Khalid led her to the table. "I heard you were staying with Ian, but didn't believe it."

"Hello, Alyssa." Courtney smiled widely. "And don't mention Daddy. If he would have a stroke, then yours would self-detonate. I had no idea you were a member here." Better yet, how *was* she a member?

"Have a seat, ladies." Khalid pulled Courtney's chair from the table as she took her seat before moving to assist Alyssa similarly. "I'll get the drinks and join you momentarily."

He turned from them as Alyssa's eyes followed him with a touch of heat.

"He's a wild man," she sighed. "But quite charming."

"What on earth are you doing here?" Courtney couldn't believe a woman had actually made it into Ian's sacred Club as a member. "How did you manage it?"

Cool blue eyes turned to regard her thoughtfully.

Alyssa was often referred to an "ice princess" with her steely eyes and soft ash blonde hair. She was from one of the most upstanding prudish families Courtney had ever known. Her family was old money, staid, conventional, and her father would likely murder her himself if he ever learned she was taking it up the butt by a man, let alone at the same time she was getting it elsewhere.

"Several of The Club members are very good friends." The other woman shrugged. "They applied for my membership and vouched for me personally. It beat taking the chance of Father learning my little hobby."

There was no bitterness in her voice, nor truly any anger, but Courtney now, as always, felt a measure of respect for her. She lived her life under a microscope at times, just as Kimberly Raddington had. A cherished daughter and heiress, the head of several charitable organizations, and often approached as a spokeswoman for those organizations.

Courtney had always admired her for her work, the warmth that she showed to only a few people, and her family loyalty. Now, she found, she had much more to admire the woman for.

"Your drinks, ladies." Khalid sat a small glass of whisky and ice in front of her, a rum and coke in front of Alyssa. "I understand Ian is currently on his way home from a meeting he left in the middle of." He was amused to no end. "Enjoy it while you can."

Courtney sighed as she lifted the glass to her lips.

"He hasn't shared you yet." They both watched as Khalid took his seat across from them.

"No." Her lips twisted in a grimace. "He wants to…" She shrugged.

How was she going to push him into anything? She was here, but just being here wasn't going to be enough.

"Courtney hasn't found the right button to push yet," Khalid informed her.

"I'm wondering if he has one," she snorted in a purely ladylike way.

"I gather she hasn't yet tripped onto Ian's sole nonparticipation kink?" Alyssa chuckled knowingly as she watched Courtney now with a suggestive look.

"I think not," Khalid murmured. "Ian would never give her such power."

"I am here," Courtney announced with a frown. "There's no reason to talk over me."

"Tell me, Courtney, how adventurous are you?" Alyssa reminded her now of a playful little cat. Her nose wrinkled engagingly, her eyes filling with laughter and fun. This was a side of Alyssa that a rare few were allowed to see.

"I'm not adventurous at all, Alyssa." She allowed her lips to curl with confidence. "I am, quite simply, without limits. What about you?"

She heard Khalid's rapid intake of breath and managed to hold her own as Alyssa reached out, running her fingers over the soft rise of her breasts. There was no arousal, but the feeling was pleasant. It wasn't an unknown touch.

"Ian's private, hidden little kink is only known to a few of us," Alyssa whispered as she watched her thoughtfully. "For some reason, Ian has always taken pleasure in seeing his woman stroked by another."

Courtney felt the flare of excitement then. It made sense. A lot of sense. All the times she had watched Ian with her maids, there had always been another woman present. She hadn't questioned it, had really not thought of it, as the extra woman had been quiet, as though waiting her turn. Perhaps she had instead, already had her turn.

It wasn't an act Courtney was unfamiliar with, but it wasn't a preference either. Then again, she had no preference outside of Ian.

"You've seen him enjoy this?" She turned to Khalid, uncertain how to proceed. Though most enjoyed the sight of two women together, they didn't enjoy seeing *their* woman with another.

"I have." He nodded. "It's one of the few things Ian keeps as quiet as possible. But, it's the only reason he gave Alyssa membership. She enjoys tormenting men in such a fashion." His lifted his drink in acknowledgement to her.

Alyssa chuckled.

"I have very rarely fully made love to a woman." She shrugged, lifting her hand back from the flushed rise of Courtney's breast. "But I do so love watching how they go insane from very simple acts. They are, at heart, charmingly weak in that area."

If Khalid's arousal was anything to go by, this was largely the truth.

Courtney bit her lip thoughtfully. Did she dare push him that hard? Well, of course she dared. She would dare most things. But what were the chances of success?

"Courtney, do not step outside your own bounds," Khalid warned her then, his voice worried.

She laughed at the concern, flashing him a suggestive look.

"Do you think I haven't done such things, Khalid?" she asked him. "When one is experimenting with her body, she tries many things." Besides, her first goal had been to be a virgin, a very experienced virgin, in Ian's bed. One did not get the experience one needed without a small amount of experimentation.

Khalid's eyes widened marginally, as they seemed to glaze again. Good Lord, the man was a lost cause at that point.

She tapped her fingernail against the table, aware of both Alyssa and Khalid watching her warily.

"Very well." She made up her mind quickly. As far as she was concerned, there was no sense in debating the matter. She would know immediately if such a thing would tempt his control. She would be able to feel it, his arousal, reaching out to her, fueling her own.

She had no intention of remaining a nun all her life, and the fact that she was unaroused with any other—male or female—unless Ian was present, was beginning to irk her to no small amount.

"Courtney…" Despite his obvious arousal, Khalid leaned forward, his expression warning.

She frowned, ire heating her expression. "Khalid, as much as your concern is appreciated, it is unwarranted. I never do anything I believe will harm me more than I am willing to be harmed. I am not Melissa Gaines." And she was growing tired of the other woman haunting the relationship she knew she could have with Ian. "I am not willing to lose every dream I've had in my life because of her destructiveness. *I*, Khalid, will do whatever it takes to make Ian see that. But never, ever, will I do more than my own conscience, or decided lack of boundaries, is comfortable with."

She was not an immature, psychotic, manipulating nutcase. She was simply a woman in love with a man who would walk away rather than risk the possibility that his hungers were destructive. A man, haunted by a death he had no hand in, a hunger he could not deny he felt, and one whose loneliness filled every part of his soul. That loneliness, that haunted ache she had glimpsed in his eyes for so long, was breaking her heart.

She needed to see laughter there. She wanted to see warmth and love. She needed to see his acceptance of her and of himself.

It was an ambitious plan, she had known that all along. There was a high chance of failure, though she refused to accept that it could happen.

"You could be a very scary woman, Courtney." His lips quirked in a gentle smile as she tossed back the rest of her whisky.

"And so I should be," she sighed as she glanced at Alyssa, meeting her reflective stare with a glare.

"I never thought otherwise." Alyssa held her hands up in surrender. "But we aren't the ones you need to convince. And we won't be the ones to hurt if the convincing doesn't work, Courtney. Ian is a dear friend of mine, and I count you as the same. Khalid and I will worry regardless of our faith in your sanity…" A smile tipped her lips. "Or your lack of it."

"Some days, where Ian is concerned, I'm all for the insanity bit," Courtney sighed, the nervous excitement running through her veins creating a hyper-energy that was difficult to tamp down.

She glanced back at Khalid, noting the tension in his large body, the obvious arousal. He was anticipating Ian's reaction to what was to come as much as she was, though for different reasons.

As he lifted the bottle of whisky he had brought to the table to refill her glass, Thom approached from his side. Leaning close, he murmured something to Khalid before turning and moving away once again.

"Okay, ladies." A gleam of anticipation filled his gaze. "Ian just pulled into the driveway. I would say the fireworks are about to begin."

Chapter Twelve

Ian stared at the back entrance to The Club, the double wood doors with their lantern lights at the side. The stately brick surrounding it gave the entrance an imposing, by-permission-only, air. And once again Courtney had broken that long-held tradition.

What was it with women lately? First Tally and Terrie had slipped through to allow Tally to seduce Lucian and Devril in a most erotic manner. Now Courtney was taking a page out of her book and revising it enough to tempt Ian's very sanity.

What it did to him to see her there, as though she were some empress of the erotic arts, tempting him to destroy them both. And she was tempting him, in ways no other woman ever had.

He quickly controlled the slight smile that would have curved his lips at the thought. She was a wildcat. She took every caress, every touch and turned it back on him, accepting every adventure he introduced her to with a hunger that never failed to surprise him. She accepted him so easily, that the firm control he had held over his deeper hungers, was slowly slipping.

She made him smile. She made the haunting loneliness he had lived with so many years dissipate. She made him want to believe…and believing was the most destructive thing he could do. For both of them.

Taking a deep breath, he stepped from the back of the limo, staring at the doors to The Club with a sense of fatalism. She was there, in the very heart of all he was. The rumormongers had nicknamed them Trojans for their dominance and their habits of sharing their women. But it went so much deeper than that. It was a part of them, who they were, what they were, and the often overriding concerns that lifestyle brought. It wasn't just any woman who could deal with the fact that her husband or lover needed to tie her up, use exotic toys on her, or allow other men to watch or touch what should be primarily his.

It went beyond possessiveness though. Not that Ian wouldn't kill the man who dared to touch Courtney without his implicit permission. Club member or not, the results wouldn't be pretty.

He shook his head. Realizing instantly that he was already accepting the fact that he couldn't hold out against her much longer. There was nothing left but the prayer that some part of the past affection would survive this new relationship when she realized it wasn't really what she wanted and that he had destroyed the innocence that was so much a part of her.

She wouldn't be the first.

Kia Stanton's sense of betrayal and fury wasn't necessarily unfounded when her husband had surprised her with his desires. Carl should have revealed his sexual tastes to her before their marriage. It had destroyed a relationship that might have worked had he been honest in the beginning.

Courtney lacked the boundaries other women did. She amazed him on a daily basis, with her view of the world, her acceptance of things she had no experience with, not just sexually, but life in general. She never made judgments, and always tried to understand each side of the coin.

She could handle his hungers.

He grimaced at the part of his sexuality that insisted that she was strong enough, hungry enough, to accept his needs. That her sexuality, her sense of self would never be threatened by the desires that ate at him.

And another part of him saw nothing but Melissa, her eyes gazing sightlessly beyond him, that damning letter lying by her side. All he could feel then was the horror, the fury, the guilt… He should have known. He should have been more careful…

"Mr. Sinclair, the door was locked." The doors swung open to reveal Matthew's dour countenance. "I locked it myself and checked it before I left. I have no idea who aided her in gaining entrance."

Khalid had. Ian wasn't stupid. He knew the other man was chomping at the bit to test Courtney's control.

"Don't worry about it, Matthew, she would have found a way in no matter the measures taken against her." He slipped his coat off as Matthew closed the doors behind them, his gaze going instantly to the closed portals of the social room beyond.

Something surged in his bloodstream. A sense of expectation, an electrified arousal. The static charge had the hairs lifting along his nape as the ache in his cock intensified. His erection tightened, his body heated, and it took a long, indrawn breath to clear the haze of lust suddenly filling his head.

Spank me, Uncle Ian… Her voice teasing, her eyes holding a gleam of untamed laughter.

God yes! Make it hurt, just a little more, Ian. Just a little more… Her screams of unabashed pleasure and sexual pain echoed in his head as he watched the small, tight entrance of her ass bloom open for his thick cock.

I won… Her unsteady laughter as they collapsed on the bed night before, drowsy, replete, the sexual battle for control still considered a draw. Ian wasn't satisfied with a draw.

Shaking his head, his jaw tightened as he forced himself to move to the doors. All he had to do was stalk to her and drag her out. No matter who stood around her… The doors opened. No matter what she was doing…

God have mercy on his soul…

Ian came to a resounding stop, shock gathering in the pit of his belly, his dick nearly pushing through his slacks as he felt his eyes widen, his lips parting in surprise.

It wasn't possible. He wasn't seeing it.

The outfit itself was control-destructive, but he could have withstood it. Ian was known for his control. And the wicked red short skirt and top, though incredibly tempting, could have been resistible.

But the rest…

He felt his mouth dry, then water, a haze of lust enveloping him, searing him as he watched Alyssa Hampstead behind her, her lips lowering to Courtney's bare shoulder, her teeth raking the flesh as her hands slowly parted the buttons on the vest Courtney wore.

Dark brown eyes flared with a heat of their own as his gaze locked with his lover's. Lust, impossibly hot, hungry, demanding, flashed in her eyes a second before the vest parted, revealing the swollen, hard-tipped mounds beneath.

He couldn't breathe. Breathing wasn't an option. He was too concerned with his eroding control to worry about breathing. Besides, if he breathed, he might have to blink, then he would miss…

"Fuck…" The long, drawn-out hiss was accompanied by the muttered groans and growls of the other men scattered about, watching as Alyssa moved around Courtney, bending, her pale pink lips opening as Courtney's hand lifted to cup her own breast and guide her nipple to the other woman's mouth.

Soft female lips puckered around the turgid nipple as Courtney almost stumbled, reaching for the edge of the table as Alyssa obviously nipped at the tender bud.

Ian was barely aware he was moving. He had to be breathing, because he had the strength to walk—no, stalk. Distantly he was aware of the intent building inside him as he moved behind Courtney, his fingers wrapping around her braid as he pulled her head back to his shoulder, his arm going around her waist to steady her as a strangled, greedy moan left her lips.

"She likes the pain, Alyssa," he growled, knowing he was cursed forever. "Do it right."

Alyssa's cool blue eyes were warm with arousal as a smile tugged at her suckling lips, but she did as he urged. And she let him watch.

Her lips pulled back from her teeth, giving him the perfect view of Courtney's hard little nipple, the areola darkening, as Alyssa tugged at it, her tongue washing over it.

"Ian... Oh God..." Courtney stared up at him, her body drawn tight, lust nearly turning her eyes black as he stared down at her.

His hand moved from her waist to her opposite breast as her hands gripped his lower arms. He gripped her nipple with thumb and forefinger, milking it forcefully as her eyes glazed with the sensations.

Wild. Untamed. She was the most beautiful creature he had ever seen in his life. But this wasn't what he wanted for her. Another woman, no matter how erotic the sight, couldn't bring her the pleasure that Ian knew another man could.

"Khalid." His voice sounded torn from his throat as he continued to stare at Courtney.

"Yes, Ian." Khalid's darkly accented voice was harsh with arousal.

"I require a third."

"With pleasure, Ian."

He heard the scrape of the chair as Alyssa slowly drew back, her gaze flickering as it met his. He would deal with her later. She knew, understood well, the only thing that would break his control. There were a few set boundaries that most women would never cross, especially in front of their men. This was one of them. It was highly erotic, in small doses, captivating.

Ian kept his hold on Courtney, her head drawn back to his shoulder, her eyes heavy-lidded now, her breathing harsh as Khalid came around the table.

"Do you like being watched, baby?" he asked her, flickering a glance at Khalid as he began to kneel before her. "Do you feel all those hungry eyes, watching you, their dicks hard, imagining what it's like to be inside your hot little pussy or your sucking mouth?"

A startled, harsh scream left Courtney's lips as she felt broad, calloused hands smoothing her skirt upward over her thighs. She was shaking in Ian's arms, staring up at him, caught by the midnight blue of his eyes, the sexual intensity, the satisfaction beginning to edge his expression.

She jerked against him, desperate to get closer as she felt the lust boiling in her body, soaking the flesh of her cunt.

Yes, she could feel the eyes, feel the arousal, the heat building around them as sweat began to dampen her body. As the skirt moved past the crotch of her panties, she felt Ian unlocking her fingers from his arms, his hands manacling her wrists as he drew them behind her back.

Khalid's fingers whispered over the wet silk between her thighs.

"I want you to come for us," he whispered, his head lowering until his lips were at her ear. "You want to be brave and bold, sweetheart? You want to know what it means to be my woman, to be a part of everything I am? Then watch them, let them see how perfectly you match my lusts."

Her eyes opened, dazed, surrounded by pleasure as Khalid slid her panties down her legs.

They were watching. She had forgotten how many men there were in the room. Surely no more than half a dozen, but they were all watching the live show as Khalid spread her thighs and moved closer.

She orgasmed the instant his tongue swiped through the soaked slit, barely glancing her clitoris. Her lips opened on a soundless moan, the edges of her vision darkening as a fist-punch of sensation slammed through her womb.

Ian chuckled, Khalid merely cupped her inner thigh and lifted her leg to give his lips greater access.

"I may have to spank you for coming so easily," he threatened her. "Maybe you need that little edge of pain to stay focused. Is that what it is, baby? Just a little, to keep you on edge."

No. No… She shuddered, tremors of sensation tearing through her as she felt the fingers of Ian's free hand moving along the shallow crevice of her ass.

If he did that, she wouldn't survive. She couldn't survive this much excitement as well as that edge.

"Watch them," he whispered at her ear as he began to draw the cream flowing from her pussy, back to the tight entrance of her ass. "Are they jacking off, Courtney? Are they getting pleasure from watching you scream in orgasm, watching your pleasure fill your face?"

A few were. She fought to breathe as she picked out the ones who sat back in their chairs, their cocks gripped in their hands, stroking themselves as Ian began to lubricate the entrance to her ass with her own juices. At the same time, Khalid, demon that he was, was slowly licking around her clit, sucking at the bare, sensitive lips as his fingers circled the ultra-sensitive opening to her pussy.

"I should bend you over this table and fuck you here and now." Her ass bloomed open over two broad fingers as a bolt of lust shook her body. "Like that idea? Do you, baby?"

She writhed against him, fighting to drive his fingers deeper inside her as she felt Khalid begin to enter her vagina with two of his as well.

"Do you want to be fucked, Courtney?" he growled. "Here and now?"

"Yes," she screamed the need exploding through her. "Fuck me, Ian."

"Maybe I should let them fuck you," he snapped. "Should I stand back, Courtney? Hold you or merely watch as they take turns working their dicks up your pussy?"

She jerked in shock.

"No." She tried to twist in his arms, held firm by the combined efforts of both him and Khalid. "You won't. I know you won't."

She liked the eyes watching her, the sense of the forbidden, the heat building around them. She could feel his anger though, his loss of control as he fought the emotional as well as the physical needs. She had broken his control. But she had done it in a manner that he would definitely punish her for.

She shrieked as his fingers buried up her ass.

"And you won't, either," he snarled. "Not without me. Not without my permission. Never."

"You bastard!" she cried then, furious that he would feel the need to declare a limit already understood by them. "Do you think I'd be here fighting for you if I desired another fucking man?" She arched, screaming, as Khalid's fingers suddenly filled her as well. "Damn you, Ian. I have to have you to get wet. How the fuck am I supposed to come without you?"

As though the furious words broke what was left of the threads of his control, he angled her head to him, lowering his until his lips could take her in a kiss that rocked her mind. She knew only touch, fingers thrusting inside her anus, her pussy, hungry lips suckling at her clit, her tongue as Ian restrained her in his arms.

"Damn you," he growled, his voice a hoarse, dark growl as the thrusting fingers, the pleasure and edge of pain, swirled within her bloodstream, sending her crashing into another explosive orgasm. "I tried. I fucking tried, Courtney. More than you know..."

He pulled back from her as Khalid followed, holding her close until the other man stepped back, before he swung her in his arms and strode from The Club.

"Get the door." He stood aside as the other man stepped easily in front of them and opened the door before following Ian through the dim hallway.

Courtney fought to breathe, her hands gripping his neck as shuddering aftershocks of her orgasm whipped through her system.

Focusing wasn't high on her list of priorities. She could hear Ian's breathing, hard and heavy, the sound of his heartbeat thundering in his chest. Every nerve of her body was sensitized, her mind clouded with passion, love and lust. And though she knew, that for the moment anger filled his system with the same desperation that the lust held, it was an anger born of fear. A fear he would lose soon, she prayed. Because until he did, there wasn't so much as a hope left for the future she had always dreamed of.

Chapter Thirteen

Courtney could not have envisioned the sheer sexual animal she was letting loose when she plotted to break Ian's control. This wasn't a man focused merely on submission, nor was he focused simply on torturing her or tormenting her.

It was the pleasure. For Ian, it was the sheer fun, the intensity, the sometimes playful teasing that went along with it. He didn't want an easy conquest. Which was a good thing, because she had no intention of being easy at any time in her life. If he wanted it, he was going to have to fight for it.

As the bedroom door opened, she jerked from his hold, surprising him with her determination to be free then wheeling away from both men.

The door closed with a subtle snick as Ian's fingers went to his shirt.

"Changing your mind?" he drawled.

He should know better.

Courtney allowed a slow smile to curve her lips as she glanced at both men, watching them undress, seeing the smooth coordination they used in getting ready.

"Done this often have you?" she asked as they shed the last of their clothing at nearly the same time.

"Often enough." Ian's hand went to his erection, his fingers curling around it as he stroked it slowly.

Khalid opted to lean against the heavy chest, crossing his arms as he watched her with a smile.

"She's going to make us work for it, Khalid," Ian informed the other man as Courtney played with her braid, opting for an air of innocence as she kept a close eye on her lover.

Oh, he was trying to be sneaky.

She moved in the opposite direction, further from the bed, careful to note where the furniture was in the bedroom and the best way to use it to her advantage.

"Did you expect her to give in easily, Ian?" Khalid was obviously still amused at both of them.

"I'm going to spank you, Courtney," he promised her, his voice lowering to a dark, rich pitch. "I'm going to rip that skirt from your body and paddle you until you come from the spanking alone."

"Oh, Ian," she shivered in exaggerated fear. "Surely you wouldn't."

Ian narrowed his eyes on her, though he felt an unwilling smile quirk his lips.

She thought she was playing them. She thought she could maneuver, scheme and plot until all things went her way.

He loved that about her. Loved how she pitted herself against him at every opportunity, challenged his dominance and his determination to make her surrender.

She was strong. It had taken him a while to see that, taken him a while to separate the past and the present, the innocence and the hunger.

Not that he wasn't terrified of hurting her. He was, more than he wanted to admit. The thought of losing her, of losing the unique, unconditional acceptance she gave him now terrified him more than the thought of her being unable to handle his hungers. If anyone could handle him, it was Courtney.

If any woman could have a hope of matching his lusts and of keeping up with him, then it was this woman, staring back at him with a challenge in her eyes and a smirk on her lips.

His Courtney.

She had always been his in one way or the other.

He shook the thoughts away. The emotion. Why worry himself with it now, when she was standing before him nearly naked, promise and determination glittering in her eyes as her gaze flickered to his erection.

There would be time later. Besides, she knew he cared for her. There was no denying that. He had always cared for her.

Courtney watched warily as Khalid moved, though he merely walked to the high chest and opened the top drawer. The drawer contained many adult toys, selected, Ian had assured her, just for her.

She hadn't yet had a chance to check out its contents.

"Suggestions, Ian?" Khalid drawled.

"The restraints are already on the bedposts." He smiled slowly as Courtney glanced at the slender chains on one post. "Get whatever you think you might use." His smile widened. "And the large tube of lubrication. She's going to be busy tonight."

Her buttocks tightened.

"Hope you hadn't intended to go shopping for a while, Courtney," Khalid commented as though it was the weather they were discussing as he began to pull items from the drawer. "Walking might be difficult."

She caught Ian moving from the corner of her eye and shifted again, drawing closer to the large chair several feet from where she stood.

"Perhaps I've changed my mind about all this sharing stuff," she announced as Ian paused.

She shot him a deliberately wide-eyed look.

"Really?" He arched his brow mockingly.

"Oh yes." She nodded emphatically. "Alyssa was sooo good, Ian. Perhaps I'd like to trade you in?"

His eyes glinted with mirth. It was amazing, seeing that laughter, this playful, dominant side that she was only now experiencing.

"We'll have to see about that." His hand lifted from his erection as he moved in on her then.

Laughing, she dodged to the side, intending to put the chair between them, to hold him off for just a few seconds longer. She wasn't nearly quick enough. Before she could do more than gasp he had her, pulling her arms behind her back and pushing her upper body over the back of the chair.

Interesting.

She watched, wide-eyed as Khalid began to move toward them, a wicked grin on his lips as her belly braced against the low back.

"Shame on you, Courtney." Her skirt proved little hindrance and was dispensed with quickly. Then a heavy hand landed on her ass as she struggled in Ian's grip. "Stay still. I want to watch this pretty little ass turn red for me."

A cry escaped her lips as his hand landed again, lower this time, creating a fiery warmth between her pussy and her ass as he toed her legs further apart.

"Ever had that sweet little pussy spanked, baby?" He leaned close, his breathing hard and heavy as he asked the question. "It's so naughty and wet. I think it needs to be spanked."

"Ian…" A scream tore from her throat as his palm connected with light force on the soaked, silken, bare folds of her cunt.

She went to her tiptoes, her eyes widening, gasping for breath as the blow was followed with a quick, hard thrust of his finger inside the milking depths of her pussy.

She nearly came.

She was so close, so sensitized by the earlier erotic play that she felt her womb rippling in warning.

"I don't think so." His finger retreated, his hand moving, only to land forcefully on her rear as Khalid stepped close to the chair.

His cock was in line perfectly for her lips.

"Open your mouth," Ian growled hoarsely as he spanked the tender curve of her ass again. "I want to watch you take it, Courtney. Open your lips and suck his cock in."

His hand landed again. Burning pleasure-pain shot through her system as another gasp escaped, only to be replaced by the dark width of Khalid's cock. The bulging head pressed past her lips as Ian landed another small strike on her ass.

She was burning, not just from the spanking, which produced its own heat, physically and sexually, but from the lust building in her veins, flowing through her body. She could feel her juices leaking from her pussy, saturating the already wet folds and dampening her thighs.

Her tongue swiped over the hot crest of Khalid's cock, her eyes rising, meeting his as the torturous pleasure continued.

"Ian, cover her fucking eyes before I come," Khalid groaned as his gaze met hers, his expression twisting erotically. "All that damned innocence while my dick fills her mouth is too much."

Ian chuckled roughly as she shuddered, her eyes widening.

She wanted to see.

She had to see.

But she was doomed to disappointment. Within seconds Ian had transferred her wrists to Khalid's grip, the other man's cock still filling her mouth as he drew the thick black silk over her eyes, secured it, then did the same with her hands.

She was blind. Helpless.

She whimpered at the sudden mental emphasis that she was now completely in their control.

Seconds later, Khalid's cock popped from her mouth as she whimpered in disappointment, only to catch her breath as she found herself suddenly sitting in the chair.

She had expected the bed.

"Come here, baby." She jerked in startled surprise as she felt Ian pulling her forward, spreading her thighs as he came between them. She felt the rasp of the chair's upholstery against her tender rear, the feel of Ian's hair-roughened thighs as he spread hers further apart.

His lips nipped at hers as she breathed in roughly and sought more of his kiss.

She could taste the faint hint of whisky, and heat, like a summer storm. The damp stroke of his tongue igniting nerve endings she had never paid attention to at any other time.

"I want to touch you," she groaned as he licked at her lips.

"You want to make me crazy," he reprimanded her, surprising her with the edge of amusement in his voice as his hands cupped her breasts, pressing them together as he lowered his head to the stiff nipples awaiting him there.

Courtney arched closer, shaking with the deepening arousal as whimpers of need passed her lips as he licked them. His tongue was damp, hot. Her nipples so sensitive that the lightest stroke had her shaking from the pleasure.

"She's beautiful, Ian." Khalid's husky, heavily accented voice was a whisper of hunger at her side. His voice was huskier, lower, pleasure filling it.

"Yes, she is," Ian agreed a second before his tongue swiped over her nipples again, drawing a low moan of exquisite pleasure from her.

"She's really horny, too," she informed them both, her tone one of desperation. "Could we do something about this now?"

Had she shocked him?

She felt him still against her for a long moment, then his lips covered a nipple, his teeth nipping, his lips drawing on her as fire began to sizzle in the pit of her stomach. Her head fell back against the chair, her feet bracing on the floor as she arched closer, desperate to press her pussy against him, for the friction needed to ease the building fury raging inside her.

"Open." A thumb ran across her lips.

Courtney was under no illusions to what was coming. Her mouth opened, wide, a muttered groan passing her lips as Khalid sank the flared crest of his cock past her lips. It was thick, hot, filling her mouth as she closed on it again and began to suck with the same devastating, teasing strokes Ian was using on her nipples.

She found that her sense of taste became elevated with the dark blindfold. Khalid's cock was just as thick as Ian's, though the head was more tapered than rounded, and the taste was wilder. A mix of lust and dry, heated nights, much like the land he came from.

Let them tease. She could tease back. Bound and blindfolded be damned. She had other ways to push them as well.

Her tongue mimicked Ian's, drawing a ragged groan from Khalid's throat as he pressed heavily between her lips, drawing back as her tongue lashed against the sensitive underside, then pressing forward again as she sucked at the burgeoning head.

He tasted of male heat and lust. A heady flavor when combined with the stimulus Ian was applying to her breasts.

She heard both men moan, the sound amplified, the desire different in each voice. Khalid was all lust and passion. But Ian, his voice was rougher, deeper, filled with an emotion that made her tremble with hope.

"She's a wicked tease, my friend." Khalid's voice was rough as he shafted her lips with obviously frayed control.

Courtney felt Ian shift, one hand moving from her breast. A second later, a scream echoed around Khalid's cock as she felt two fingers plunge deep inside her cunt, separating the pulsing tissue as fire lanced through her womb.

Khalid held her head steady as he continued to fuck his cock in and out, past lips that fought to maintain suction even as she struggled to breathe. Ian's lips drew frantically at her nipple as his fingers scissored inside her vagina, stroking alternate nerve endings and forcing her quivering flesh into submission.

And he wasn't letting her come.

Deliberately, backing off, surging forward, stroking, tormenting, he kept her on the edge of her arousal as light began to swirl within her vision, proof that the intensity of the sensations was destroying her mind.

Suddenly, Khalid's cock popped free of her mouth, his laughter drifting around her as she uttered a protesting cry and attempted to follow for more. Ian's fingers slid from her pussy and she was suddenly left devoid of any touch.

"That was mean." She shifted her legs, searching for Ian with her feet as she felt the cool air of the bedroom caressing her overheated flesh. "Come on, Ian, you don't have to torture me."

But she knew he would.

She was looking forward to it.

"Come on, baby."

She gasped as Ian's voice whispered at her ear again. He helped her from the chair, steadying her when her legs quivered beneath her, and led her to the bed.

"You've been a very bad girl, Courtney." She couldn't tell now if he was amused or serious. "You'll have to be punished for that."

Oh, hell yes. She was sure as hell hoping so.

"Ohhh, are we going to get kinky, Uncle Ian?" she teased him breathlessly then jumped, startled, as his hand landed on her ass in a burning caress.

"Be quiet, before I gag you," he ordered, his tone of voice dark, forbidding as he laid her on her stomach and released the restraint on her wrists.

Not that she had time to do much more than slip and attempt to run her palm up the thigh nearest her before they had captured both wrists once again and attached the padded cuffs to them, stretching her out in the center of the bed.

Her ankles were next, though there was quite a bit of slack in the small chains she could hear clinking together. Once they had her restrained, they began to play in earnest.

She was placed on her hands and knees, gasping, as she felt Ian move behind her while Khalid stretched out beside her, his head moving beneath her body. Almost instantly his wicked tongue began to play with her saturated pussy as his fingers found her burning nipples.

That was bad enough. That pleasure at its most extreme, simply because he absolutely refused to allow her release. But Ian, demon that he was, began to up the ante.

His hand landed on the sensitive cheek of her rear, causing her to jerk at the fiery wash of sensations it produced. She would have been more comfortable if it had hurt. Rather it singed, causing her to twist and press back for more as Khalid hummed against her pussy.

She could feel her juices pouring from her vagina as her flesh began to heat, to melt for the two men so intent on making her insane. Losing her sight had only served to emphasize that of touch, as she knew Ian meant for it to do. The lightest caress was more intense now, more destructive.

"What a pretty, sweet little ass," Ian crooned as he parted the curves. "Stay still, baby, let me get you ready." He patted her rear as she felt the tapered end of the tube of lubrication gel being inserted into her rear.

She arched, moaning deeply at the sensation of the wand penetrating that dark channel.

"I do nothing but live to hear you scream in pleasure anymore," he growled, and by the tone of his voice, that thought didn't seem to please him.

"I live to scream for you—" She arched wildly as she felt Khalid's tongue curling around her clit as the cool sensation of the gel began to fill her ass.

She was breathing harshly now, her hips twisting as she fought to drive her clit further inside his teasing mouth.

Ian's hand landed on her ass again, harder.

"Stay still, little cat," he ordered harshly. "It's going to be a very long time before you get to come again. Save your strength."

In that moment she began to suspect that perhaps Ian hadn't yet shown her all the different facets of his sexuality. His voice was darker, deeper, the pleasure throbbing just beneath the surface was thicker than ever before.

The nozzle was removed from her anus then, sliding free of her as she moaned heavily at the rasp against the tender nerve endings. Khalid slid from beneath her body as Ian moved from behind her, lying along her side and beginning to play in earnest.

"Come here, baby." Ian's lips found hers, an amazingly tender kiss as his tongue licked at her lips, his hands burying in her hair as she cried out at the overwhelming pleasure.

Because for all Ian's tenderness, his gentle kiss, Khalid had now turned into her tormentor. Moving behind her, his hand began a rhythmic series of light slaps against her rear, alternating every few seconds with an underhanded burning smack to her sensitive pussy.

She tried to breathe, to scream against the sensations ripping through her, but Ian's lips caught each cry, his encouraging moans fueling the haze of lust surrounding her.

As his tongue slid past her lips once again, Khalid speared two fingers deep inside her pussy. As Ian licked at her lips, Khalid curled his fingers and stroked against the ultra-sensitive flesh high within the very depths of her vagina.

She was shaking, torn between ecstasy and torment, certain there was no way to survive the sensations. With each slap to her tender flesh, the flames burning over her body became worse, sensitizing her, awakening nerve endings she had no idea she possessed as the tension in her body began to build higher.

Her womb ached, burned. Her clit was so sensitive that even the air caressing it was too much for the delicate mass of nerves, yet it wasn't enough. They kept her hanging on a precipice so sharp, she could feel the bite of hunger growing with each second.

"Ian..." She screamed his name as she felt Khalid parting the cheeks of her ass, the broad crest of his cock smoothing along the crevice.

"Now we get kinky, baby," he growled, his voice darker as she felt him come to his knees beside her. "Now I watch. Do you remember the times you saw me with your maids, sweetheart? What was I doing?"

She whimpered at the memory.

"I was watching, watching how easily they accepted any pleasure I chose for them after we had finished driving them as high as possible. But I didn't have to drive you, did I, baby." His whisper was edged with mingled awe and lust. "You were right there waiting on me, weren't you?"

"God, yes," she cried as she felt Khalid's cock tuck at the opening to her ass.

"There's a good girl," Ian crooned, his hand moving to her hair, pulling the braid to the side as he turned her head. "Open for him, Courtney. Let him in. Let me see just how brave and beautiful you really are."

It wasn't his words that caused her to push against the heavy erection seeking entrance, it was his broad hand landing heavily against her rear as his cock smoothed over her lips.

Her mouth opened as her anus relaxed. At once, both cocks entered their desired destinations she felt the last of any sanity she possessed begin to unravel. The wide crest of Ian's erection pierced her mouth as fire began to bloom in her ass, streaking through the delicate nerve endings as it encompassed her cunt, her throbbing clit. She was a mass of needy, burning flesh now, accepting whatever they were willing to give.

It seemed to last forever, that first penetration of her body by Khalid's cock. Stroking, working slow and easy into the entrance as she fought for a harder, deeper stroke.

She would have begged for it, but Ian's cock was filling her mouth, stealing any chance to speak, to beg, to scream.

"I'll not last long, Ian," Khalid groaned heavily as her muscles flexed around him, struggling to accept the width it was taking. "Save the dramatic stuff for later, dammit."

Ian grunted at the request, but drew back slowly, dragging his cock from her mouth as he released the restraints from her body, then lay down beside her.

"Oh God..." The scream ripped from her throat as she was lifted, pushed further onto the cock impaling her ass as Khalid brought her back, flush against his chest and Ian slid beneath her.

Tremors of agonizing pleasure were attacking her nerve endings as she clenched around the erection penetrating her ass, stretching her, burning her as she fought to adjust to it. But she was given no chance to adjust.

Ian's hands adjusted her legs over his, then gripped her waist as they began to slowly lower her.

"Ian, I can't stand it..." She jerked in their grip, feeling Khalid's cock stroke, shift and caress the hypersensitive flesh it penetrated.

"Too bad, baby." She felt his cock press against the opening of her pussy, Khalid buried deep inside her, remaining still as she once again knelt on the bed, only now, Ian lay beneath her, prepared to penetrate the ultra-tight recesses of her pussy.

"Now, you take all I am, Courtney," he growled. "Everything. Starting now..."

If she had known pleasure before, it was nothing compared to what Ian began to show her. With Khalid buried deep in her ass, Ian began to work his cock into her pussy, its narrow channel protesting the burning impalement of Ian's erection. Short, easy thrusts worked her open, made a way for the heavy weight of his cock, and sent her senses careening.

She could hear herself begging, pleading, but she wasn't certain what she begged for. As he worked his cock inside her, his lips surrounded a nipple, his teeth rasping, nipping the tender peak as hard hands held her hips in place until he finally, agonizingly, slid every broad inch of his cock inside her.

The dual penetration was nothing like the toys they had played with. Her senses were spinning now as they began to move within her. Four hands stroked her, caressed her, two voices urged her on in her pleasure, as two heavy, wide cocks began to fuck her with hungry demand.

She could feel the wave of her climax building, though she realized the slow, measured pace the two men were using would never throw her quickly into climax. Once more they were torturing her, building the tension inside her until she was certain she would never survive it.

"Feel, Courtney," he whispered as he tucked her head against his chest, his lips at ear. "The pleasure and the pain, the fire and ice. Feel it, baby, let it have all of you. Let me have all of you."

He already had her.

Her fingers clenched into his shoulders as she fought to hold on, though there was no fear of her moving any more than the two men taking her wished. Their cocks burned inside her body as they thrust heavily into her, the rhythm building, each stroke sending the clawing, electrical impulses of pleasure soaring within her.

She couldn't breathe. She couldn't exist. She felt the explosion begin in her belly, felt it expand, detonate, overtake her as her soul began to melt in the conflagration overtaking her.

Ian and Khalid's voices were lost in the madness as the orgasm surged through her. Surged through her and refused to stop. Over and over it convulsed her body, as each stroke triggered another, sent her surging, screaming, then repeated the process until she felt something inside her fly free.

The final, shattering release ripped through her as Ian exploded inside her, filling her with the white-hot wash of his semen and Khalid shuddered above her, obviously in the throes of his own release.

Sandwiched between them, drifting in a sea of lost reason, Courtney felt, for once, sated, all her senses satisfied as she heard Ian's rumbling growl of complete male satiation at her ear. Something she hadn't heard before. His voice, whispering her name, a tremor—perhaps of acknowledgement that she was his match—vibrating deep within it.

Exhaustion filled her. Like a person starving, then sated, she closed her eyes to glory in the relief.

"I think she handled that pretty well." Khalid collapsed beside Ian as he cuddled Courtney against his chest, his face still buried in her neck.

"Fuck off." Ian's voice was lazy, sated, thick with emotion.

Khalid wondered if he would face the emotion though.

He chuckled as though such heavy thoughts weren't a part of his after-release mentality.

"You've overdramatized what happened before, Ian." He scratched lazily at his chest. "Stubborn bastard."

Ian grunted as he turned, placing Courtney between them as Khalid leaned up to dispose of the condom he had donned before taking the woman. As much as Ian liked to share, he didn't like his playground drenched in another man's seed.

"She's so damned wild she amazes me," Ian sighed as he turned her to her back, chuckling as she growled irritably at being moved.

"Wild as the wind," Khalid agreed, watching as Ian's fingers curled around a still flushed, swollen breast.

Her nipples were still hard, the flesh of the areola darkened from her passions. She murmured appreciatively as his thumb rasped over the tip. Her eyes remained closed, but her expression was one of drowsy, returning sensuality.

"Come here, little wind." Ian sighed deeply as he pulled her into his arms then, tucking her protectively against his chest. "Sleep. For now."

Khalid wondered if his friend had any idea how revealing that move was. Never, with all the women he had seen Ian share, had he been prone to cuddle them when the sex was over. And never had his voice been so deep, so filled with emotion. He loved the girl, but admitting it would be as hard as finally sharing her had been. Ian was set within the life he had deemed would be his years before. And Courtney, soft, sweet, inherently innocent, was everything he had ever feared of corrupting. Realizing that Courtney saw it as a part of the love she felt for him, a part of herself, not corruption, would be the hardest battle the two would face.

Khalid sent a prayer to God that his friend would realize this before it was too late.

Chapter Fourteen

Courtney came to awareness slowly the next morning. Beneath her, Ian slept, his arms holding her as she lay draped over his chest. Beside them, Khalid breathed deeply as well, separated from them by nearly a foot as he sprawled naked on his stomach.

The night before had been…intense. Hours upon hours of sexual greed whipping like lightning around them.

How many different ways had they taken her? She couldn't remember. All she remembered was Ian's dark voice, urging her higher as each touch sent her careening over edge after edge of intensity.

He had held her as Khalid fucked her. Fucked her as Khalid held her. They had held her, lips and teeth and tongues eating at her, sending her screaming into orgasm after orgasm as she finally relinquished herself into their hands, into their hungers.

It had been an amazing experience. As though Ian had been making up for time and delayed need, he pushed every limit had had ever suspected she had. Only to learn, there were no limits.

A smile curved her lips at the thought. He was such a stubborn man.

"You should be sleeping." His hand moved over her unbound hair, stroking it lazily as he turned her over his body until she lay between him and Khalid.

She opened her eyes, staring up at him, seeing the lack of tension in his expression now.

"I kept up." She smiled up at him, daring him to deny she had.

He snorted at her declaration, his blue eyes slumberous, filled with warmth as his hands caressed down her back.

"You lost it," he charged. "You didn't make an hour."

"But I kept up," she reiterated, a smile tugging at her lips.

"That you did." His smile reached his eyes as his thumb smoothed over her swollen lips. "You definitely kept up."

And her body ached in remembrance, in areas she didn't know could ache.

"I'll run Khalid off after breakfast." His hand cupped her cheek. "We'll have a nice, quiet day alone. If you like, perhaps dinner tonight at The Club." Wry amusement touched his eyes. "I may as well give Matthew permission to allow you there, it's obvious you can't be trusted to follow the rules."

"What rules?" She widened her eyes innocently, keeping her voice soft, quiet. The atmosphere of intimacy was a balm to the worry that had filled her for so many weeks.

A grin curved his lips.

"You are a wild woman."

Her heart exploded as he leaned forward, his eyes open, touching his lips to hers as though in benediction. The touch was rife with unvoiced emotion, a tender, almost tentative caress that had her heart filling with joy.

He would need more time, she knew. Accepting her as she was, pushing aside his past and giving her all of himself hadn't been easy. He would have to feel his way a bit longer before he allowed his heart the same freedom.

She could wait. She had endless patience, and for now, her love for him sustained her. She had pushed past this first, difficult hurdle. The rest would come in time. Because she knew Ian, no temptation, no hunger, no need was strong enough to break his will, unless he wanted to be broken.

"Oh God, I need a shower. All this sappy crap is getting sticky." Khalid's amused voice vibrated drowsily beside them.

Courtney rolled her eyes as Ian sighed.

"I could have told you he was a problem," he informed her with gentle mockery. "You'll wish he hadn't been present when you pulled your little shenanigans last night."

Satisfaction blazed within her.

"Was I complaining?" she asked, and cuddled closer as she ran her hand down his chest to the early morning erection awaiting her.

Heat filled his expression then. Acceptance.

Her fingers curled around the impressive width, a murmur of pleasure leaving her lips as she began to make her way down, her lips caressing his chest as his hands tangled in her hair.

Not to be outdone, Khalid was joining in the games. She felt his lips at her lower back, his fingers traveling up her thigh.

"She's tender," Ian gasped as her teeth rasped his stomach. "Be gentle, Khalid."

She felt Khalid pause, as though the harsh order were an unusual one.

"Always, Ian," he promised as his fingers whispered over her wet, swollen pussy. "As gentle as a spring rain."

As she neared the delectable erection awaiting her consumption, a loud, furious commotion outside the bedroom door had her eyes widening in alarm.

"I don't give a goddamn what his orders are, get the hell out of my way!" The harsh order was accompanied by other voices, raised in protest, in alarm.

"Fuck. Fuck." Ian jumped from the bed, jerking the comforter over her as Khalid followed suit, grabbing at their pants and rushing to dress.

The bedroom door slammed open to reveal her father.

He was furious.

His gray eyes trained on Courtney with narrow-eyed fury, his still muscular body shaking with his anger.

"Daddy, what are you doing?" Shocked, surprised at the rage that seemed to whip through the room, she stared back at him, kneeling in the center of the bed as she held the comforter around her. "Why didn't you tell me you were coming?"

Her mother came around him, obviously upset, her dark eyes meeting Courtney's in sympathy.

"I'm sorry, darling," she sighed wearily. "I had no idea where we were going until it was too late, and he stole my cell phone." She cast her husband a disgruntled look.

"Courtney, get out of here." Her father's voice vibrated with his anger.

He looked like a raging bull, his face flushed, his eyes glittering as they trained on Ian.

"Why?" She rose slowly from the bed, careful to keep the blanket around her as she moved to stand in front of Ian.

Unfortunately, Ian wasn't having it.

"Go to your room, Courtney." He backed up her father's order with a gentle demand of his own as he stood carefully distant from her.

"I will not." She stared between the two men, her brows tightening in a frown as she glared at her father. "You couldn't have waited until we were at least dressed? Or allowed the butler to inform Ian you were here?"

"And miss this?" His hand swung out to encompass the bedroom as he sneered the question. "Not likely."

"Miss what?" she snapped back, her own anger brewing now. "What were you missing, Father? Something that was entirely none of your business."

"Courtney." Ian stepped closer to her then, drawing her to him as her father clenched his fists, his lips flattening furiously. "Let me handle this."

"There is nothing to handle." She shook her head, uncertain, unwilling to leave the room while her father was so furious.

She had rarely seen him so enraged. Each time she had, someone had ended up hurt. Not her or her mother, never anyone undeserving. Until now.

"I can't believe this," her father snarled. "Goddammit, Ian, you were my best friend. I trusted you with her."

Courtney could feel her own fury, her own pain rising with each word out of her father's lips. He had raised her to think for herself, to be a person separate from him and her mother. He had praised her willingness to always see beyond what her eyes detected, and now, he could see no more than the fact that Ian had taken her to his bed.

"What does your friendship have to do with anything, Father?" she questioned him angrily. "*This* is none of your business."

"You're my daughter," he snapped.

"I'm a grown woman, not a child," she reminded him, fighting to hold back her tears, feeling Ian, despite his physical closeness, drawing further away from her.

"Courtney." He lowered his head to her ear, his voice soothing, cool. "Let me handle this."

Her breath hitched in her chest at the tone. Once again, Ian had drawn within himself, and she feared this new development might be a hurdle she couldn't defeat.

"No." She shook her head, turning to him, staring up at him, seeing the chill in his eyes, his regret, as fear began to sink deep inside her heart. "He's just angry, Ian. I'll talk to him…"

"The hell you will," her father snarled behind her. "Ian can discuss this one."

She could see the pain Ian was hiding so carefully. What had she done? He counted her father as one of his few, true friends, and now she had come between them. Without the time it would have taken for Ian to see how he truly loved her, he was being torn between his friendship and his lusts.

"Daddy." She turned back slowly, staring beseechingly at the father who had always praised her, spoiled her, taught her to fight for what she believed in. "Daddy, please don't do this. Please leave, just for a few moments."

She was trembling, fighting her tears as her gaze met her mother's, pleading for her help.

"Courtney, I will tell you one last time to step from this room." His voice lowered, his tone that of command. One she had never refused to obey in her life.

She was breathing harshly now, seeing everything she had fought these weeks for crumbling at her feet.

"No."

He moved toward her.

"Dane, stay the hell back from her." Before Courtney could protest, Ian had pushed her behind him, his arm holding her in place as Khalid cursed violently.

Dane stopped, glaring at the three of them.

"Do you think I would hurt my only fucking daughter?" he snarled, as Marguerita placed a delicate hand on his arm. "After the hell I survived thinking I had lost her and Marguerite both, you think I would ever raise my fucking hand against her?"

"Dane, don't let the past repeat itself with Courtney," she begged him then. "Please, let us leave the room for now. This can wait. Please do not do this thing."

"Dammit, Marguerita, she's our daughter. Do you think he didn't know what he was doing…?"

"Do you think she didn't," Marguerita argued furiously then. "You are making the same decisions my family made for us, Dane. Denying her a choice. Only your methods are different."

Courtney laid her head against Ian's back, a sob shaking her body as she fought to hold back the sound.

Ian would never, ever forgive her now.

"I will remind you, wife," he snapped. "It was not your best friend, nor mine, who betrayed *us*. But I'll be damned if I'll let Ian break her heart."

"Stop," Courtney cried out raggedly, jerking away from Ian, her fists tightening in the comforter she held around her until she faced both men, blinking back the liquid pain threatening to fall from her eyes. "Do you think he tricked me into his bed?" she yelled furiously. "Don't you think he did everything to keep me from it? I seduced him—"

A sharp, mocking laugh met her words.

"You're a baby, Courtney. Ian's a hell of a lot older and more experienced. He knew how to say no."

"No." She shook her head desperately. "I love him…" She ignored Ian's flinch, knowing the damage caused by her father's arrival would be difficult to repair. She prayed it wouldn't be impossible. "Please, Father, I'm begging you…"

"And does he love you?" her father snarled, turning to Ian. "Answer me, Ian," he sneered. "Do you love her?"

Everything inside her began to crumble. The second stretched out to eternity as Ian stared back at her, regret darkening his eyes. All sound muted within the room, all but the sound of her heart as she stared back at him, her gaze locked with his, her heart breaking as she watched the denial coming.

There was such regret in his eyes. Affection, yet, it was there, the same affection that had always been in his eyes for her. But there was no love, no realization.

"I'm sorry, Courtney…" His voice was soft, filled with apology. "Your father's right. I should have denied you."

She felt something crash inside her, fragmenting. A whimper passed her lips, though she had promised herself if this day ever came, she wouldn't cry. She wouldn't regret.

Surely he just didn't realize he loved her. That was all it was, she assured herself.

"That's okay..." Her eyes were burning as she fought her tears, her sight cloudy as she fought to find a way, any way... "It can come..."

He was shaking his head, his expression closed, cold.

Oh God.

She felt her knees weakening. Felt her heart exploding in her chest.

"Go to your room while I talk to your father." His voice was cold. Final. "Nothing lasts forever, Courtney. Not even the wind."

She felt the blood leave her face. A horrible sense of unreality closed in on her, darkening the vision at the edge of her eyes, stealing the breath from her chest as she stared back at him in dazed, mind-numbing pain.

"Stupid bastard," Khalid muttered, shaking his head at Ian's response.

She turned, forced herself to tear her gaze from Ian's and to face her father once again.

He was watching her, the fury of moments before replaced with something else. Regret? Realization?

"I love him," she whispered again, feeling the single tear that escaped her control. "With everything inside me. I can forgive you this. But I won't forgive anything further. You will leave this room with me."

He opened his lips to speak.

"Please, Daddy. For me."

They clamped shut as his gaze cut to Ian, brooding, filled with anger.

"Courtney." Her mother moved forward slowly, reaching out to her, her expression twisting as Courtney flinched away.

"No." She shook her head tightly as she turned to Ian. "I'm sorry."

She was sorry her father had arrived. That she had destroyed one of the true friendships he had known. She was sorry she had pushed when she should have stayed clear. So many things she was now sorry for.

Her father was right, in so many ways. Only a child believed in fairy tales. And healing Ian, being with him, being loved by him, was the greatest of all dreams.

He stood still, staring back at her with a dark, forbidding frown.

"I'll pack." She tried to clear her throat of her tears. "I'm truly sorry, Ian."

She moved past them all, determined to hold back the tears, to gather the broken fragments of her soul together until she could find the space she needed to repair them.

Her father cursed softly as she passed him, but other than that, not a word was spoken as she slowly left the room.

The door closed behind her, leaving Ian to endure the silence and the condemning stares of those now watching him.

No matter how many times he had taken Courtney, how depraved he and Khalid had gotten the night before, the innocence that was so much a part of her had remained. She had looked at him as she always had, her eyes filled with light, with purity. As though nothing could mar the untamed spirit inside her.

But in one brief second, he had watched it die. The pain from seeing that was more debilitating than the day he had found Melissa, staring back at him in empty accusation.

"Well, I hope the two of you are quite satisfied with yourselves." Marguerita's voice was cold, furious. "You remind me of two little boys on a playground, standing off over a favored toy that belongs to neither of you."

Ian watched her silently as he tried to make sense of what he had seen in Courtney and why it was ripping his soul apart.

Why now? Why would that innocence die within her eyes as she stared back at him with such bleak pain? Surely she had known, had understood, that he had lost his ability to love years ago. Hadn't he?

"She's my daughter," Dane snapped. "If I had any clue he would touch her—"

"Oh shut up, Dane," Marguerita sighed, her voice lacking fury, but filled instead with disgust. "You refuse to admit she's a woman, not a child. You've been hiding your head in the sand for years, unwilling to admit that as she grows older, so do you. And in doing so, one day, she will leave our home for another. I knew exactly why she was coming to Ian, and what she planned to do. Had you been man enough to listen to reason the past hours I've been arguing with you, you would have understood that."

"He's too old for her—"

"She's wanted him since she was a teenager. Be damned glad she waited this long rather sneaking into his bed when she was sixteen, as she once threatened to do," she snapped, her eyes blazing as she turned back to Ian. "And I do believe you are as pathetic as any man it has ever been my misfortune to meet. Why my daughter should love one so clearly determined to be miserable for the rest of his natural life, I have no idea."

He stared back at Marguerita in surprise.

"You know, Ian." Her voice trembled as she spoke. "I remember something you told me once, after you and Dane rescued me from that hell my family consigned me too. When life was a bleak, ugly little hole I had no idea how to climb out of. You told me nothing mattered but love. Nothing was so innocent, so pure, as true love. I just watched you destroy the very thing you once said you would treasure above all things. Pure, innocent love. May God have mercy on your soul." Then she turned to her husband. "And pray he has mercy for you as well. For it will be a long time before I do. Now, I go to give what comfort I can to my daughter. If she will allow it—" Her voice broke. A reminder, that because of them, her daughter had flinched from her, unwilling to be comforted in their presence.

Ian stayed silent. He heard every word she said, felt them like knives in his gut, but all he could see, all he could truly remember was watching that purity slowly die in Courtney's gaze.

As the door slammed closed behind Marguerita, he stood, facing the man who had been his dearest friend.

Dane was watching him soberly now, the fury of moments before having dissipated in the face of his daughter's pain, and his wife's fury, perhaps. He watched Ian thoughtfully, his eyes narrowed, the cold gray depths reflective.

"Well, you two have truly managed to fuck up what began as an otherwise perfect morning." Khalid picked his shirt and shoes from the floor as he moved to the door himself. "And let me be the first to say that Marguerita summed it up quite well. You are both pathetic."

He slammed the door behind him as well, leaving Ian and Dane alone to face each other.

"She's my baby. You're my best friend." He pushed his fingers wearily through his dark blond hair as he faced Ian now. "Thinking of her, in bed…" He grimaced. "Dammit, I don't want to think of my child, my baby, doing that stuff."

Ian grunted at that.

"I won't let her take the blame." He shrugged. "As you said, I could have said no. I could have warned you and let you come after her."

"But she's an adult," Dane spoke over him. "As Marguerita keeps pointing out, she's not a child anymore."

Ian shifted uncomfortably. He wished Dane would just fucking hit him. It would help alleviate the ache growing in his chest.

"She loves you," Dane sighed as he pulled himself from the chair then. "I didn't believe it. Not when Marguerita and

Sebastian argued so fiercely. I couldn't imagine she could understand the depth of acceptance it takes to love men such as we are. But as my wife is always eager to point out, our daughter has her grace, not just my stubbornness."

Courtney was hurting.

Ian pushed his fingers through his hair as he turned from Dane, unconcerned with the other man's bitter realizations.

Damn it to hell, he could feel her hurting. As though something had ripped a hole in his soul when he watched that light die in her eyes, he could feel her pain. It hadn't lessened when she left, but had only grown stronger, affecting his breathing, his sense of reality.

Nothing lasts forever. He had made himself believe that over the years.

Nothing endures. Nothing lasts. Nothing is permanent.

But Courtney was. Her love was. From the moment he first met her, a wild little girl with big doe eyes, she had watched him with the same unabashed emotion. The same innocence.

He had carried her out of her grandparents' estate in the dead of night while Dane went after Marguerita. Her arms had been tight around his neck, her little voice whispering, "thank you", "thank you", over and over again. And from that day forward, she had watched him with that same, overwhelming innocence.

The innocence of love.

She was shameless. As honest in giving of herself as she was in how she viewed life. One of the few who endured simply because they loved.

What had he done?

Chapter Fifteen

One Month Later

The pain didn't go away.

The aching loneliness refused to abate.

And dammit, she was fucking horny and couldn't get off.

Courtney paced her room, dressed in the comfortable black cotton lounging pants and matching top. Her hair was loose, flowing down her back, the ripple of the strands against her shoulders reminding her of Ian. He had liked her hair. Many times he had wrapped it around his hand, holding her head back as he came over her, his cock working inside her as he whispered how tight, how hot she was.

She stopped at her window, staring silently into the gardens below. She couldn't cry anymore. She had cried until she felt she could fill the oceans with her tears.

There wasn't even anyone to blame, except herself. It would have been easier, she thought, if she could have hated someone else for the pain. She had known going in that making Ian realize he had a heart would be a difficult journey at best. But in her immaturity, in her own belief in herself, she had believed she could accomplish that goal.

She hadn't considered failing. And in not considering it, had not thought of the harm she could cause if she did fail.

She had hurt not just him, but her father as well. Two men who had forged a bond in pain years before were now no longer friends. The two men she loved most in the world had been irreversibly hurt by her foolish actions.

And she was alone.

A dry sob tore at her chest at the thought. She now slept alone, she wept alone.

Drawing in a deep breath she turned back to her bedroom, considering it as she had been for most of the morning. Her mother had suggested refurnishing her suite, changing it. But perhaps it was time for more.

She had lived with her parents all her life. After finishing school, she had come home, unwilling to commit herself to college at that time, eager to be the adult she thought she was. She had built her life around her dreams of Ian, and now that life no longer existed. It was time to build a new one.

It wouldn't be as fine as the one she felt she could have had with him. The laughter and heat, the sharing. She could have grown in his arms, become anything she wanted to become and still be Ian's woman. She had known that. She had thought there was time to make the decision of where her education would continue, and how she would fill her life.

Perhaps, rather than refurnishing, it was time she left instead. Time she forced herself to step away from the protection and the love her parents' home afforded her, and forge her own life.

She had a multitude of things she enjoyed. Decorating, training the horses on her father's estate for the competitions they were often entered in, she even liked the charity work she often helped her mother with. She could turn any of those into a career.

She especially enjoyed...Ian.

It seemed there were more tears after all. Another slid down her cheek as the loss threatened again to overwhelm her.

"No more tears," she chastised herself severely as she moved to her closet. "Change instead."

Change required energy. It forced one to stay busy, to push all other things to the rear and focus solely on what must be done. It was the only answer to the life she now faced. She had accepted, at least for now, until she could cope with losing everything she had believed would be hers, she would be alone. But that didn't mean she had to wallow in the pain, nor did she have to let it worsen.

She pulled a chic dark gray dress from the closet along with matching pumps. She would need her own apartment, a place of her own. Then she would enroll in college as her father kept encouraging her to do. She would slowly rebuild her life. It wasn't her dream, but it would do.

As she laid the dress over the bed, a soft knock at her bedroom door interrupted her thoughts.

"Come in," she called out, watching warily as the door opened and her father stepped into the room.

He was a handsome man for his age. Still well-developed, his sandy blond hair as thick as ever, his gray eyes turbulent. He had always been her strength as she grew up. Ready to protect her, to guide her, or merely to laugh with her. She had always believed there could never be a man more perfect than he was. Except Ian.

"Going out?" He glanced at the dress, moving further into her room as she watched him, aware that letting her go would be difficult for him.

He had so loved and spoiled her, all her life. He had taught her many of her greatest accomplishments and had cheered her on ahead of everyone else. He had taught her confidence, taught her strength. He had helped her find the best of what she was inside herself.

"Yes." She glanced at the dress, then back to him. "I'm going apartment hunting."

She didn't have to imagine how it would affect him. His eyes instantly darkened with an instinctive protest as his big body tensed. He couldn't know how hard it was for her as well, though. Leaving the only security she had known besides Ian's arms, would be one of the hardest things she had ever done.

"A rather sudden decision, isn't it?" he growled. "No one has asked you to move out."

"I know, Daddy." She smiled softly. "It's just time, I think. Perhaps it's time for college as well." She shrugged restlessly. "I can't spend my days just drifting. And after so many parties, it becomes rather boring. I…I need something more…" She glanced away from him, unwilling to look as she hurt him further.

"You can live here and go to college," he suggested.

She could, but living with her parents wouldn't accomplish the growth she needed. She needed to learn how to dream dreams that didn't include Ian. She couldn't do that here, where all her dreams of him had begun.

"No." She breathed in deeply. "I need to be on my own, I think. It's time I grow up."

How a woman who had indulged sexually as she had with Ian could utter those words, she wasn't certain. She felt ages old. And yet, as uncertain now as she had felt during the time her parents had been apart.

He lowered his head, pushing his hands forcefully into the pockets of his slacks as he nodded slowly.

"It's hard, letting you go." He cleared his throat, staring around the room as he blinked several times. Hard. "Hard to let go of the years I lost and remember you're not a baby anymore."

Courtney bit her lip and found there were many more tears. Tears she would shed later rather than now.

"You taught me to follow my heart, Father," she whispered huskily. "That's what I must do."

He nodded. Cleared his throat again.

"Ian called," he announced as his head rose.

She flinched. She couldn't help it. The pain built inside her until she was certain it would take her to her knees. He hadn't called her. Not even once.

"Is he doing well?" Any news of him was better than nothing.

She worried about him, she admitted. Though she doubted he needed her concern. She was terrified she had added more pain, more guilt to his already haunted eyes. The thought of that was nearly as painful as losing him.

"Yeah." He nodded firmly. "He sounded tired though."

She stared back at him calmly, despite the agony resonating through her.

"You're talking to him again then?"

"Yeah." He nodded again. "I was…worried about him." He shifted his shoulders uncomfortably.

She had worried as well. She talked to Khalid often, though he rarely had any real news of Ian.

"I'm glad he's well." She fought the trembling of her lips as she smiled back at him. "Now, I really need to get dressed…"

"He asked about you." His eyes met hers, a question forming there.

Pain curled through her chest, making it difficult to breathe.

"I hope you told him I was well?" Her smile wobbled as she met his gaze.

"I told him he fucking broke my daughter's heart," he finally snapped. "What the hell was I supposed to tell him, Courtney?"

"That I am well," she answered, her voice thickening with more tears. "He needs know nothing more, Father. I am alive. I am healthy. I am not suicidal. Nothing more should concern him."

He grimaced in disgust.

"You haunt this house like a ghost," he growled. "Even Sebastian is worried. The bastard wasn't supposed to break your heart."

"For pity's sake, what do you think I'm going to do?" she yelled back at him. "Did you have Ian thinking I'm going to kill myself because I couldn't gain his heart? What would make you believe I'm so weak?"

"I did no such thing," he informed her fiercely. "But that doesn't mean I can't tell him what a sorry bastard he is."

"Argh. You are as insane as any man I have ever met. It is no wonder you and Ian are so close." She threw her hands up in surrender. "First, you do not want him to be with me, now you would chastise him for *not* being with me. Make up your mind, Father, before you make yourself crazy."

He grunted at that. "He didn't have to hurt you."

"He did not hurt me." It was no more than the same argument they had fought for the past month. "I hurt me, Father, don't you understand that? I was wrong to push him..." The tears came again. "Would you just stop speaking of him? Please..."

"Why, so you can forget me?"

She stared in shock as Ian stepped into the room.

Her eyes widened as heat began to fill her body, racing through her bloodstream, chasing away the chill that held her in stasis for so many weeks.

He looked horrible. His face was haggard, lined with weariness, his deep blue eyes filled with shadows.

Her head whipped around to her father, staring at him in mute shock.

"He called from the limo." He shrugged. "He wanted to see you. It's your life, Courtney," he finally sighed, his gray eyes concerned, finally filled with acceptance. "I can't live it for you, and to be honest, I'd just fuck it up further if you let me." He turned to Ian then. "I'll be downstairs when you're ready to talk."

He turned and left the room, leaving her alone then with the man who had haunted her for most of her life.

Why was he here though? Did he worry that she would somehow meet the same end that Melissa had?

"If he has led you to believe I would hurt myself, then he is playing a very cruel game with you," she bit out fiercely. "You must remember I inherited my scheming heart somewhere. It was obviously him. You know how he gets when he's angry, Ian. He'll let you believe whatever you like."

She couldn't believe he was here. She stared at him, eating him with her gaze, caressing him with her eyes as she longed to with her hands. How tall and strong he looked. His sun-darkened flesh, the thick black hair, his wicked blue eyes. He stood before her dressed in low-slung jeans and a white silk shirt. Boots covered his feet, giving him a rakish stance. And between his thighs… He still lusted for her. His cock was hard, pressing against the material in a bid to be free.

Her body responded to that knowledge, her breasts swelling, her nipples growing hard and sensitized as he continued to watch her.

"I know how Dane is." He crossed his arms over his chest as he watched her solemnly. "You disappoint me though."

"Me?" Her brows snapped into a frown as his words finally sank into her head. "How could I have disappointed you? I left. What more could you wish?"

"Did I ask you to leave?" He arched his brow questioningly. "I don't recall asking you to do anything of the sort. You drove me crazy for weeks, finally got what you wanted and then you just up and left."

She blinked back at him, her hands waving nervously.

"I had caused you such trouble…"

"No more than I expected." He grunted. "Don't you think I knew your father was a little smarter than you were giving him credit for? I knew he would get suspicious. You were the one who thought you had him fooled."

She flushed at the reminder.

"I didn't want to make things worse..." Her throat tightened with regret. Why hadn't he understood that? And why wait a month to berate her for it?

He stepped further into the room, bringing with him the unique scent that she had always loved about him.

"You made things much worse," he growled then. "You left without saying goodbye. That hurt my feelings, Courtney."

She shook her head, watching him in confusion.

"How?" She frowned trying to figure that one out.

"I was furious with you." He stopped in front of her, staring down at her, his expression lightening as he saw whatever it was he was searching for within her gaze. "I am still furious with you. Which means, I may well have to punish you severely. Later..." She gasped when he touched her, his arms going around her, one hand tangling in her hair to draw her head back. "Much later..."

His lips came down on hers forcefully, his tongue spearing between them as they parted in surprise and conquering any protest she would have made. Emotion hit her like a tidal wave, swamping her in pleasure, in an arousal that tore brutally through her system.

This would not do at all.

Reality slammed forcefully into her head, her heart as she jerked back from him, tearing herself from his arms as she stared back at him, fury erupting inside her.

"Your feelings were hurt?" Incredulity swept through her. "How dare you stand before me proclaiming such a thing? How dare you in all your fucking male superiority dare to say such a thing to me?"

Weeks. Weeks of agony, of sleepless nights tore through her. The days of pacing the floors fighting to understand how she could have possibly been wrong, how her heart, which had always led her right, had fucked up so horribly, and *his* feelings were hurt?

"Courtney..." His voice hardened.

"Do not 'Courtney' me," she snarled, pointing her finger furiously at his chest, trembling with her fury. "I stood before you, my soul bare and bleeding and not once..." She held up her finger imperiously. "Not even one time, neither by look nor by word did you even hint that you should feel any a single tender emotion for me. That you gave one whit for the agony resounding through my soul."

"You got your sense of drama from your mother," he growled, frowning back at her as he propped his hands on his hips. "Let me know when you're finished chastising me and we'll talk."

"Finished chastising you?" She smiled. It was all teeth. "Oh dearest Ian, I have finished chastising you. You may return to the cold comfort of your Club, and the even colder depth of your bed. Alone."

She couldn't believe it. Could not believe his daring, his nerve.

His eyes flared with sudden anger.

"You will listen to me," he snapped. "Don't push me, baby. I've been pushed far enough."

"I have yet to push you, Ian Sinclair," she yelled, furious, as she stomped to the door. "I have yet to show you what an arrogant all-knowing prick I now believe you are. You may leave." She flung the door open, fury pulsing through her.

She hadn't come in a month. No orgasms. No pleasure. No sexual pain.

She had cried until her pillows were drenched.

She had made her mother cry. She had brought tears to her father's eyes.

She had suffered. For what? So he could arrive in her home, in her bedroom and say his feelings were hurt?

Phfft! on his feelings.

"You damned little wildcat." He stomped to her, jerking the door out of her grip and slamming it closed before jerking her back in his arms, restraining her hands behind her back and drowning her furious scream with his lips.

Lips that ate at hers. Lips that slanted across hers as his tongue forced its way into her mouth, licking at her, devouring her.

She hadn't had an orgasm in a month.

She had drenched her pillows in tears.

And he was here now. Kissing her as though he could not taste her enough, his cock pressing hard and demanding against her stomach as he arched her into his embrace. He consumed her senses, forging past the fury to the soul-deep hunger for his touch, the satisfaction only he could bring.

She needed more. She had to be closer, to draw the heat of him into her, to hold this small, unexpected touch forever to her heart.

"You left me, Courtney..." he growled against her lips, nipping at them erotically as her eyes opened drowsily to stare back at him. "You can't leave me, baby. Never again. Not ever again."

She would have spoken, she would have questioned the surprising declaration if his hands didn't seem to be everywhere at once, divesting her of her clothing, stroking her, sending her senses spinning with his touch.

She was weak, and she knew it. He might not love her, but before she had to walk away from him forever she could touch him once last time, take him into her body and remember forever how perfect it was.

You can't leave me... Never again... Not ever again...

The words vibrated through her mind.

"No. Wait..." She turned her head from him, trembling, pleasure and pain vibrating through her body. Pleasure from his touch. The pain of losing him. "Ian... Oh God, yes..."

His lips covered a hard, up-thrust nipple heatedly, drawing on it, sucking it deep into his mouth as his teeth rasped against it and his hands pushed the loose pants from her hips.

She was lost then. Nothing mattered but his touch, his hand lifting her to the bed as he followed her down, his amazing dexterity as he laved her nipple and quickly stripped the clothes from his own body.

Finally, he was naked. Hot and hard, his body tense and ready as he wrapped his arms around her, holding her tight as his lips moved once again to hers. The kiss opened her soul. Pleasure flooded every cell of her body, every corner of her spirit as his hands cupped each side of her face, holding her still as his head lifted.

Her breath caught at what she saw in his gaze. Emotion, bright, intense, adoring emotion.

"I love you, Courtney," he whispered, his expression twisting painfully as he watched her. "I didn't know how much I could love until you were gone. Until your laughter no longer filled my home, your wicked high jinks no longer made me crazy. Until I stood in that damned club and knew, without you by side, my life was as empty as my bed was without you in it. I didn't know what love was, until I saw my refusal to admit it drown all the sweet innocence in your eyes. I love you."

She stared back at him, certain she couldn't be hearing the words that had her heart beating in wonder, her soul filling with warmth, just as he was slowly filling her aching, once empty pussy.

She gasped, arching to him as she felt his cock working inside her. Slowly. So slowly as she moaned, needing more.

"Look at me, baby," he whispered when her eyes would have closed to better savor the dream she was certain this was.

"I'm going to wake up," she whispered tearfully. "I'll wake up and you'll be gone again."

"Never..." His hips bunched, then a strangled scream left her throat as he pushed forcefully inside the snug tissue clasping him so tightly.

Okay, that didn't feel like a dream.

Well, it did, but not the sort of dream you wake up from. It felt like paradise, a burning ecstasy searing her from the inside out as she fought to accustom herself to the feel of his cock inside her once again.

She fought to catch her breath as she felt him seat inside her fully, his erection a heated brand, nudging against her cervix, sending electrified sensations whipping through her body, tightening her womb.

It had been so long. It seemed as though it had been years since he had touched her, taken her. Since she had known the forceful dominance of his possession.

"You're so hot, baby," he growled, holding her head still as he sipped at her lips, stared into her eyes and began an intoxicating rhythm between her thighs. She tightened her pussy, needing him deeper, needing to feel him to her very soul as he took her.

"There you go." He smiled against her lips as she lifted to him. "Let me have you, baby. Let me feel how hot and sweet your pussy milks my cock."

She bucked beneath him, driving him further as she began to shudder with the pleasure, hard tremors whipping through her muscles as she began to shake with her need to climax.

"Good..." he groaned, moving faster now, fucking her hard and steady, his cock moving forcibly, stroking the ultra-sensitive tissue, sending her senses careening as she felt her body tighten in nearing explosion.

"Watch me, baby." He began to move harder. Faster. "Let me see your eyes as you come, Courtney, keep them open."

Open. Her eyes were open, and she gasped for breath beneath his kiss, shuddering, whimpering cries leaving her throat, building to a strangled scream as she jerked, exploded and felt her cunt melt around the steady, hard thrusts of his erection.

His face tightened, his lips pulling back from his teeth in a snarl of pleasure as he slammed inside her. Once. Twice. Then he tightened, jerking in the throes of his own release as his seed began to spill inside her in hard, steady pulses.

"I love you…" She cried against his lips, her arms tightening around him, tears falling from her eyes. "Oh God, Ian, I love you…"

Weary, spent, Ian collapsed beside her as he pulled her into his arms and lifted her to draw the comforter back before jerking it over them and settling in the bed as Courtney rested beside him.

She hadn't woken yet, which meant she must not have been sleeping.

"I thought I had lost you forever," she whispered against his chest, feeling his hands move over her back in a comforting stroke as he sighed heavily.

"You stole my heart, and I hadn't even realized it." He kissed the top of her head gently. "What happened with Melissa terrified me, Courtney. I thought she was innocent. Thought I had hurt her, even though her father swore that wasn't the case. I spent the last week in Texas with him. Finding out the truth. Learning things I hadn't known about her. Putting it to rest."

It wouldn't have been easy for him, she knew, facing the past after all these years.

"I wouldn't have come to you if I hadn't known what I wanted, Ian." It hurt that he hadn't trusted her love. "If I hadn't known my own heart and needs."

"It wasn't you, Courtney. It was me." He drew her back, leaning over her as her head rested against the pillow. "Believe that if you never believe anything else. It was my fears and the residue of guilt I had for my lifestyle and the excesses that are so much a part of me. I always felt love would ease it, take the need from me. It hadn't with Melissa, and I always felt it had destroyed her. And you..." His lips kicked in a grin. "You reveled in them. I had to realize myself what love was before I could realize how much I truly loved you. If you hadn't left, I wouldn't have been forced to make the discoveries I did. You saved us both in doing that. But..." His hands tangled in her hair again. "Never again. You won't leave me again or I promise you, you won't enjoy the spanking I'll give you in payment."

Everything inside her heated, lit from within, and lived. He loved her, just as she had known he would. Just as she had known he should.

And as Ian watched her, he watched the fragile glimmer of innocence that had lit her eyes when he entered the room, glow to full, vivid life. Love. Pure, innocent, joyous love. There were no shadows in her eyes, no pain, only acceptance and the sweet emotion he had missed so desperately in the past weeks. For the first time in his life, Ian knew he belonged.

Her lips curved slowly. "Hmm," she hummed at the thought. "Spank me, Uncle Ian. Spank me so hard..."

And he knew there was no taming a wild, shameless wind.

Chapter Sixteen

"Well, they haven't come down yet." Dane glanced to the stairs, a frown creasing his brow as his wife moved beside him.

"Hmm, perhaps they are still…talking…" He heard the suggestive tone of her voice and stared down at her reprovingly.

She shook her head at him, giving him that hopeless look that only she could perfect.

"He's still too old for her," he muttered.

She chuckled knowingly. He was nearly ten years her senior as well.

"I don't want to hear it," he informed her before she could open her mouth to remind him of that fact. "That's us. This is our daughter."

His baby.

He shook his head, drawing away from the marble entryway and moving back into the dimly lit living room where he once again threw himself on the couch to await his daughter.

Marguerita sat down beside him, cuddling into his embrace, her head resting against his chest as he propped his chin against it.

She was his laughter. His life. He had nearly lost her once and he never let himself forget what life had been like without her. Devoid of laughter, or warmth. He was devoted to her, he would die for her. Just as, he knew, Ian would do for Courtney.

He had seen it in the other man's eyes as he stood at the door hours before.

"Kill me now," he had ordered Dane fiercely. "Because life without her fucking sucks."

It was then he had known Courtney hadn't been wrong. She had captured the heart Dane had feared his friend had lost years before. It was disconcerting though, knowing the sexual experiences his daughter would share. It was weird enough just knowing she would be sleeping with Ian. The perverted bastard.

"And our daughter is a grown woman." He stared at her as she moved, coming before him before straddling his thighs suggestively, her silk dress falling back from her shapely thighs as they hugged his hips. "And I would say, she will likely be quite busy for several hours." She leaned down, her lips moving over his neck as his palms cupped her rear.

His Marguerita. Perfect. His life and breath.

"Hmm, we might have a few hours to kill." His head fell back on the couch as her teeth raked beneath his chin. "Here, or the bedroom?"

He knew her well though. She was shameless, a wanton who reveled in his touch, who met his passions with needs and desires of her own and never hesitated to state them.

"Hmm, do you really want to move?" she whispered, her breath hot, her voice a husky whisper of desire.

"Not that far." He lifted her dress further as he turned her and laid her back on the couch. "Don't scream too loud." He flashed her a devilish smile. "The children are still awake."

She laughed, a throaty sound of joy, of amusement and his heart tripped in happiness, as it always had.

His Marguerita. And if Ian was as smart as Dane had always thought he was, then Courtney was in very capable, very loving hands…

Why an electronic book?

We live in the Information Age—an exciting time in the history of human civilization, in which technology rules supreme and continues to progress in leaps and bounds every minute of every day. For a multitude of reasons, more and more avid literary fans are opting to purchase e-books instead of paper books. The question from those not yet initiated into the world of electronic reading is simply: *Why?*

1. ***Price.*** An electronic title at Ellora's Cave Publishing and Cerridwen Press runs anywhere from 40% to 75% less than the cover price of the exact same title in paperback format. Why? Basic mathematics and cost. It is less expensive to publish an e-book (no paper and printing, no warehousing and shipping) than it is to publish a paperback, so the savings are passed along to the consumer.
2. ***Space.*** Running out of room in your house for your books? That is one worry you will never have with electronic books. For a low one-time cost, you can purchase a handheld device specifically designed for e-reading. Many e-readers have large, convenient screens for viewing. Better yet, hundreds of titles can be stored within your new library—on a single microchip. There are a variety of e-readers from different manufacturers. You can also read e-books on your PC or laptop computer. (Please note that Ellora's Cave does not endorse any specific brands.

You can check our websites at www.ellorascave.com or www.cerridwenpress.com for information we make available to new consumers.)

3. ***Mobility***. Because your new e-library consists of only a microchip within a small, easily transportable e-reader, your entire cache of books can be taken with you wherever you go.
4. ***Personal Viewing Preferences.*** Are the words you are currently reading too small? Too large? Too... *ANNOYING*? Paperback books cannot be modified according to personal preferences, but e-books can.
5. ***Instant Gratification.*** Is it the middle of the night and all the bookstores near you are closed? Are you tired of waiting days, sometimes weeks, for bookstores to ship the novels you bought? Ellora's Cave Publishing sells instantaneous downloads twenty-four hours a day, seven days a week, every day of the year. Our webstore is never closed. Our e-book delivery system is 100% automated, meaning your order is filled as soon as you pay for it.

Those are a few of the top reasons why electronic books are replacing paperbacks for many avid readers.

As always, Ellora's Cave and Cerridwen Press welcome your questions and comments. We invite you to email us at Comments@ellorascave.com or write to us directly at Ellora's Cave Publishing Inc., 1056 Home Avenue, Akron, OH 44310-3502.

2239190

Made in the USA